MERCY

ALSO BY BRETT BATTLES

THE JONATHAN QUINN THRILLERS

Novels

Becoming Quinn

The Cleaner

The Deceived

Shadow of Betrayal (U.S.)/The Unwanted (U.K.)

The Silenced

The Destroyed

The Collected

The Enraged

The Discarded

The Buried

The Unleashed

The Aggrieved

The Fractured

The Unknown

The Vanished

Novellas

Night Work

Short Stories

"Just Another Job"—A Jonathan Quinn Story

"Off the Clock"—A Jonathan Quinn Story

Eden Rising

Dream Sky

Down

THE ALEXANDRA POE THRILLERS

(Cowritten with Robert Gregory Browne)

Poe

Takedown

STANDALONES

Novels

The Pull of Gravity

No Return

Mine

Night Man

Novellas

Mine: The Arrival

Short Stories

"Perfect Gentleman"

For Younger Readers

THE TROUBLE FAMILY CHRONICLES

Here Comes Mr. Trouble

MERCY

THE NIGHT MAN CHRONICLES

BRETT BATTLES

This one is for Corri.
A friend and a fan and a fellow BHS graduate,
whose life, like so many others' during the pandemic,
ended much too soon.

CHAPTER ONE

You know what I hate?

Unpopped kernels in my popcorn.

I'm chomping away and all of a sudden I bite down on one, and my tooth feels like it's going to split in half. I swear I can still feel the sensation hours after this happens.

Why am I thinking about popcorn right now? Because I'm sitting in a storage room next to one of those big, glassed-in, theater-type popcorn machines, and even though it's clean, it still reeks of butter and stale popped kernels. It's mounted on a cart so it can be wheeled into whichever banquet requests it. The room holds a bunch of stuff like that, separated into themes. The popcorn machine is part of the Hollywood theme. I've also seen a Western-theme grouping and a Vegas theme complete with roulette and craps tables.

Where am I that would house all these kinds of things in a single storage room?

Why, El Palacio Banquet Experience, of course.

From its brochure:

Choose from our nine distinct banquet halls for your next wedding, party, or company event. We offer full catering and a themed experience you will remember for a lifetime.

Why am I in a big building full of banquet halls, especially since no one's throwing weddings or parties these days? That would have to do with something else I hate—people who take advantage of other people, especially ones who are going through hard times.

I can't do anything about the popcorn smell, but I can address the asshole problem. In fact, it's kinda become a specialty of mine.

El Palacio Banquet Experience is in Santa Ana, California, which is south of L.A. in Orange County. The city is the marginally smaller and less famous neighbor of Anaheim, home of Disneyland. The banquet building is a locally owned place that, according to research my friend Jar and I have done, is booked solid months in advance when a pandemic isn't raging across the planet.

I'm here to make sure the damage the business suffers does not extend beyond the effects of the mandatory shutdowns needed to keep the virus in check.

Which brings us to Marco Tepper and Blaine Lawson.

These two pieces of work have been causing trouble down here, south of what we sometimes affectionately call the Orange Curtain. They've been smart about it, and for the most part have been good at mixing up their tactics to keep the police from connecting the string of crimes they've committed.

They seem to be operating with two distinct goals. The first is enrichment by theft. To that end, they've hit over a dozen businesses but never two alike, and never ones that are within five miles of another they've robbed.

As for their second goal...let's call it stress relief. These crimes occur at places where they can bust up a lot of things and spray-paint the walls. They probably steal a few things while they're at it, but it's not the primary goal.

What the businesses all have in common is that they have closed for the pandemic. This means it's often days—and in one case, almost two weeks—before the crimes are discovered. Even worse is the fact they're small businesses, whose owners are already hurting from the lost income of being forced to close and can't fall back on corporate help.

I try not to look at the news too much when I don't have to, so Jar's the one who brought to my attention the articles about the crimes. Most were small mentions in local papers or community websites. Only a couple showed up in the *Orange County Register*, but even then, neither article was very long.

"I think it is the same people behind each of these," she said.

On first blush, I was skeptical. Like I said, no two crimes have been committed in the same way. But I trust Jar's instincts so I couldn't just dismiss it out of hand.

It took us a week to tie everything together and another four days to uncover Marco's and Blaine's names.

Turns out they've been playing a variation of the bully game since they attended middle school together. They're twenty-seven now.

Marco is the only one who's gone to college. He's smart but has a temper that can get the better of him. Which is why he was kicked out of school for behavioral issues and didn't graduate—apparently, he hadn't reacted well to the grade a professor had given him. To be honest, after reading his school file, Marco's lucky the cops weren't called in.

Since high school, Blaine has burned his way through a series of entry-level service jobs, none of which he could hold on to for more than a year, and most not even six months.

Marco has been able to get better jobs, but his ability to stay in them is on par with his friend's.

When the virus hit and everything shut down, both were let go from their positions. Instead of finding other jobs, they apparently decided to take advantage of others' misfortune. I'm sure this string of burglaries and vandalism isn't their first foray into this kind of behavior. They're too good at it for that to be true. I do think, however, the pandemic has allowed them to accelerate their activities.

Which, ultimately, is what helped Jar and me identify who they are.

"Three blocks away," Jar says over the comm in my ear. She's been watching for their arrival via the camera on our drone, which is flying high above the banquet hall building.

"Copy," I say.

The time for waiting is over.

I exit the storage room and walk down to El Palacio's main lobby. Normally, the place has a few security lights that are always on, but I've killed the power to them so the only light in the entire facility is the little amount wandering in through the windows. Thanks to my night vision goggles, I have no problem seeing.

The banquet building has multiple entrances, but I know exactly which one Marco and Blaine will use. They've tipped their hand. It's a door in back. I could meet them there when they arrive, but I want them to get a little comfortable first.

My gut tells me that before they start their reign of destruction, they'll come to the lobby and scope everything out first. That suits me fine. I trade the large storage room for a maintenance closet at the edge of the lobby, just large enough for a bucket and a mop and a few shelves filled with cleaning supplies. And me.

What I like about the closet is that its door is painted to look like the rest of the wall, so it's all but invisible to the casual glance. It doesn't even have a doorknob. A push on it pops it open.

Once I'm closed inside, I lift my goggles from my eyes, turn on my phone, and activate the app that will allow me to view the video feeds, not only from the drone but also from the cameras I've placed throughout El Palacio.

Thanks to my day job, I have access to a wide array of...let's just say items not available to the average citizen. I'm not saying you wouldn't be able to buy cameras and drones, but I doubt they'd be the same ones I can get. Then there are some of the other items I have with me that you could never lay your hands on.

Working in the world of intelligence and secrets has its advantages.

Being inside El Palacio—or, in Jar's case, just *out*side—has nothing to do with how we make our living, however.

This is what we do between jobs. A hobby, if you will.

"Here they come," Jar says.

On the drone shot, a dark gray Dodge Durango is coming down the street that runs behind the complex. It's the latest in a series of vehicles Marco and Blaine have stolen. This is the third job in a row they've used it, which means, if they're sticking to their pattern, they'd be dumping it for something new before the night is over. But they will not be sticking to pattern.

The Durango turns down the side of the property, then across the front, and finally down the other side before turning onto the back road again, the two vandals checking for potential problems. The only vehicles in the parking lot that surrounds the building are five identical delivery vans with the El Palacio Banquet Experience logo on the side. This, I'm sure, is exactly what the men were hoping to find.

They park the SUV on the street, directly across from the door they intend to use. They have no need to worry about being seen by neighbors. This is a business district, and all the shops and restaurants in the area have also been closed for a few months.

The reason we know which door they'll use has to do with a visit Marco and Blaine paid El Palacio three days ago. The complex is surrounded by cameras outside. Technically, no one should be able to approach any of the businesses without being recorded. When Marco and Blaine showed up previously, they were dressed in the uniform—stolen from a former job—of a heating and AC repair company. Using the industrial ladder they'd brought, they climbed onto the roof, where they readjusted the cameras to create an uncovered corridor to their selected door. Since the cameras are not actively monitored, no one caught the change.

Well, *we* did. But we've left the cameras as they are, because their current positions serve our purposes, too. We have placed our own camera in a spot that allows us to see the door and the area that runs from it to the street.

I switch to that feed in time to see Marco and Blaine climb out of the Durango. They are dressed in dark clothing and each is carrying a bag that I'm sure contains the tools and cans of spray paint they plan on using inside. They are both wearing face masks, which, in the current climate, makes them look like pretty much everyone else.

Blaine's head swivels from side to side as they approach the building, while Marco's gaze stays fixed on their destination. When they reach the door, Marco crouches down to pick the lock.

I'm looking forward to seeing how they deal with the alarm. While all the other places they hit had security systems, no alarms have ever been triggered. Jar and I have a pretty good theory as to what's going on, but this will be the first time we see Marco and Blaine in action.

It takes Marco an excruciating two minutes to get both locks undone. I had them open in about twenty seconds. Of course, picking locks was part of my training. Whenever it took me longer to open a lock than the time limit my mentor had given me, he was fond of saying, "You're dead. Do it again."

Marco rises back to his feet and the two men talk for a moment, the door still closed. The moment Marco pulls it open, I switch to the camera I put in the back hallway. A *beep-beep-beep* emits from the alarm control panel just inside. Marco strides up to it, confident and unhurried. After he opens the panel, he pulls a piece of paper out of his pocket, glances at it, and punches a code into the keypad.

The beeping stops.

Marco probably thinks this is the most ingenious part of his plan. But it is the weak point that first led Jar to think all the crimes were connected. Every single place he and Blaine have broken into has an alarm system from the same company— SecurTrax Solutions, based in Costa Mesa.

We knew Marco and Blaine—well, probably only Marco— had either figured out a way to hack into a SecurTrax system, or they'd gotten their hands on the access codes for each of their targets. Looks like it's option number two. Which means there has to be a third person in their little operation. Someone who gives them the codes, and who subsequently removes any traces of Marco and Blaine using them from the SecurTrax log systems. We know this is true because there's never any record of the alarms being shut off.

Now that we know for sure what's going on, it should be simple enough to figure out who this inside person is, but we'll leave that job for the police.

Marco and Blaine have turned on flashlights and are walking down the hall. Every time they pass a door, they peek inside but do not enter. Just like I predicted, they are taking a look around before they start rampaging. They're probably looking for the main office, where they can find info on anything that might be worth stealing.

As they near the lobby, I can hear their voices without the aid of my electronic bugs.

"Hey! Look at all this!" Blaine says.

His eyes are on the glass cabinets displaying several antique urns along the back wall. I'm sure he's imagining the fun he'll have smashing them up.

"Come on," Marco says. He points across the lobby to the hallway leading to several other banquet rooms. "The office should be over there."

They walk past my door without even glancing in my direction, and head toward the other side of the room.

I slip my phone into my pocket, pull my black ski mask over my face, and retrieve from my bag the two specialized guns I've brought with me.

Up to this point, Marco and Blaine have remained pretty much unscathed. The only problem they've run into happened at a kitchen supply store in Brea, where, unbeknownst to them, a security guard had been recently hired. Luckily for Marco and Blaine—and not so much for the guard—they saw the man first and beat the living crap out of him. He'll live, but he's still recovering from his injuries.

Marco and Blaine are unaware of my presence. And they won't be as lucky this time. Have I mentioned I don't play fair?

As soon as they enter the office, I sneak out of the maintenance closet, walk past the office door, and stop three meters down the dark hall to wait.

Between the sounds of drawers being opened and closed, I can hear the two men talking. I haven't heard any smashing yet. I've been afraid I might have to let them do a little of that before I act, but hopefully that won't be the case.

When Marco's voice turns excited, I know they've found something of interest. He follows this up with, "It says it's in the storage room. Come on."

The office door swings inward, and two flashlight beams dance into the hallway. One of the beams momentarily points in my direction, but the men's attention is aimed toward the lobby and neither notices me.

I let them take a couple of steps away from me, then I clear my throat.

Both men jerk in surprise and whip around.

Marco snickers at the sight of me. "Oh, buddy, are *you* in the wrong place tonight."

I have no doubt they're going to rush me, but before they can, I point my guns at them.

This is not what Marco expected. His expression switches quickly to one of innocence. "Whoa, hold on there. No need for any trouble."

He takes a tentative step toward me, so I raise the gun that's trained on him a little higher. This stops him in his tracks.

"Why don't you put those down," he says. "And we can talk about this."

There will be no talking. Just like they will never see my face, they will never hear my voice. Not now. Not ever.

"I can take him," Blaine whispers, as if I can't hear him.

"Shut up," Marco hisses back, then to me says, "No one's going to rush anyone. Now please, lower those guns, buddy. You don't want to hurt anyone."

Needless to say, my hands remain in place.

Marco's eyes narrow. Poor boy. I'm trying his patience.

For a second, his gaze slips from me to the gun. Then he does a double take, his eyes returning to my weapon. "What the hell are those?"

It's not an unreasonable question.

My guns are not the bullet-shooting kind. They're dart guns, but nothing like the kind I had as a kid that dispensed plastic darts with rubber suction-cup tips. The darts these hold are carbon-fiber tubes topped by a needle that can deliver all kinds of drugs into a target. My colleagues and I often fill them with a knockout drug like Beta-Somnol. But that's not what I'm using today.

"Those don't even look like guns," Blaine says. "They look like toys."

They don't look like toys, but they do look odd. I'll give him that.

While Marco still seems a bit wary, I can see in Blaine's eyes that he's decided I'm not a threat. His head moves forward a beat before he lifts his foot to make his move on me.

I pull both triggers at the same moment.

I'm naturally right-handed, but I have worked hard to be ambidextrous when it comes to things like weapons, as that ability could—and has—saved my life. So both darts fly true and hit their targets in almost identical spots mid-torso, just below the ribs.

Blaine goes down first because he was already in motion. He tries to stand up again, but can't even get both feet under him before he slams back onto the carpet with an expulsion of air.

The moment the dart hits Marco, he looks down at it, as if not understanding what just happened. When his mind catches up, he tries to grab the cylinder, but it's already too late and a moment later he joins his friend on the floor.

I lower my weapons and walk over to them.

"What did...you...do...to us?" Marco asks, his words coming out in a labored staccato.

What I've done is inject them with something we call the little helper. Unlike Beta-Somnol, which would knock out Marco and Blaine for hours, the little helper puts them in a state of paralysis without causing unconsciousness. The length of time this lasts depends on the dose. In their case, they should be able to move their fingers and toes in about six hours. The rest will come back slowly after that.

I pluck out the darts, then walk back to the maintenance closet where I left my bag. Both men try to shout to me, but it's more of a panicked whisper. Though the little helper does not prevent victims from talking, it does weaken the ability to put any force into a voice.

After putting the guns and used darts in the bag, I walk down the other hallway, out of earshot from my new friends, and say into my comm, "They're down. How we looking outside?"

"Nice and quiet," Jar says.

"Give me a few minutes to get them in place before you make the call."

"Just say the word."

I have to smile. *Just say the word* is not a phrase Jar would have used even six months ago.

When we'd come up with the plan for tonight, my biggest concern was moving the drugged bodies. But in the hour I spent waiting for Marco and Blaine to arrive, I did a little poking around and discovered a furniture dolly in the storage room.

I maneuver Blaine onto it first. He's the larger of the two, and I always like getting difficult things out of the way first. I tie him down with a couple of bungee cords that were also in the storage room. It's not that he might put up a fight; I only want to avoid him accidentally rolling off and forcing me to load his ass back on. I then transport him, his bag, and my bag to the Camelot banquet hall.

His eyes dart back and forth the entire trip, his breaths coming in panicked bursts. Occasionally he whispers to himself things like, "What am…" and "I need…" and "How can I…" Never once do I hear a full thought.

The Camelot room is lit only by the dim glow from one of the outside floodlights, seeping through a row of high windows along the north wall. Except for the two chairs sitting next to each other near the dance floor, the room is empty. I have a feeling the chairs are normally used by a bride and groom, as they are large and heavy wooden things, adorned with carvings of horses and knights and dragons. I place Blaine in the one on the left, setting his forearms on the chair's arms.

Marco is more talkative on his trip. He starts off with threats like "You're…making a big…mistake," and "You're going…to pay… big…for this." But as we're wheeling down the hallway, his tactic changes. "If you let…us…go now, we'll…leave…this place…alone." Then, "Hey…you need…anything? TV? Computer? I can…get… you whatever you…want…if you…look…the other way."

When we enter the Camelot room, he changes from bargaining with me to asking, "What are you…bringing us…in here…for?" and "What are you…going…to do…to us?"

I put him in the second chair, then return to the hallway, close the door, and toggle on my comm.

"Ready to go here," I say.

"Any problems?" Jar asks.

"Not a one."

"I'll make the call."

"Copy."

Inside the room, I can hear Marco and Blaine talking, their tones desperate. When I walk back in, they immediately shut up.

I open my bag, which is sitting on the floor behind the chairs, and extract twelve heavy-duty zip ties and a roll of duct tape.

"What's that...for?" Marco asks as I step back where they can see me.

I set the tape and all but four of the ties in his lap. It's as good a table as any. I zip-tie each of his wrists to an arm of the chair, and then do the same with his ankles to the chair's legs. Four more ties and Blaine's also secured in place.

I use a few more ties on their arms, closer to their elbows, then grab the tape. Once again, I start with Marco, wrapping the tape around his chest to secure him to the back of the chair, and then do the same to Blaine.

Taking a step back, I examine my handiwork.

The tape is overkill but I knew that going in. It's more for show than anything else, a kind of psychological weapon meant to convey to Marco and Blaine how really screwed they are. And by the looks on their faces, it's working.

After putting the roll of tape away, I carry my bag over to the door, where I can pick it up on my way out. From a covered recess built into the wall near the exit, I remove a remote controller and walk back to the chairs.

"Look, we didn't mean...anything," Marco said, exerting a bit more control over his voice now. "We were just going...to take a...look around, that's all. We...shouldn't have come. We're sorry...all right? Come on...please. Just...let us go."

"Why can't I move...my arms?" Blaine asks. "What...did you do to me?"

I turn my back to them and push one of the buttons on the remote.

A motor hums to life.

"What the hell...is...is that?" Marco asks.

In answer to his question, a large screen begins descending from the ceiling. Once it stops, it hangs four meters in front of them.

Another push of the remote and a projector hidden in a faux ceiling beam lights up the screen.

I imagine the system is meant for showing montages of a happy couple's life together or something similar. Tonight's show will be a little less romantic but equally satisfying.

I move behind the chairs again and click my mic three times, letting Jar know the projector is on.

A moment passes before an image appears on the screen. It's a static shot of a dark space, with details hard to make out beyond a few shadowy forms. Then Jar switches the input from visible light to night vision, and the room comes into focus.

Marco gasps when he realizes what he's looking at.

Blaine remains clueless. "I don't get...it. It's...a room. So what?"

"Look," Marco hisses.

Blaine is quiet for a second, then says, "Oh...crap."

Oh, crap, indeed.

What they are looking at is the storage room they rented at a facility in the city of Orange, where they keep all their ill-gotten goods, and where, I suspect, they've done most of their planning.

Superimposed in the top right corner of the image is the time, indicating this is a live shot. Whether Marco and Blaine notice this or not, I don't know. But they'll figure it out soon enough.

I click my mic once. A query, which Jar has no problem interpreting.

"Two minutes out."

I click again, this time to let her know I understand.

"Why are you...showing us...this?" Marco asks. "We-we don't know...what this...is."

I almost blow it and laugh. I mean, it's funny because a

moment ago Marco all but said, *That's our place.* He may be the smarter of the two but he's no Stephen Hawking.

Seconds go by without any change to the image.

Marco again says he doesn't know what he's looking at, but his tone is half-hearted at best. After another thirty seconds, he says, "Okay...yes...it's ours, okay. We're...we're sorry."

"Yeah, man," Blaine jumps in. "We're...sorry."

"All of that...you can...have it," Marco offers. "Just let us...go."

"Pulling up now," Jar informs me.

Marco's and Blaine's pleas continue, their voices growing more and more desperate.

I'm not going to lie. I'm really enjoying this.

"Switching back to visual light mode," Jar warns me.

The picture on the screen reverts to the dim image we first saw.

"What's happening?" Blaine asks. "Why is it...dark?"

Over the Camelot banquet room's speakers come the muted sounds of footsteps. Blaine hasn't heard them because he's been blathering, but I'm betting Marco has.

The steps go silent, and for a moment all is quiet. Then, at the same time we hear the screech of the metal roll-up door being opened, light floods into the storage space.

Marco lets out a shocked curse under his breath as several police officers, weapons drawn, move into the room.

"What are...they doing there?" Blaine asks. "How did they... find out?"

"I swear to God...if you say...another word..." Marco says.

"What? What...did I...say?"

On the screen, the cops continue until they reach the back.

"Clear," one of them shouts.

"Clear," another says.

The men lower their weapons and begin looking around. It

doesn't take long before one of them approaches the table in the back corner.

We have a special camera focused down on it and Jar switches to that one now.

On the table is the notebook Marco used to work out the details of his and Blaine's activities. He's been pretty diligent about ripping pages out and getting rid of them once a job is done, but success has bred laziness, and the notes for the last few jobs are still in the book. He is cryptic in his writing, so it will take a bit of work to figure out what the notebook contains, but I have every confidence the police will succeed.

There's something else on the table, too. Something Jar and I added just before we came here. It's a printout of a map, a small section of Santa Ana that features El Palacio Banquet Center. Written in pencil right next to the center's name is today's date.

"Got something here," the cop at the table says.

Another officer comes over, probably the man in charge, and the first guy points at the map without touching. The newly arrived cop looks at it for a moment, then touches his mic.

"This is Sergeant Yates. We have a possible location on the burglar suspects."

Our map might have been a little on the nose, but it has done the trick. The sergeant's reporting of it is my cue.

I tap the remote again, turning off the projector and sending the screen back into the ceiling. I then walk toward the door without looking back at Marco and Blaine.

"Hey! Hey! Where...are you going?" Marco calls. "You've got to...get us out...of here! Whatever you want! I swear...I'll give you...anything!"

I don't react. I simply put the remote back where I found it, head to the exit, and grab my bag.

"You son of a...bitch! We.... You'd...better watch your back... because we will...find you!"

When I enter the hall, I'm tempted to close the door behind me, as a symbol of how little his words mean to me. But I want to keep things easy for the cops so I leave it open. The moment the police see it, I'm sure they'll check the room.

I also leave open the door I use to exit the building. Then I walk two blocks to where Jar waits in the van we rented for the job.

"Any news?" I ask as I climb into the driver's seat.

"Four units inbound," she says. "ETA three minutes."

I start the engine. "I guess we should get going."

We're eastbound on W. Santa Clara Avenue, almost to the I-5 freeway, when a pair of Santa Ana police department cruisers race past us in the other direction, emergency lights flashing, sirens off.

Some days are really good.

CHAPTER TWO

A nd some days aren't.
         Technically it's not really a new day. We finished at
El Palacio Banquet Experience around sixteen hours ago, at
1:30 a.m. It's now 5:13 p.m., and Jar and I are in the living room
of my Redondo Beach townhouse, watching the local news.

All day I've been feeling pretty satisfied. Taking down a pair
of lowlifes like Marco and Blaine has a way of doing that. The
inflation of my ego never lasts long, but today it sticks around for
even less time.

Your first thought might be that Marco and Blaine have
somehow escaped or avoided blame for their activities. That's
not the case. They're locked up, and probably won't be
breathing free air again for a while. We've left a few clues at the
storage locker that will ensure they receive credit for every
single thing they've done.

My mood has more to do with something a reporter just said
on the news.

"According to a source, the two men had entered the business with plans of vandalizing the facility. Before this could be
achieved, they were thwarted by an unnamed individual

wearing a stocking mask, who incapacitated them and left them tied up for police to find."

If he had stopped there, I could've lived with it. It is what happened, and it would be hard to hide that for long. It's what he says next that has elevated my blood pressure.

"This brings to mind the capture of Miles Deveaux, the so-called Valley Heights Rapist, in January. In a press conference last week, Mr. Deveaux's attorney, Carl Swanson, related a similar story about his client's capture, and suggested that the masked man was the true criminal and had framed his client. One has to wonder if the two cases might be connected. Or perhaps it's a case of imitation being the best form of flattery. This is Benjamin Aguilar in Santa Ana, for KCAL News."

Carl Swanson's claim about who's really responsible for the crimes Deveaux is accused of is bullshit. No one will ever believe him. The DNA evidence alone will snuff out that theory in a hurry if he dares float it in court.

But the part Benjamin Agular wondered about? That's true. The two events are connected.

The fact that someone has noticed isn't good.

I should have changed my mask.

No, what I should have done was never take on another one of my little hobby jobs so close to home. I keep telling myself that, and I keep ignoring it.

While I should take comfort in knowing there's no way to connect me to the masked man, it's hard not to feel unsettled by even tangential connections.

Things get worse by ten p.m.

Raul Staggs, a reporter at KTLA, has grabbed on to the story a bit tighter. Under a montage of shots from both the Deveaux case and the arrest this morning of Marco and Blaine, he reiterates what Aguilar reported, then plays clips from an interview he did with Swanson in which the lawyer reveals details of

Deveaux's "imprisonment" at the hands of a masked man. (Full interview to be available on the station's webpage tomorrow.)

There are undeniable similarities between what happened to Deveaux and what happened to Marco and Blaine.

What can I say? I use what works.

When Staggs finishes his conversation with Swanson, I think the worst of it is over, but I am woefully wrong. His report cuts to a small yard in front of an apartment building. Staggs, in a voice-over, says, "Late this afternoon, we received a tip that there might be another incident connected to the masked vigilante."

What connection? I don't know this house.

The shot cuts to a different angle on the same yard, this time focused on a girl maybe fifteen years old, sixteen at most.

I narrow my eyes. She looks vaguely familiar, but I can't place her.

Voice-over again. "Kalee Walsh says she encountered the man last fall."

I relax a little. It has to be something she's made up in hopes of getting her face on TV.

"My friend Gina and I were in the store, grabbing a soda."

"That would be Park's Mini-Mart?" Staggs asks.

"Yeah. That's right."

My blood turns cold. This isn't a made-up story and she's no fame hound. Well, I mean, she might be, but she's not lying.

A new shot, this one featuring Park's Mini-Mart. It's one of several stores that occupy the street level of a building not far from the I-10 freeway.

Staggs's voice continues over the shot. "You may recall in September of last year, Park's Mini-Mart was the location where the gang known as the Masked Raiders were finally captured."

Yes. Masked Raiders. It's a stupid name but no one asked me.

"Kalee Walsh and her friend Gina Rodriguez were inside the store with the store's owner, Mr. Park, when, according to Kalee, the masked vigilante entered and tasered a member of the Raiders who was also inside."

Back to Cali. "When the wires hit him, he dropped to the floor. I've never seen someone go down that fast. The guy with the mask—"

"The masked vigilante," Staggs says.

I want to reach through the screen to strangle him. I hate that name almost as much as I hate Masked Raiders.

"Uh-huh. He told Mr. Park he'd taken care of more of them in the alley, and that Mr. Park should call the police. He told us not to mention that he was there, so we didn't."

"Until now."

A nod. "I heard about what happened last night at that wedding place, and that someone in a mask stopped those guys. It sounds a lot like the person who helped us."

New shot. Staggs on the sidewalk in front of Park's Mini-Mart. "I attempted to confirm the story with Mr. Park but he declined to be on camera, and only said he didn't know what the girl was talking about. Is it possible this is where the masked vigilante got his start? This is Raul Staggs in—"

I shut off the TV.

"We should call him," Jar says. "He is using the wrong nickname."

I glare at her. "That's not helping."

She's referring to something that happened in Northern California, soon after the incident at Park's Mini-Mart. Yeah, another hobby mission, where one night I was spotted on the roof of an apartment complex, wearing—you guessed it—my ski mask. The local paper assumed I was a robber and labeled me Night Man, something Jar enjoys reminding me.

I don't like the name, but I have to admit it's better than the

Masked Vigilante. And while her suggestion to call Staggs was a joke, I can't deny the idea has a bit of appeal.

Nickname aside, I'm agitated. I guess I should be thankful no one has linked the Masked Vigilante to the larger missions I've undertaken, like the one in Northern California, but that knowledge does nothing to ease my stress.

I'm pretty sure the only thing that will eventually make me feel less paranoid is if I stop.

Not just doing projects in the Los Angeles area, but doing them altogether.

As soon as this thought enters my head, I sense Liz nearby, frowning.

I'm not saying forever, I tell her. *I'm just saying for now. Lie low for a while. That's all.*

Not long ago, I would have said the words aloud, but now that Jar's living here, too, I keep my conversations with Liz in my head. I'm not sure how Jar would react if she knows I receive visits from my dead girlfriend now and then.

Ghost Liz is the one who pushed me into doing these projects in the first place. I know that sounds crazy. Mainly because it is.

I know she's not real. She's just my subconscious talking to me in her voice.

With her mannerisms.

And knowing things I don't actually know.

Hold on. What I mean is, she tells me things I think I don't know but probably do on some level.

Except when there's no way I could have known.

Ugh, this is why I don't like thinking about it too much.

The bottom line is, it's time to take a break.

Whatever you wish, Liz tells me, then disappears.

Her words aren't the comfort I'd like them to be. I know Liz. She doesn't give up that easily.

Which is why my shoulders are still tense.

"How about some *Overwatch?*" Jar suggests.

I shrug. I know she's trying to distract me, but I'm not sure I feel like doing anything other than crawling into a hole and burying myself alive.

With a little more prodding, though, she wins me over. She even grabs me a beer while the videogame is booting up.

Two hours later, I'm still annoyed but my stress level has dipped into the almost normal range, and I finally feel like maybe I can sleep.

We turn off the console and I give Jar a hug goodnight.

We've gotten into the habit of doing that before going to bed. For a person who isn't great with physical contact, she's become good at hugging.

What we've never done is kiss. I'm not saying the urge isn't there for either of us, but I think we both know we're not quite ready to take that step yet. By the same token, we sleep in separate rooms, Jar downstairs in one of my guest rooms, and me up here in the master.

We're a couple.

But we're not.

But we are.

It's confusing, I know. Especially with Liz still hanging around. But it's working for us so we roll with it.

I gotta say, not my best night of sleep ever.

Not only did I lie in bed for a couple of hours before I slipped under, but after I did, I didn't stay that way for long. My sleep was like a stone skipping across the surface of a lake. Asleep for a bit, awake for a bit, asleep for a bit—you get the idea.

At 5:40 a.m., after staring at my closed eyelids for about thirty minutes, I realize I'm finished for the night so I get up and take a shower.

When I walk into the living room, Jar is sitting on the couch, drinking a mug of coffee and watching *Back to the Future*. This is not a surprise.

A: She doesn't sleep much.

B: Coffee is like water to her.

And C: *Back to the Future* is one of her favorites. I've pieced together from odd bits of conversations that she watched it a lot when she was teaching herself English, so it's like comfort food to her now.

I shuffle into the kitchen, pour a mug of coffee for myself, and take a seat beside her. On the screen, Marty has just left the prom and is in the town square with Doc Brown, about to travel...well, back to the future. The movie's almost done, which means Jar's been up for a while. Again, not surprising.

She leans against me, her eyes never leaving the screen, and for a few minutes, I forget all about the news reports from last night.

If you didn't know Jar, you wouldn't realize what a minor miracle it is for us to be sitting here like this. I've mentioned it already but it's worth noting again. Human contact is not one of her strong suits. Also on that list would be: small talk; lying (even the tiny white lies people tell every day), with the exception being when a job calls for it; and understanding why people ask questions with answers that are—to her, anyway—obvious.

She only recently turned twenty-two, but before she was even a teenager, she'd experienced more hardship than most people who live into their nineties. That and the fact she's somewhere on the spectrum caused her to self-insulate, if you will. It's only been a little over a year that she's started to let others in.

Basically, since she started working with me and my partners on the day job.

We work in intelligence, on projects that take us around the world at a moment's notice. At least we did. We've been suspended for the last—what is it?—whoa, almost two months now. We didn't do anything wrong. We just happened to be on a job that went sideways through no fault of our own. But until the investigation is complete and we're cleared, we're on hiatus.

On the screen, the movie comes to an end in a flash of headlights and the rolling of the credits to the music of Huey Lewis and the News.

I'm about to ask Jar if she's hungry, thinking I might whip us up a couple of omelets, when she picks up her phone, unlocks the screen, and shows me a picture of a Winnebago Travato camper van.

"That's, um, nice?" I say.

"It will be ready for pickup at noon. But it is in Tustin so we should leave by eleven."

"And why would we be picking this thing up at noon?"

"Unnecessary question."

Like I said, not a fan of questions with obvious answers. Unfortunately, the answer isn't so obvious to me, so I say, "Indulge me."

She sits up, her eyes rolling. "Because I reserved it."

I huff a laugh that I should have probably held in, but it got away from me before I realized it.

Her eyes narrow. "You promised to take me on a road trip, remember? When will there be a better time?"

We've been talking about a road trip for a while. Jar's exposure to the States has been limited to the few places where we've done some work—both on my personal projects and on missions from our day job. She's been keeping a list of places she wants to see. It's grown pretty long and would probably take us a year of constant traveling to complete.

We don't have a year. At least, I don't think we do. The day job is bound to come roaring back to life at some point. Could be tomorrow. Could be a month from now. Likely it'll be somewhere in between. So we should have a week or two at least.

And given the press attention the Masked Vigilante is receiving, now is the perfect time for a getaway.

I push off the couch. "I guess we should get packed."

CHAPTER THREE

We spend the first night in the parking lot of a Walmart in Henderson, Nevada.

I didn't even know that was a thing, but apparently it is. Turns out, most Walmart locations are happy to let RVs drop anchor for free in their parking lots. This was a tip from the rental agent when we picked up the Travato.

I had thought about taking Jar on a drive down the Vegas Strip. Sure, the casinos are all closed but the lights are still on, and if you're in the area, it's worth a look. But we left the L.A. area later than planned so I'm a little beat.

The reason for the delay was a good one, though. The Travato has a trailer hitch, and it turned out the rental place had motorcycle trailers, too. So we rented one and made the return trip to Redondo Beach to pick up my Yamaha.

We're on the road again before the sun comes up, and reach Hoover Dam just as the sky is lightening. The structure is the first item on Jar's list to be checked off.

There are usually tours that take you inside, but not these days. As a reminder, the world is on fire, in a slow-burn, don't-get-too-close-to-me kind of way. Nothing fun is open. While it's not an ideal situation for our little adventure, it also means most of the places we'd like to visit won't be very crowded.

We walk the top of the dam and gaze out at the Colorado River below. After a few minutes of watching the water stream away, I hold out my phone so that we are both in frame and say, "Smile."

"Must we?" Jar asks.

"It's proof that we were here."

"I don't need proof that—"

"Just smile."

I snap the shot.

It's a good one. I'm not sure I'd call the expression on Jar's face a smile, but she doesn't look completely uncomfortable so that's a win in my book. I send the picture to one of our partners in San Francisco, knowing she'll appreciate it, then Jar and I head back to the camper.

Our final destination for today is the Grand Canyon, and we reach it in just a few hours. All the national parks closed in mid-March and stayed that way through April. Though the pandemic is still with us, most of the parks have reopened, albeit with limited admissions and none of their usual amenities available.

Jar scored us a two-day pass and a camping spot inside the park, but when we get there, we realize we probably could have just bought a pass upon arrival. Hardly anyone else is around.

I don't know whether you've been to the Grand Canyon or not so let me set the scene. After you enter via the south entrance, you drive through a few miles of flat forest. And while it's nice to look at, it's a little different from the view you have before you arrive at the park's gate. Even when you get to the visitor's center (currently closed), you still can't exactly see what all the fuss is about.

But then you walk over to the trail along the rim and...wow.

Normally, the only times I've ever seen Jar look stunned is when she's confronted with a social interaction to which she doesn't know how to respond. This time, the surprise on her face is triggered purely by the view in front of us.

It's a glorious, crystal-clear day, the temperature probably hovering around twenty-two degrees Celsius (seventy-two degrees Fahrenheit for the metrically challenged). The last time I was here, I was a teenager on a trip with my family. Summer vacation, probably, because I remember it being a lot hotter. It was also hazy, making the other side of the canyon look out of focus. That's not the case today.

Neither of us say a word for at least fifteen minutes. Out of the corner of my eye, I watch Jar slowly scan the canyon, then scan it again.

She's the one who finally breaks the silence. "It's...magnificent."

I smile. Magnificent is not a word I've heard her use before, but it doesn't surprise me. Her English vocabulary is better than many native speakers'. You might notice she just used a contraction. It's something we've been working on. There's still room for improvement but I have no doubt she'll get there.

We spend several hours driving along the rim, stopping now and then for another look. At around three, we head for our campground. Like elsewhere in the park, the entrance has signs warning us to keep our distance from others. It's almost laughable. While the campground probably has more than a hundred spots, I count only eight of them being used, each space far from other campers.

Our spot puts us on the northwest end, our closest neighbors a couple of sedans parked together with three tents set up behind them. They're about fifty meters to the south, and about the same distance to the east is a big Winnebago RV. You know the type—as large as a bus? It makes our Travato, which is also a Winnebago, look like a VW Bug.

Since this is a vacation, my first order of business is to take a nap.

Don't judge me. In my day job—and often on my little side projects—I get very little sleep, so I've learned to grab it when I can.

When I wake, the sun is much lower in the sky, and Jar has a fire going in the pit a few meters outside the Travato's door. She's looking at her computer and sitting in one of the foldout chairs that came with the camper.

I grab one of the books I've brought along and head out to join her.

The temperature has dropped several degrees, and while it's still nice enough, I welcome the warmth of the fire as I plop into the chair next to Jar.

"Hey," I say.

She grunts a hello without taking her gaze off her screen.

She's engrossed in a movie or TV show of some sort. I glance at it for a few seconds to see if I can figure out what it is, but it's not familiar. I open my book, *The Midnight Library* by Matt Haig, and start to read.

I've probably polished off ten pages when I hear Liz's voice say, *Take a walk.*

I grimace and try to focus on the book.

Now would be good, Liz says.

It's kind of weird having your dead girlfriend living in your head. Especially when you're sitting next to your new girlfriend, who's not really your girlfriend, though kind of, but not really, but maybe.

Sometimes I think my life's a mess.

Now, Liz says.

I push out of my chair and set my book on it.

Jar taps her space bar, stopping the video, and removes one of her wireless earbuds. "Where are you going?"

"Need to stretch my legs. Thought I'd go for a walk."

"I'll come with you."

She closes her computer and gets up.

As Jar walks over to put her computer in the Travato, Liz says, *Please*.

I scoop some dirt onto the fire to put it out as I ask in my head, *Which way?*

Instead of receiving an answer in words, I feel a pull to the north. It's not strong, but it's definitely there. It's also completely my imagination. I mean, it has to be, right? I'm not really being haunted by Liz's ghost, so she can't possibly be using her "para-normal" abilities to guide me anywhere.

That would be ridiculous.

And yet, as I've learned over the many months when she's been talking to me again, it's better to heed her suggestions so I head north.

I hear the Travato door close behind me and Jar jogging to catch up with me.

When she reaches me, she hands me a face mask and asks, "Where are we going?"

"I'm not sure," I say, pulling the bands over my ears.

I can feel her giving me a sideways look but I don't react. Like I said, Jar doesn't know about Liz.

Wait. Let me rephrase.

She *does* know who Liz was. Knows about the relationship Liz and I had. She was there when Liz was shot about a year and a half ago. But if she knows about Liz and my continued conversations, she has never let on. Besides, she'd think I'm crazy.

Hell, even I think I'm crazy.

We take a path north out of the campground, toward the canyon rim. When we reach a fork, Liz's tug pulls me to the left.

It would be a lie to say I'm not getting a little anxious. The last time Liz led me down a trail like this, I ended up finding a dead body. I'd prefer not to do that again.

The path, which has been concrete to this point, narrows as it transitions to packed dirt. The brush to either side is filled with the budding green of spring growth. I can almost feel the pollen in the air, and remind myself to take an allergy pill when we get back to the camper so that I don't end up sneezing all night.

The path forks again, the main trail continuing straight west, while a smaller, less used one veers off a bit more to the north. Unsure which way Liz wants me to go, I slow my pace.

North, she finally says.

"This way," I tell Jar, and swing onto the smaller path.

I can feel Jar's gaze on my back, but I choose to believe this is because the new path has forced us to walk single file, rather than because she's wondering about my sanity.

I get a glimpse of the canyon through a gap in the brush. It can't be more than thirty meters to our right.

I silently ask, *What are we doing here?*

Typical of Liz, she does not answer. Maybe she thought I needed some exercise.

Then I hear a voice. It's coming from somewhere ahead and is barely audible above the rustle of wind through the brush.

"What was that?" Jar asks.

She's heard it, too. I didn't think it was Liz's voice but it's nice to know for sure.

"I don't know," I say.

When we hear it again a few seconds later, I note a tone of panic I didn't pick up before. Both Jar and I start to run at the same time.

I'm not sure if it's due to the sound of our feet or the person has stopped talking, but I don't hear the voice anymore. I'm not even sure exactly where it came from. We've gone twenty meters already and it's possible we've already passed it.

Then Liz says, *Here*.

I turn to my right, into the brush on the canyon side. Behind me, I hear Jar slide to a stop on the path before following.

"Help me! Please!" The voice is directly in front of us but still muffled. Which is strange, because it's not that far to the edge of the canyon.

I try to peek ahead, but I don't see anyone through the breaks in the bushes.

I weave left and right, literally taking the path of least resistance, until the tall brush we're in is replaced by small scrubs all the way to the canyon's lip.

I stop. There's no one here. I look left and right but we are the only ones around.

I cup my hands around my mouth and yell, "Where are you?"

"Please! I'm down here. Please help me!"

Jar and I rush to the edge of the canyon because—*of course*—the person needing help is on the other side.

In case you've never been here, the Grand Canyon for the most part does not have guardrails, so you can walk right up to the very edge and, if you're as unlucky as the guy crouching on a ledge about two meters below us can attest, you can go over the side, too.

He's in a precarious spot. The half-meter-long ledge is just wide enough for his shoes to fit side by side. About the only good thing is that the canyon wall is not a sheer drop like it is in some places. But the slope is still steep, and if he slips off the ledge, he'd be in for quite the long slide before he stops again. He might survive it, but he wouldn't be in good shape.

He's clutching something in his right hand that looks like a stuffed animal. He looks too old for something like that, but who am I to judge?

"Please, get me up!" he says.

When I first glimpsed him, I thought he was probably in his twenties, but now as he stares up at us, hope in his eyes, I realize he's a lot younger, maybe sixteen or seventeen.

He's pressing his body against the canyon wall, his arms thrown out on both sides, hugging the rock. And he's not wearing a face mask, which is becoming an unusual sight these days, even when one is out alone.

"Can you raise your hands above you head?" I ask. If he does, they might be high enough for us to grab.

The speed at which panic replaces the hope in his gaze has to be some kind of world record. "Are you kidding?"

"Okay, okay. We'll figure something else out. Just don't move."

"Where would I go?"

I take several steps to the left to get a better look at the ledge he's on. It appears stable but there's no way to tell for sure, and it's possible the whole thing could shear off at any moment.

"What's your name?" I ask.

"Evan."

"Evan, I'm Nate. I'm going to need you to hang in there for a little bit longer."

"No, no! You have to get me up now."

"To do that, I'm going to need some rope. We have some in our camper. It'll take me a few minutes to get it, but I promise I'll be right back. Jar will stay here with you."

"Jar?"

"I'm Jar," Jar says.

"That's your name?"

"Is that a problem?" Jar asks.

Apparently realizing how insulting he sounded, he says, "No. Um, sorry. I, uh, was just asking. Hey, uh, did you see anyone else up there?"

"Anyone else?" I ask, looking around. "Should there be?"

He hesitates then says, "I thought I heard someone right before you showed up."

"Just us as far as I know. Now you sit tight. I'll be right back."

I race toward the campground. About halfway there, I'm hit with the sensation someone's watching me. Without breaking stride, I glance over my shoulder, but the trail behind me is empty.

The rope is in one of our gear bags, which is stowed in the storage area under the Travato's cushioned bench seat. We may be on vacation, but I've learned if I'm going to be away from home for more than a day, it's always best to take the tools of my trade with me.

I grab a hank of rope and am running back down the trail in less than half a minute. At the same spot as before, I once again feel the sensation of being watched. Someone must be hiding in the brush. If Evan wasn't on the verge of taking a fast trip to the bottom of the canyon, I'd take the time to find out who it is.

When I reach the canyon rim again, I'm happy to see that Jar is calmly lying near the lip, looking over the edge, talking to Evan.

As I stop next to her, I hear Evan say, "Is that him? Is he back?"

"He is," she says. "Just a few more moments now."

"Please hurry."

I unwrap the rope and tie a loop on one end that's large enough for Evan to fit through, then take the other end and run it around the base of the biggest bush I can find. I give it a tug. The bush jitters, but I think it will hold.

Satisfied, I return to the canyon lip and look over. "You ready?"

"Yes! Hurry, please."

I hold the looped end of the rope over the edge so he can see it. "I'm going to lower this down to you. I want you to put this over your head and under your arms so that it sits in your armpits and straps across your chest. Make sure to put the knotted end at your back. Got it?"

"I...I'm not sure I can do that."

"It'll be fine. I'll talk you through it."

"Oooookay."

I lower the rope until it dangles against his body. "Very slowly, move your left arm to your chest."

"I don't want to let go."

"Keep it slow and steady and you should be fine."

Evan does not look convinced.

"It's the only way we're going to get you out of there," I say.

His fingers curl toward his palm, then, like an inchworm, he slides his arm toward his body until his hand rests on his chest.

"Excellent," I say. "Now slip your arm through the loop, then raise the rope high enough so you can get your head through it, too. Remember what I said before. The rope goes under your armpit, and the knot at your back."

He gets his arm through with no problem, but the moment he bends his head forward to move it into the loop, he starts to lose his balance and slams back against the dirt wall.

"Ohmygod. Ohmygod. Ohmygod."

"You're all right," I say. "You're not going anywhere." While his left arm is in the loop, his head is not. "I need you to try again. But this time, don't lean your head forward. Just put the rope over the top."

"I can't."

"You can, Evan. Once the rope is over your head and your

other arm, I can pull you up and you'll be standing here with us in less than a minute."

Evan closes his eyes and takes a deep breath. At first, I think he's too scared to do anything, but then he brings his left arm back in, raises the rope over his head, and reaches back out to hug the wall. Then his right arm moves slowly to his torso and through the loop.

"Good," I say. "Really good. I'm going to pull on the rope now. Just a little at first to make it tight. Okay?"

He nods.

Using the lever of the bush, I do as I described, until the rope hugs his chest and the knotted end is raised behind his head.

"You ready?" I ask.

"Yes! Get me off of here."

I don't yank him up but pull at a steady rate, sliding him up the canyon wall. As soon as his torso is above the lip, Jar twists him around so that he can lean forward onto the ground. Once he can get a leg over the lip, I stop pulling and let him crawl the rest of the way to safety.

He lies there on his stomach for several seconds and then rolls onto his back, clutching the worn-looking stuffed tiger he's been carrying tight to his heaving chest.

Jar and I both move a socially acceptable two meters away. I disentangle the rope from around the bush and begin rolling it up.

When Evan finally opens his eyes again, I say, "Are you okay?"

"I...I think so." He sits up, pulls the loop off him, and drops it to the ground.

"You might have some bruises from the rope," I tell him as I coil up the last of it.

"Okay," he says as he jumps to his feet. "Um, thanks." And without another word, he runs back toward the path.

I stare after him. I didn't really expect him to hang around for social hour, but I thought we might get more than just "um, thanks." After he moves out of sight, I look at Jar. "Kids these days, huh?"

"He is troubled," she says.

"He's a teenager. By definition he's troubled."

Her eyes narrow in a grimace as she studies me. "How did you know he was here?"

Oops.

Not only is she asking something I don't want to answer, but I've failed to keep the surprise of her question off my face. I try to cover it with a comically raised eyebrow and say, "ESP."

"You turned off the path at exactly the right spot."

"It was just a guess."

She gives me a *hmmm* and starts walking toward the path.

She bought my excuse, right?

Yeah. I don't think so, either.

CHAPTER FOUR

Instead of returning to the Travato, Jar and I continue on our walk.

I wish I could appreciate the surrounding beauty more than I am, but Jar's not talking to me. At least not with anything more than single-word replies.

Which is *awesome*, by which I mean it totally sucks.

But what am I supposed to do? I certainly can't tell her Liz guided me to Evan. The only thing I can play is the it-was-a-lucky-guess card, but it would probably just make her more suspicious.

So I'm stuck with mostly silence, which turns to thoughts of Liz and what she did today. Leading me to Evan like that? I mean, it's great, but it also makes me feel uneasy.

Check that. Uneasy is too mild a word.

It makes me feel...well, shaken.

How can I continue to believe she's just a figment of my subconscious when she does things like this? Things that I have no way of knowing about?

Stop it, stop it, stop it.

She can't really be here. She can't.

I decide to do what I have done all the other times I was struck by this existential crisis. After considering the situation just long enough to make me feel troubled, I push the thoughts as far to the back of my mind as possible and lock them away.

Obviously this isn't a permanent solution, but it will get me through the present.

Jar and I watch the sunset from a canyon lookout point along the path, the last vestiges of the day playing out across the opposite rim as the canyon itself grows dark.

Not only is it a feast for the eyes, but the view is powerful enough to break through some of Jar's defenses, and she leans against me as we watch the final rays of the sun disappear.

Above us, the stars begin to shine, and soon a whole swath of ancient light dots the sky. With the night comes a chill in the air, which finally gets us moving back to camp.

I think everything is back to normal again until I catch sight of the Travato. I put the campfire out before we left but it's roaring again, and in its flickering glow I see the silhouettes of two people sitting at the picnic table that came with our campsite.

A glance at Jar tells me she's seen them, too.

For the life of me, I can't figure out who they are. Squatters? Park rangers? People who were cold and thought nothing of using our firewood to warm up?

It's not until we're about twenty meters away that I realize one of our visitors is Evan.

With him is a balding man in his mid-forties, if not older. His stomach sits as firmly on his lap as the grimace resting on his face. I can see the latter because neither of them is wearing a mask.

As we near the fire, the man stands up and prods Evan to do the same. The older guy is a bear of a man—that stomach of his hangs off a body that has to be at least a hundred and ninety-six centimeters (six foot five).

"Evening," he says. His voice is deep, scratchy. A smoker.

Jar and I stop on the other side of the fire, leaving a good four meters between us and them.

"We're sorry to disturb you," the man says. "It's, um, my understanding that you helped my son."

When the man says *my son*, Evan, who is standing behind him, looks at the ground as if wishing he was anywhere else but here.

"No big thing," I say. "Just happened to be walking by."

"Said he slipped and got trapped between a couple rocks and would have still been there if you hadn't stopped to help him. Doesn't sound like nothing to me."

That does not sound anything like what I did.

But seeing no reason to dispel the kid's lie, I say, "He'd have eventually worked his way out on his own. He wasn't really in any danger."

The man looks back at Evan, taps him hard on the arm, and nods at me.

As Evan moves closer to the fire, I notice a slight discoloration on the right side of his jaw. It could be just the flicker of the flames, but I don't think so.

"Thank you for helping me," he says.

"You already thanked me. You don't need to do it again."

"*I'll* tell him what he needs to do and what he doesn't," Evan's father says, a flash of his annoyance now directed at me.

I smile and make no other response.

The man takes a breath. "Sorry. The boy's got me a little…. It's all right. Look, I wanted to say thank you, too."

He takes a step as if he's going to walk around the fire to us.

Before he can, I hold up a hand in the universal signal to stop. "Don't worry about it. Happy we could help."

The man halts, seems to take in our face masks for the first time, then snorts a laugh. "Sure." He nods back at a lump of something sitting on the picnic table. "The wife sent over some cookies. She made them this morning." He forces a smile. "You have a good night now."

He grabs Evan by the arm and heads into the darkness, toward the big Winnebago down the road. Before Evan completely looks away from us, several expressions cross his face that seem to say *thank you* and *I'm sorry* and...well, the last isn't so much directed at us. It's more a sense of impending dread. Like he knows his evening is far from over and the worst is yet to come.

When they are out of earshot, Jar says, "I do not like Evan's father."

"*Don't* like him." I say this unconsciously, my inner tutor popping out to help her with contractions.

To her credit, she doesn't scowl at me like she probably should. "I don't."

"For the record, neither do I."

We sit by the fire as the night continues to cool. At some point I go inside the Travato, warm up some chili on the stove, and carry our bowls back outside.

We talk little as we stare at the flames and eat. This is not unusual for us. Comfortable silences are more the rule than the exception in our life together. Only something's not quite comfortable about this silence.

I don't know about Jar, but I'm having a hard time not thinking about Evan and his father. Every once in a while, I catch noises coming from their campsite, nothing loud enough to determine the cause but they make me uneasy.

It's nearly ten p.m. when we put the flames out and head inside the camper. As we do, I notice the fire at the Winnebago is still lit, so either they're staying up late or letting the flames burn unattended, which is against campground regulations, not to mention common sense.

Jar and I break out the PlayStation and play *Overwatch*. Yes, we've brought it with us. Gamers gotta game.

Except my focus is divided and I keep getting killed. I can't help but glance out the window every twenty minutes or so to see if the fire at the Winnebago is still going. It is.

After about two hours, when Jar says, "Maybe we should check," I realize she's been looking out the window, too.

Intuition, or maybe you'd call it suspicion, is a hazard of our day job. It would be great if I could turn it off when I'm not on a mission, but I've never found the switch. Right now, the feeling that something's wrong is hitting both of us hard.

We leave the TV on and set it to play a movie on Netflix so that the screen will continue to flicker. In the glow, we grab a few items from one of the storage bins and head out through the driver's door, which is on the opposite side of Evan's Winnebago. Though it's pretty cold out, we've opted to wear sweaters instead of jackets, as they will allow us to move a lot more quietly.

There are six campsites between us and the big Winnebago. In each is a cleared area with a fire ring and picnic table. The areas between the sites are dotted with a light cover of brush and the occasional tree. We stay low enough that our silhouettes are indistinguishable from the ground cover. We're aided in this effort by the fact moonrise is still a few hours away.

The campfire by the Winnebago is still burning, though it's beginning to lose strength. As we near, we can see the picnic table and some chairs similar to the folding ones we brought with us. They sit empty. The lights inside the RV are off, which I take to mean everyone's gone to bed.

My jaw tightens in annoyance. The rule about unattended fires is not the kind you want to ignore. An unwatched fire could be a death trap for anyone in the area.

I'm contemplating whether I want to make a big deal out of it by pounding on the RV's door and making Evan's father put the flames out or just doing it myself when Jar taps my arm. I glance at her, and she points at the ground near the firepit, a mixture of concern and uncertainty on her face.

For a second or two, I think the lump on the ground is a pile of supplies the family left outside. But then I realize it's a person, curled in a fetal position, facing the dying flames.

The air is chilly enough that sleeping outside couldn't be comfortable, even in a sleeping bag next to a fire.

But this person isn't in a sleeping bag, and has just a stocking cap and a jacket on over his clothes.

I lead Jar to the edge of the campsite. Though the person is facing away from us, I have no doubt it's Evan.

I scan the area to make sure I didn't miss anyone else. The person at the fire is the only one outside. I check out the RV. The only window facing the fire that doesn't have a curtain drawn is the one on the front passenger side.

Because the Winnebago is backed into its parking space, I don't have a great view through the window from where I am.

Check, Liz whispers.

I motion for Jar to stay where she is, then sneak across to the road that connects the campsites and move into the bushes on the other side, where I will have a better view.

Someone is sitting in the front passenger seat. The starlight provides more than enough illumination for me to see the person is bald and big. Unless Evan's father has a twin brother, it's the boy's dad.

I can't imagine this is where he spends most of his night, so what's he doing? Keeping an eye on his son? If so, he's not looking out the window. In fact, he appears to be leaning back in his seat.

One of the items I've brought with me is a pair of binoculars that has several modes, including night vision. I flip the switch and zoom in on the RV's cab.

It's Evan's father, all right. And from his closed eyes and slack-jawed mouth, I'd say he's asleep.

Hmm.

Something is leaning against his right shoulder, rising several centimeters above it. Maybe a stick or the handle of a broom. Hard to tell even with the binoculars. Whatever it is, I don't like it.

I watch him for several seconds to make sure he is asleep, then I move to the edge of the road and pick up a small branch that's fallen from a tree. While holding the binoculars to my eyes with one hand, I use the other to wave the branch in the air to see if the motion will stir the man. He doesn't even twitch.

I quietly approach the front of the Winnebago.

I can hear his snores now. They're not terribly loud but they are satisfyingly rhythmic. And I have a feeling it would take something dramatic to wake him up.

I move in close to get a good look at the thing leaning against his shoulder. My eyes narrow.

It's not a stick. And not a broom handle, either.

It's the barrel of a rifle, which I'm guessing is meant as a scare tactic to keep Evan in line. Even if the man doesn't plan on actually pulling the trigger, anytime you involve a weapon—especially only as a prop—the chances of something going wrong loom large.

I peek over at the fire.

Is Evan being punished because he went off on his own this

afternoon? Or is it because he got himself into trouble and needed someone else's help to get out of it? I think about the story Evan made up about getting stuck in some rocks, and wonder how much worse his punishment would have been if his father knew the truth.

A reflection of the flames where there shouldn't be any catches my attention.

Tiny and thin. There and gone.

I creep out from the RV, take a few steps toward the fire, and see it again. It's low to the ground, not far from Evan's legs.

I tiptoe a little closer, staying as quiet as possible.

I'm about two meters from Evan when I realize what's reflecting the fire. Strung from a leg of the picnic table to Evan's right ankle is a length of fishing line. It's thin, so it could easily be broken with a sharp tug. But it's not a physical restraint. It's a mental one. If, in the morning, the string is broken, Evan's father will assume his son went somewhere—never mind the fact that the filament could snap if Evan merely tries scooting a little closer to the fire.

It's simple and brutal and inhumane. And I don't for one moment believe this is the first time something like this has been used on the kid.

Evan's father is not just an asshole. He's a monster.

A thousand different things that Jar and I could do run through my mind:

Call in the park police.

Cut Evan free and hide him in our trailer, then turn him over to the authorities with pictures of what's been done to him.

Yank open the Winnebago's door, drag Dad out, and show him that he's not the only one who can be brutal.

But everything I come up with has issues:

Would the park police have experience dealing with child abuse? Or would they accept Dad's explanation when he tells them he was only trying to teach his son a lesson and, perhaps, went a little overboard?

Would the spotlight be turned on Jar and me for sticking our noses in other people's business?

Would the retaliation against Evan be worse than the initial punishment in the days following our attempt to help the kid?

And as satisfying as using Dad as a punching bag would be, would I soon find myself in a federal jail on assault charges?

If the campground was more remote and not in the middle of a national park, I could probably get away with feeding Evan's dad a little of his own medicine. Here, there are too many things that could go wrong.

Still, we can't just walk away and do nothing.

I'm turning toward the brush to rejoin Jar so we can talk over our options, when I hear the catch of a breath.

Evan is looking at me over his shoulder, his eyes wide in surprise. I jam a finger to my lips, hoping that will keep him quiet.

He glances past me at the RV window where his father sits and looks back at me, saying nothing.

I creep over and crouch down beside him. In a whisper, I say, "Do you want us to get you out of here?"

"What? No!" His reply is louder than it should be. He realizes it and shoots a glance back toward his father at the same time I do. His father remains asleep.

"You should go," Evan whispers, his volume much lower than before. "I'll be okay. Everything will be fine in the morning."

I glance down at his legs and raise an eyebrow, making it clear I've seen the fishing line. "That's not normal."

"It's...it's okay. As long as it's still there in the morning, he'll leave me alone."

I notice the discoloration I saw on his jaw earlier has grown darker. "You're going to freeze out here," I say.

"It's not that cold."

The truth is somewhere between the two. I can't leave him like this.

"You never saw me, understand?" I whisper. "No matter what happens, I wasn't here."

"What do you mean, whatever happens?"

"Do you understand?"

"I, um, I understand."

"Hang in there. It's going to be all right."

From the pile by the picnic table, I grab a couple pieces of firewood. But before I can add them to the pit so Evan will have a little more warmth, he whispers, "Please don't. He'll know some of the wood's missing. I...I'm not supposed to use any."

Though the level of my fury has just quadrupled, I put the wood back and disappear into the brush.

Jar is waiting where I left her. I tell her about my conversation and explain what I want to do. As expected, she's in full agreement.

While she stays to keep an eye on Evan, I hurry back to the Travato, where I retrieve a small piece of equipment I didn't think I would need. On my return trip, I angle my course to come at Evan's campsite from the back, and sneak up to the rear of the Winnebago. After taking a picture of the vehicle's license plate—it's from Colorado—I lower myself onto my belly, wiggle underneath the vehicle, and identify a spot on the undercarriage that will suit my purposes. From my pocket, I extract a tracking bug and adhere it to the spot. No one will ever notice it.

I slip back out, rejoin Jar, and we return to the Travato.

My mobile phone is not like your mobile phone. It can utilize both traditional cell phone networks and satellite networks, and has levels of encryption and security that are not available to the general public. Just one more perk of working in the secret world.

It also has dozens of apps you won't find in any app store. Some we've purchased from vendors who operate in a legally gray zone. Most, though, have been engineered either by Jar or one of my other partners.

I select one of the latter apps. It's a call disguiser, if you will. First, it will display to the recipient a phone number different from the one I'm actually using. Yeah, I know spam callers can do this. But my app goes a little deeper, and if anyone traces one of my calls, the evidence would convince them the faux info they receive is correct.

Another aspect of the app is that it allows me to change my voice. Sex, age, tonal qualities— all these parameters can be adjusted. Some of the settings work better than others, but I've used it enough to know which combinations sound best with my voice.

I adjust the settings to that of a raspy-voiced, seventy-year-old man, then select a phone number with an El Paso, Texas, area code and set the phone's current location as a campsite at the other end of our campground. I make my call.

I reach a voice message, which, at this time of night, is to be expected. It provides me with an option to be connected to the Grand Canyon's division of the United States Park Police. I push the appropriate button.

"Park Police," the voice of a young man answers.

"Good evening," I say, sounding tentative. "Sorry to bother you so late."

"It's all right, sir. What can I help you with?"

"It's probably nothing, but...well I saw something kind of strange."

"Yes, sir?" He's sounding interested now.

"I have a hell of a time sleeping. You'll know what I mean

when you get to my age. Sometimes I take a walk to relax. That's what I was doing. I just got back."

"You saw something strange on your walk?"

"Well, I'm not sure. It seemed strange."

"What was it?"

"Someone sleeping on the ground by a campfire."

"I'm not sure that's—"

"The thing is he, or I guess she—I don't know, I couldn't tell —wasn't using a sleeping bag. He was just lying there in the dirt, but he had a perfectly good RV right there next to him. He looked like a kid. Maybe a teenager. I don't know. It didn't feel right, though. You know what I mean?"

"You're sure it was a minor?" His tone has become concerned.

"I think so, but who can tell ages these days?"

"Why don't you tell me where you saw this and we'll check it out."

I give him the name of our campground and the spot number being used by the Winnebago. When he asks for my name, I say, "Oh, I-I-I don't really want to be involved. Just passing on what I saw."

"I understand, sir. But it would be helpful if—"

I hang up.

He calls back. (FYI, if someone calls one of my faux numbers, it gets routed back to my phone, with a notation on my screen so I know what number was called. Helps me keep my lies straight.) Since I have nothing else to say to the man, I send the call to a voicemail that will greet him with a generic outgoing message.

Now we wait.

A quarter hour passes before we see headlights turn onto the road that runs by our camping spot. When the vehicle reaches the Winnebago's site, it stops. I raise the binoculars. As I suspected, it's the park police. The officer turns off his head-lights but leaves his engine running, then climbs out of the driver's seat. His partner, a woman, exits the other side.

I swing the binoculars over to the Winnebago, expecting to see Evan's dad come barreling out, but the RV remains quiet.

The cops walk up to the front end of the campsite, where the woman turns on a flashlight and points it toward the embers of the now almost dead fire. When the beam lands on Evan, it stops moving.

For a moment or two, the cops seem unsure what to do. Then they approach Evan.

I know the exact moment they spot the fishing line attached to his leg, from the way the woman moves her light from Evan to the picnic table and back. She leans down and shakes his shoulder.

The way Evan jerks in surprise makes me think he dozed off. Either that or he's good at faking it, which, given the apparent relationship he has with his father, wouldn't shock me.

The officers talk to him for several seconds before the male cop walks back to the Winnebago. It looks like he's going to knock on the door, but then he turns his head back toward the fire as if he's been called.

Evan, who's sitting up now—carefully, to not break the fishing line—is looking at him, his mouth moving.

The officer turns back to the RV. Instead of knocking on the door, he moves up to the front passenger window and raises his hand to tap on the glass. He pauses and leans in closer.

This is the moment I've been waiting for.

For a beat, everything is quiet and calm. Then the cop whips out his pistol and barks something back at his partner.

He's seen the rifle.

The woman pulls out her own gun at the same moment she raises her radio with her free hand and speaks into it.

All the commotion must have finally woken Evan's dad, because the cop near him raises his gun high enough to be seen and probably barks something at the window, though I can't tell for sure since the cop's back is now turned to me.

I should have placed an audio bug in the area so we can hear what's going on. But I *am* on vacation so I guess I can excuse myself for not thinking of everything.

I'm wondering how the cops are going to play this since it's only the two of them. I get my answer about a minute later when the Winnebago's side door opens, and a woman about the same age as Evan's father steps outside. She has that scared and confused look of someone who's been unexpectedly woken from a dead sleep. She's wearing a robe, and her hair's in a loose, chaotic halo around her head. Exiting behind her is a preteen boy. Ten, maybe? Twelve? Hard to tell from where I am.

The female cop has them stand against the side of the RV, facing her. The boy moves close to his mom (I'm assuming that's who she is) and leans against her. He's holding something in his hand. A stuffed animal, I think. It looks like the tiger Evan was clutching when we pulled him off the ledge.

For the next four minutes, not much of anything happens. Then I see the lights of three vehicles coming down the campground road, at a much faster pace than how the first sedan arrived.

Two of the vehicles are park police, while the third belongs to the ranger service, bringing seven new people in all. The two rangers stay back by the road while the cops hurry over to where the woman cop is standing.

She's clearly the one in charge. She directs two of the new arrivals to join the first cop at the window to watch Evan's father, then she and two of the others enter the Winnebago. The final officer stays outside to watch Evan, the woman in the robe, and the other boy.

I can't see what they're doing inside because of the curtains over most of the windows. But when the cops outside the front passenger window step away and lower their guns, I know the officers inside have removed Dad from his seat.

Soon, they exit the side door with him, the rifle being carried by one of the officers.

What happens next is a whole lot of nothing, at least from Jar's and my point of view. Conversations are had, and two of the cops go back into the Winnebago—to search it, I assume. To us, it just looks like a bunch of milling about.

Again, I can't help but be annoyed I didn't plant an audio bug over there.

In the end, the entire family is split between police cars and driven away, Dad the only one in handcuffs.

Am I pleased with our endeavors tonight?

Not as much as I'd like.

Unless Dad ends up in jail for several years starting tonight, I'm under no illusion this will stop him from mistreating his son. All we've done is put a finger bandage on a gaping wound. At least Evan won't be spending the entire evening out in the cold.

The last two people to leave are the park rangers, who do so only after making sure the fire in the pit is out.

And then darkness returns to our little bit of paradise.

CHAPTER FIVE

Someone is pounding on the Travato's door.

I go from deep sleep to wide awake before the second rap. It's a habit you have to develop in my line of work. Grogginess is a quick way to an early death.

The faint light coming in through the windows tells me it must be around dawn.

Jar is lying beside me, a grimace on her face.

Yes, sometimes we do sleep together, like when we're camping. But we don't *sleep* together. At least not yet. And, I don't know, maybe never?

Ugh. It's all so complicated.

After a brief pause, the knocking returns.

I climb out of bed, pull on a shirt to go with the gym shorts I slept in, and peek out the window to see who it is.

If anyone was wondering how long Evan and his family would stay as guests of the park police, the answer is apparently until just a few minutes ago.

Dad is at the door, and he doesn't look happy.

I had a feeling he might suspect we were the ones who

turned him in. Of course, it's possible Evan told him we came by, but I'm hoping the kid kept his promise to me.

I'm not expecting this visit to be more than a bit of bluster, but I'm also not going to greet the man unprepared. I set a collapsible baton on the bench seat next to the entrance, where it will be easy to grab, and open the door.

"What the hell, man?" I say. "We're asleep."

"So were we when you called the cops on us last night."

"When I what?"

I'm a good actor. I mean, *really* good. You have to be in my world, which is why back when I was a baby spy, my mentor had me take acting lessons. Lucky for me, Los Angeles has some of the best teachers in the world.

Evan's dad is not buying my routine, though. "I know you called them! You need to stay out of our business. Understand me?"

He's puffing his chest out, all tough guy-like, so I step outside to remind him that he might be taller than me—not to mention wider, though I guess I just did—but I'm not a scrawny kid tooling around the countryside. To emphasize the point, I move right into his personal space.

"I don't know what the hell you think I did, but I do *not* appreciate getting woken up at the crack of dawn. So you either take it down several notches, and ask me nicely about what's bothering you, or you turn around and head back to your little camper, have a cup of coffee, and think about how much of an idiot you look like right now."

Unsurprisingly, he doesn't back down. "I know you called them."

"The cops? What do they have to do with anything? And why would I call them on you?"

When he hesitates, I sense he's beginning to wonder if he's made a mistake. Which tells me Evan has kept his promise.

The man takes a step back. "Just...leave us alone."

"Buddy, I was never bothering you in the first place."

He glares at me for a moment before heading back toward his Winnebago without another word.

I watch him until I'm sure he won't return, then I step back inside the Travato.

Jar is up and has the coffee going. She's also set one of our dart guns on the counter near her, in case things with Evan's dad got out of hand. I assume she's loaded it with some of the Beta-Somnol-filled darts, which would have knocked him out for a few hours.

That's Jar, always on the ball.

I make us some breakfast and we eat inside, watching Evan's camp.

I have no idea if the boy's family was planning on leaving today, but they're doing so now. Evan and the younger kid (Evan's brother?) are collecting the items left outside the RV and putting them away. Through the window, we catch glimpses of their mom doing similar chores inside. Every once in a while, Dad sticks his head out the door and yells something at the boys. What a lovely family picture. I wonder what daily life is like back home.

As I watch the two boys work, a memory tickles my brain. Three, actually.

The first is when Jar and I were looking down at Evan on the side of the canyon, holding a stuffed tiger and asking, "Did you see anyone else up there?"

The second, from moments later, when I was retrieving the rope from the Travato and had the feeling someone was watching me at the same spot on my way there and back. The sensations were fleeting, but definitely there.

And the third memory, late last night, when the cops came and Evan's mom and brother (again, assuming that's who they are) exited the RV. More specifically, the brother and the stuffed tiger he was holding.

Had the younger boy dropped it and Evan gone down to retrieve it? Is the boy the person Evan had asked about? Had he been the one watching me?

I file all this away as a point of interest, and take another sip of my coffee as the last of our neighbors' camp is stowed away.

Once all the storage-area doors are closed, Evan says something to the younger boy, who takes a seat at the picnic table. Evan moves to the edge of the campsite closest to ours and picks up a branch. After a glance back at his RV, he looks in our direction for several seconds, then kneels down.

My interest is piqued enough that I grab the binoculars, but bushes are in the way so I can't see what he's doing. When he climbs back to his feet, he looks our way again, and then, with obvious reluctance, begins walking toward the Winnebago. As he passes the picnic table, his brother stands and joins him.

Evan lets the other boy enter the RV first. After his brother disappears inside, Evan looks back at us for a third time before he, too, enters the vehicle.

Five minutes later, the Winnebago is gone.

"Want to take a walk?" I ask.

"Yes, please," Jar replies.

Evan has left us a message in the sand.

THANK YOU

It's nice to be appreciated, but the words are not making me feel as good as they should, because all I can think about is how crappy his life must be.

And no, that's not a tear gathering in my eye. That's...dust.

Like a sudden breeze, I feel Liz appear beside me. *Follow them*, she whispers.

I take a breath and close my eyes. *This is supposed to be a vacation. I'm not sure Jar will want—*

"We should follow them," Jar says.

I swear these two must have meetings behind my back.

But the truth is, I think we should follow them, too.

After I snap a picture of Evan's message, we walk back to the Travato, pack up, and head out.

Evan's father's name is Charles Price.

He seems like the kind of guy who'd go by a nickname, though. Maybe Chuck. Possibly Charlie. Definitely not Chas.

Let's call him Chuckie, shall we?

We know Chuckie's name because Jar looked up the Winnebago's license plate in the Colorado Division of Motor Vehicles database, and hunted down the driver's license for the man listed as the owner. The picture on it is definitely that of Evan's father.

Unless they've moved, Chuckie Price and family live in Mercy, Colorado. Jar tells me the town is in the farm-covered plains in the eastern part of the state. The last census put the population at a bit more than twenty-six thousand. A decent size. Big enough to be called a small city and support an array of fast-food joints, a Walmart, a county hospital, and four grocery stores.

There are three high schools in town—Mercy High, the big public school; St. Catherine's, a private Catholic school; and Grover High, the alternative school for those who can't attend one of the others for whatever reason. I only mention these because when searching Chuckie's name, Jar came across an article in the *Mercy Sentinel*—the local newspaper—about the Mercy High football team, which includes a line that mentions Charles Price as one of the volunteer coaches.

Six kids with the last name of Price attend the Mercy school district. As a sophomore at Mercy High, Evan is the oldest. Behind him comes a girl named Marina, who's a freshman, then a boy named Cody in seventh grade at Richmond Middle School. Next are a girl and a boy—Brooke and Sawyer—both in fifth grade, and finally a boy named Lucas in kindergarten. Brooke and Lucas attend Pierce Elementary, while Sawyer goes to Riverside.

Sawyer is Evan's brother. We know this because the parents listed on both of the boys' records are Charles and Kate Price. The parents of the other four kids are Steven and Melissa Price. Maybe they're relatives of Evan's family, or maybe they just happen to have the same last name.

Jar has been trawling for only easy-to-find info, so she hasn't discovered anything about Evan's mom other than the woman's name. She can dive deeper later if we think it's necessary.

Honestly, I'm not even sure what she's already learned is necessary.

We don't know what our end game is here. Are we only following the Winnebago to make sure Evan isn't punished again tonight? Or is our goal to make sure Chuckie learns to stop treating his kids like trash? That seems like it could be a longer-term project and I'm not sure we can commit to that.

The problem is, it's not in Jar's and my nature to turn our backs on someone in Evan's situation. Which is why we follow the Prices all the way to Albuquerque, New Mexico, reaching the city just before noon.

Instead of staying on the I-40, the Winnebago transitions onto the I-25 when it reaches the middle of town, and heads north for a few miles before exiting and pulling into the parking lot of a McDonald's.

I use the opportunity to stop half a block away at a gas station to fill up. The Prices are on the move again before I'm done. New Mexico has mandated no eating inside restaurants for the foreseeable future, so the Prices' order would have been to go.

On their way back to the interstate, they drive right past the gas station. I notice Evan sitting by the rear window, staring outside. I worry he might've seen me, but if he did, I'm sure I would have noticed some kind of reaction. He was simply sitting there, as if he was looking through this world into an entirely different one.

When our tank is full, we pick up some lunch ourselves and head out. No need for any rush, after all. The tracker tells us exactly where the Winnebago is.

The land north of Albuquerque is a wide open space, covered with scattered brush that rises no more than a few feet above the ground, and bordered on either side by mountains. The view is both monotonous and beautiful.

Soon enough, we reach Santa Fe. The city sits nearly two thousand feet higher than Albuquerque, which means the temperature is several degrees cooler here than where we stopped last.

My assumption is that the Prices will stay on the I-25 all the way to Colorado, but you know what they say about assumptions.

Just before the interstate bends to the southeast, the Winnebago exits and heads north into town. We follow.

We've been off the freeway for almost ten minutes when Jar says, "They're turning." She's looking at her laptop, keeping tabs on the tracking bug's location.

"Stopping somewhere or onto a street?"

"Hold on...stopping. Gas station."

I turn off the road two blocks before the station and work my way through the neighborhood, until I'm approaching the main road again just a block away from the Prices. Twenty meters shy of the intersection, I pull to the curb.

Though a building blocks our view, we are literally a stone's throw away from the Winnebago. I'm half tempted to send our drone aloft to take a peek, but it's the middle of the day. Someone would surely see it and wonder what we're doing. Which might lead them to call the police. People are very sensitive about drones these days, as if they're not being spied on in a thousand other ways all the time.

The Winnebago has a massive eighty-gallon gas tank, so we sit there for a while before Jar says, "They're leaving."

I wait until they've gone a couple of blocks, then pull back onto the main road.

"They're turning again," Jar says a few minutes later. The Prices have barely gone a mile from the gas station. "Into a residential area, it looks like."

"Maybe they've moved here," I say.

We've discovered nothing that would back this up so it's pure speculation, which is likely why Jar doesn't comment on it.

Instead of turning into the neighborhood myself, I pull the Travato into the parking lot of a supermarket three blocks away and park in an empty corner near the road.

Leaning over, I take a look at the map on Jar's screen. The red blip representing the Prices' Winnebago is moving down East Buena Vista Street. It makes two turns and stops in what appears to be the middle of the road. After remaining there for nearly a minute, it turns off the road onto one of the properties, where it travels about twenty meters before stopping again.

When it's clear the RV is going nowhere soon, Jar switches to Google Maps and brings up a satellite image of the neighborhood. The homes in the area are large, and most sit on equally large pieces of property. The Prices have stopped at one of these places, the fenced-in land at least an acre and a half, running from the street in front to the street in back.

Jar determines the property's address and hunts down the owners.

They are not Charles and Kate Price, but a couple named Tyler and Kristen Bacca. I would like to note this does not preclude the possibility the Prices are renting the place, so my speculation could still be correct. I keep the thought to myself, though.

We watch the dot for another twenty minutes.

"I don't think they're going anywhere soon," I say.

Jar glances at me and then back at the map. It's about as much of an acknowledgment as I'm going to get that she thinks I'm right.

"Let's take a closer look."

It feels nice to get my motorcycle off the trailer and onto the road. It's a Yamaha MT-07, black with red rims. A fun bike to tool around on.

I can't help but feel the desire to air it out as soon as we leave the parking lot, but I resist.

It takes a little over a minute to reach the road where the Prices stopped. The property has an automated metal gate sitting across the entrance. That's likely why the Winnebago paused for so long before turning onto the driveway. Beside the gate is a speaker box guests use to make their presence known. Chuckie probably walked up to it to let the occupants know he and his family were there. Or maybe he made Evan do it. Who knows?

The gate is connected to a six-feet-high wall that we know from the satellite image surrounds the property. It's plastered to match the adobe-style houses that are prevalent throughout the area. Combined with some trees in the yard, it prevents us from seeing even a hint of the house or the Prices' Winnebago.

I drive around the block, to the back side of the lot. I'm hoping there's an exit we couldn't see in the photo, but the wall is solid all the way across.

One thing is for sure—this place is expensive.

We don't know anything about the Prices' financial situation, but if they're renting this house, they must be doing pretty damn well.

"Seen enough?" I ask.

"For now."

Instead of returning to the Travato, I take us on a drive through town. We are on vacation, after all.

It's a gorgeous day, the air crisp and the sky clear. The kind of day that makes you want to be outside. But the roads and the sidewalks aren't as full as you'd normally expect. Shoutout to the virus for keeping everyone inside.

The southwest adobe-style architecture I noted earlier extends to pretty much everywhere. The houses, the stores, the medical offices, the car repair shops. Even the state capitol building is finished in the ubiquitous tan and burnt orange color scheme.

Huh. Ubiquitous. I don't think I've ever actually used that word in a sentence before, but *man*, is it appropriate now.

Most of the businesses appear to be open, though with signs in their windows reminding customers that masks are mandatory and only a limited number of people are allowed in at one time. Most restaurants are also open, their signs reading TAKEOUT   ONLY   or   OUTSIDE   DINING AVAILABLE.

What a fun little world we're living in right now.

We stop at a coffee shop and sit at one of the tables on the sidewalk.

Jar asks the question that's apparently been on both of our minds. "What do we do now?"

I take a sip of my latte, then say, "We could head up to Taos. It's not that far. Take a drive through the mountains. Or we could go south to Carlsbad. I hear the caverns down there are pretty cool. Roswell's in this state somewhere. That's on your list, isn't it? We could go check out the aliens." I start humming the theme song to *The X-Files*, a show I introduced her to and we've been making our way through.

Jar apparently isn't a fan of my musical skills, as she cuts me off with, "We are not going anywhere."

"All right. Then I guess we could stay here."

"Better."

We both take another sip.

"So," Jar says, "what do we do now?"

The first thing we do is return to the Travato.

While I put the bike back on the trailer, Jar goes inside to find us a place to stay for the night. Not that we're entirely sure we're going to stay. That'll depend on what the Prices do. But it will be helpful to have something lined up in case we need it.

By the time I join her, she's already reserved us a spot at the Los Sueños de Santa Fe RV Park & Campground. It's several miles southwest of the house where the Prices are, but is closer than either of the city's two Walmarts.

With our accommodations taken care of, Jar sets to work on finding out whatever else she can about the Prices. I could help her out—I'm not too shabby at this kind of research myself—but

Jar is several levels better than I, and I'd probably end up "uncovering" things she's already discovered.

So, even though it's only four p.m., I decide to cook us dinner.

My pork chops are browning very nicely, thank you, when Jar says, "The women are sisters."

"I'm sorry?"

"Kate Price and Kristen Bacca—they are sisters."

"Huh. Are the Prices renting from them or visiting?"

"Visiting. From what I can tell, the Price family still lives in Mercy."

"Then chances are they're staying the night."

"There is no way for me to know that."

Here's the thing about Jar. Her default setting is to avoid answering questions with speculation or flat-out guesses. I'm not saying she never does that. It happens, but often with great reluctance. It's something she's been working on, to mixed results so far. Let's just say, I have greater confidence that she'll be free and easy with her use of contractions long before she overcomes her aversion to voicing suppositions.

But given that evening in rapidly approaching and the Winnebago hasn't moved an inch, the Prices are most likely going to spend the night at Aunt Kristen and Uncle Tyler's.

I plate the pork chops, put a healthy scoop of rice beside them, and add several spears of steamed asparagus to each serving.

"He owns a car dealership," Jar says as I carry the dishes to the table.

"Chuckie's a car salesman?"

"Chuckie?"

This is when I realize I haven't shared with her my nickname for him. "He seems like a Chuckie."

The variations in what Jar can convey in the roll of her eyes is pretty astounding. Annoyance, disgust, pity, intellectual superiority, among other expressions. I have been at the receiving end of all of them.

Right now, I'm being hit with a healthy amount of why-do-I-put-up-with-you. The answer is because I'm cute and funny. I don't tell her this, because I have a feeling it would subject me to a less than agreeable reaction. But I know the truth.

"The Prices have some money, then," I say. Which makes sense, given how much the Winnebago probably set them back.

"Unless he is hiding a bank account I cannot find, not as much as you might think."

She shows me Chuckie's bank balances. He's got eighteen grand in savings, and a little over three in a checking account. He also has an investment account with fifty-seven thousand in it, but that's it.

Eighty thousand dollars is nothing to sneeze at, but it does not seem like much for a car dealership owner. He doesn't even have enough to pay for his sons' college. (If they're planning on going and he's planning on contributing, that is.) In fact, he's one bad medical problem away from going broke.

"Does he have a retirement account?" I ask.

"Not that I could find."

I sit down next to her. "Any criminal record?" I ask, because if I called the cops on him less than twelve hours after meeting him, surely someone who's known him longer has called the cops, too.

"He has a DUI from four years ago, but that is all I can find."

"No police visits to his house?"

"Not in the records."

"What about hospital visits? The wife, either of the boys?"

"I have not checked for that yet."

While the bruise on Evan's jaw might have been caused by

his stunt at the Grand Canyon, my senses tell me Chuckie was behind it. And there's no way it would be the first time he's been physical with his son. Still, there's a good chance Jar won't find any medical records. Abuse victims often forgo treatment if it is not absolutely necessary because that's what they're told to do.

Jar has found a few other items, but nothing that appears to be too important.

We watch an episode of *The Boys* on Jar's computer while we eat. When the Prices still haven't moved by the time the dishes are cleaned and put away, I drive us to the RV park.

The place is basically a big oval road, lined on both sides by campsites. Nothing fancy, but perfect for our needs. After we get the Travato settled into our assigned spot and hook up the electricity to charge the batteries, I roll my Yamaha off the trailer again, and we walk the bike out of the park to avoid making a lot of noise.

It was crisp earlier but as we ride back toward where the Prices are, it feels downright frigid now. Maybe not to people who live around here, but it sure does to an L.A. guy like me. I can't even imagine how Jar, who grew up in the tropics, is feeling right now. Probably like an ice cube. And yes, we're both wearing jackets and gloves but they're not helping as much as I'd like.

Though the traffic is even lighter now than when we drove to the RV park, the traffic lights seem to be conspiring against us, and it takes us nearly fifteen minutes to get back to the neighborhood where the Winnebago is parked.

Streetlamps are a rarity in the area. There are none on both the street Evan's aunt and uncle live on and the road behind their property. What keeps the area from being completely dark is the glow from exterior lights on many of the houses.

Three blocks away, we find a road that has only a few houses on it, one of which is under construction. I kill the engine and we get off, then Jar follows me as I roll the Yamaha behind the unfinished house. The spot keeps us out of sight of the neighbors and anyone who might walk by on the street.

Jar extracts our drone from inside her backpack. The craft is palm-sized and has a battery that will keep it in the air for at least two hours. Its camera has both zoom capability *and* a wide-angle option that can give an excellent overview of a large area. Like my binoculars, it has several modes—infrared, thermal, polarized, night vision, and the standard day vision. The craft comes with several shells, so you can change its outer housing to match the current color of the sky and basically turn the drone invisible. But the best part, and the main reason it costs so much, is the whisper tech that keeps the engine and rotors all but silent.

Before leaving the Travato, Jar attached the night shell to the drone. She passes the craft to me and I hold it out in my hand. Using the controller app on her phone, she sends the drone into the night sky.

I look down at her screen. A graphics interface for the controls overlays the feed from the camera but doesn't distract much from the view.

We watch the feed as the drone comes at the Baccas' house from the street along the back of the property. The area immediately on the other side of the wall is mostly brush and dirt, well maintained. This runs all the way up to an outdoor living area consisting of a wide, arcing deck; an outdoor kitchen; an over-sized swimming pool; and an extra large Jacuzzi. No one's using the area tonight, but I imagine that would change as summer approaches.

The drone is currently too high for us to see through the back windows of the house, but there's no missing the spill of interior lights falling onto the patio.

Jar flies the craft in a spiral pattern over the lot, just like I trained her to do. With few exceptions, it is critical to start any recon with an overview of your subject before taking in any details. In addition to giving you a sense of the place, this also allows you to look for anyone lying in wait, ready to spring a trap.

Not that anyone will be springing a trap here.

The house is a big one, but we already knew this from the satellite image. What wasn't quite as clear in the photo, but is now, is that part of the structure on the west side is a three-car garage. The driveway that leads up to it curves past the front of the house and loops back to where it started. Parked at the side of the driveway, about six meters in front of the garage doors, is the Prices' Winnebago.

Interestingly, there are lights on inside it, too.

I wonder if the family is staying in the RV instead of the house. I remember as a kid visiting some of my parents' friends in Northern California somewhere. I think their last name was Forrester. They also owned an RV, though much smaller than the Prices', and me and the two Forrester kids, who were both around my age, got to spend the night in it. I thought it would be fun but it was kind of a nightmare. Not because of the RV, but because the older kid was an asshole, and I ended up staying awake most of the night to make sure he didn't punch me in the face while I slept.

Whoa. Repressed memory alert. Sorry about that.

Side note: William Forrester, wherever you are, I haven't forgotten you.

Jar finishes her circuit of the building and returns the drone to the rear, where she lowers it until she has a good view of the back of the house. From the number of windows and the way they are positioned, I'm guessing the place has at least four rooms along the backside. A kitchen, for sure, because we can see a large sink and what looks like an island beyond it. We can also see a living room—or maybe bonus room if that's what they're calling it—just beyond a set of French doors to the deck. Past this is a small, frosted window that I'm sure belongs to a bathroom. The last several windows are covered with curtains. They might all be for one bedroom but there's more than enough space for two.

Chuckie is in the living room, sitting on a couch, his arm around his wife and his mouth moving. He has the look of someone telling a story. Kate, on the other hand, looks as if her mind is a million miles away. I'm betting this isn't the first time she's heard this tale. Chuckie's main audience is the only two others in the room. They are both adults around Chuckie's and Kate's age, so presumably they are Kristen and Tyler Bacca. Kristen sits in an easy chair at the end of the couch nearest her sister, while Tyler sits in an identical chair at the other side.

The sisters look a lot alike, though there's a lightness to Kristen's bearing that I have yet to detect in Kate. What I find most interesting is the Chuckie-Tyler dynamic. Tyler looks small compared to Evan's dad, both leaner and probably a lot shorter. But make no mistake, he doesn't look subservient to his brother-in-law at all. If anything, he looks the king and Chuckie the jester.

We see no signs of Evan and Sawyer. And if the Baccas have children, they aren't around, either.

"Check the Winnebago," I say.

Jar flies the drone back over the house.

The RV's curtains have not been drawn, allowing us a clear view inside.

Evan and Sawyer are sitting next to each other at a table, looking down at a book. From the book's position—mainly in front of Sawyer—and the way Evan glances intermittently at his brother, I get the impression Evan is helping his brother with some schoolwork.

I think back to when I was a sophomore in high school. My little brother is only three years younger than me, so the gap between us is less than that of the Price boys. If I'd been told to help him with his homework, I wouldn't have been happy about it. I wasn't a jerk or anything. It's just the age. I'd have done it but would have been annoyed the whole time.

Evan does not look annoyed. If anything, he looks encouraging. He even smiles and nods occasionally.

Huh, maybe I *was* kind of a jerk. Does this mean I have to apologize to my brother for crimes not committed?

Jar hands me her phone, giving me temporary control of the drone, then pulls out two sets of comm gear from the backpack. After she dons hers, she hands me mine and takes her phone back.

I push the earpiece in and say, "I won't be long."

Sticking to the shadows, I work my way to the street that runs along the back of the Baccas' house.

When Jar flew the drone around the property, I looked for signs that the Baccas have dogs and saw none. But the lack of proof is not proof itself, so it's still possible one is roaming around somewhere. If so, I'm prepared. One of the things we purchased at Walmart was a bag of doggie treats, and I have several tasty Snausages in my pocket.

When I reach the Baccas' wall, I whisper into my comm, "Ready."

"You're clear," Jar replies.

"Copy."

I pull myself over the barrier and drop into a crouch on the other side. I hold still for an entire minute, waiting for any reactions to my arrival.

The night remains undisturbed.

I creep along the back until I reach the southwest corner, then head along the west wall toward the front of the property.

As I get closer to the house, I start to hear muffled voices and laughter coming from inside. I could easily sneak over to the swimming pool and get close enough to hear what's being said, but I'm not interested in Chuckie's stories.

The gap between the wall and the three-car garage is only two people wide. Unfortunately for me, the Baccas have chosen to use the space to store old pieces of wood and a few discarded chairs. This makes my way forward more like a *Ninja Warrior* obstacle course than a simple path through. I'm able to negotiate most of it with some twists and turns, but about three-quarters of the way through, I come to an obstacle I can't just scoot around. I could move one of the chairs blocking my progress, but since there's nowhere to put it, I'd be forced to carry it all the way to the end of the passageway. Instead, I suspend myself between the fence and the garage wall like a human arch, and move up until I'm high enough to shuffle over the chairs. After I clear the hazard, I work my way down until I can drop back onto my feet.

I pause in the darkness at the front corner of the garage and study the Winnebago. It'll only take me a few seconds to reach it, but I need to make sure Evan and Sawyer won't see me.

Let's be honest. I've been in infinitely more dangerous situations than this. Ones where crossing a similar stretch of ground could have cost me my life. What I am doing right now is like getting up for a glass of water in the middle of the night. Sure, I could stub a toe or trip over something on the floor, but for the most part it's something I should be able to accomplish with my eyes closed.

Neither of the boys is looking through the RV's windshield, nor has anyone come out of the house. Staying low, I make my way to the side of the Winnebago that faces the fence, and stop under the window directly across from where Evan and Sawyer are sitting.

"That's right, keep going," Evan says, his voice barely muffled by the wall of the RV.

I hear Sawyer next, his young voice speaking with the cadence of someone who is still learning to read. "'The...baaa-ker...took the...man's...order...and...'" He goes on like this for several more sentences.

When he stops, Evan says, "Very good. You understand what's going on?"

A pause. "The baker is making a cake for the party."

"That's right. Let's find out what's next."

Sawyer begins reading again.

I would like to note two things. First, Sawyer has a way of talking that is...different. I don't mean when he's reading, I mean his normal voice. It's not really monotone but it's monotone adjacent. I'm not saying he sounds disinterested, because I think he's enjoying what he's reading. I'm just noting the fact, that's all.

Second, Evan is a great kid, and you will not convince me otherwise.

I don't just want to help him now. I *have* to help him.

In case it isn't clear, I've returned to the Prices' Winnebago to rectify my previous error. From my pocket I withdraw one of the four listening bugs I've brought. They're small, thin, square pieces of plastic that have an adhesive on the back to hold them in place. But even with their tiny size, they'd be noticed if I am not careful about placement.

Ideally, it would be great to hide them inside the RV, but for obvious reasons that's not an option at this time. But they're powerful enough to pick up conversations inside the Winnebago even if they're placed on the outside.

I don't know how familiar you are with big motorhomes these days, but most have sections called slideouts that, um, slide out when an RV is stopped for the night, to give the occupants more room inside. The Prices' Winnebago has three of them. One next to the side door by which I am standing, and two on the other side—one at the back and the other across from the door where I am. The last is the slideout that contains part of the table the boys are using.

I remove the protective cover off one bug and carefully attach the disc to the underside of the slider next to me. This portion of the RV will move back into the vehicle when the slider is retracted. The bug is small enough that it won't interfere with the mechanics, and is in a spot that can only be noticed if someone gets on his or her hands and knees and performs a thorough examination of the area. Later, when the sliders are all put away and the RV is back on the road, the device should be almost dead center under the floor.

I creep around the RV to the slider that Evan and Sawyer are sitting in and put another bug underneath it.

In case the bugs somehow get knocked off the slider when it's moved into stowed position, I have an alternate location in mind for the final two. Like every RV I've ever seen, the Winnebago has several storage compartments, accessed from the outside. The holding spaces stretch under the camper's floor.

Naturally, the compartment doors are securely shut, but their locks aren't particularly complicated and I'm able to pick the first in short order. From what I can tell, the space beyond goes under the kitchen area. I place a bug as far in as I can without actually climbing all the way through the opening, then I shut the door and relock it.

For the final bug, I pick the lock for the compartment closest to the front of the vehicle. I'm at first doubtful I'll be able to get it close enough to the cab to pick up any conversations in there, but when I lift the door, I see that the compartment extends a good meter more toward the front of the vehicle than I assumed.

Currently, the compartment contains a couple of folding chairs but nothing else. I carefully move these to the side, and slip into the compartment to my waist so I can place the bug as far forward as possible.

I've just pulled off the protective plastic when Jar says, "Charles and Kate have just exited the house."

Crap.

I hastily shove the bug against the compartment's ceiling and start to pull myself out. I barely get a few centimeters when my jacket gets hung up on something.

Double crap.

"Fifteen seconds from you," Jar says.

Even if I am able to free the snag, there's no way I can get out of sight in time. I have only one option and it's not a great one. I reverse course and pull my legs inside, which ironically releases my jacket from whatever it was caught on.

"Five seconds."

I twist around, grab the back of the compartment door, and pull it tight into place, making it look like it's closed.

The footsteps round the front of the RV and pass right by me.

A woman's voice. "It's okay," said in the tone one uses when meaning *it's not a big deal* and *you're overthinking*. I assume it's Kate.

The only reply she receives is a grunt. That's definitely Chuckie.

The Winnebago's side door creaks open, then the vehicle rocks slightly as Evan's parents climb in.

"What are you still doing up?" Chuckie says. His words come quick and angry.

Evan says, "We, um...uh...I was—"

"What time is it?"

"Um...nine...forty-two."

"I *told* you to have him in bed by eight thirty."

"Charles," Kate says, "they were just looking at a book."

"Sawyer wanted a-a story. I was just helping him read it."

"See, they weren't doing anything wrong."

"You were told to have him in bed by eight thirty," Chuckie says, as if he heard neither Evan nor Kate.

"I-I'm sorry. I'll do it now. Sawyer, come—"

"No. Your mother will put him to bed. You, outside."

"Charles, no," Kate pleads. "Not here. You can't do that here."

I'm sure some might be upset that she doesn't stop at *you can't do that*. But my sense—albeit based on a very small sampling of data—is that Kate Price has very little influence over her husband, and saying that he can't do whatever he's going to do *here* is a way of utilizing what little sway she does have.

Silence in the RV.

In my mind I see Kate looking at Chuckie while Chuckie stares daggers at Evan, whose gaze is on the table as he remains unsure what to do.

When Chuckie finally speaks, it's in a low growl I strain to hear.

"Put him in bed, then you, too. And I don't want to hear a word."

Movement above, but by whom? Did Chuckie say that to his wife or his older son?

A few seconds later, I hear Kate say, "Can I get you something? Maybe some water?"

"I don't want any damn water," Chuckie snaps. "I just want to sleep."

"Okay. I'll get the bed ready."

Movement toward the back of the Winnebago, where the main bedroom area is. I'm guessing that's Mom, which probably means the instructions to put Sawyer to bed were given to Evan.

A temporary peace has returned to the Price household.

I have two choices. Either I wait here until I'm sure everyone's deep asleep, or I get out now while the Prices are still moving around, when their noises could cover any sounds I make. As you might imagine, hanging around for what could be a couple of hours does not sound like a fun idea.

I push the compartment door open and stick my head outside. Most people would likely get out as fast as they could if they're in a similar situation, but the chances of being heard would skyrocket. I take my time to carefully extract myself.

After I'm all the way out and the door has been lowered into place, I lock it again.

When I reach the wall at the back of the Baccas' property, Jar says "Welcome back."

"Thanks. Are the bugs working?"

"They are."

"Did you hear—"

"I heard. We are doing the right thing."

You are, Liz concurs.

I nearly jump. I hate it when she sneaks up on me like that.

Thanks, I say in my silent voice, then I hop the fence and make my way back to Jar.

CHAPTER SIX

I wake just after seven a.m., feeling well rested.

I slept great. I mean, *really* great. It's not that I sleep bad most nights—I don't. But I think finally getting back to work has eased something inside me that I didn't know was so tense. Granted, it's work for my hobby and not the day job, but it stretches the same muscles, both real and metaphorical.

Yikes. Suddenly I'm a philosopher. I'll try to temper that a little, but no promises.

Per usual, Jar is already up and working at her computer. I sometimes wonder what would happen if she gets eight hours of sleep. Could she keep going for days then? I'm not going to ask her out of fear she would actually try it out.

"The Prices up yet?" I ask as I make myself a cup of coffee.

"I hear some movement but no voices yet," Jar says.

Which probably means Chuckie is still asleep, and whoever is up—maybe Kate, maybe one of the boys, maybe all three—is making as little noise as possible to not wake the lion.

"What are you doing?" I ask.

She turns her computer just long enough for me to see the screen. On it is today's *New York Times* crossword puzzle. She's taken to doing them every day, though she has yet to finish one without considerable help. Not only is English not her first language, she doesn't have the cultural knowledge to decipher many of the clues. Still, it's surprising how much she does figure out on her own. I give her four months, six tops, before she's knocking them out in record time.

I retrieve my own laptop and sit across from her. I check the news first and read an encouraging report on a possible vaccine for the virus. It's still in the trial phase, but scientists are upbeat about its potential to fight off the pandemic. It's funny—this thing has been with us only since the start of the year, so just under five months, but it feels like it's been here forever, and any reports about potential vaccines seem like fantasies that will never happen.

I guess it's a case of I'm-not-going-to-believe-any-of-it-until-someone-is-shooting-the-cure-into-my-arm type of thing.

And now I'm Doubting Thomas. What the hell is going on with me this morning?

I skim through the rest of the news and then click over to YouTube, wanting to find something funny to put me in a lighter mood. I'm watching a video montage of people trying to ice skate for the first time when Jar sits up and says, "He's awake."

I click pause as she turns up the volume on her computer.

"...because that's what we're going to do, that's why," Chuckie's saying.

"All right, then that's what we'll do," Kate replies in a calming voice. "But....they're going to wonder why we left without saying goodbye. I know you don't want that. Why don't we have breakfast first? They should be awake by the time we finish."

Though I don't hear it, I imagine that Chuckie takes an exasperated breath right before he says, "Fine."

When the conversation seems to end with that, I ask Jar, "They're leaving?"

She nods. "The father said he wanted to leave right away so they could be home by lunchtime. The mother would like to say goodbye to her sister first."

"Why the sudden desire to get out of there? Did he get a phone call or something?"

"I did not hear him taking a call."

"Maybe he got a text or an email."

Jar says nothing to this, as she has no way of knowing the answer.

It's possible Chuckie had a falling out with Tyler and Kristen the night before. He *did* seem agitated last night when he and Kate returned to the RV. Or maybe he just isn't a big fan of his sister-in-law and her husband. Whatever the case, if they're getting back on the road, we need to do the same.

I take a quick shower, get dressed, and go outside, where I unplug us from the RV park's electrical system and make sure my motorcycle is securely in place on the trailer.

Since we know where the Prices are going, we don't need to wait around to follow them. We leave Santa Fe while they're still eating breakfast.

From the New Mexican capital, there are two basic routes to Mercy, Colorado. According to Google Maps, the longer trip is actually faster by nearly a half hour, thanks to the majority of the route being on the interstate. I'm guessing this is the way Chuckie will go. The second choice is a bit more scenic and travels through the tail end of the Rocky Mountains, on a two-lane highway for the most part.

Since we're still technically on vacation, I see no reason not to take this second option. I mean, we might as well enjoy the view as we stalk the Prices, right?

I still believe we're doing the correct thing, but what's not clear to me yet is what our endgame will be. Yes, our goal is to make sure Evan and his brother and their mother are safe, but it's not like we can keep watch over them for the rest of their lives. So, we'll have to either come up with a permanent solution to improve their lives, or at some point we'll have to let them fend for themselves.

I hear a whispered *not that* in my ear. Is it surprising Liz isn't a fan of leaving the Prices on their own?

No, it is not.

Once again, we are embraced by another gorgeous day. The bright blue sky is streaked with just enough clouds to emphasize how wide it stretches. And on the ground, the greens of spring tinge the brush all around us.

Jar stares out the window toward the mountains off to our right, taking everything in. Though I can't see it, I know she has an earbud in her right ear. While she's enjoying the beauty of northern New Mexico, she continues to monitor Evan and his family.

If there is any question as to how she can listen in on the bugs with them being so many miles away from us, the answer is simple. Our bugs have cellular technology built into them. It's basically like calling up a phone, which allows us to listen in from pretty much anywhere in the world. I don't want to beat a dead horse but it's more day-job tech.

We are almost to Taos when Jar says, "They're finally leaving."

"Did they get to say their goodbyes?"

"They did."

By my calculations, we have a seventy-five-minute head start on them, which means, even if they take the faster route, we will reach Mercy before they do.

If you've never been to the western half of the country, you might not fully grasp just how open the land is out here. After we pass Taos, it's pretty much all empty plains and mountains clear into Colorado. I'm talking miles and miles and miles of nothing but nature. You could fit dozens of Chicagos out here and still have room for more.

The border between states is marked by an old wooden sign that reads WELCOME TO COLORFUL COLORADO. A little while later, we cross the mountains. It's not as dramatic a view as the ones seen from the road that passes between Denver and Grand Junction, but it's still beautiful. When we come out the other side, the land before us lies flatter than any I've ever seen.

Welcome to the western edge of the Great Plains.

By the time we near Mercy, the open prairie transitions into tilled farm fields. We've also come far enough east that the Rockies have slipped below the western horizon, leaving nothing but flatland in all directions.

I grew up near both the ocean and the mountains in southern California, and I know from experience that if I go too long without being close to one or the other, I get a little antsy. It feels odd not to see land jutting skyward or to know the edge of the continent isn't a short car ride away. What I'm saying—and I mean no disrespect—is I think I'd go crazy if I had to live someplace like this permanently. Of course, others might drive themselves mad growing up where I did, knowing the earth could start shaking at any moment.

We are all the products of where we grew up, I guess.

The small city of Mercy comes at you in drips and drabs at first. A farmhouse here and there. Then a few more, getting closer and closer to one another. Just past a combo gas station/convenience store, we pass a sign that reads:

MERCY
CITY LIMITS

ELEV 3598 FT

The town sits along a spur of the Arkansas River, the
entirety of Mercy on the west side. On the other side of the river
we see only farms. Along the main drag, we pass a row of fast-
food joints, a dental office, and a place called Barkley's Hard-
ware Supply, where you can also rent a U-Haul truck.

The deeper into town we go, the older the buildings
become. Most of them are well maintained, though a scattered
few look empty and in need of work.

Downtown is centered around a quaint, two-story city hall
building, complete with four Greek columns flanking the
entrance. Next to this is Dornan Park, a lovely grass-covered
area with a large gazebo where, I imagine, the high school band
plays concerts on all the appropriate holidays. It sits beside the
river and slopes down to the water.

If Mercy was any closer to Los Angeles, it would be
crawling with film crews using it for commercials and TV shows
and movies. It has that Middle America quality to it that Hollywood loves.

Most of the businesses appear to be open, and a lot of the
people who are out and about aren't wearing masks. I'm
guessing the pandemic has either barely touched the town or
everyone is in a state of denial. Coming from California where
things are—shall we say—direr, I am appalled by and slightly
jealous of these people's innocence. Whether they want to
admit it or not, though, no amount of disregard will keep the
virus from coming.

Jar does a search for campgrounds and RV parks in the area.
Turns out Mercy is not a big stop for vacationers, and the only
official place for trailers and such is the Dornan Mobile Home
Park, whose website says it has a few spots for overnight stays.

This does not appeal to me. Mobile home parks have permanent residences on site. Likely, a lot of them. And I'd be willing to bet the temporary spots for people like us are located at the rear of the property, and every time we leave or come back, we would have to drive by all the trailers. I'm not sure how long we'll remain in town, but I would like to keep a low profile while we're here. Dornan Mobile Home Park is not the way to do that.

Lucky for us, there's a Walmart.

The superstore is located on the western edge of town. I park in an empty area near the northwest corner of the lot. After it gets dark, I'll move to a less conspicuous spot behind the building, where we will be unseen from the road.

I hop out of the Travato and roll my Yamaha off the trailer. As I bring it around the side, Jar exits the camper, carrying our two helmets and a jacket for me. As much as I would like to take a break after the long drive, Chuckie Price apparently has a lead foot, and the hour-plus lead we once had on them has shrunk to twenty minutes, leaving us no time to relax.

I take care not to rev the engine too loudly as I drive us back through town. Even then, we get the occasional curious look from pedestrians and people in other cars. With a population of over twenty-six thousand, the town is more than large enough that its residents can't know everyone who lives here, but every town has those folks who can sense whether or not someone belongs.

I've yet to see anyone of Asian descent around, and I have little doubt we'd be getting even more curious looks if Jar wasn't wearing her helmet. So far, the people have been mostly Caucasians and a few Hispanics. My sampling size is small, of course, but I don't see that mix changing very much.

We're waiting on a side street, near the south end of town where the highway enters Mercy, when the Prices' Winnebago drives by. I pull out at a leisurely pace and follow it. I figure they're heading home. That would be the first place I'd want to go after a long trip. But I'm wrong.

Instead of turning onto the road that would take them to their house, the Prices continue up Central Avenue—which is what the highway is called on the stretch running through town —all the way to the north end of town, where they pull into Price Motors.

We already know it's a Ford dealership, but when the lot comes into sight, I get the impression from the choices available that Price Motors does at least an equal amount of business in used vehicles of different makes and models.

I pull to the curb on the opposite side of the road at about the same time the Winnebago stops near the showroom. I'm not worried about being noticed. It's a four-lane road and we're parked in the shade between two cars.

Jar pulls out her phone and turns on the speaker just in time for us to hear Chuckie say, "Stay here."

This is followed by Kate saying, "How long are you going to—"

"I said *stay here*."

When the side door of the RV opens, Chuckie is the only one who gets out. He marches over to the glass door of the show-room, yanks it open, and strides inside. I see him for only a few more seconds before he disappears into the building.

Over Jar's speaker we hear Sawyer say, "I'm hungry."

"I'll make some lunch as soon as we get home," his mom says.

"There's food in the refrigerator."

"Honey, we'll be home soon. Let's just wait."

"But I'm hungry now." He's not whining. If anything, he sounds confused by her responses.

"We're not eating here," she says, exasperation creeping into her voice. I'm not sure why she doesn't want to give him some food now, but I have a feeling it has to do with Chuckie. Maybe he'd be angry if they eat without him. Or maybe she's just too tired.

Sawyer is not on the same wavelength. "Why not?"

Voice rising, she says, "Because—"

Evan jumps in. "Here. Eat this. That should hold you over."

There's a moment of quiet before Sawyer says, "Thank you, Evan."

"You're welcome."

After that, no one says a word.

I wonder what Evan gave his brother. Part of a saved candy bar? A cookie he'd stashed away? Maybe it was a piece of fruit from the counter.

Whatever it was, good on Evan for deescalating the situation.

It's ten minutes before Chuckie comes striding out of the building. After he reenters the Winnebago, we hear the creaks of the RV's floor as he moves to what I assume is the driver's seat. He utters not a word, nor does anyone else, their silent response likely a habit honed over who knows how many years of living under Chuckie's abusive reign.

The next sound is that of the engine starting, and then we're all on the move again.

This time, they do go to their house.

It's a white, two-story, clapboard home sitting on a corner lot in a quaint neighborhood. Separating the yard from the sidewalk is a waist-high, white picket fence. A nice home, where you might expect a dad to be playing catch with a kid in the yard, or the whole family giving a dog a bath.

The place has two driveways, one off each of the roads that go by it. On the side where the main entrance to the house is located, the driveway is short and leads to a detached, two-car garage. The driveway off the side road is longer and doesn't end at the building. It extends into the backyard about fifteen meters. Unlike the front driveway, this one is closed off by a gate that looks like it rolls to the side behind the picket fence.

The Winnebago stops in the middle of the side street, just shy of this second driveway. Evan gets out and hustles over to the gate. He's still in the process of removing the padlock and chain holding it closed when Chuckie taps the RV's horn. Evan flinches but he doesn't look back, as if he expected to hear the honk at some point. After he moves the gate out of the way, Chuckie pulls the RV onto the driveway. Evan then closes the gate from the inside and reconnects the chain.

Jar and I have been watching from half a block away. As much as I'd like to stay a bit longer, we've been here probably longer than we should be, so I turn the bike around and drive us off in the opposite direction.

We pick up lunch on the way back to the Travato and take it inside the camper to eat. I pick up my burger to take a bite, but I set it back down before I do and look out the window.

"What?" Jar asks.

Without looking over, I say, "What *what*?"

"You're thinking about something. What is it?"

"You know, sometimes people like to think and not talk."

"Hmmm," she says, the left side of her mouth ticking up in a grimace.

She continues to stare at me, which I'm sure she knows is unnerving.

Her stare causes me to squirm a little. Hoping it might get her to leave me alone, I reach for my burger again and take a bite this time.

Her gaze does not falter.

I sigh and say, "I'm worried that there might not be anything we can do to help them."

Jar keeps her gaze on me, as if she's expecting me to say more.

So I try to explain what's in my head. "We both know Chuckie's a class-A pri—"

"I do not like the name Chuckie," she says.

"Which means it's perfect for him, right?"

She glances away, thinking, then says, "Continue."

"People like Chuckie are never going to stop abusing their families. But unless he does something big that we witness and can do something about, what we're left with is a bunch of little things that can be brushed away."

"The incident at the campground was not a little thing."

"And look how easily he got out of that."

A frown. "Little things can be just as damaging. How can we ignore them?" This is something she knows from experience. Her childhood was not exactly ideal.

"Yes, they can be just as damaging. The problem is, if we try to act on any of them, it'll be easy for him to deny he did anything wrong. And it'll be our word against his, because chances are Evan and the rest of his family won't back us up."

From the look on Jar's face, she knows I'm right. It's not that Chuckie's family is fine with what he's doing to them, but shielding an abuser from blame is a common reaction of those abused.

"We could be here a long time before he does something big enough we can react to," I say.

As Jar stares at the table, the wheels of her mind turning, Liz materializes beside her.

Actually, *materialize* isn't the right word. I don't really *see* Liz as much as I feel her presence. It's often sudden and looming, like she's floating just above my shoulder. You might think it's less jarring having her sit across the table from me, but I tense even more when she seems to be buddying up to Jar.

Speaking of Jar, it's as if Liz's appearance has jolted her from her thoughts, because a second after my dead girlfriend shows up, Jar looks at me again and says, "We can't do nothing."

The words could have been spoken by either woman.

Hell, *I* could have said them. Because despite how I've been playing down our chances of helping, I also know that doing nothing is not the answer.

Ugh.

It's hard enough being ganged up on by Jar and Liz together. Now I'm doing it to myself, too?

"We do not have anywhere to be right now," Jar said. "Let's give it a little time, see what happens."

Yes, Liz whispers. *Time.*

Practical brain is telling me I should argue the point, but practical brain has been shoved aside, and sense-of-justice brain has taken over. "If we're going to be here more than a couple of nights, then we probably need to find someplace to stay that's not as *public* as here."

A hint of a smile on Jar's face. "I can look into that."

"And we'll probably need a less conspicuous vehicle, too."

"I can also—"

"No, I'll take care of that."

Jar nods while Liz radiates relief, and then disappears again.

CHAPTER SEVEN

W e need to bug the Prices' house.

Not just with audio bugs but video, too. That might sound extreme, but it's the one way to ensure we know what Chuckie is up to. Getting inside won't be easy, however. During the daytime, we would need to worry about their neighbors seeing me sneaking around. Mercy seems the kind of place where a person's not going to turn a blind eye to suspicious activity and would call the cops without hesitation.

Nighttime's problematic, too, because the Prices will be home. And it won't help that the house is older. Moving around it will inevitably involve trying—and likely failing—to keep the floor from creaking.

The issue is solvable but it will take a little thinking. Which is exactly what I'm doing while I drive to the north end of town, where all the car dealerships are located.

No, I'm not going to Price Motors. That would be tempting fate. Thankfully, Chuckie doesn't have a monopoly on vehicle sales in Mercy. There are three other dealerships. One Dodge/Chrysler outlet, and two that deal exclusively in used cars.

I don't need something new. In fact, I'd rather have something that has a bit of wear and tear to help it blend in.

I stop at the first used car lot and peruse the vehicles from my bike. I see a couple of sedans that look okay, but I'd rather not settle for okay.

I drive the block and a half to the other used car dealer, a place called—I kid you not—Auto Manic, and after a quick look from the curb, I pull onto the lot. A vehicle in the front row has caught my eye.

I'm barely off my motorcycle when a middle-aged guy in a yellow shirt and brown tie hurries out of the old construction trailer that serves as Auto Manic's office, waving and smiling in my direction.

"Good afternoon! How you doing today? Welcome to Auto Manic. I'm Kyle Remick."

He sticks his hand out toward me as I'm pulling off my helmet. I immediately retrieve my mask from my pocket, put it on, and fold my arms across my chest. *He's* not wearing a mask, and there's no way I'm touching that hand.

"Oh, yeah, right," he says, lowering his arm. "Hold on."

After shoving a hand into his pants pocket, a confused look crosses his face. He puts his other hand in his other pocket, but his expression does not change.

"Don't go away. I'll be right back."

I wouldn't say he runs back to his office—it's more a fast walk with pumping arms—but I bet that's what he thinks he's doing.

Though he's told me to stay, I head over to the vehicles lining the street. What I don't do is go to the one I'm interested in.

The trick with these guys is not to tip your hand. The vehicle I approach is a ten-year-old Honda Civic EX coupe, fading blue with gray interior. I see no scratches or visible dents, and the tires appear to have at least another year of treads left on them.

It's...fine.

It's just not $8,750 fine. That's the price listed in the window. Fair market value on a Civic in this condition is more like $6,250. Twenty-five hundred bucks is a hefty markup.

The door's unlocked so I lean inside and pop the hood. As I raise it, I get a glimpse of Kyle rushing back outside, his hands fumbling with a mask he's trying to attach to his ears.

I look at the engine. It's clean, which I take as a good sign. The battery will probably need replacing soon, but all the hoses look in decent shape. My inspection is merely superficial, of course, but it's enough to give me the impression that Kyle and company aren't trying to offload a lemon.

Kyle reaches me a moment later, huffing under his mask. Once he's caught his breath, he says, "Honda Civic—can't go wrong with one of these."

I say nothing and continue rooting around the engine like I'm looking for something specific. I'm not.

"This one's in great condition," Kyle goes on. "Had her on the road the other day and she just zipped along."

I give him a sideways glance, then return my gaze to the motor. After a moment, I let out a *hmmm* and straighten up. As I shut the hood, I say, "This your only Civic?"

He looks surprised. "Uh, at the moment, yes. Is there a problem with this one?"

Instead of answering, I scan the lot, donning a disappointed expression.

"We can take it out for a test drive," he suggests. "Once you get a feel for her, I'm sure you'll find she's what you're looking for."

I don't know if it's just me, but I don't like it when people refer to cars or, really, any kind of vehicle as a she. I might make an exception for big ships, but otherwise no. Why? I don't like the implied ownership of a woman. Sorry if that sounds too sensitive. (Not really sorry.)

"Whadda you say?" he asks. "I can get the keys and be back here in less than a minute."

He actually leans to the side as if getting ready to sprint back to his office, a come-on-let's-do-this smile on his face.

"I don't think so," I say.

The smile slips. "Sure, sure. Maybe there's something else I can show you."

"Maybe."

"I, uh, I didn't catch your name."

"Matthew," I say. It's the name on the fake ID I plan to use for my purchase. I have dozens of IDs in other names, though I've brought only a few on the trip. They're not the kind you can pick up just anywhere. Mine (and the ones Jar has) have been crafted by experts to withstand the harshest scrutiny. You could even look them up in the appropriate official databases and they would check out as genuine.

"Nice to meet you, Matthew. I'm Kyle. Kyle Remick. In case you didn't catch it the first time."

"I caught it."

"Oh." He laughs uncomfortably, then to cover this, he turns to the lot and says, "I've got a couple Ford Tauruses, a Chevy Malibu, and a, um..."—he looks around—"a Sentra here somewhere. Ah, there it is. The black sedan. Just came on the lot yesterday. Haven't even had time to move it up front yet." He pauses before adding in an enticing, almost singsongy voice, "It's only three years old."

I let him show me the Sentra and one of the Tauruses, but I continue to act dissatisfied.

When we're finished with the Ford, I say, "I'm just not seeing what I'm looking for. Sorry."

"What *are* you looking for? I can make some calls and I'm sure I can find it."

I start walking back toward the front end of the lot. "It's all right. Thank you for your time."

"No need for thanks. It's what I'm here for. But I'm serious about helping you find something."

We're almost back at the Civic. "I'll think about it."

The disappointment in his eyes tells the story of a man who's heard that line from a parting customer many times before, only to never hear from the person again. Ever the optimist, though, he pulls a business card from his pocket and holds it out to me. "Here's my number. Call me anytime."

I take the card. "Thanks."

I head toward the sidewalk, passing between the Civic and the Ford F-150 crew cab pickup that originally caught my eye. As I reach the front of the truck, I stop and look back at it.

"Hey, Kyle," I say.

He's already started walking back to his office, but he stops at the sound of his name and looks back.

"What can you tell me about this one?" I ask.

It will take me two trips to get my motorcycle and my new truck back to the Walmart parking lot. The first is to bring the bike back. It's about twenty centimeters longer than the truck bed, so I have to fit it in at an angle.

Kyle has kindly provided me with a two-by-eight board that I use as a ramp. He also made a call to one of his friends who sold me four straps that I use to tie the bike in place.

Jar exits the Travato as soon as I drive up. She eyes the Ford. "I was expecting something smaller."

"Have you looked around?" I ask. "Everyone's driving a truck."

"That is not true."

Maybe I exaggerated a little bit. It's more like every fourth vehicle is a pickup, but the gist of what I said is valid. The truck will not stick out as we drive it around town. Plus, it gives us options that a sedan would not.

Also, I've always wanted to own a truck, which might have played some part in my decision. But I'm not going to tell her that.

After I roll the Yamaha onto the trailer, I get back into the truck.

"Where are you going?" Jar asks.

"I left something at the dealership. I'll be right back."

Another thing about the truck that may have swayed me was that it comes with a hard plastic cover that encloses the bed and can be locked. This will allow us to carry stuff in the back without anyone knowing what's there. I had to take the cover off to fit the motorbike, hence the reason for trip number two.

After Kyle and one of his fellow salesmen help me get it back on, I return to Walmart.

I'm not the only one who has completed their task this afternoon.

Jar has lined up two rental places for us to look at.

The first is a farmhouse about three miles outside the city. The farmland around the place is apparently owned by a corporation that has acquired many other farms in the area. The death of the family farm by big business is a pattern that's been happening all across America for decades now.

The house sits back from the road a good two hundred meters, and is reached via an isthmus-like driveway, lined on either side by recently planted fields.

The house is half hidden behind a small copse of trees. It's a one-story place with a basement. About fifty meters behind the house is a faded white barn. Jar tells me the owners are using it for storage so it's not part of the rental deal.

Jar retrieves a key that's hidden in a pot on the side of the house, and we take a look through the interior. Someone renovated the place ten or fifteen years ago so it's more modern than I expected. It has three bedrooms, none particularly large; two bathrooms; a living room/dining room combo; and a decent-sized kitchen. It's partially furnished, which is good since we forgot to bring our furniture with us on vacation.

I like the anonymity of the place. No neighbors in sight, and little chance someone could sneak up on us without us knowing. But it *is* farther from town than I would like it to be.

We head to the second place, where we're met by the property manager, Mr. Hansen. The home is back within city limits and only five blocks from the Prices' house. That fact alone is very appealing.

The downside? It's one half of a duplex, and from the toys strewn across the shared front yard, the other half is home to a family with more than one child. That could be a problem. While children don't hold a monopoly on curiosity, they are more likely to act upon it. I am not a fan of prying eyes.

I'm also leery about sharing a wall. In part because I don't want to be jolted awake by voices from the other side, but mostly because I don't want anyone listening in on *our* conversations.

My fears are placated by our potential landlord while he gives us a tour of the inside.

"The builder put extra insulation between the units," he explains when we enter the bedroom that shares a wall with the neighbor. He pats it. "They're also double thick. Someone could be yelling on the other side and you'd never know it."

I'm not sure I completely buy that, but I do like that the

barrier is not a traditional wall. Besides, this room and a bath-room are the only rooms that butt up against the other half of the duplex. There's another bedroom and bathroom we can use to avoid this end of the house entirely.

We tell Hansen we'll get back to him and we return to the Travato.

"Well?" Jar asks. "Which do you think we should take?"

"I'm kind of thinking we should take both."

She cocks her head, an eyebrow raised.

Whoa. I've actually surprised her. That doesn't happen often.

"Hear me out," I say. "The duplex is close but not too close to Evan's house, so it's perfect for keeping an eye on things. But the Travato won't fit in the driveway, so we'd have to park it on the street. I don't like that idea. The farmhouse is too far away for us to be going to and from all the time, but it would be a good place to hide out if the need arises. *And* it has plenty of room for the Travato."

She considers my explanation and then nods. "I'll call the landlords."

I'm guessing the rental market is a bit depressed at the moment, because both landlords are eager to get us into the places.

We go by both of their offices and fill out the paperwork. Like I said, our aliases are solid, with excellent histories that will make us look like dream tenants. I briefly consider using a different ID than I did when buying the truck but decide against it. Better to be known around town by one name than two.

Our credit checks go as expected, and soon enough each landlord whips out a lease for us to sign. Both originally ask for a year but we talk them into six months. Our cover is that we're freelance web designers who work from home, and are trying out the area to see if it's someplace we'd like to settle long term.

Am I going to pay six months' rent on each? Not unless we somehow end up here a lot longer than I expect. But we will be sacrificing our deposit.

In case you're wondering how we can afford all this, Jar and I make good money. I mean, *really* good. It also helps that my day-to-day expenses aren't that high, and Jar's are next to zero. In my case, I've been doing my day job for about a decade now and I have a lot saved up. So, I have no problem spending a little cash to help someone in need. It's a solid investment as far as I'm concerned.

Hansen, the duplex owner, says that since the place hasn't been used for a couple of months, he wants to tidy it up before handing over the keys. He tells us to come back tomorrow afternoon, with a cashier's check for first month's rent and the security deposit. Even though we also won't be able to pay Mrs. Turner, the property manager of the farmhouse, until tomorrow, she says, "You know where the key is. Just go on in anytime."

Looks like we won't have to stay in the Walmart parking lot tonight.

But once again, we have a transportation dilemma.

The only kind of vehicle Jar has ever driven is a motor scooter. And while she can likely drive a full-on motorcycle, my Yamaha is too big for her.

Not sure if I've mentioned it or not, but Jar is small, like under one hundred fifty-two centimeters (five feet). She's slight, too. Though I'm sure she could quickly learn how to drive a four-wheel vehicle, I'm not about to start giving her lessons today.

We drive the Travato to the farmhouse, pulling the Yamaha in the trailer. The property has plenty of places to park, but the one I like best is a spot behind the barn, where the camper can't be seen from the road. Although the house has some furniture, it has no sheets or blankets or plates or silverware, so we'll probably be spending our nights in the Travato when we're out here.

We'll figure out how to hook up electricity and water to the camper later. For now, we just roll the bike off the trailer and ride it back into town. But we do not return to the Walmart parking lot, where the truck is. We go to the duplex, where we've been given permission by Mr. Hansen to leave the bike in the garage.

To get back to Walmart, we walk.

It's maybe a mile and a half and doesn't take that long. Even so, by the time we reach our truck, the sun has set.

Since we're here, we go inside Walmart, pick up a few things, and load them into the covered bed of the truck. Next we hit a fast-food drive-thru and head out of town.

As we leave Mercy, Liz joins us in the cab.

I tense.

She usually doesn't show up just to hang out. But for the first kilometer past the city limits sign, that seems to be exactly what she's doing.

I'm starting to relax a little when Jar quickly sits up and says, "Look."

She points ahead to the right, at a flicker of orange-yellow light between some trees, maybe a kilometer away.

A fire.

Could be someone burning trash, but it's late for that.

A bonfire?

When Jar says, "I think we should check," Liz's presence dims. She doesn't completely fade away, but I get the sense that what she wanted to tell me has been handled by Jar.

Which means those flames are probably not from a bonfire.

"Find us a way there," I say.

If you've been on roads in farm country before, then you know they tend to be laid out in large grids to accommodate the fields. This means intersecting roads tend to be few and far between. And by the time Jar says, "There should be a road coming up in about seventy meters," the fire is behind us.

I slow in anticipation, expecting a four-way intersection with another paved road.

"Right there," Jar says, pointing not far ahead.

"Where? I don't see it."

But then I do. It's a dirt road that only goes off to the right.

I take the corner faster than I would like, the pickup's back end fishtailing on the loose dirt. Once I get us back under control, I stomp on the accelerator and the truck flies down the road, kicking up a cloud of dust behind us. I didn't expect to put the pickup through this kind of workout so soon, but I'm happy it seems to be handling things without complaint.

The road passes through a gap in a row of trees that runs off to either side, like a giant wall. Which, in a way, is what it is. The line separates the fields fronting the road we were on from the fields fronting the road where we're headed.

"Can you see the fire?" I ask.

Jar's looking out her side window. "No, the trees are in the—wait. There it is. It looks...big."

I'm tempted to push the pedal all the way to the floor, but we're already going faster than we should on this kind of road in the dark, so I hold my foot steady.

Ahead, I see the ends of the fields on either side of us and know that's where the next road must be. I ease back on the accelerator, and this time I'm able to make the turn without the truck threatening to flip over.

Back on asphalt now, I do shove the pedal to the floor.

I can see the fire now. It is big. Too big to be a controlled blaze.

"Two driveways away, I think," Jar says. "About three hundred meters." We pass the road leading to a farmhouse seconds later, and not long after that, Jar points again. "There, there!"

At the far reaches of the truck's headlights, I see a mailbox on the right side of the road, and just beyond it, the beginning of a long driveway.

When I turn down it, my breath catches in my throat. It's not just one structure burning—it's three. A house and a barn and a small outbuilding. They are all separate fires, the land between them untouched by flames.

We race down the driveway to where the road widens into a large open area at the side of the house, and we skid to a stop near a Chevy Silverado. A middle-aged woman stands a few meters away from it, staring at the burning home. When she hears my door open, she looks over as if just realizing we're here and runs to meet us.

"Please, he's inside," she says. "He should have been out by now."

I look at the house. Except for the fact that it's two stories, it looks a lot like the place we just rented. The flames are concentrated on the right side, at the back. Of the three burning buildings, it looks as if the fire here started last.

"My brother, he-he went in just a few minutes ago," the woman says. "He wanted to make sure no one was inside."

I start to pull my face mask out of my pocket but then stop and ask, "Do you have a towel or a blanket or something like that?"

"A blanket, I think."

She runs to her pickup.

Jar, who has joined me outside and is already wearing her mask, says, "You're going in."

I glance at her and nod.

She looks as apprehensive about the idea as I feel, but we both know we didn't rush over here to just watch a house burn down.

The woman returns a moment later with a dirty green blanket.

I grab it from her with muttered thanks, and run to a water spigot sticking out of the ground near the front of the house.

Even though the flames are on the other side of the building, I can feel the heat as I soak the blanket with water. As soon as I've drenched it, I drape it over my head and down my back, and pull the two sides together in front of me, leaving a small gap to see through. It is not the perfect outfit to wear running into a burning house, but it is better than nothing.

Jar gives me a worried nod, which I return, before I enter the house through the partially open front door.

It's too dark to see much of anything, so I hold the blanket with one hand, pull out my phone with the other, and switch on its flashlight. I pass through an entryway into what I'm assuming is the living room. It has no furniture or anything hanging on the walls. The room is smoky, but since the fire hasn't reached this part of the house yet, it's not as bad as it could be. I can hear the blaze roaring down a hallway that leads farther back, so it won't stay this way much longer.

"Hello?" I yell. "Do you need help?"

Dammit. I should have asked for the man's name.

I rush to the left to a doorway that leads to another room. It's smokier here, so I crouch down to stay below the bulk of it.

"Hey! Anyone in here?"

I sweep the flashlight beam through the room. I thought it was the kitchen but it's not. A dining room, maybe? Whatever it is, it also has no furniture. Through an open door on the other side, I can see the beginnings of what has to be the kitchen. It's smoky back there, too, and though it's mostly dark, an intermittent flicker of light tells me the fire is beginning to breach its walls.

I don't want to go in that direction but I need to find this guy. I pull the blanket as close around my face as possible and hurry to the kitchen doorway. Even with the wet cloth in front of my face, I can't help but breathe in a bit of the smoke and cough it back out. I'm not going to be able to stay here more than a few seconds.

I shine my light across the kitchen floor. The moment I'm sure no one is in the room, I retreat to the front of the house. The two choices I have left are the hallway that leads toward the fire, and the stairs to the second floor. Well, I do have a third choice: head back outside. That would be the smart decision, but I can't bring myself to do that yet.

I step into the hallway and immediately know if the man's down there, he's out of my reach. Flames are licking the walls at the end of the corridor, and the smoke is heavy and thick.

I move over to the staircase. It's not that great an option, either. As I'm sure you know, smoke rises. Which means no matter what, there will be more of it at the top of the stairs than here at the bottom. I suck in some air through the not-quite-as-wet-as-it-was-earlier blanket, and head up.

When I reach the top, I crouch so low that I might as well be on my hands and knees, to stay below the thickest part of the smoke . I have, at most, a minute before I need to get out of here. It's probably more like thirty seconds.

The hallway's empty except for me. If the man is up here, he's beyond one of the four doorways I can see. Fire is raging in the two rooms at the far end. The only good thing about that is, the light from the flames provides enough illumination for me to pocket my phone.

I move to the first doorway and peek in. Empty, of furniture *and* people.

I move across the hall and down a little farther to the next entrance. No furniture here, either. But sprawled on the floor near one of the windows is a man.

I rush to him. He's unconscious, his breaths labored.

I jerk the blanket off me and manhandle him over my shoulder. He's not tall but he is a bit pudgy, so it takes some effort to get him in place. Once he's set, I wiggle the blanket back over both of us.

Back in the hall, the flames are starting to come up through the floorboard, and I know the house won't remain standing for much longer. I hurry down the stairs, trying not to cough but failing.

When I reach the bottom, the living room is a hell of a lot smokier than it was the last time I was here, and I become disoriented. I pause just long enough to remember where the front door is and then turn to my right.

I know I've reached the entryway when my shin smacks against the built-in bench. I stagger backward a step, wincing. For a second, it feels like the guy over my shoulder will slip off, so I readjust his weight. Then, ignoring the pain in my leg, I stagger out the front door.

Jar is at my side before I make it more than a few steps. She pulls the blanket off, drops it on the ground, and guides me away from the house.

The woman joins us a moment later.

"Is he all right?" she says. "Oh my God, is he all right?"

"Please, give them some room," Jar says.

"I can't tell if he's breathing."

"Ma'am, please."

I can't see if the woman has done what Jar asked, but at least she doesn't say anything else.

When we reach the trucks, Jar helps me set the man on the

tailgate of the Silverado. As soon as he's lying down, the woman tries to move in again.

"Hold on," I say, as gently as I can. "Let me check him first."

"Are you a doctor?" Not an accusation. Hope.

Instead of answering, I check the man's vitals. He's breathing. His pulse could be stronger, but I don't think he's in imminent danger of dying on us. He could probably use some oxygen soon, though.

"We should call for an ambulance," I say.

"They're already on the way," Jar says.

"Is he going to be all right?" the woman asks.

"He breathed in a lot of smoke so he'll need treatment for that, but I don't think it's life threatening."

The woman's whole body seemed to sag in relief. "Thank you. Thank you so much."

Before I can say, "You're welcome," I feel a cough coming on, so I nod and quickly move away before I hack up some of the smoke I brought out with me.

"Are *you* all right?" Jar asks, her hand on my back.

"I'm fine."

"You were in there a long time." She pauses. "I did not... enjoy that."

I couldn't have been in the house for more than three or four minutes, but it probably felt a lot longer to her.

"I'm sorry."

"You had no choice."

That's another one of the things I love about Jar. She understands the world that she and I inhabit. We are not like most people. We don't watch danger from afar. We face it head-on.

Which brings up something else I should mention. Do not *ever* try to do what I just did. I have trained for years to operate under intense pressure, and even with all I know, one wrong move and I wouldn't have made it out of the house. You, most likely, would have collapsed inside. As much as you may feel the need to be a hero, dying won't help anyone.

We hear the sirens for a good minute before two fire vehicles, an ambulance, and a pair of sheriff's cars turn down the driveway to the house.

Which is also right about the time the back half of the house collapses.

CHAPTER EIGHT

I f I obeyed my instincts, Jar and I would have left before the authorities arrived. But I was worried the man would take a turn for the worse, and if that happened, his sister would not have known how to help him.

My backup plan of slipping away in the subsequent chaos of the firefight is also thwarted, this time by the pair of sheriff's cars that the deputies have parked at the end of the driveway, basically cutting off the isthmus to the main road.

And of course, after I've been checked by the EMTs and given some oxygen to be safe, the deputies want to question us.

This does not make me happy.

Don't get me wrong. I've been questioned by the police before. I've even spent some time in the uncomfortable company of the FBI. But whenever possible, I try to avoid the attention of authorities. Unfortunately, today is not going to be one of those days.

The deputy's name is Daniel Olsen. He's around thirty-five, so a handful of years older than me. He's a skinny guy for a deputy, but tall. The kind of guy I can easily imagine having played guard on his high school basketball team.

We're standing near the police cars to avoid being in the way.

None of the structures are salvageable, so the firemen are focused more on keeping the fire from spreading to the nearby trees than stopping the buildings from burning down. It's an act of kindness to the owners actually, saving them from having to spend the extra money on demolishing the parts of the house and other structures that wouldn't have burned. Or maybe that's saving the insurance company money. Whatever the case, it won't be long before all three buildings are piles of charred rubble.

Olsen takes our names first. Matthew Dane for me, and Kara Chen for Jar. He then asks us to tell him what happened.

We tell him the truth. We spotted the fire and rushed here to see if anyone needed help, and we found the woman, Carla Wright, who told us the man—her brother, Harlan Gale—had gone inside and not come out.

"So you decided to go in after him?" Olsen asks.

"Yeah," I say with a shrug.

"You could have gotten yourself killed."

"Or I could have found him and brought him out...like I did."

"You should have waited until we got here and let us handle it."

"He would have been dead by then."

Olsen isn't trying to be an asshole. He's only saying the things he should to someone who did what I did.

"You're from around here?"

It's hard to miss the I-don't-recognize-you tone underlining his question.

I'd like to say something other than what I'm about to, but we've already started laying down the foundation of our faux history with our landlords, so it's best to stick with what's already out there.

"We just arrived today, actually."

This is met with a raised eyebrow. "Today?"

"That's right."

"You've never been to Mercy before?"

"Just virtually."

His eyes narrow.

"Online," I clarify.

"Oh, right."

I give him our spiel about web design, looking for new places to live and giving Mercy a try. It sounded a lot less suspicious when we told it to our property managers than when we say it to a cop.

"I'm guessing you have no idea who could have set the fires?" he says.

It's kind of a trick question. Even though it's obviously an act of arson, given the three separate fires going at the same time, no one has actually said as much to us. Would Matthew Dane, web designer, have guessed as much? I'm thinking no.

"They were set on purpose?" I say.

"We seem to have ourselves a serial arsonist."

Okay, now this is news. "This isn't the first time?"

"Not even close." He glances at his notepad to get himself back on track. "Didn't see anyone running away when you drove up? Or any cars driving off?"

"The only people we've seen are Ms. Wright and Mr. Gale."

He thinks for a moment and cocks his head a little. "What were you two doing out this way?"

"We were going to check out a house we might rent. It's not too far from here. When Kara spotted the fire, we came here instead." The only reason I don't say we've already rented the farmhouse is that he might see us in town, possibly even going into the duplex, so I don't want him to get too curious about us.

Another car arrives, and the man who climbs out— a civilian, from the way he's dressed, probably in his fifties—walks over to one of the other deputies.

"You always rush to fires?" Olsen asks.

I repeat what I told him when he started questioning us. "We thought someone might need help."

"And we were right," Jar adds, a tad more annoyed than she needs to be.

"I wouldn't advise doing that on a regular basis. You might not have gotten out."

The civilian approaches us, smiles, and says, "Good evening, Daniel."

"Evening, Mr. Mygatt," Olsen says.

The older man looks back at the house. "Thought we might be past all this."

"Apparently not."

Mygatt's gaze stays on the fire for a few more seconds before he looks at me. "You're the one who saved Harlan's life?"

I shrug as if it was no big deal, and say nothing.

"I'm not sure whether to thank you or curse you out."

"I'm sorry?" I say, genuinely confused.

Mygatt chuckles. "Harlan's my cousin. We have a kind of, um, tempestuous relationship. I was just kidding about the curse-you-out part, though. He and I may get on each other's nerves from time to time, but I'm glad he's still around." He leans toward me and stage whispers, "Besides, I can give him a hard time about this for years." He turns his attention to Olsen.

"I didn't mean to interrupt. When you're done here, I would like a word."

After Mygatt walks off, Olsen asks us for contact information and I give him one of the numbers that will ring to my phone.

He writes it down. "Thanks. If we have any other questions, we'll give you a call."

"That's it? We're free to go?" I ask.

"That's it."

"Would it be possible for someone to move one of your cars so we can get out?"

He glances at the driveway. "Oh, yeah. Sorry about that." He cups a hand over his mouth. "Hey, Dalby! Move your car out of the way. These folks are leaving."

A deputy who was standing near the back of the fire trucks —Dalby, presumably—jogs over to one of the sheriff's cars and climbs in.

As Jar and I get back into the truck, Carla Wright hurries over, waving her hand to get our attention. I lower my window.

"You're leaving?" she says.

"You've got plenty of help here now. We're just in the way."

"I wanted to thank you for saving my brother."

"You did already."

"I did?"

I nod.

"You didn't tell me your name, though, did you? If you did, I don't remember it."

I did, but there's no reason to remind her of that, too. "I'm Matthew and my girlfriend's name is Kara." That's part of the fake history Jar and I had fleshed out before we checked out the rentals. Since we'll be living together, it's either that or pretend to be married.

"You live in Mercy?"

"We're staying in the area."

"I'd love to drop something by to thank you for what you've done."

"That's not necessary."

"Please, I insist."

"We're just about to move into a new place. Why don't you tell me where you live and I can drop by? Would that work?"

"Perfect. Thank you." She gives me her address and I put it into my phone. She glances back toward the ambulance, which looks like it's also getting ready to leave. "Better make it the day after tomorrow. I'll probably be busy with Harlan tomorrow, making sure he's doing okay."

"Day after tomorrow it is," I say, having no intention of paying her a visit.

"Late afternoon."

"Sounds good."

She hurries to the ambulance and climbs into the back, just before one of the EMTs closes the door.

We wait for the ambulance to leave first. As it heads for the driveway, I notice Mygatt standing off to the side, pointing his phone's camera lens at the blaze. From the way he interacted with Olsen and the other officers, I wonder if he's a fire inspector or someone like that.

Once the ambulance is speeding down the drive, I take my foot off the brake and get us the hell out of there.

During the drive to the Travato, I can't help but think about the fire. Based on what Olsen said, this wasn't the first case of arson. But why burn down an empty house, and a barn, and whatever that third building was? From what I've read, most people who purposely set fires are driven either by a love of flames or a love of money. Sometimes both. If you're doing it for the insurance money, you'd want to do it so that it looks like it was caused by faulty wiring or something similar. You wouldn't have burned your house down in such an obvious way.

All very strange.

But also not our problem.

The Travato is a welcome sight. This will be only our fourth night staying in it, but seeing it now feels a little like coming home.

Maybe I'm just overreacting to my experience at the fire. Which is kind of odd, given the more intense experiences I've been through in my life. Of course, it's been almost two months now since we've had any work. I mean, on the day job. Obviously I've done a few things on my own—like dealing with Marco and Blaine and hoisting Evan off the side of the Grand Canyon. Still, the relative inaction must be playing with my senses, right?

The air inside the camper is only marginally warmer than it is outside. And with my clothes still damp and no roaring blaze nearby to fight off the cold, I begin to shiver.

Noticing my condition, Jar flicks on the heater, but it'll take several minutes to warm up the place.

"Why don't you take a shower?" she says. "That should help."

The Travato has an adequate but small shower. We don't keep the water heater on all the time, so it'll take nearly as long as the room heater to warm up.

"In the house, I mean," she says. "The water heater there is on."

"You checked it?"

"You did not?"

When we did our walk-through of the house earlier, I did note that the power was on, but no, I didn't check the water heater. Leave it to Jar to be even more thorough than me.

I grab a change of clothes, a bottle of shower gel and a towel, and walk to the farmhouse, where I use the shower in the master bath since it's the largest. I stand under the hot stream, face upturned, as all the ways the evening could have gone wrong run through mind.

Fire is unpredictable. Fire does not care about anything. If you are in its path, fire will turn you into fuel at its first opportunity.

I don't like fire.

It's an enemy that takes great effort to tame, and often the only thing that can be done is to flee. If, that is, one has a way out.

I've been lucky in my career and have had to get up close and personal with fire on only a few occasions. Most of those instances were brushes with flames that didn't last very long. Tonight's interaction was one of the longest. There was a moment at the bottom of the stairs, with Harlan over my shoulder, when I wasn't sure which way to go. I figured it out quickly enough, but I'd be lying if I said the potential of burning up with the building didn't cross my mind.

Which is probably the reason it takes a bit longer than it should for my shivering to abate.

When it finally does, I wash my upper body and hair, and then reach down to remove my prosthetic right leg. The device is waterproof, which is great, but the sock over my nub is not. I keep the prosthetic in the shower with me so I can clean it, too, and toss the sock out. It lands on the floor with a wet *thwack*.

My right leg ends just below the knee, the visible reminder of an injury I received back when I was an apprentice. It almost ended my career at a point when my career had barely begun. If I'm honest, though, losing the leg has made me better at what I do than I probably would have been if it didn't happen.

It focused me, and taught me to come up with solutions I

wouldn't have otherwise thought of for certain problems. It still does. I'm not sure someone can say this about themselves or not, but what the hell, I'll throw this out there. The injury and its aftermath have made me not only better at my job but also a better person.

I have multiple prosthetics. The two I use the most are the one I wear when I go for a run, and the one I think of as my everyday leg. It's the latter that I've been wearing today and just took off. It's surprisingly comfortable, and makes me look like I'm not missing a limb at all—except, of course, when I'm wearing shorts. It also has five built-in secret compartments. For example, the one on the outside of the calf contains a specially built knife for unexpected situations. In the other compartments, I can hide things like IDs and cash and whatever else I may need to stash away, as long as it's not too big.

When I finish, I towel off, get dressed, and head back to the Travato.

Jar has warmed up the burgers and fries we picked up before we left Mercy. I'm not sure they taste any better than they would have if left cold, but I wolf them down anyway.

"Maybe we should wait until tomorrow," Jar says.

She's talking about the task we'd planned on doing tonight, before we knew I'd be running into a burning house.

Still...

"I'd rather not waste the time," I say.

"You look tired."

"Since when has that stopped us from doing anything?"

The frown she gives me is...let's call it *dubious*.

I glance at my watch. It's only a little after nine p.m., so we still have plenty of the night to work with.

"How about this?" I ask. "I'll grab a nap and we can go in a couple hours."

She still doesn't look convinced, but she also doesn't put up an argument.

I set the alarm on my phone, as I'm pretty sure Jar has no intention of waking me. Then I lie on the bed and within moments am asleep.

CHAPTER NINE

By midnight, I'm awake and ready.

I'll never admit it to Jar, but when my alarm went off, I really had to fight the urge to roll over and sleep the night through.

We head back to Mercy.

At this time of night, the place is a ghost town.

The only businesses open are a few gas stations, though none of them seem to have any customers. The few bars we pass are closed. I assume that's due to the pandemic, though maybe operating hours for places like them are different here in Colorado than they are in California.

The only other occupied vehicle we see is a police sedan that crosses through an intersection three blocks ahead of us. As soon as it disappears from view, I turn down a side street and park at the curb, just in case the cop decides to circle back and check on us.

Sure enough, half a minute later, the sedan drives through the intersection behind us, down the street we were on earlier. But neither of the two officers inside looks our way.

I give it another two minutes, and then we're moving again.

Taking side streets, we work our way to a road about halfway between our duplex rental and the Prices' house. I find a spot to park that's not directly in front of any house. Though all the windows of the nearby residences are dark, Jar scans them with our binoculars to make sure no one is watching us.

"We're clear," she says, and lowers the glasses.

From her backpack, she withdraws our comm gear and hands me a set. Once our radios are in place, I open my door as quietly as possible and slip outside. Jar climbs across the cab and exits the same way.

Our goal tonight is to get an up-close look at the Prices' house, and hopefully figure out how I'll get inside it to plant our bugs. While I don't expect to actually enter tonight, I have an array of audio and visual bugs with me on the chance that opportunity strikes. It's a limited supply, probably enough to cover the house, but not much more than that. Vacation, remember?

Staying in the shadows, we work our way to the street that runs by the side of the Price property, where the entrance to the driveway the Winnebago used is located.

The neighborhood is as quiet as if we were in the middle of the deserted countryside, which means we have to be extra careful to not make a sound. One moderately loud misstep and we'd probably wake up a half dozen people. Thankfully, there are no streetlamps on this particular block, though one does sit on the road that runs in front of the Prices' house, just across the street from their front door.

This does not mean the side street is completely unlit. An outdoor light on the back of the Prices' house illuminates the space between the building's rear entrance and the RV.

I doubt someone forgot to turn it off. Chuckie doesn't seem like the kind of guy who'd put up with that kind of error. I have a feeling it's on because he wants to deter anyone from trying to mess with his Winnebago. Which is kind of paranoid for a small city like this. While I'm sure things go missing now and then here, motorhomes are hard to hide, and I'd be willing to bet that the number of vehicle thefts in Mercy per year can be counted on one hand.

Using the binoculars, Jar checks the windows of the house for signs of life. The Prices, like most of their neighbors, appear to have turned in for the night.

Once she gives me the okay, I sneak across the road to the gate that closes off the driveway. Unlike the picket fence that separates the rest of the Prices' property from the public side-walk, the gate is made of chain link. It's also high enough that I can't just step over it.

I give it a gentle shake, thinking maybe I can hop it. The chain link feels tight to the frame, but not tight enough to be soundless. So much for going over the top.

I'd rather not go over the picket fence, either. As I'm sure you can understand, I like to avoid pointy things between my legs whenever possible.

Thankfully, I have other options.

The easiest of these is via the backyard of the neighboring house behind the Prices'.

The fence between the two places is six foot high, made of wood, and looks solid. This same fence encloses the neighbor's entire backyard, and while it's taller than the picket fence, it's less spikey, and as a bonus, includes an unlocked gate next to the house. Before I open it, I toss a few pebbles into the yard to wake up any sleeping dogs. When nothing happens, I lift the latch and push the gate open.

A half minute later, I've hopped over the back fence and am now standing in the Prices' yard, hidden from the house by the Winnebago. I crouch here for a whole minute and wait to make sure my arrival has gone unnoticed, then I creep along the RV to the front end and peer around it.

A deck juts out from the house about five meters and runs nearly the length of the structure. The rest of the yard is covered with grass that's in the early stages of making a comeback from a dormant winter.

The only entrance into the house that I can see is a sliding glass door at about the midpoint of the deck. Curtains are pulled across the glass, but it's a pretty fair guess that a living room is on the other side. From the other windows, I determine the kitchen is to the left of the glass doors, while immediately to the right is a bathroom. On the other side of the bathroom, two more windows belong to what is probably a bedroom or den. It, too, has curtains closed. Along the second floor are multiple windows—another bathroom and what I assume are two bedrooms, if not three.

I creep onto the deck and step up to the sliding glass door. From my pocket, I remove my phone and a wand-like device and attach them to each other. After opening my alarm detection app, I move the wand along the frame of the door.

The house has an alarm system but it's a standard model, used by a lot of home security companies. Which means it's well known to my software. I tap a button on my screen and thirty seconds later, the red warning that reads ACTIVE ALARM switches to a green INACTIVE ALARM.

Again, the purpose of this trip is not to actually go inside. But now that the detector knows the way into the Prices' system, the next time I tap DEACTIVATE, the delay will be a second or two at most. I turn the alarm back on.

Sliding glass doors are among the easiest to break into. Which is why a lot of people put something in the tracks to block the door from being opened. Glancing through the glass at the bottom of the frame, I'm not surprised to see the Prices have done just that. Looks like an old broom handle. Problematic, but not impossible to deal with. As for the door's lock, I've dispatched dozens like it with ease in the past. If I go in this way, the lock will not be the problem.

"Someone's coming down the street," Jar whispers in my ear.

I glance back at the picket fence but don't hear anything from that direction. "Car?"

"On foot. Sounds like one person. From the west."

That would be from somewhere beyond the neighbor whose backyard I passed through. I listen for footsteps but can't hear any.

"How close?"

"A block and a half."

"Copy."

Someone out for a midnight stroll, I'm guessing. If the person continues in this direction and glances into the Prices' backyard, he or she will likely spot me if I stay where I am, so I sneak off the deck and move around its north side, farthest from the street.

A few seconds after I'm hidden, I finally hear the steps. They're light, either of someone who is small or someone trying to avoid making too much noise.

Since Jar isn't giving me an update, I'm guessing the walker is near her.

The area I'm in is dark enough that I can look around the end of the deck without worrying too much about being seen.

The steps are getting close, and I should be able to see the person any second.

When I do, the walker is a lot closer to me than I expected. In fact, the person, who is wearing a hooded puffy jacket, is on the sidewalk right next to the Prices' fence. My next surprise comes when he or she stops at the long gate and looks at the house. I can't help but think the person knows I'm here. But there's no way that's possible.

Nothing to see here, I mentally project toward the walker. *Keep it moving.*

The person stirs as if hearing me, and for a moment I'm impressed with my telepathic powers, but my self-esteem takes an immediate hit when the walker moves over to the picket fence on the other side of the gate, removes three of the pickets as if they were being held in place by tape, and slips *through* the fence into the Prices' backyard.

What the actual hell?

After the pickets are put back in place, I watch the walker approach the house for as long as I can before I pull back out of sight. I don't hear any steps moving onto the deck, and realize I must be hiding where the walker is headed.

Seriously?

I do the only thing I can and squeeze under the deck, no more than five seconds before the person comes around the end of it.

It's Evan.

He continues past me for a few more steps, then stops and looks back, as if sensing he's not alone. When he doesn't see anyone else, he disappears into the area between the house and the detached garage. Though I can't see what he's doing, it sounds like he's climbing up the side of the building.

I want to take a look, but that would entail sticking my head out from under the deck, so I resist.

When the climbing stops, I hear a faint scraping sound, followed by more movement, and finally a repeat of the scraping. After that, the night goes silent.

"Are you all right?" Jar asks. "Were you seen?"

Evan has probably moved out of earshot but I don't know for sure, so I click my mic once to let her know I'm okay.

After another fifteen seconds, I allow myself to crawl out from under the deck.

Evan is indeed gone.

A trellis, lightly populated with vines, runs up the side of the house, stopping less than a meter below a pair of second-story windows. These are the only windows on this side of the house. Clearly, Evan climbed up the trellis to one of them. I'm curious about how the structure can hold his weight. It doesn't appear to be strong enough.

I move in closer and give it soft tug. I'm right. The whole thing should have pulled off the wall before Evan made it halfway up.

So why didn't it?

I look around. Near the other end of the area, closest to the front side of the Prices' home, is a covered walkway that leads from a door on the side of the garage to a door on the house. Beyond this is a full-size fence, running from house to garage. In other words, I'm in the most private outside area of the property.

I pull out my phone, put my fingers over the flashlight, and turn the light on. Controlling the beam in this way, I shine it at the house.

Poking out from the lattice at various points are wooden arms about the length of my hand. Each has a notch near its outstretched end, where I'm guessing small potted plants can be hung. There are no pots hanging on any of them right now, but I bet it's a project one of the family members will take on soon enough.

And by one of the family members, I mean Evan.

How can I know that?

Because I don't think he'd want anyone else to deal with them.

While most of the hangers are nailed directly to the lattice, six are not. They *look* like they are, but in fact they're attached to heavy-duty metal brackets that are screwed into the side of the house. I test one of them. It is solidly in place.

Evan has created a climbing wall, hidden in plain sight.

I'm impressed. I mean, *really* impressed.

I turn off my light and look up. The window straight above me leads to the corner room in the back of the house, and has to be the one he went in. Which I take to mean it's his bedroom.

I open the alarm detection app on my phone again and reconnect to the Prices' system. One of the options on the app allows me to see a log of alarm activity. The last thing listed in the system is that it was armed at 9:04 p.m. (FYI, my software prevents the log from noting any activation or deactivation that *I* might do.)

Either Chuckie deemed it unnecessary to put sensors on the second-floor windows, or Evan has found a way to turn his off without raising suspicions.

I admire his handiwork for a moment longer before turning to the garage. I've been here longer than I planned, but still have a few things I'd like to do before I go. I move over to the garage's side door and run an alarm check. I discover a contact sensor on the door, another on the roll-up door out front, and a motion sensor that I'm guessing covers a majority of the interior. The three sensors are on their own node, meaning they can be turned on or off independently from the house. I deactivate the garage node and pick the locks on the side door.

It's a two-car garage, half the area taken up by a workbench and boxes, and the other half by a current model Ford Premium Fastback Mustang. I believe its color is officially called Twister Orange. It is a vehicle meant to be seen. The kind driven by hotshots and glory hogs and men who think more of themselves than they should.

We know from DMV records that the Prices have two registered vehicles, both in Chuckie's name. They are the Winnebago and a five-year-old Ford Explorer. I'm betting the Explorer is used by Kate, and that her husband takes whatever car from his dealership he's interested in.

I turn off the car's alarm, place a combo listening/tracking bug underneath the driver's seat, and exit the garage, resetting everything to the way it was.

I consider planting some of our bugs near windows to pick up conversations inside, but as I said, our supply is limited, so I settle for using a single bug next. Best would be the kind designed to pick up voices through glass, but the ones I have with me are a more general type.

I choose a spot on the kitchen window that's hidden from view from the inside by a curtain, and from the outside by the lip of the planter box hanging from the sill. The bug is tiny so that'll help, too. I just hope it works the way we need it to.

When I finish, I creep over to the fence where Evan passed through.

The kid has some serious skills. Whether you push or pull on the pickets I saw him remove, they feel nailed in place like all the others. What you have to do is slide them up about two centimeters and *then* move them away from the fence. He's cut slots into the backs that are wide enough at the bottom for a nail head to fit through, but above that is a narrow channel only the nail's shaft can traverse. He's even put a dummy nail head on the outside of the picket and painted over it, to match the look of the regular ones.

If he was maybe six or seven years older, he'd make a prime candidate for being my apprentice.

I use Evan's exit, put the pickets back in place, and move across the street to where Jar waits.

"Explorer?" I whisper.

"Taken care of."

Along with keeping an eye on my back, one of Jar's tasks was to see if the Prices' Explorer was parked nearby, and if so, do to it what I did to the Mustang.

"The person who crawled through the fence—it was Evan, was it not?" she asks.

I nod and tell her about how he gets in and out of his room. Which reminds me there is one more bug I should install before we go.

I place the video bug in the tree directly across the street from the RV gate, and aim it so that its field of view includes the modified portion of the fence. This way we will know if and when Evan goes out again, and if I'm in the area, I can use the opportunity to sneak into his house the way he snuck out.

It's been quite the night and I'm exhausted. We return to the truck and drive back to the Travato. Less than ten minutes later, I'm asleep.

CHAPTER TEN

R emember that guy at the fire last night? The one Olsen called Mr. Mygatt?

Guess what?

He's not only the publisher of the *Mercy Sentinel*, he's also one of its reporters. Am I pleased to find this out? I'm sure you know the answer to that.

The story of the farmhouse fire is front-page news, at least on the *Sentinel*'s website. Jar found it while I was still sleeping this morning. She'd been curious if there was more information about the incident.

There is, but there's so much more, too.

THE MERCY ARSONIST STRIKES AGAIN
LOCAL MAN INJURED

Fire brought down another house just outside Mercy last night. This time it was the former residence of the Baldwin family, located on North Edwards Road. The property's current owner is Gage-Trent Farming. According to fire chief Davis

Leonard, the fire appears to have been started not long after sunset.

When asked if the blaze was the work of the Mercy Arsonist, Leonard would only say that investigators will determine the cause later. But the similarities to past incidents are impossible to ignore. Not only did the house burn, so did a barn and a horse stable, the only other buildings on the property. Like with the other fires, the buildings were not in use.

Local business owner Harlan Gale and his sister, Carla Wright, were the first to spot the fire, and rushed to see if anyone needed help. Gale entered the house to make sure no one was inside. While there, he was overcome by smoke and collapsed.

Mercy newcomers Matthew Dane and Kara Chen arrived soon after Gale entered the house, having also spotted the blaze from the road. Dane ran into the building using a wet blanket as a shield, found Gale, and carried him outside.

Soon after, the county fire department arrived, and EMTs transported Gale to Mercy County Hospital, where he is currently listed in stable condition.

"Harlan would have died if that nice couple hadn't shown up," Wright said. "I can't thank them enough."

When asked why he risked his own life to save someone he didn't know, Dane said, "I did what anyone else would have done."

I never said that.

I barely spoke to the guy. In fact, I don't remember him even asking me that question. But as much as being misquoted annoys me, what's worse is the fact that Jar and I are mentioned in the article at all, even if we are only identified by our aliases.

I can't seem to stay out of the news these days. Have I been cursed or something? Because that's exactly what it's starting to feel like.

At least we didn't stick around long enough for him to take a picture of us. That would have been disastrous. Imagine Chuckie sitting down at his computer and checking the *Mercy Sentinel* to see what happened while he was away. Or maybe he's the kind of Luddite who still receives a physical paper. Right there, probably at the top of page one, would be a picture of the two people he (rightly) thinks called the cops on him at the Grand Canyon.

Jar snaps me out of my thoughts by saying, "There have been six other fires like this since January. Always empty houses, five owned by Gage-Trent, Incorporated, and one by Hayden Valley Agriculture. The companies have been buying up farms in this part of Colorado for the last several years. The last fire was ten days ago, at a farm five miles south of Mercy."

I skim the news article she's brought up on the earlier fires, and frown. "As interesting as that all is, we're not here to solve anyone's fire problems, remember?"

Jar gives me that of-course-I-remember look. "I was only thinking it might prove helpful to have an awareness of what is going on around here."

"Fair point," I concede. "I wonder if the police have a suspect yet?"

"They do not."

"You've checked their files."

"Of course I have."

"What a surprise," I say, as deadpan as I can.

I expect a glare in response, but she seems to be purposely not looking at me, as if there's something else on her mind but she doesn't want to mention it. That's all right. I'm pretty sure I know exactly what it is. She's thinking that since we're in Mercy already, it wouldn't hurt to poke around a bit and see if we can find out anything about the fires.

I glance around the room, sure that Liz is around here somewhere. But I can't see her, nor do I feel her presence. I guess she's leaving this up to Jar. I don't need to be visited by a ghost to know both women feel the same way about this.

And while I can sympathize with their position, I'm not as keen on getting drawn into anything else. We're here because of Evan and his family, and that's where our focus should remain.

I'm also aware that stating it like that will not go over well, so to placate both Jar and Liz, I say, "Keep tabs on the situation. If something catches your eye, let me know."

Jar nods, her gaze still turned away. "Good idea."

On our way into town, we take the long way and drive by the location of last night's fire.

The only thing still standing is a two-meter section of the house's northwest corner. The rest of the building, like the barn and the stables, lies in a blackened heap.

I'm sure Jar would like to drive up for a closer look, but two cars are parked near where we were last night and at least three people are walking around the remains. It would not be smart for us to be seen there again.

We spend some more time in Walmart, buying blankets, sheets, a pair of blow-up mattresses, a couple of folding chairs, and a portable card table. Luckily, though the duplex is empty, it has curtains so we don't have to worry about being leered at by people walking by.

While we're eating lunch at a sidewalk table in front of a restaurant called Mercy Me, I get a call from Mr. Hansen.

"I just wanted to let you know the place is ready anytime you want to move in. Just stop by here first with the check and I'll give you the keys."

"That's great, thank you," I say. "We'll try to be there within an hour."

"Perfect." He pauses, and I think he's going to tell me good-bye, but instead he says, "I read the paper this morning. You and Miss Chen were at that fire last night?"

Gulp.

"Oh, um...we just happened to be driving by."

"Sounded to me like you saved Harlan Gale's life."

"It wasn't as dramatic as all that. I'm sure he would have gotten out on his own."

"I don't believe that for a minute," Hansen says. I can hear a smile in his voice, as if I'm his son and he's a proud dad.

This day just keeps getting better and better. Ugh.

"Gotta run," I say. "See you in a bit."

"Sure, sure. I'll be waiting."

After Jar and I finish lunch, we swing by a bank to get a cashier's check. It's kind of a baby boomer way of paying for things, but Hansen's a card-carrying member of that demographic, so it's not surprising that's how he wants to do things.

I half expect the teller to say something about the *Sentinel* article when I hand her my ID, but she shows no sign of recognition. She is younger so she probably doesn't read the local paper, at least not first thing in the morning.

We arrive at Hansen's office a little after one p.m. The moment we walk inside, he jumps up from his desk, beaming from ear to ear. That's right. He's not wearing a mask. Of course, until this moment, he's been the only one in the office so he can be excused for that.

"Matthew, Kara, so glad to see you!"

Jar and I stop a few steps inside the door, but he's coming right at us and thrusting out a hand to shake ours.

I hold up my palms. "Whoa, Mr. Hansen. Good to see you, too, but, um—"

Jar cuts to the chase with, "Mask."

Hansen takes another step, then stops and laughs. "Right, right, right. It's good to get into that habit, isn't it?"

He retreats to his desk, grabs a blue disposable paper mask, and straps it across his face. When he comes back, he brings with him a thin stack of papers and a pen.

"How are you two doing this morning?" he asks. "Any effects from the fire?"

"We're fine," I say.

"That was very brave of you."

"It really wasn't that big of a deal."

He chuckles. "That's not what I heard. I talked to Curtis a few minutes ago, and the story he told me is a little more exciting."

"Curtis?" I ask. I really don't want to continue this line of discussion, but I have no idea who he's talking about.

"Curtis Mygatt. He owns the *Sentinel*. Says he met you at the fire last night."

I force a smile and say, "I have your check for you."

By two p.m., all our Walmart packages are inside the duplex, which means technically we're moved in. Hansen has done us the favor of transferring the utilities into our names and has used his clout to waive any deposits.

"The least I can do for what you've done," he said when he told us.

One of the main rules in the world of secrets is to always

keep a low profile. The rule also applies to the practice of my hobby. And yet here we are, having already broken it within a few hours of arriving in Mercy.

Really stellar work there, Nate. Outstanding.

"What's wrong?" Jar says.

"What do you mean, what's wrong?"

"You groaned."

I thought I restricted my discontent to inside my head. No sense in lying about it, though. "Just thinking about the news article."

"It is unfortunate, but in a few days most people will forget."

Most people, perhaps, but I doubt Hansen will be one of them. And certainly Harlan Gale and Carla Wright won't forget. Nor, I suspect, will the sheriff's department.

"I hope you're right," I say.

The doorbell rings.

Jar and I exchange a look before we head for the entrance. It's probably one of our new neighbors, coming to say hi. Maybe even our building mates.

When I pull the door open, I almost laugh from a combination of absurdity and panic. Standing on the other side of the threshold is Curtis Mygatt—owner, publisher, and no doubt lead reporter of the *Mercy Sentinel*. He's either obtained our address from the cops or his friend (and our landlord) Mr. Hansen.

He smiles and says, "Mr. Dane, Miss Chen, good to see you again."

"Good afternoon, Mr. Mygatt," I say. "What can we do for you?"

"I wanted to welcome you to your new home."

"Uh, thank you."

"You're in a great location here. Close to a lot of shops, nice neighborhood. I'm sure you're going to be very happy."

"I'm sure we are."

He continues smiling at us, and I have the distinct feeling he's expecting us to invite him inside. That is not going to happen. I say, "We appreciate you stopping by," and take a step back to shut the door.

Mygatt says, "I was also hoping you might have a few minutes to talk."

"About what?"

"Last night. Mercy." He smiles again. "You two."

Do I want to shut the door in his face and sneak out a back window? You bet I do. Thank God for those acting classes, though. I contort my features into a look of disinterest and say, "I'm not sure there's much to say."

"I'm sure that's not true. Look, I just have a few questions you might be able to help me with, that's all. Nothing big."

We might as well get this over with. "Go ahead and ask. We'll answer as best we can."

"It may take a few minutes. May I come in?"

"We literally just got the key for this place thirty minutes ago. We're nowhere close to ready for guests yet."

"Of course, of course. I should have thought of that." He flashes that smile again. "Tell you what. How about I buy you a cup of coffee, then? I bet you could use a break."

I do some quick calculus, weighing whether telling him we don't have time today and avoid him at all costs after that would be smarter than taking him up on his offer and getting it over with. It's a close call, but better a solved problem that's behind you than an active one still looming in the future. "That would be very kind. Thank you. We'll need to clean up first. Can we meet you somewhere?"

"Of course. How about we go to The Smiling Eyes? It's a coffee shop over on Central, about five blocks from here."

"Sounds perfect."

The Smiling Eyes is on a corner, at the end of a row of businesses that include a flower shop, a mini-mart, and an antiques store. Tables are set up on the sidewalks outside the coffee shop, along both the main street and the side street. A makeshift counter has been placed in the doorway to keep anyone from going inside. The owner of the coffee shop seems to be taking the pandemic more seriously than most of the other places in town. I appreciate that.

Mygatt waves to us from one of the tables along the side road as we walk up. "I told them to expect you. Just give Greta my name."

Greta turns out to be the woman at the counter. She's probably around my age and looks to be part Hispanic. She's both friendly and clearly in charge, which makes me think maybe she's the owner.

Once our drinks are ready, we join Mygatt.

"I know it's a busy day for you so I appreciate you giving me some of your time," he says as we sit.

"Thank you for the coffee, Mr. Mygatt," Jar says.

"Yes, thank you," I say.

"No need for any of that mister stuff. You can call me Curtis."

Jar and I both take sips from our cups.

"How long have you two been in town?" He asks this as if it's small talk, but I have no doubt it's one of the questions on his list.

I'd like to tell him we've been here a while, but it's a question he probably already knows the answer to from the cop last night, or our landlord.

"A day," I say.

"You mean to say yesterday was your first day here?" He is a mediocre actor at best, the surprise in his voice achingly forced.

I nod.

"Wow. That's quite the welcome. But don't you worry. Most days around here are a lot quieter than that."

"I hope so."

"If you don't mind me asking, what brings you to Mercy?"

I do mind, but again, he won't be the first we've told. I give him the web designer story.

"So, what you're saying is, you're giving us a test drive."

"You could say it that way."

"I hope you don't let last night weigh too heavily in your final decision. Mercy's a great place. A lot of good people. Good values, you know? Family. Community." He glances at Jar. "We even have a few Asian restaurants in town. I'm sure you'll like them."

Nothing like a little casual racism over coffee.

Jar's time in the States has been limited, and from her non-reaction, I'm guessing her being called out as "different" has gone unnoticed.

But it pisses *me* off, and I have to rein myself in when I speak to keep my ire from showing. "You said you had some questions?"

I know he's already started asking them, but I'm pretending I don't realize that.

He leans forward. "I'd love to hear about last night from your perspective. Starting from when you spotted the fire."

I shrug. "Not much to tell. Kara saw it first and we went to find out if there was anything we could do."

"What were you doing out there in the first place?"

"Just driving around. Getting a feel for the area."

He nods. "And when you got to the house?"

"The woman, um..."

"Carla Wright."

"Yeah, Ms. Wright told us her brother had gone inside."

"Missus," he says, as if that should have been obvious. "Did she say why?"

"He wanted to make sure the house was unoccupied," Jar says, speaking for the first time since we sat down.

"Did he see someone?"

"You'd have to ask him," I say.

Mygatt nods again. "So that's when you decided to go inside?"

"Shouldn't you be writing this down?" I ask. "Make sure that you don't forget something or misquote us?"

If he catches my dig at the lack of accuracy in this morning's article, he makes no sign of it. Instead, he taps the table next to where his phone is sitting. "Recording everything. Easier that way. When I used to take notes by hand, conversations wouldn't flow as easily." He pauses briefly. "You don't mind, do you?"

I most certainly do mind, but what I say is, "I guess not. But you really should tell people before you record them."

"You're right. It's just that some people get a little uptight about it." He brushes it away with another one of his smiles. "You were going to tell me about deciding to go into the house?"

"We couldn't just leave him in there."

"Carla said something about a blanket?"

As I start to tell him about the blanket and the water, Jar pulls out her phone, acting as if she's just received a text, and starts tapping on the screen. I'm pretty sure there is no text.

Mygatt asks me about the rescue and I describe that, too. By the time I finish, Jar has returned her phone to her pocket and is focusing on the conversation again.

Mygatt asks a few additional questions, trying to tease more details out of me, but I don't give him anything worthwhile.

"You're very modest," he finally says.

"I don't know about that."

"See, there it is again. It's a good quality. Means you're a good person, Matthew. Not that there was any question about that."

Saying thank you would be weird, so I keep my mouth shut.

"Where do you two call home?" he asks. "I mean before coming here."

"California. The Bay Area."

"San Francisco?"

"Not too far from there."

"Sounds nice."

"It is. It's just expensive."

"That's why you're looking for someplace new?"

"One of the reasons."

He continues to ask about our lives for a few more minutes, and I continue to give him vague answers. When he runs out of questions, he picks up his phone and says, "May I take a picture of the two of you?"

"Why?" I ask.

"I'd like to do a profile piece on you guys," he says as if he's giving us a gift. "You're new to town and you're heroes. People are going to want to know about you."

Holy crap. No, no, no, no, no.

"Wow, that's very nice of you," I say. "But we'd rather you didn't."

He looks confused, like he can't conceive why we wouldn't want the attention.

"We'd like to get to know Mercy on our own terms," I explain. "If you publish an article about us, like you said—people will know who we are. That's not going to make it easy for us to settle in."

I can see my words starting to take effect.

"If you really want to do a story about us, maybe it could

wait a few weeks," I say. "Give us the chance to see if we like it here first." There's still some wavering in his eyes, so I add, "If you do that, you'll be able to include our decision on whether we stay or not."

Now he's starting to tip in our direction. "'Fire Heroes to Permanent Residents,'" he says, trying on a headline. "I'll have to work on that, but I like the idea. How long are we talking?"

"Four weeks?"

"How about we check in with each other in three?"

"Sure. Three will work."

———

When Jar and I are back inside the cab of the truck, I ask, "The recording?"

"Corrupted," she says.

"Nice work."

As I suspected, that text she pretended to receive was actually cover for her to hack into Mygatt's phone and destroy the audio file of our conversation. Mygatt will be annoyed when he finds out but glitches happen, and as far as he knows, he'll be having a follow-up conversation with us soon enough. Hopefully that will be enough to keep him from getting too mad.

We will not be having that follow-up, however.

CHAPTER ELEVEN

The biggest item on my to-do list is to install those bugs inside the Prices' place, but over the next few days, the house is always occupied.

Not by Chuckie, of course. He goes to work around seven every morning and doesn't come home until seven in the evening, when, in the grand tradition of the 1950s, he expects dinner to be on the table and everyone seated and waiting for him. We know this from conversations we've picked up via the bug. It's limited in how much it can detect but at least it's working.

Kate and Sawyer are the ones who haven't left. Evan is home most of the time, too, though he did go out once on Wednesday to the grocery store, on his bicycle.

I've been hoping he'd sneak out of the house again. Though that would mean I'd be going inside while the rest of the family is home, I can work with that. Evan's escape route has remained unused, however.

But today is Friday, and I can't help thinking that Evan, like any true teenager, will see sneaking out of the house at the start of the weekend as a birthright.

We are monitoring the Prices from our duplex. Chuckie's running a little late tonight and doesn't arrive home until 7:42 p.m.

This does not change the routine for the rest of his family. Like on the previous nights, Kate has apparently been watching for him from the window. Before he's even pulled into the garage, she yells out, "Dinnertime! Hurry up! Hurry up!"

Jar and I hear the boys coming downstairs, followed by the now familiar sound of dining room chairs scraping on the floor as they sit.

When Chuckie enters the house, Kate greets him with the same, "Welcome home, honey. How was your day?" she says every night. If he responds, our bug doesn't pick it up.

The next five minutes are dotted with the occasional sounds of movements but little else. Finally, after the creaking of another chair, Kate says grace, and the sound of silverware clinking signals that the family has started to eat.

I don't know about you but when I was growing up, our dinner table was always filled with conversation. My parents are talkers, and they believe in making sure everyone is involved in the discussion. When I was young, my dad especially liked coming up with hypothetical situations and asking my brother and me things like, "Pretend you're out hiking and you find an ancient city. What does it look like?" and "If you could invent something that hasn't been invented yet, what would it be and how would it work?" and "What if a spaceship landed in your backyard and you were the first person on Earth to meet beings from a different planet? How would you communicate with them? What would you talk about?" Sometimes we pretended we didn't want to play along, but secretly I really enjoyed it and I'm sure my brother did, too.

My point is, meals were—and still are—noisy affairs at my

house. The opposite seems to be true for the Prices, albeit this is based on a small sample size.

I don't know how they stand it. It feels unnatural. Oppressive, even. The worst part: no one's allowed to leave until Chuckie finishes eating.

I know we've already established that he's not a good man, but I feel it bears repeating.

This guy is a supreme asshole.

The sound of eating finally tapers off. Unsurprisingly, it's Chuckie who speaks first. Every night since we've been listening, it's gone this way. On Tuesday, he said, "The steak was a little well done." On Wednesday, "Go finish your homework." And yesterday, "I've got work to do. No one bother me."

Tonight, it's "Barry called. He wanted to make sure we're bringing your potato salad tomorrow."

"Tomorrow?" Kate says. "What's happening tomorrow?"

A long pause before Chuckie says, "The *barbecue*." The tone is very are-you-an-idiot.

"They're still having it?"

"Of course they are. Why wouldn't they?"

"No reason," she says quickly, a forced lightness to her tone. "I just hadn't heard anything, that's all."

"Well, it's on, and we're going."

"Great."

A chair pushes back from the table.

"I'll be in my office," he says.

Chuckie walks out of the room, and a few seconds later we hear the faint sound of a door closing. The den, I'm guessing.

"All right, let's get this cleaned up," Kate says.

I sit back. If the pattern remains unchanged, very little else will be said in the house for the rest of the evening.

"They should not be going to a party," Jar says.

"No, they shouldn't."

Though the pandemic hasn't hit this area hard yet, there have been a few cases, so it won't be long before it spreads as widely as it has elsewhere. Unfortunately, following CDC recommendations to limit social gatherings doesn't appear to be high on a lot of people's priority lists around here.

Their bad choice is our good fortune, though. "If they're all going to be gone, it'll be the perfect time to get inside," I say.

Jar frowns. "Not perfect. It will be daylight."

She means the neighbors problem, but I have an idea for how to deal with that.

After I tell her what it is, Jar thinks about it for a few seconds and says, "That might work, but it is still risky."

"I'm open to other ideas."

At the moment, she has none.

She sets up her computer to alert us if anyone at the Prices' house says anything else, and we make our dinner—a best-we-can-manage version of *pad see ew*—then settle in and watch *Samurai Gourmet* on Netflix.

At 11:48 p.m., after we just started the eleventh and penultimate episode in the series, Jar's computer bongs with an alert.

I pause the video while she picks up her laptop. It's kind of late for conversations at the Prices' and I figure it must be someone saying goodnight. But upon looking at her screen, Jar bolts upright.

"It's Evan," she says. "He is leaving."

She angles the computer so I can see it. On it plays the video feed from the bug I left in the tree across the street from the house. He's sneaking along the back of the house, toward the picket fence.

"Come on," I say. "Let's see where he goes."

We rush out of the house, Jar bringing her backpack and laptop, me bringing jackets for both of us. After I pull the truck onto the street, Jar hands me a set of comm gear. I shove the earpiece into place and tap the mic to activate it.

"Check, one, two," I say. "Check."

"You're good," Jar says.

"Evan?" I ask.

"He is almost done removing the pickets from the fence."

We're still two blocks away, and I'm worried he'll disappear into the night before we have him in sight. I gun the engine and race faster than I should down the residential streets.

Just ahead, the corner with the street that runs past the side of Evan's house comes into view. It's the same street Evan used when walking home on the night I watched him climb up the side of his house. Which gives me an idea.

I pull to a stop just short of the curb. "Follow him. I'll track your phone."

Without hesitating, Jar jumps out of the truck, leaving her laptop behind for me. I pull out again and speed to the corner, then turn so that I'll drive right by Evan's house. It's dark enough on this block that he shouldn't be able to see my features if he looks, but I'm betting he'll keep his head down until I've passed.

That is, *if* he's still in the area.

I keep an eye out for him as I drive by but the street looks deserted. I drive past his house and continue for another block before I turn left.

I want to pull to the curb and wait for Jar to report, but I also know if Evan was hiding somewhere as I passed by, it needs to sound like I've driven away, so I go three blocks north before stopping.

"Anything?" I ask over the comm.

Two clicks, which means no.

Crap.

Did we miss him? If we did, then I have a feeling we're out of luck, because I doubt we'll spot him again until he returns.

I begin counting off the seconds. When I hit thirty, I'll go pick up Jar.

Jar clicks her mic three times as I reach seventeen. Something's happened.

"Evan?" I ask.

One click. Yes.

I snatch up Jar's laptop and type in her password. I'm pretty sure I'm the only person on the planet who has reached this level of trust with her. I open the tracking software and select Jar's phone from a set of potential devices, which includes all the phones belonging to our colleagues at work. It's a way we can keep track of one another when necessary.

A map of the surrounding area appears, and on it a red dot showing me where Jar is located. The dot remains stationary, about a dozen meters from where I let Jar out. Then it starts to move, going west down the street that runs by the side of the Prices' house.

I take a road that runs parallel to the one Jar and—presumably—Evan are on, heading in the same direction. When I'm two blocks behind them, relatively speaking, I slow to avoid getting ahead of them.

After relaying my new position to Jar, I say, "Give me three taps if he turns toward me, and four if he goes the other way."

She taps once to acknowledge my instructions.

Three minutes go by without any change. Even at my reduced speed, I am still gaining on them, and have closed the two-block gap to less than one.

"He's getting into a car," Jar whispers in my ear, her words coming in a rush. "Come get me."

I whip the truck around and double back to the intersection

I just passed, then take that road to the one Jar is on. Before I reach the corner, I kill my headlights and make the turn.

About a block and a half in front of me, I see the rear lights of a sedan speeding away and assume it's the one Evan is in. Jar steps out from between two parked cars ten meters ahead. I stop just long enough for her to swing the door open and jump in, then we're off again.

I nod toward the sedan's taillights. "That's them, right?"

As she says, "Yes," the sedan turns right and disappears.

I flick on my headlights and race ahead.

"How many were in the car with him?"

"Three."

"Were you able to see them?"

She nods. "The dome light came on when he opened the door. Teenagers. Two boys and a girl. I have never seen any of them before."

The road the sedan turned onto is one of the main arteries in town. They're heading in the direction of the business district. When we reach the intersection, I do what my grandmother would call a California stop, slowing the vehicle enough to check no one's coming but never bringing it to a full halt.

The sedan is a little more than three blocks ahead of us.

If this was a normal Friday night, I'd assume they're headed to one of the fast-food places on Central Ave., most of which would probably be open until at least midnight. But we all know these aren't normal times, and I highly doubt any of those places are staying open late these days, if they're open at all.

The sedan does turn onto Central, though. By this point, Jar and I are only a block and a half behind it. I stop (normally, not California style) at the intersection with Central and make the turn.

Evan and his friends blow right past the McDonald's and Wendy's and Sonic and KFC—which are all closed—and continue toward the south end of Mercy. No more than a handful of other cars are out, so I ease back on the accelerator and let Evan's sedan grow its lead on us to nearly two blocks.

Time and again, I anticipate them turning off the road into one of the neighborhoods, but they keep going straight. When it becomes clear they are planning on heading into the country-side, I say, "Do you have goggles?"

"Yes."

She digs into her bag and pulls out a pair of night vision goggles. They're not the fanciest pair we own, but they're more than adequate for my needs.

I angle the truck toward the side of the road like I'm going to park, then turn off our headlights. As soon as we're dark, I pull on the goggles and press down on the gas again to continue our pursuit.

If Evan and his friends were professionals, I would have to do a lot more than douse our lights to hide our presence. But they're not, so my little trick should be adequate enough to make them think they're on the road alone.

Four miles outside town, they turn right onto a county road, and three-quarters of a mile after that, they slow and then stop in the middle of the asphalt. I take my foot off the pedal, shift into neutral, and let our truck roll to a stop without touching the brakes.

Jar has pulled out binoculars from her backpack and trained them on the sedan.

"Are they getting out?" I ask.

"No."

"Then what are they doing?"

"I cannot tell for sure. If I had to, um…guess, I would say they are talking."

It's nearly another minute before the sedan starts moving

again. When it does, it's traveling at only about half the speed as before, giving me the sense they're looking for something.

We match their pace.

After about four hundred meters, the sedan turns left.

"Is that a driveway or..."

Jar checks the map on her computer. "It's a road."

When we reach the intersection, I'm not sure I should take the turn. The road is two-laned but narrower than the one we're on, and is cracked and dotted with patches. I don't want to be caught on it if Evan and the others decide they've gone the wrong way and suddenly come back.

I stare at the taillights of the sedan. The vehicle is about a hundred and fifty meters away, still moving slowly.

Screw it, I think, and take the turn. If the sedan comes back this way, so be it. We'll just make sure they don't see our faces.

Newly plowed fields surround the road for the first half kilometer, after which a grove of trees, maybe thirty meters thick, springs up on both sides. When the sedan reaches the farmland just past the grove, its brake lights flash on again.

Once more I let the truck roll forward on its own momentum. The sedan swings to the side of the road, and all of its lights go off.

I tap the accelerator enough to get us just inside the grove, then pull the truck off the road.

Jar is holding the binoculars to her eyes again. "They're getting out."

"All of them?"

A pause, then, "Yes." She goes quiet for a few more seconds. "They're crossing the road. And...are walking into the field." She stares through the glasses for another moment before lowering them. "The trees are in the way. I can't see them anymore."

I had a friend in college who grew up in the desert, south of

Palm Springs. He'd tell us about the high school parties they had out in the middle of nowhere, away from town. "The best part," he'd say, "was that we could get ourselves into trouble and out of it again, without our parents or the police ever being the wiser." I have to admit, I was a little jealous. Being a city kid, our parties were always at someone's house, which were more often than not shut down before they could really get going.

I'm wondering now if Evan and his friends are heading to their version of a desert party. Perhaps a kegger at a barn, where they could make trouble without anyone else knowing about it. The only problem with this idea is that there aren't any other cars around.

Maybe it's just a party of four.

This would be a great opportunity to break out the drone, but it's back at the duplex. Which means if we want to know where Evan and his friends are going, we'll have to follow on foot.

I throw the truck into reverse. This turns on the backup lights, but I'm no longer worried about being spotted by Evan. There's more than enough growth between us to block the lights from his and his friends' view.

Once we have backed out from the trees, I turn onto a dirt road—really more of a path—that runs between the grove and the farm field abutting it. I kill the engine. Now, if Evan and the others leave before we do, it would be highly unlikely for them to see our vehicle.

Jar and I climb out, jog back to the main road, and move down it toward the now empty sedan. It's breezy tonight, the cool wind blowing from behind us and rattling the leaves in the trees.

When we reach the far end of the trees, we stop, and I use the binoculars to scan the field where the others went. I spot them walking along the edge of the farm next to the trees, about halfway to the back end of the field. Unlike where we left the truck, there is no path here, only a meter-and-a-half strip of land that separates the field from the grove.

Staying low, we sneak over to their sedan. While I attach a tracker to the undercarriage, Jar takes a picture of the license plate. We then cross over to the strip of land the others are on and follow them. To reduce the chances of being seen, we keep as close to the trees as possible, our silhouettes mixing with the shadowy trunks. The bigger problem is noise. The breeze is moving toward Evan's group, and will carry any extraneous sounds toward them.

About every five steps, I raise the binoculars to check on the others' progress. The fourth time I do so, they are gone.

I hold out a hand, stopping Jar, then sweep my gaze through the area ahead.

There they are. They've walked into the field and are moving away from the trees.

I shift the glasses ahead of them to see if I can figure out where they're headed.

About seventy meters in front of them are more trees, though much fewer than those in the grove beside us. They are scattered around an unplowed area that appears to be where a house should be. Only there is no house.

But something is there. It's low to the ground, and hard to make out through the trees and a wide line of brush. It might be a structure, or it might be a pile of fertilizer. No way to tell from our angle.

We continue on along the woods, taking even more care as it's a lot easier now for Evan and his friends to glance back our way. Thankfully, their attention remains focused on their destination. As they near the tree-dotted area, they crouch and continue forward at a much slower pace, like they're worried they might be seen by someone ahead.

This idea is reinforced when, instead of going straight onto the unplowed land, two of them go left toward the back of the farm, and two go right toward the main road. They are circling the area, in what I can only assume is an attempt to make sure no one else is around.

The duo on the front side of the property arcs around to the roadway that runs to the main road where the sedan is parked, and stops.

The other two have halted also. They are about thirty meters closer to the back of the property than from where they started.

I switch back and forth between the pairs, waiting for something to happen. At around the ninety-second mark, a dull light appears in the hand of one of the teens at the front and is raised to his or her ear. A phone.

I sweep the binoculars back to the others. Though I don't see a similar light, I can see one of them holding a hand to his or her ear.

Fifteen seconds later, all four of them start walking toward the spot they were surveilling, which I take to mean they believe the area is deserted.

Jar and I kneel down next to the trees, then take turns watching the teens through the binoculars for the next twenty minutes. More like *try* to watch them, as most of the time they're hidden from view by bushes or trees or both. One thing we have no problem seeing are several camera flashes. Again, we are talking teenagers here, so they're probably taking selfies.

When they finally leave, they head down the driveway back to the county road.

While I know Jar and I could return to our truck without the others being the wiser, we've bugged their sedan so we don't need to keep them in sight to follow them anymore. Besides, I really want to get a look at whatever it is that drew them out here.

We remain where we are until Evan and his friends are in their sedan and headed back to Mercy—or wherever their next stop is—then we take the same route across the field that they took earlier.

We're not even halfway to our destination when the breeze lets up for a few seconds—and the air becomes tinged with a smoky, ashy odor.

My first thought is of the Mercy Arsonist and that it's actually the kids and they've started a fire. I begin to run, hoping we can put the blaze out before the flames can do much damage. The closer I get, the more overwhelming the smell becomes. Oddly, the area ahead remains dark. Not a flicker of flames in sight.

That doesn't make any sense.

"Slow down," Jar says from not far behind me. "No reason to run."

I continue on for a few more steps before I realize she's right.

There's no fire for us to put out. No wrongheaded deed Evan and his friends have done that I need to rectify.

Whatever happened here happened before any of us arrived.

We reach the end of the field and step onto a wide area of fresh grass.

The *something* I glimpsed earlier that was hidden behind trees and bushes, that I thought might be a building? It's the charred debris of the home that once stood here. The wreckage is not from an old fire, though. It isn't even the remains of a fire that happened earlier in the week. This fire happened today, and if I had to guess, no more than six hours ago.

Tire tracks made by large vehicles are everywhere, and the

ground around the foundation is soaked with water, leading me to the obvious conclusion that this house received the same emergency response as the house fire we were at on Monday night.

Someone has wound caution tape around the blackened pile of wood, with the words ACTIVE INVESTIGATION DO NOT CROSS printed on it.

If I had to guess, I'd say the emergency vehicles left at most two hours ago.

About eighty meters behind the house are the burnt remains of a barn. That location, too, has caution tape strung around it.

While I take a closer look at the house, Jar sits on the ground and pulls the laptop out of her backpack.

I've had more than my share of experiences dealing with the aftereffects of fires. One time, years ago when I was an apprentice, my mentor (and now partner) had me meet him at the scene of a house fire. Ironically, that was also in Colorado, but at a resort area in the Rockies. I arrived first, and got it in my head that it would impress him if, before he arrived, I could figure out what had happened. Not only did I fail to figure out anything, my partner was, shall we say, less than pleased I had trampled all over the crime scene. Which was why I soon ended up on my back, in the snow.

To be young and arrogant and naïve. I sometimes miss those days.

But not really.

I've had a lot more training and experience since that job, and though I might have been way out of my element back then, these days I could give even the best fire investigators a run for his or her money.

There's no doubt in my mind this fire was deliberately set. The fact that the barn has burned down, too, is all the proof I need. But while it might seem obvious it was started by the same person or persons who set the fire on Monday, I won't rule anything out just yet.

I move around the house until I'm at the back. Though it was impossible for me to conduct a similar investigation at Monday night's blaze due to the fire crews, it was still apparent the ignition point had been somewhere at the rear of the house. I'm looking for signs that the same is true here.

Before this house burned down, it had sat about a half meter above the ground, on the concrete walls of what had been its basement. Here in the back are two narrow basement windows, near the top of the concrete. The glass is missing in both, either blown out by the fire or knocked out by the water used to fight it. Or broken by the arsonist.

I kneel beside one window and shine my phone's flashlight inside. Much of the house has collapsed into the basement, which explains why the pile above is not high. I lean my head through the window and shine my light on the wall below me. Scorch marks on the inside lip of the window, and on the cinder block going all the way to the floor. Next to the wall are a few small pieces of burnt wood and several broken glass jars, the remains of what was likely a shelving unit and the objects it held.

Here's the thing about fires. They like to go up, not down. Sure, it's possible the shelf caught on fire after the floor above it collapsed into the basement, but what I'm seeing is telling a different story, one where the flames started from below.

I shine the light around again, hoping to spot the ignition point, but see nothing definitive.

I climb back to my feet and dust myself off, then continue around the house until I reach Jar again.

"Anything?" I ask.

"The fire department received a call reporting the fire at six twenty-one p.m.," she says. "It took them seventeen minutes to get here. According to the logs at the sheriff's department, deputies arrived four minutes before the fire department and reported that no one was at the house. The fire was out by eight-oh-eight and everyone was gone by nine fifty-five p.m."

"Is it on the *Sentinel*'s website yet?" I ask.

"Not yet."

"Then how did Evan and his friends know about it?"

"I don't know." After a pause, she tentatively adds, "A police scanner?"

"Perhaps," I say. "Good thought."

I hope she's right, but I can't help thinking there is another reason. Like maybe they had forehand knowledge it was going to happen.

Dammit. We're going to have to do exactly what I didn't want to do, aren't we?

As much as it pains me, I say, "I think we should take a closer look at all these fires."

Jar only nods, though I'm sure she's pleased. It's what she's wanted since Monday night.

The only surprise is that Liz doesn't make an appearance to join in on the silent gloating.

CHAPTER TWELVE

Tracking data shows us that Evan and his friends have returned to Mercy and gone to the McDonald's on Central Ave. When we drive by, we see them parked in back of the closed restaurant, with two other sedans and an old VW van.

Some of the occupants—probably all, though we have no way of knowing—are leaning against the vehicles and talking to one another, in a more typical teenage activity than checking out the scene of an arsonist's handiwork.

"Should we try to get close so we can hear what they are talking about?" Jar asks.

"I doubt what they're saying is very interesting."

Jar becomes contemplative, as if that's not something she would have considered on her own. Which I'm sure is probably the case. Jar basically went from being a young kid straight into adulthood. I'm not sure she's ever had friends her same age.

By the time we return to the duplex, it's almost one a.m. I'd been hoping to be asleep over an hour ago, but Evan's excursion put a crimp into that plan. What this means is that I'll get less rest than I wanted.

Won't be the first time.

At 4:20 a.m., Jar shakes my shoulder and says, "Time to get up."

If you're tracking stats, my total sleep time is three hours and seven minutes.

Jar has been up long enough to have made me some coffee and a bowl of oatmeal, which I appreciate. I don't have a lot of time to spare. The sun will be up in about an hour and I need to be in place before then.

While I down my meal, Jar shows me the backpack she has prepared for me. "I would have included a few apples, but they can be noisy and...aromatic. So, I am afraid you will have to be satisfied with granola bars. There are ten. I would not advise eating them all. I have also given you four bottles of water. You should be careful how much you drink, too, because—"

I hold up a hand. "I get it."

With a nod, she zips up the bag.

"If I'm caught, you're going to have to call in some help," I say.

"Then do not get caught."

"That's the plan."

"Good."

Breakfast done, I pull on a sweater and light jacket. Both are black, like my pants and T-shirt and shoes. To finish off my noir ensemble, I don a black face mask and black stocking cap, then slip the straps of my backpack over my shoulders.

Jar turns off the lights and peels back the curtain on one of the front windows to peek outside.

"It's clear," she says. "Be careful."

"Don't have too much fun without me."

"What kind of fun are you expecting me to have?"

There are times I forget Jar is Jar. "It was a joke."

A frown and a *hmmm*.

I open the door and step outside.

The night is still as dark as it was at midnight, but it won't be long before the eastern sky starts to lighten, so I head off at a brisk pace, pretending to be someone out for a little early exercise. At this speed, it takes me five minutes to reach the Prices' house. Like on Monday night, I come at it from the side street, but instead of using the neighbor's yard, this time I enter the property via Evan's removable pickets.

You may be asking yourself why I'm here so early if the house won't be empty until the Prices leave for the barbecue, presumably sometime this afternoon. Simple. Like I said before, getting onto the property during daylight would be more challenging. Much easier to sneak in while it's dark and hide in their yard until they're gone. Hence the reason for the granola bars and bottles of water.

To avoid spending more time than necessary in the halo of the backyard light, I move along the fence toward the back corner of the lot, and then hurry over to the RV. I pick the lock to the door of the forward storage unit, open it, and slip into the hold.

This is where I'll be spending my time until the family leaves, which I figure will be no earlier than two p.m.

Seems like the perfect opportunity to take a long nap.

It turns out I have miscalculated.

In retrospect, I should have anticipated this might happen. But I'll be honest, it didn't even cross my mind. Hell, Jar didn't even think of it, and she seldom misses an angle.

I spent most of the morning slipping in and out of sleep. It was kind of fun in a way. I kept jumping from one dream to the next. Though I can't remember what the dreams were about, I do recall they were filled with excitement and adventure. I'm pretty sure Jar was in all of them. Beyond that, I've got nothing but a sense of sleep well spent.

This state lasted until around noon, at which point I dug into my hoard of granola bars. They're the soft, chewy kind in case you're wondering, the kind that's unlikely to cause any unnecessary noises or leave crumbs.

Every half hour, I checked in with Jar. She was monitoring the only bug we have at the house, and keeping a close eye on the feed from the camera across the street.

When two p.m. passed without any signs that the Prices were leaving, I started growing antsy. At three, I began to seriously worry that the barbecue had been cancelled and we somehow missed hearing them talk about it.

But then, at 3:12 p.m., Jar said, "Charles just shouted, 'Ten-minute warning.'"

I relaxed a little. "Finally."

"He could mean any number of things."

"I guess we'll see."

At 3:20, she said, "He just shouted 'Let's go' several times."

"See, they are leaving."

"Maybe," she conceded.

A minute passed. Then two.

Then Jar again, "I think we have a problem."

"What's wrong?"

"Charles, Evan, and Sawyer just came out the back door."

The words were barely out of her mouth when I heard Chuckie shout from maybe half a dozen meters away, "Kate, come on. We're going to be late."

Though I understood why Jar was concerned, in my head I'd half convinced myself they'd left the house through the back door because the barbecue was within walking distance.

But then Chuckie said, "Get the gate," and I heard footsteps jogging toward the driveway entrance behind the RV.

"Evan is opening the rolling gate," Jar said. "Kate has just exited the house. She's holding a pan of something.... Charles has just closed the door behind her.... Now he and Kate and Sawyer are walking toward the RV."

As I said, I have miscalculated. Which explains why I am still lying in the Winnebago's storage compartment as the vehicle bounces down the streets of Mercy, on its way to wherever this barbecue is taking place.

Dammit, dammit, dammit.

I was *right there*.

At the house.

I should be inside the place at this very moment. Fifteen to twenty minutes is all I would need, then I'd be back in the RV waiting for dark. It was a good plan. A great one, even. One that ninety-nine times out of a hundred would have worked.

Daaaaaammmmmmmit!

I hope the barbecue isn't too far away. If that's the case, Jar could walk over and watch the area so I can sneak out. But the prospect of that scenario is slipping further and further away with every passing minute.

"Which way are we headed?" I whisper. I'm not worried about the Prices hearing me. The sounds of the road should be enough to obscure my voice, but no sense in taking chances.

"North. You are almost out of town."

"Well, isn't that just awesome."

"You are being sarcastic, correct?"

"Yeah. Very."

Looks like we've blown our big chance for placing bugs

inside the Prices' house. Let me rephrase that. Looks like *I* blew it. I'm the one whose bright idea it was to use the Winnebago.

"You are in the countryside now."

Have I said dammit yet? Probably too much. Sorry. It's just...

Never mind.

Dammit.

It's another twenty minutes before the RV slows to a crawl and takes a right turn. From the roughness and the sound of particles smacking into the undercarriage, I'm guessing the new road is not paved.

Jar says, "It looks like...ou...to...ake."

"Repeat that. You're breaking up."

This time when she speaks, the signal is worse, and all I pick up are a few vowels and maybe a syllable or two.

"If you can hear me, I can't hear you."

Our comms piggyback on the mobile services of the area we're in. But wherever we're headed now appears to have lousy cell coverage. I have a solution for that. I can route my comm directly through my phone and use the satellite function. The only problem is that doing so will only work if my phone has direct line of sight with the satellite, i.e., it needs to be outdoors.

My experience—albeit limited—in the Mercy area leads me to speculate that the dirt road we're on is actually a driveway and we're headed to a farm. If that's the case, we should be stopping any second now.

Only we don't stop. The Winnebago bounces around for another ten minutes, the dirt road twisting and turning.

When the ride finally ends and the RV's engine turns off, I experience a few moments of false silence, as my ears adjust to a world without the whine of the motor and the pounding of the road less than a meter under my head.

The first noise I hear is from the Prices above me, making

their way to the side door. The RV rocks a little as they exit, and then the door slams shut.

I close my eyes, focus on the sound of their movements, and determine that the family is heading straight out from the passenger side, toward the destination. In the distance, I hear laughter and talking and a splash of water, which leads me to guess this home has a swimming pool. None of the sounds are closer than thirty meters, and some are maybe even forty or forty-five away.

I'm torn about what my next move should be. Part of me wants to slip out and see what's going on. My initial mission of breaking into the Prices' house may have been put on hold, but perhaps I can learn something from observing them at the barbecue.

The other part of me is saying I should stay right where I am. The Prices are my ride back to town. I don't want to find myself in a position where I can't return to my hiding place before they leave. And I absolutely don't want to be seen by anyone when I climb out.

I concentrate on the sounds outside again, this time focusing on any that might be near the vehicle. At first everything is quiet, then I pick up the crunch of moving tires from a vehicle heading toward my position. The noise of compacting dirt grows louder by the second, until the vehicle rolls up next to the driver's side of the RV and stops.

I hear doors open and people getting out.

"The Reubens are here," a woman says. "I thought you said they weren't coming."

"That's what Lee told me," a man replies. "I guess their plans changed."

"Thank God. At least there's someone we can talk to."

The man laughs.

Someone else must be with them, because right before they walk off, three doors close in rapid succession. I listen as they walk past the Winnebago and head in the same direction the Prices went, until once more all I can hear is the racket from the party.

If I'm going to get out, I need to do so on the driver's side since it faces away from the gathering. And with the arrival of the new car beside us on that side, my chances of exiting the storage area without being seen have increased.

I scoot up to the access door and listen. What I hear are the chirps of birds and the sound of a light breeze fanning leaves. What I don't hear is the approach of another vehicle or sounds of people walking or talking or milling about.

I pull out my gooseneck camera from my bag. It's basically a long, flexible tube with a small camera lens on one end and a connector on the other that plugs into my phone.

After the two devices are attached to each other, I release the latch on the compartment door and push it slowly upward, my ear attuned to any sudden sounds outside that might indicate someone has noticed the movement.

All remains quiet.

As soon as the gap between the door and frame is wide enough, I slip the end of the gooseneck outside and twist it to look left and right. The space between the Winnebago and the vehicle parked next to us is unoccupied. Even better, the neighboring vehicle is a Chevy Tahoe SUV, so it completely blocks the compartment hatch from anyone who might be on the other side of it.

One of the first things my mentor taught me was to understand that no situation is static. If you come upon an opportunity, you take it, lest it disappear while you're deciding what to do.

Which is why I open the door wider and slip outside without a second thought, pulling my backpack with me. I don't want to lock the hatch in place, as leaving the latch undone will make it easier for me to get back inside later. But I don't want the door to appear to be open, either. I pluck a twig off the ground that's about as wide as the gap between the hatch and its frame, stick it into the space, and break it off so that the only thing left is the end of the twig in the gap, holding the door in place.

Works like a charm.

I peek through the windows of the Tahoe. About twenty-five meters beyond the SUV is a wide grove of trees, which is a lot better for me than the farm field I was expecting to see there. The area between the Tahoe and the trees is also unoccupied. Perhaps the bad luck I've had today is finally starting to go away.

I glance to my left, looking for the road we arrived on. When I find it, I'm surprised to see that the grove of trees extends all the way around the parking area up to it and starts again on the other side. We seem to be inside a small forest, not a mere copse. As for the road, no one is on it.

I move around to the other side of the Tahoe and head toward the trees, keeping the Winnebago between me and the party goers. Once I'm safely in the woods, I find a spot from where I can see what's going on.

Here's another thing I was wrong about. The Prices have not brought me to somebody's farmhouse. The barbecue is taking place at a lakeside park. The lake appears to be about three hundred meters across and another four hundred wide, and like the parking area, is surrounded by trees.

As for the party, it's drawn quite the crowd. Which explains why there are so many vehicles in the parking area. I count eight sedans, seven pickup trucks, five SUVs, and four RVs besides the Prices' Winnebago. There has to be at least sixty people at the park, and though I'll need my binoculars to confirm, it doesn't appear many of them are wearing masks.

Super-spreader event, anyone?

Do these people not watch the news?

All I can imagine is they're suffering from a mass case of the It's Not Going to Happen to Me Syndrome.

It almost makes me want to run over there and slap each of them in the face to wake them up, but that would entail getting near them and that's not going to happen. The sight actually makes me feel a little worried about riding back with the Prices, even with the floor between us and me wearing a mask.

Off to one side of the park is a dock that juts into the lake, and several people have congregated there. Near the dock is a building that I'm pretty sure houses toilets. The only other permanent structure is a covered area with picnic tables near where the majority of the people are. A banner hangs from the columns that hold up the roof.

I pull out my binoculars.

The sign is professionally printed and reads:

47th Annual Mercy Chamber of Commerce Barbecue
Sponsored by Gage-Trent Farming

Interesting. Gage-Trent is the owner of six of the burned-down houses, including the one I ran into.

I check out the crowd nearby and realize I've underestimated the attendance. I can see more than sixty people just in that area. Throw in those over by the docks and a few other stragglers and there must be at least eighty attendees, if not a hundred.

I see Chuckie laughing it up with a couple of other guys. Kate's not too far way, speaking with a small group of women and one older man.

Though there are four permanent barbecues just outside the covered area, they're not being used. Someone has brought one of those long, barrel-style grills, above which waves of heat are distorting the air. It doesn't look like they've started cooking anything yet.

I briefly wonder if they're having this so far from town to avoid getting shut down by the police, but then I spot two officers I saw at the fire. They're drinking beer and joking with everyone else.

I shift the binoculars over to the dock area. The people there are younger, high school and below, I'd say. Evan is there, his legs hanging over the side of the dock, his feet almost touching the water. There's a brown-haired girl sitting next to him, not too close, but not too far away, either. Sawyer's there, too, but he's sitting on the ground a few meters from where the dock starts. He's alone and swaying slightly, like he's keeping time with music.

Interestingly, the dock dwellers are all wearing masks, including Evan and his friend. (I can't tell if Sawyer is—his back is to me—but I assume so.) It gives me a little hope about the future.

One thing for sure, this party is just getting started. And it'll be a while before anyone goes anywhere.

I slip deeper into the woods until I find a clearing, then I link my comm to my phone and switch to satellite mode.

"Nate for Jar," I say.

When she doesn't reply within a few seconds, I repeat my call.

Dead air.

"Jar, come in."

Another five seconds of nothing, then, "I'm here, I'm here. Sorry. Are you okay?"

"I'm fine."

"You are not in the RV." She's not asking this. She knows I couldn't have called her otherwise.

"I had an opportunity to take a look around. We're at a lake with a park next to it."

"Grayson Lake," she says. "It is listed as a county recreation area."

"How far from Mercy are we?

"Twenty-three point seven kilometers north-northeast."

Which means I definitely don't want to miss my ride back.

"Have the Prices met up with their friends?" she asks.

I snort. "It's a little bigger party than just a barbecue with friends. This is a sponsored event."

"Sponsored?"

I describe the scene.

"That is very unsafe," she says.

It finally registers on me that she's been talking in a low voice this whole time. Not a whisper, more like she's in a library. But it's still unusual.

"You're still at the house, right?"

A pause. "I am in *a* house."

"What the hell does that mean?"

"Exactly what I said. It's no place you should worry about."

"Well, I wasn't worried until you said that."

Silence falls between us as I wait for her to give me a straight answer. But she's good at this kind of game and remains quiet.

Keeping my voice as calm as possible, I say, "Jar, where are you?"

She lets out an annoyed breath. "Since you cannot bug the Prices' house, it is up to me. That is where I am."

"Are you crazy?" I blurt out.

"I had an opportunity to take a look around." Jar is particularly adept at throwing my words back at me when it suits her.

"So, you just waltzed into their yard, in the middle of the day, and broke into their house?"

"I do not know how to waltz."

"I think you're missing my point. The sun's up, remember? Someone probably saw you."

"No one saw."

"How can you possibly know that?"

"This is a small community. Someone would have come to check by now, or would have called the police and I would be in jail."

"This is the barometer you're using?" I say, and then something else dawns on me. "Wait. How long have you been there?"

"Inside? A little over twenty minutes."

The Prices and I have been gone for around three quarters of an hour at this point. If you figure it took her around ten minutes (maybe even a bit more) to walk over and sneak onto the property, and another three to five to plan and prepare, she must have decided to do this as soon as the Winnebago pulled out.

I know the anger I'm feeling is actually worry that she's undertaken this task without me being close in case anything goes wrong. I also know Jar is more than capable of pulling things like this off without me. I'm being overprotective, which —you don't have to tell me—is not a good look. I guess what bugs me the most, other than my worry, is that we didn't discuss things first. We usually do that before jumping into something like this.

Well, not always, but at least seventy-five percent of the time. The other twenty-five percent is usually me doing something stupid on my own. I'm just not used to being the one on the outside. Which, again, is a me problem.

I take a deep breath and say, "I'm guessing you're almost done, right? You don't have enough bugs to cover everything."

As I mentioned, we're short on bugs and I have the majority

of our remaining stash with me. I left only a few behind in case something came up for which we might need one.

"I have enough for the important areas. And there is no need to rush. You can warn me when the family is on the way back. So, I am taking my time."

Her words don't make me feel any better.

"You have an exit plan?"

"That is a stupid question. Of course I do."

"Do you want to go over it?"

A couple of annoyed breaths, then, "I will wait until dark and slip out the backyard."

I don't like the idea of her staying there that long, but it's pretty much what I was going to do. And I highly doubt the Prices and I will be coming back before sunset.

"What about the backyard light?" I ask. We're pretty sure it automatically comes on at night, which means it would light her up when she leaves.

"I have killed the power to it," she says. "I made the breaker look like it has tripped. See? I will be all right. Now, if you stop wasting my time, we can both get back to work."

We sign off, with promises to let each other know if we have any problems.

My chest is still tight with concern, which is weird. If any of the other operatives I work with on my day job were in the Prices' house, I wouldn't give it a second thought. And Jar is as good as they are, so it shouldn't matter.

But it does. Because—

I close my eyes tight and try to avoid going where that thought was headed.

Hey, idiot, I tell myself. *Get it in gear*.

After a deep breath, I open my eyes, my head clearer than it was before. Wow, it's been a while since I let my emotions control me that much.

I focus on the task at hand.

As I see it, I have three choices of what to do next: I can watch the picnic from here in the trees, I can go back to the Winnebago and take another nap, or I can try to move in closer and see if I can pick up more information.

I'll give you one guess as to which I choose to do.

CHAPTER THIRTEEN

Staying in the woods, I skirt around the parking area and make my way toward the lake. The trickiest part is crossing the entrance road. I choose a spot thirty meters from where it meets the parking area, make sure no one is coming or going, and then sprint across.

The rest of the way is slow going due to the abundance of undergrowth and my desire to create as little noise as possible. Thankfully it's spring, so it's mostly new bushes that bend but do not break as I sweep by.

When I near the water, I head west until I'm just a few meters from where the trees end and the park begins, a short baseball toss away from the dock.

I pull out my binoculars again.

Evan has not moved from his spot, though the girl sitting with him has inched a little closer. They are facing the trees I'm hiding in, which allows me to get a good look at them. I'm pretty sure the girl is the same one who was in the car with Evan last night. She has long dark brown hair, brown skin, and a bright smile. She likes him. There's no missing that. I get the sense he likes her, too, but doesn't know what to do about it.

After I take a picture of the girl, I turn my attention to the others in the area.

Standing near the end of the dock are five teens—three guys and two girls. Two of the guys are half a head taller than the other kids and look a year or two older. Probably upperclassmen. They seem to be holding court, joking with each other and occasionally smiling at the girls. The third guy is trying to stay involved but he's outmatched.

I've been there, buddy. It gets better.

I don't recognize any of them so I move on. There are four additional teens on the dock, and three more on shore sitting on the grass. Sawyer is still there, and still alone. He's looking at what appears to be a magazine and definitely listening to something over earbuds. I can see the white cord dangling down the front of his torso into a shirt pocket.

One of the teens sitting on the grass catches my eye. No question—he was in the sedan last night. No one else rings a bell.

After taking pictures of everyone, I reposition to a spot that gives me a better view of the bigger crowd by the barbecues.

Conversations are being had everywhere, many with an animated quality probably being helped along by beer or whatever alcohol is in the Solo cups a lot of people are holding. If I had a directional microphone with me, I could listen in. Jar and I have one but it's back home in California, as I did not anticipate needing it on vacation.

I find Kate talking with a different group of people from the last time I spotted her. She looks more relaxed than I've ever seen her, which I attribute to the fact Chuckie is nowhere near her.

Huh.

I don't actually see Chuckie anywhere.

I scan the crowd again. Nope. He's not there. Maybe he's

beyond the crowd, walking around the edge of the lake. Hard for me to see that area through everyone.

I look over to the parking area. A couple of guys are standing next to the open tailgate of a pickup, but neither of them is Chuckie. When my scan reaches the Winnebago, I stop. While I see no one standing outside it, I pick up movement through the window near the side door.

I increase magnification.

Someone is definitely inside the RV. The interior is too dark for me to make out who it is, but I assume it's Chuckie. I know where the rest of his family is, and I can't imagine he's the kind of guy who would let someone else go inside the Winnebago without supervision.

Four minutes later, my guess is confirmed when the side door opens and Chuckie and two other men exit the vehicle.

The man in front looks to be in his sixties and is husky in that former athlete gone to seed kind of way. He's also bald and trying to make up for the lack of hair on top with a goatee and mustache that have both been dyed black. From his wrinkles, I'm guessing he's trying to look younger than he really is. The other guy is probably about twenty years the bald man's junior and the same height as Chuckie, but in better shape. Like go to the gym every day good shape. He still has all his hair, too, though it's kept military tight.

All of them, including Chuckie, are wearing shorts. Mr. In Shape is wearing a green polo shirt, while Goatee and Chuckie are both wearing Hawaiian shirts. I don't think I've mentioned this yet, but a lot of people at the party are wearing Hawaiian shirts. Must be a theme.

I'm curious what Chuckie and his friends were doing inside. Lucky for me, we have the vehicle bugged. And unless Jar has accidentally deactivated the auto-record feature, whatever they talked about should've been uploaded to the cloud.

Check that, *will* be uploaded. The relay needs a signal, and that won't happen until the Winnebago is back in range of a cell network. Which means I can't listen to Chuckie and his friends right now.

I take pictures of the two men I don't know, in case the conversation turns out to be interesting.

The men stand next to the RV for a few minutes, finishing their conversation. By the way they're leaning toward one another, and the occasional glances both Chuckie and In Shape give the area around them, I get the sense they don't want anyone else to know what they're discussing.

Well, well, well. My interest has been piqued.

When they finish, Chuckie gestures to his friends in a way that says *go on, I'll be right there*. He then goes to one of the RV's back storage doors and opens it. From inside, he pulls out a couple of folding chairs, shuts the door, and heads back to the barbecue, a chair under each arm.

I watch the party for another thirty minutes and take pictures of as many of the participants as possible. When I finish, I know I've done pretty much all I can here, short of going out and mingling with the crowd, which is definitely not going to happen.

I walk back through the trees the way I came. Before I return to the Winnebago, I check in with Jar. She's finished bugging the house and is apparently sitting on a stool in the windowless pantry, watching *The Umbrella Academy* on Netflix. Which, she points out, I am interrupting.

After reassuring each other that everything is fine with our respective situations, I sneak to the RV and crawl back into my hiding space.

Around 7:45 p.m., I start hearing car doors opening and closing and engines starting. The party is coming to an end.

When I hear someone approaching the Winnebago, I think, *Finally, I get to go home.* But the person gets into the vehicle to the RV's right and leaves. The next time it happens, my reaction is a bit more subdued, which pays off because this time it's the Tahoe that drives off.

I'm beginning to wonder if the Prices are planning to be the last to leave when I hear Chuckie's voice yelling, "You bet! I'll give you a call next week. Have a good night!"

Something bumps against the Winnebago's side, then I hear the jangle of keys, followed by the side door being unlocked.

"Let's go. I'm tired," Chuckie says.

The first to enter does so with light steps. Sawyer, probably.

"Don't forget the chairs," Kate says from near the door, then enters.

"Catch," Chuckie says. I hear keys again, this time flying through the air before hitting something and falling to the ground. "Jesus! What's wrong with you?"

"Sorry," Evan says.

"Put those away and let's get out of here," Chuckie says.

I hear movement at the same place I heard something bump against the RV, and I realize that both sounds were likely caused by the chairs I'd seen Chuckie pull out earlier.

Which is why I'm expecting to hear the door to the rear storage area open. From where I am, I can't see it due to the Winnebago's support structure so I'm not worried about being discovered.

Or I *wasn't* until a key enters the lock for the hatch, on the front passenger side of the vehicle.

There is nowhere I can go.

After my initial *oh, crap* moment passes, my rational mind

kicks in. Evan doesn't need to look into the hold to slide the chairs inside, so there's still very little chance he'll see me.

When the leg end of the first chair passes through the door, the only parts of Evan I see are his waist and hands, backlit by the orange sky of the recently set sun.

As the chair legs get near me, I scoot back a little to make sure they have enough room. When the other end enters the compartment, Evan lets go of the chair and his hands disappear long enough to grab the second chair.

He shoves it inside on top of the first chair, with a little more force than he needs to, in what I'm guessing is a passive-aggressive show of annoyance. I can't say I blame him, but the problem is this micro outburst caused one of the legs of the second chair to get hung up in the cloth seat of the first. When the chair unexpectedly stops wanting to go in, Evan tries the very male thing of shoving it harder a few times to see if that'll take care of the issue.

It does not.

What I'm hoping he'll do is pull it out and try again, in which case I'll grab the leg before it can get caught and guide the chair into place.

What he does instead is lean down to see what's wrong.

I hold very still, hoping the darkness of the storage space is deep enough to conceal me.

Evan eyes the chair and spots the problem almost right away. He pulls the chair back enough to free the leg and then pushes it in again, watching its progress to make sure it doesn't get stuck again.

That's when he sees me.

He freezes, confused, then starts to pull away, scared.

I do the only thing I can think of to save myself, and whisper as loudly as I dare, "Evan."

This stops him. He leans down to the opening again, probably thinking I'm one of his friends, who for some unknown reason is hitching a ride. When he sees me, his brow furrows, not recognizing me.

I whisper, "I helped you, now you help me."

His head cocks, still not understanding. But then his eyes widen as he realizes who I am.

Before he can say anything, I put my finger to my lips.

Not even a beat later, Chuckie yells from inside the RV, "Evan! Move it!"

Evan and my eyes are still locked, my finger still in front of my mouth. I twist my head slightly and raise my eyebrow, silently asking if he'll keep my presence a secret.

After another beat, he nods, shuts the door, and climbs into the RV.

"What the hell took you so long?" Chuckie's voice is filled with accusation, as if he's sure Evan was up to no good.

I prepare myself to bail out and run if Evan reveals what he saw. But the boy only says, "A chair got stuck."

"How in God's name did a chair get stuck?"

I'm guessing Evan shrugs his answer, because the next thing I hear is Chuckie swearing again and telling Evan to sit as the Winnebago's engine fires to life.

As soon as the signal indicator on my phone shows a couple of bars, I shoot Jar a text, telling her we're on our way. She responds by letting me know she's already back at the duplex.

I know we've reached the Prices' house when the RV slows and Chuckie says, "What the hell? Who messed with the light?"

He's talking about the backyard light. I'm the only one in the vehicle who knows the answer to his question, but I choose to remain silent.

After Evan opens the gate, Chuckie pulls the RV into its parking space.

I figure I have two minutes, tops, before he gets the light turned back on, so I can either wait here until everyone's gone to sleep or get out as quickly as I can now. The latter is definitely the more desirable course, as I have a feeling if I stay out here too long, Evan will find a way to pay me a visit.

The moment I hear Chuckie exit the passenger side of the Winnebago, I slip out of the hold on the driver's side and move to the rear corner of the RV nearest the street. When I hear the back door of the house swing open, I creep down the backside of the vehicle and peek around the edge at the house, just in time to see Kate and Sawyer go inside. Evan follows, but before he enters, he glances back at the Winnebago. I duck out of sight before he can see me, and wait until I hear him go in.

The moment the door closes, I hurry over to the removable pickets and let myself out. I barely make it to the other side of the street when the Prices' backyard light flicks on.

Jar stares at me. "What?"

"There wasn't much I could do about it."

She's reacting to news of my encounter with Evan.

Her brow is creased in worry. "Should...should we leave?"

It's a question I've been considering, too. I've had the whole ride back to process it, so I shake my head and say, "Not yet."

In the day job, if something goes wrong, we don't simply abandon a mission. There are always exceptions, of course, but I don't feel this qualifies as one. Yes, Evan knows we're in Mercy. And yes, that is a problem. But if we're smart about things, this evening's hiccup will be the only time our paths cross with his.

I say as much to Jar. She looks as though she's not

completely convinced but doesn't argue. I know she doesn't want to leave, either.

"How did you get into their house without being seen?" I ask.

Turns out the answer is the drone, which she used to make sure the streets and nearby yards were unoccupied when she approached the Prices' place. This did not eliminate the risk of someone looking out a window, but there are only three windows in other houses that have a direct view of Evan's secret entrance to the Prices' yard.

When I ask how it went, she opens her computer and brings up feeds from the cameras she's hidden. She only had five, and placed one in the dining room/living room area, one in the upstairs hallway, one in the kitchen at an angle to also pick up some of the downstairs hallway, one in Chuckie's home office, and one in the garage. She also had six audio-only bugs and used three of them—in the master bathroom, in the entryway, and at the far end of the living room, in case the camera can't pick up conversations in that area.

I have to say, for the owner of a car dealership, Chuckie is not living as high a life as I expected. Sure, it's a nice, four-bedroom house—five if you count the downstairs den—and the kitchen has been recently renovated, but I imagined someone in his position to have an even bigger house, maybe on the edge of town where he would have more acreage. The pandemic would explain a recent drop in business, but the Prices have clearly had the house for a while. Perhaps business has never been that good.

It's something to look into, and I mention this to Jar.

The corner of her mouth slides upward in a mischievous grin. "I had some time, so I took a look through his office."

"And?"

"I found many interesting things. The first being the door."

"The door?"

"He keeps it locked."

I frown, not fully understanding. Keeping an office door locked is not exactly unusual.

She adds, "With two deadbolts."

"Oh. That seems excessive."

"It is."

"Is he just paranoid? Or is there a good reason?"

She opens the feed from the camera in his office. It's a wide-angle shot from a side wall, with an entrance to the left, three cabinets—two filing and a closed-door metal one—straight ahead, and a wooden desk with a large executive-style leather desk chair to the right, in front of the window to the backyard.

I take a longer look at the closed cabinet. On the door is a numbered dial, and below this a three-spoked handle that can be spun, like the handle of a safe. Because that's exactly what it is. Not for money, though.

A gun safe.

"Did you get a look inside?" I ask.

She nods. "Three shotguns, three rifles, and four pistols. The rifles are a .22 and two thirty-aught-sixes. The pistols, three 9mms and one .40 caliber. There are also at least three full ammunition boxes of each type."

While that might explain the double locks on the office door, they still seem a bit excessive. The gun safe is a Marshall MN58, if I'm not mistaken. A good brand. Solid. Hard to break into without the appropriate skills. So more than secure enough on its own.

Which in my mind means the locks aren't there just for the guns. They've been installed because Chuckie doesn't want people—specifically his family—going through his stuff.

Speaking of...

"You said you found many things?" I say.

Jar closes the feed and clicks on a folder on her desktop. Inside are several image files. She opens them all and toggles through them.

Not photographs from a camera. Screen grabs.

"From Chuckie's computer?" I ask.

She shoots me an annoyed look as if that should be obvious. "Like I said. I had time."

Each image is of a different document. Loan statements, utility bills, insurance bills, vehicle information for several cars, brokerage statements, bank statements, and a few emails.

She enlarges one of the bank statements. It's for his checking account from last month, and shows a beginning balance of $3,758.21 and an ending one of $3,141.98. In between, there are approximately thirty transactions. Only three are deposits, while the rest are withdrawals for bills or other payments.

On first blush, it seems normal enough. Money going in and money going out, and the difference in the balance from the start of the month to the end not too large, albeit in a negative direction.

Jar shows me statements for the four months before that. They each start with a balance between five hundred dollars and just over a thousand dollars higher than they end with, meaning the account has steadily been trending downward.

"Is he transferring money into his other accounts?" I ask. I know from her preliminary check a few days ago that he has both a savings and brokerage account.

She shows those statements to me. The savings account has $18,391.17 in it, and the brokerage $57,464.03.

"I looked at statements for each going back two years. Up until the summer before last, the savings account had $340,000 in it and the brokerage almost $700,000."

"Whoa." That's over $960,000 gone in twenty-one months. "He must have other accounts."

"It's possible, but I have not discovered anything else." Allow me to translate. That's Jar speak for it's highly unlikely.

"Then where did the money go?" I ask.

"I have been trying to discover that but have come up with nothing so far."

"What about the deposits to his checking account? Maybe some of the deposits come from the missing cash."

"If so, it was not done directly."

"Then he must be using the money to keep his business afloat."

"That is what I have been thinking, too. I've accessed the accounting files for Price Auto and am in the process of downloading them. There is a lot to go through, so it may take some time."

Money woes could partially explain Chuckie's persistent foul mood. A downward financial spiral is not a great mix with an already volatile personality. I'm not saying it excuses anything, just that it could be a trigger.

But going through all those records will take time and we already have a lot on our plate. "We can call JP if you want. He really knows this stuff and you can concentrate on other things."

JP is a forensic accountant, and a living encyclopedia on all things financial. It's not often that my colleagues and I need his services, but when we do, his help is always invaluable.

She considers the idea and nods. "I will contact him."

That's another thing about Jar that's different from most people. Ego is never a problem. If it makes sense for someone else to do something, she's all for it.

"Is there anything else?" I ask.

"Perhaps, but I am not sure if it is important or not." She brings up another document. "Look at this."

It's an email to Chuckie, from August 17, two years ago.

Mr. Price:

This is to confirm your meeting tomorrow with Mr. Neuman at 10:30 a.m.

If you have any questions, please let me know.

Sincerely,
Tara Kerns
Executive Assistant to the Regional Vice President
Hayden Valley Agriculture
cc: Vince Neuman, Isaac Davis

Jar brings up a second letter, dated one week later.

Dear Mr. Price:

We consider this matter closed. Please do not attempt to contact us again.

Vince Neuman
Regional Vice President
Hayden Valley Agriculture
cc: Isaac Davis

"That sounds ominous," I say. "Did you find anything that might tell us what the meeting was about?"

"I couldn't find any other communications or documents that mentioned the company. Charles...*Chuckie* has continued to visit their webpage a few times every month since then, however. The last time was on Tuesday." The day after we arrived in Mercy. "He checks the bio page for Vince Neuman every time."

"That sounds obsessive."

She gives me an oh-there's-more look and says, "And he always uses incognito mode."

I can't help but snort.

Incognito mode is great if you don't want your significant other to search your browser history and find out what you've been looking at, but that's pretty much where your anonymity ends. Your internet provider and the websites you view will know you stopped by. Which means if you end up doing something nefarious that makes the police curious about your internet habits, all they would have to do is get a search warrant for your records from your provider and they'd know exactly what you've been up to.

Or you can do what Jar has done and hack into the internet company, without worrying about search warrants or permission, and take a look yourself.

I can't imagine Chuckie is trying to hide the fact that he visits the Hayden Valley website from his family. Double-locked door aside, I'm sure they've been trained not to go into the den, and even if they did, they wouldn't care that he's been visiting an industrial farming company website. Which probably means he thinks he's preventing Hayden Valley—and anyone else who might be interested—from knowing what he's doing.

She shows me a few more of the documents, but nothing stands out as being important. She then asks about my afternoon at Grayson Lake.

"Not much more than what I've already told you. A lot of people hanging out together."

She shivers as if cold. "So stupid."

"Yeah, kind of what I was thinking, too. Unfortunately, I was too far away to hear any conver—" I stop myself. I forgot about the visit Chuckie had made to the Winnebago with his two friends. "Can we check the bugs in the RV? Somewhere around, um, four-fifteen to four-thirty, I think. Could be a little later than that." I explain why.

It takes her just over a minute to find the audio and play it back.

The first thing we hear is the RV's door open and Chuckie saying, "Go on in. Have a look around." His voice is muffled but clear, the bugs having no problem picking up the sounds through the Winnebago's floor.

"This is nice," another voice says. It's deep and kind of rusty, the kind of voice that only comes with age, so I'm guessing it belongs to the older man.

"Thanks," Chuckie says. "It beats staying in tents."

The door closes and for several seconds we hear only the floor creaking.

Then: "Looks clear." A third voice. Younger, stronger. Mr. In Shape.

The silence returns for about fifteen seconds.

"Two?" Chuckie says.

"We're almost there," the old guy says. "Pressure time."

Someone grunts a short laugh. I think it's Chuckie but I can't be sure.

"Questions?" the old guy asks.

"No," Chuckie replies. His words are followed by a sound too faint to identify. Then, "How about a beer?"

"I wouldn't turn one down."

"Stop," I say.

Jar pauses the playback.

"That noise right after Chuckie tells him no—can you turn up the volume and play it again?"

Jar isolates the segment and lets it roll. The noise is louder, but I still can't make out what it is. Jar noodles with the settings and then plays it again, this time on a loop.

Three times through and I think I've got it. "Paper."

"Yes. Like it's being folded."

"Go back to that gap after the one guy said it was clear. Where everything was quiet."

Jar does so, keeping the adjusted settings where they are. In what was silence before, we can hear something in the same movement-of-paper vein we just heard.

A picture forms in my mind. "So, the old guy—"

"The old guy?" Jar asks.

"The raspy voice." When she nods, I go on. "He pulls a piece of paper out of somewhere...his pocket, say. And he hands it to Chuckie. After Chuckie looks it over, Old Guy asks if he has any questions, Chuckie says nope and sticks the paper in his own pocket. How's that sound?"

"There is no way to know for sure."

"Yeah, I know. It's a guess. Just want to know if you think it fits."

An uncomfortable look crosses her face. "It...fits the sounds we heard."

"Play the rest."

The conversation that follows the offer of a beer is strictly small talk—questions about the Prices' recent vacation, comments on the high school's decision to cancel the upcoming graduation ceremony, and general scoffing at how some people are overreacting to a virus that, in Chuckie's words, "isn't any worse than the flu."

Idiotic stuff, yes, but none of it shines any light on the exchange of the paper, nor does it touch on anything else that might be of interest to us. That is, until In Shape says, "We should be getting back. We don't need people wondering where we've been."

It's not a lot, but it confirms they don't want anyone to know what they're doing.

"Here, I'll take those," Chuckie says.

We hear bottles clinking together and then crashing into what I assume is a trash can. The door opens, and we hear the Winnebago groan as the three men exit.

"Just one other thing," the old guy says.

He's outside now, so his voice is not only muffled but fainter, due to him being farther from the bug. Jar turns up the volume before he speaks again.

"The weatherman mentioned a storm coming through midweek. Do not let it slow anything down."

"Before and after?" Chuckie asks.

A pause. "Right after."

"Understood."

"Good."

"Better if we don't all return together," In Shape says.

"You guys go ahead," Chuckie says. "I need to grab a couple of chairs anyway."

From the moment they stepped out of the RV to this point in the conversation, I saw them through the binoculars. So when we hear Old Guy and In Shape moving away, I tell Jar, "You can turn it off. There's nothing else."

If I'm right about the exchange of a piece of paper, I'm betting we can see Chuckie do something with it when he gets to his house. Before I can mention it, Jar opens the feeds from the Prices' house in a grid pattern, and sets the playback time to when the family arrived home from the barbecue.

We see Chuckie enter the house first. He stops at the light switches next to the door and flips the one for the outside light down and back up, then looks into the yard. When he sees the light is still out, he marches through the house into the laundry room.

"The fuse box is in there," Jar says.

We don't have a camera in the laundry room so we can't see what Chuckie does. We only see him exit a minute later and go over to the kitchen window. When he looks out from there, the light is back on. I'm sure he's wondering why the breaker went off, but he's not doing anything about it now.

Instead, he heads to his office, which he unlocks, enters, and locks again.

Alone now, he reaches into a pocket of his shorts and pulls out a folded piece of paper. (Yay, me!) He opens it and looks at it.

I'm hoping he'll set it on the desk so that we might be able to make out what the message says, but when he does set it down, he's already folded it again.

He unlocks one of the four-drawer filing cabinets—because of course he keeps them secured—and pulls out the second drawer from the top. It contains files stuffed with papers. He reaches for the file at the very back, but instead of removing it, he pulls it and all the files in front of it toward him, creating a gap between the last file and the back of the drawer. From there he removes a manila envelope that has been folded several times, creating a package about the size of a stack of money.

For a moment, I think that's exactly what's inside, but when he unfolds the envelope, he pulls out a smart phone.

I look at Jar, raising an eyebrow. "You didn't find that?"

She grimaces. "No. But I should have."

"Relax. I'm just giving you a hard time. I'd have missed it, too."

This does not seem to make her feel any better.

Chuckie holds down a button on the side of the phone until the screen lights up. The device wasn't just asleep; it was completely off. Once it's booted up, he opens one of the apps and begins typing. Though we can see the screen, it's tilted in a way that makes reading what he writes impossible. We also can't see which app he's using, though I'm willing to bet it's some kind of message app.

Once he's done, he shuts off the device, puts it back in the envelope, and returns the package to its hiding place in the drawer.

From his desk, he retrieves an unused business-size envelope and places the folded piece of paper in it. He sticks a piece of tape on each end of the envelope, opens the bottom drawer on the other filing cabinet, and tapes the envelope to the underside.

The guy has obviously watched too many bad spy movies. If I'm looking for hidden documents, the bottom of a drawer would be one of the first places I check.

None of what we've seen proves Chuckie's up to something nefarious, but it sure feels that way. And while it doesn't seem directly related to his behavior toward Evan and the rest of his family, anything that can give us leverage over him is fair game.

So, do I want to see what's in that envelope?

Yes. Yes, I do. Very much.

But just as important is that phone. If we can clone it, we can track what's being sent and received.

"We have to go back in," I say.

Not surprisingly, Jar is on the same wavelength.

CHAPTER FOURTEEN

When I wake at six a.m. the next morning, it feels like I've slept in.

Last night, Jar and I stayed up for a while, working out our next steps, but were still able to get to bed at a decent hour. At least I was. Who knows what time Jar turned in?

It's Sunday, and I'm hoping we'll have the opportunity to get back into the Prices' house this morning. Small-town life in America often revolves around church. And I'd be willing to bet, whether Chuckie is religious or not, going to church is part of his routine, if for nothing else than to mingle with potential car buyers.

Should I have left in the predawn hours and hidden in the Winnebago again in anticipation? Maybe, but Jar's successful trip during the daylight yesterday makes me think we can pull it off again.

I take a shower, get dressed, and head into the living room, where I expect Jar to be up and waiting for me. She's there all right, sitting at the card table. Or should I say, *leaning onto*? Her head rests on her arms, which are lying on the table just in front of her computer. The laptop is open, but the screen is dark.

I tiptoe into the kitchen, start up the coffee maker, and set about making some breakfast. We have only one frying pan, so I put the sausages on first and use one of our disposable paper bowls to make the French toast mix. As I do, I watch Jar, sure it won't be long before the smell of the coffee or the meat will wake her.

It's not often that I can look at her like this. If I do it when she's awake, she'd wonder what's wrong with me. I guess anyone would.

Her hair, the darkest of dark brown, is usually kept in a ponytail or some kind of bun clipped to the back of her head. This morning it's free, flowing over her shoulders and draping over her upturned ear. When she's awake, it's hard for me not to focus on her eyes, as they're the window into what's in her mind, so it's nice to have a moment to take in the rest of her face —the gentle nose that widens a bit at the end, the small but rounded cheeks, and the mouth that can smile as wide as a noontime sunbeam or grimace like a tiger ready to pounce.

I sometimes forget how small she is. There are times, though, when I swear she's as big as I am. Her drive, her determination, even her physical abilities far outshine what people expect. Which is why I make it a habit of not underestimating her.

I can't imagine not being around her all the time. If I try, I feel panic building. And if I think about it too much, guilt sets in, and I feel as if I'm betraying Liz. She's been gone well over sixteen months now, but there are times when it feels like she was alive just yesterday.

She's as much as told me I need to move on. I'm kind of surprised she hasn't shown up right now to do the same. Then again, her appearances have...lessened as of late, which I'm guessing is her way of helping me disconnect from our shared past.

I mean, that's what she'd be doing if she were a real ghost and not just my subconscious playing games.

God, I really need therapy.

Jar moans, low, like a hum, then her eyelids slowly part. For a moment or three, our gazes lock, and I see the hint of a smile on her lips. Then she blinks and quickly sits up, her expression neutral again.

"What time is it?"

"Around six thirty. I'm making French toast and sausage."

She takes a deep breath and opens her eyes wide, forcing herself to wake up. "That, um, sounds good."

"I know blow-up mattresses aren't the most comfortable, but I gotta believe they're better than sleeping like that."

"I did not—*didn't* mean to sleep here. I was just resting."

"For how long?"

She looks toward the ceiling, thinking, then says, "Five hours and ten minutes. Maybe eleven."

Five hours is *a lot* for her. "Are you feeling all right?"

She frowns at me as she gets out of her chair, then walks to the back of the house without saying a word.

After breakfast, we begin monitoring the bugs at the Prices' house. Church is indeed on their schedule, but while they're eating, Chuckie announces he has work to do and will be staying home, torpedoing Jar's and my plan.

If this news upsets his wife, she keeps it to herself and only says, "Okay."

When breakfast is done, he locks himself in his office while the others clean up and get ready to leave. The first thing Chuckie does is retrieve the phone from the filing cabinet and turn it back on.

After it powers up, it vibrates softly, indicating it has received a message. Chuckie reads the screen, types in a reply, hits SEND, and turns off the phone again. He then sits at his desk and wakes up the computer.

For the next twenty minutes, he looks at reports from his dealerships, adding notes here and there, basically doing what he told his wife he needed to do.

While this is going on, the boys come down the stairs, dressed in shirts and ties and slacks and nice shoes. Evan has Sawyer take a seat in the living room and says, "Don't go anywhere. I'll be right back."

Evan enters the downstairs hallway and sneaks down toward his father's office. When he reaches the door, he leans in close, listening.

In the office, his dad continues to look at spreadsheets, unaware his son is so close.

I don't know what Evan is hoping to hear, but I doubt it's the clack of Chuckie's keyboard.

I've got to hand it to him. He's taking quite a chance. If his father suddenly opens the door and finds him there, Chuckie would be furious.

What finally gets Evan moving is not his father catching him eavesdropping, but his mother saying, "Okay, time to go," as she heads down the stairs.

Instead of returning to the living room, Evan slips into the guest bathroom, quietly shuts the door, and flushes the toilet. He then exits and walks into the living room as if he was up to nothing unusual at all.

This kid has some seriously good instincts.

"You both look great," Kate says to her sons. "Grab your jackets."

As they do this, she walks a few steps into the hallway and says in a raised voice, "Charles, we're leaving."

Chuckie turns from his desk and replies, "All right. Bye."

I can see disappointment on Kate's face, like she was hoping he might come out and give her more than a few words through the door. But there's resignation in her look, too, the kind worn by someone who's grown used to this kind of disappointment.

In the office, Chuckie is out of his chair now, standing next to the door, listening in the same manner his son did less than a minute earlier. I can't tell if he hears Kate walk away, but he definitely hears the front door open and shut, because as soon as it's closed, he leaves his office and moves to the end of the hallway. We don't have a camera that gives us an angle on what he's looking at, but it's easy enough to guess that he can see out the front window from where he is, and probably all the way to the SUV Kate uses, which is parked at the curb.

The sound of an engine rumbles to life, then its pitch intensifies as the vehicle is put into drive. Before the noise completely fades away, Chuckie moves closer to the window, watching his family leave. He hangs there for a minute, no doubt to make sure they don't suddenly return, then hurries back to his office, where he retrieves the hidden phone, turns it on, and stuffs it in his pocket. Next, he removes the envelope hidden under the file drawer and puts it in the other front pocket of his jeans.

Back in the hall, he locks up his office, rushes through the house and out the side door facing the garage.

Crap.

"Come on," I say, and grab the keys to the truck and the bag containing our drone.

Jar snatches up her backpack and slips her laptop inside as we hurry out of the house. It's not that we're going to lose him. The tracker on his Mustang will let us know where he is at all times. But I don't want to be too far behind him when he arrives at his destination. If this trip is secret enough that he doesn't want his family to know about it, I don't want to miss anything.

By the time I pull out of our driveway, Jar has the tracking app open. "He just turned north on Central Avenue."

It takes two minutes before we have eyes on him. In another two, I've closed the gap between us and the Mustang to half a block.

The thought pops into my mind that maybe he's having an affair. A hidden phone would be good for that, and meeting up with his lover when his family is otherwise busy would be ideal. But Chuckie doesn't really need excuses like church to find some alone time. From what we've seen, he's away from home twelve hours a day during the week, at a place where he's the boss, and can come and go at will. If he wants to conduct a secret liaison, he could do it anytime.

And then, of course, there's the paper the old guy gave him yesterday. Why would Chuckie be bringing that to a girlfriend or boyfriend?

No, wherever he's headed has to be about something else.

Two blocks before he reaches the north end of town, Chuckie turns left onto Schoolhouse Drive. I slow to give him a bit more of a lead before I take the turn, too. The first few blocks are lined with homes, none too big, none too small. A nice neighborhood. Then again, I haven't seen a bad one in this town yet.

I keep expecting Chuckie to pull up in front of one of the houses or turn down a side street, but he continues straight.

Soon, the houses give way to Timothy Morgan Elementary School, which in turn passes the torch to Mercy High School. The latter is spread out on both sides of the road. Most of the classrooms and buildings are on the left, and on the right are the gymnasium and fields for almost any sport you could think of. Attached to the gym is an indoor swimming pool that's apparently available for the whole town to use in normal times. A temporary sign strung above the entrance reads:

POOL CLOSED TO THE PUBLIC UNTIL FURTHER NOTICE

The shutting down of the public pool is not surprising. Despite the obvious reluctance of many...Mercy-ites? Mercites? Mercians? Mercenaries? (Heh, heh. That last one's funny.) Despite the obvious reluctance of many in town to take the pandemic seriously, a statewide mandate has meant in-school attendance stopped at least a month ago and all classes were switched to online.

Mercy High sits near the northwestern corner of town, and once we pass it, we enter an area of scattered homes and businesses with plenty of land between them.

A quarter mile on, Jar looks up. "He's slowing."

As I ease back on the gas pedal, the Mustang's brake lights come on for several seconds before the car turns off the road to the right, into what appears to be a parking lot in front of a small building. Not a home. Some kind of business, I believe.

"Pull in there." Jar points at a larger building on the driver's side of the road, about sixty meters ahead.

I do as she directs.

A sign on the front of the building identifies it as Mercy Storage. Its parking area arcs around the front of the building and down both the east and west sides. Behind the structure is a fenced-in parking lot, about half full of RVs and boats on trailers and other vehicles people apparently don't have room for at home.

The building has only one window, and it's at the front next to the entrance. The room beyond it is dark, and a sign in the window reads OFFICE CLOSED. A keypad is mounted to the wall next to the door, which I'm guessing allows people with stuff stored inside to enter whenever they need to. Apparently no one is interested in doing so at the moment, because the main parking lot is empty.

I take us to the west side and stop at an angle facing where Chuckie pulled off the road. Though there are several vehicles parked over there, the Mustang's orange paint job sticks out from the crowd.

"What is that place?" I ask. "A bar?"

"It is not a bar."

Jar hands me the binoculars and removes the drone from its bag.

I adjust the focus and take a look at the building. It's square with a metal roof and a glass door entrance. Definitely a business, but I see no signs identifying what type it is.

Windows on either side of the door are large enough for me to see some clothing racks and shelves inside the building. A retail space. What kind, I'm still not sure. Even at max magnification, I can't narrow things down further.

One thing I can see is Chuckie. He's inside talking to a man behind a counter. The store appears to be otherwise deserted. Which begs the question, where are the people from the other parked cars?

With what appears to be a laugh, Chuckie turns from the counter and heads for the door.

I glance at Jar. She's about to open her window to send the drone aloft.

"Forget that," I say. "He's leaving."

I reach out to shift the truck into reverse, but before I can, Jar says, "Are you sure?"

"He's leaving the store right now."

"Look again."

I frown and narrow my eyes. She seems to know something I don't. I raise the binoculars.

"Yes, he's leaving. He's walking back to his car." I probably say this with a little more sass than I should.

"Just wait."

"For what? He's leav—"

I stop myself. While Chuckie has indeed returned to the Mustang, he's opening the trunk. From inside, he withdraws a golf bag. I switch my view back to the building, this time focusing on the area beyond it. The land is so flat here, it's hard to see much of anything.

"Is he at a golf course?" I ask.

"Driving range," Jar says.

"You could have told me that at the beginning."

"I take it he is *not* leaving?"

I look at Chuckie again. He's walking toward the building, the bag strapped over his shoulder. "Not leaving," I say through gritted teeth.

She's gracious enough not to look too smug as she opens her window and holds the drone outside. With a few taps on her phone, the device lifts into the air and disappears.

For the next twenty minutes, we watch from above as Chuckie hits balls on the driving range. On occasion, he shares a word or two with one of the other golfers, but mostly he seems to stick to himself. Twice, a guy who works for the range brings Chuckie baskets of balls and removes the empty baskets.

When the employee starts to bring over a fourth basket, Chuckie checks his phone, waves the guy off, and works on the few balls left in the current basket.

"I think he's finishing up," I say.

I start the truck. There's one more thing we need to do, and it involves getting as close to Chuckie as possible.

As I pull back onto Schoolhouse Drive, Jar, who's been monitoring the drone feed, says, "He has hit the last ball."

I speed down the road and turn into the driving range parking lot. Two cars from the Mustang a slot has opened up. I pull into it, turn off the engine, and Jar and I lean our seats back into the crew cab section so that we're below window level. Jar then transfers control of the drone to my phone.

I watch as Chuckie reaches the building and starts to walk past it. "Here he comes. Anything?"

Jar has opened a new app on her phone. "Not yet."

Chuckie pauses at one of the shop's windows, waves to the man inside, and continues on.

When he's about three vehicles away from us, Jar says, "Contact. They're both on."

I let out a relieved breath. We've both been worried he's turned off his secret phone, but Jar has picked up signals from both the phones he's carrying.

She taps her device several times and watches a progress bar on the screen.

Chuckie walks past the back of our truck, without so much as a glance in our direction. When he reaches the Mustang, another car pulls into the lot and parks a few vehicles away on the other side. Chuckie opens the trunk of the Mustang and places his bag carefully inside. As he shuts it again, the driver of the other car gets out of his vehicle and says loudly, "Morning, Charles."

"Hey, Robert. Good morning. How are you?"

On the drone feed, I watch them meet up halfway between their vehicles and shake hands. They talk—maskless—for a few minutes. They're far enough away from us, and from the bugs in the Mustang, that we can't hear what's being said. The conversation appears jovial, like a couple of old friends shooting the breeze. Soon enough, they're saying their goodbyes and Chuckie heads back to the Mustang, while Robert returns to his car and pulls out his clubs.

"You're almost out of time," I say.

"I need forty-five seconds."

Chuckie will be gone before then.

Which means it's up to me to buy more time.

I start the engine, back out of our space, and pull in behind the Mustang a second before its reverse lights come on.

Chuckie slams on his brakes and I slam on mine, like I'm as surprised as he is about how close we came to hitting each other.

He can't see our cab from where he is, but he can see that our truck bed is still partially behind him. He honks his horn twice.

"Have you got it?" I ask.

"Almost."

"I can't stay here."

"Hang on."

Another honk, this one longer, more irritated.

"*Jar.*"

A third honk, which I'm sure is about to be followed by Chuckie getting out of his car to see what the hell is wrong with us.

"Okay," Jar said. "Done."

I hit the gas and speed over to the exit. Instead of turning left and heading into town, I go right. Given Chuckie's sparkling personality, I'm sure if I went in the other direction, he would tailgate us for a while and maybe even try to find out where we were going.

As it is, when I look in the rearview mirror, I can see his Mustang sitting at the parking lot exit, as if he's debating whether he should follow us or not. In the end, he chooses to let us go, which I think has more to do with wanting to get home before his family returns from church than deciding against teaching us a lesson.

Once he's out of sight, I make a U-turn and head back toward town. Just before we reach the driving range, I stop long enough for Jar to recall the drone, which, after we drove away, automatically went into hover mode.

We make our way back to the duplex, monitoring the Mustang's homeward journey to make sure we don't cross paths.

We pull into our driveway at about the same time Chuckie exits his garage and enters his house, so we stay inside the truck and watch him on Jar's phone. As I expected, he's made it back before Kate and the boys. After grabbing a Coke from the fridge, he heads into his office and returns the secret phone to its place in the filing cabinet.

I expect him to do the same with the note, but he sits down at his desk and starts surfing the internet. It's possible he's forgotten he has it, but that doesn't seem likely. I would think the note isn't something that would slip his mind so easily. Plus, putting the phone back should have been a reminder to do the same with the envelope.

But he just sits there, looking at his spreadsheets.

The only other possibility is that he gave the envelope to someone. That would explain hiding what he was up to from Kate.

The question is, who received it?

"What if he gave it to someone at the range," I say. "We know he talked to the guy inside the store. And there was the other guy, the one who brought him the balls."

"And the man when he was leaving," Jar says. "Perhaps when they shook hands."

I like that idea a lot. "Just the three possibilities, right?"

"He could have talked to someone else before the drone got there."

That's true. It would have had to be a brief conversation, because the amount of time from when he moved out of view of the binoculars and into the view of the drone was short. Of course, he wouldn't need much time to pass the message along.

"It is also possible he did not give it to anyone at all," Jar says. "And instead put it someplace for someone to find later."

Also a good thought.

In fact, if I had to rank the likelihood of what happened, I put that at the top of the list. Second would be handing it off to the guy who arrived when Chuckie was leaving. Chuckie had checked his phone right before turning down the offer of another basket of balls. He could have received a text letting him know the guy was almost there, and then transferred the paper during the handshake.

I think for another few moments. "Why don't you stay here and check the video. Maybe you can figure out if and when a handoff occurred. I'll go back to the range and have a look around. If we're lucky, the note will still be there."

Jar nods and shrugs on her backpack.

"If Chuckie leaves his house, let me know," I say.

She nods and climbs out of the truck. "Be careful," she says before closing the door.

CHAPTER FIFTEEN

A s I pull into the driving range parking lot, I smile. Not only is the Cadillac CT5—belonging to the man who shook hands with Chuckie—still here, the space next to it is empty.

I park there and get out, casually looking around to make sure I'm alone. No one else is around. I attach our second-to-last tracking bug to the Caddy's undercarriage. Maybe this guy has nothing to do with the paper in the envelope, but best to be prepared in case he does. I then take a picture of the sedan's license plate and send it to Jar, with the message:

The guy who shook with Chuckie.

I head over to the store and go inside.

The retail space isn't particularly large, about thirty square meters (325 square feet, give or take). More than half the floor space is taken up by three circular clothing racks—one filled with golf shirts, one with golf pants, and the last light jackets. In a corner is a display of bags, and along the back wall are the shelves I saw before, on them balls and tees and other golf para-phernalia.

At the west end is the counter, behind which stands the same guy I saw Chuckie talking to. When I look his way, he says, "Good Morning. Welcome."

"Morning."

"Anything I can help you with?"

"Just looking at the moment."

"Cool. I'm here if you need me."

"Thanks."

I check out the rack of shirts first, and browse through enough of them to confirm that none have pockets where the note could have been placed.

The pants rack is next. While these definitely have pockets, each pair of slacks is hung with the pocket openings pointed at the floor. I doubt Chuckie would risk his paper falling out by accident.

The jackets, on the other hand, are prime suspects. I spend more time there, slowly working my way around them as if I'm seriously considering buying one. The rack turns, allowing me to remain on the side opposite the service counter. There's no need for me to worry, though. The clerk's attention is focused on the golf tournament playing on one of the four TVs mounted throughout the room on the walls.

The jackets are a bust and I move on to the golf bags. It would be easy enough for Chuckie to have dropped the enve-lope into one of them, but they're all empty. I scan the room, and see nowhere else the note could have been left without the clerk potentially noticing it.

I head over to the counter. When I near, the clerk peels his gaze from the TV and says, "Find something?"

"A lot of things, but I'm going to have to pass today," I say with a smile. "I have a question. I'm new in town. Used to do some golfing at my old place."

"Where's that?"

"Northern California."

"Whoa. A Cali guy."

I smirk. "You know, no one calls it Cali out there."

"Really? I thought everyone did."

"Sorry."

"Huh. So, um, what brings you to Mercy?"

"What brings anyone anywhere?"

"Work?"

"Got it in one." Before he can ask me what I do, I say, "I'm wondering how much it costs to use the range."

He points at a sign at the other end of the counter.

½ Basket $3

1 Basket $6

2 Baskets $10

3 Baskets $12 Best Deal!

The BEST DEAL! part is in red ink.

"Ah, I should have looked around before I asked," I say.

"A lot of people miss it."

"I don't see a sign about clubs. Do you rent them?"

"Don't have any?"

"I do, but haven't shipped them out yet. Wasn't sure I'd have the opportunity to use them here. Now I'm regretting it."

"Hold on," he says, then disappears through an open doorway into a room behind the counter. When he returns, he's holding a golf bag with several clubs in it, both woods and irons. "We do rent them, but seeing as you're new here and this is your first time at Mercy Driving Range—this is your first time here, right?"

"Yeah, first time."

He lifts the bag over the counter, and I help him set it on the floor by my side.

"You can use these for free today."

"Seriously? That's very kind of you. Thank you."

"You're welcome. Still going to have to charge you for the balls, though."

"Of course. I'll take, um, three baskets, I guess."

"That'll be twelve dollars."

After I pay, he says, "You can use tee box number seven. Paul will bring you your baskets." He grabs a microphone from under the counter, turns it on, and says into it, "Number seven, three fulls."

The range has twelve tee boxes, all but three of which are being used. Wooden signs with the appropriate numbers are posted behind each tee box, box number one being closest to the store and the rest moving west from there. Cadillac Guy is in box number four. There's another man in box six, but no one in box number five between them.

As I make my way to my spot, the guy I saw bringing Chuckie balls—Paul, I assume—jogs toward me, carrying a bucket.

"Morning, morning," he says as he reaches me.

He has the weathered face of someone who's spent a good portion of his life outside so it's hard to put an exact age on him. I'd say somewhere between forty-five and fifty-five, though he could be younger. Like the majority of the people in this town, he's white.

"Morning," I say, and nod at the basket. "Those for me?"

"Yes, sir. Is here all right?" He hovers the basket over a spot at the edge of the box.

"Yeah, that should be fine."

He sets it down with a smile. "When you're ready for your next one, just give me a shout and I'll bring it over. I'm Paul, by the way."

"I'm Matthew."

He starts to extend a hand, then pulls it back and seems to notice my face mask for the first time. "Sorry." He fumbles in his pocket and pulls out his own mask. After he puts it on, he taps the side of his head. "I keep forgetting that. I need to remember. Sorry, sorry."

I wave off the apology. "We're all trying to remember."

"Yeah, I guess we are. Well, um, have at it." He gestures at the range and turns back toward the shed attached to the rear of the store, where I'm guessing the range balls are kept.

Before he leaves, I say, "Hey, Paul?"

He turns back around.

"I've been known to have a bit of a hook. Any way I can move over there?" I gesture to box five. It's the only one that's open between me and the east end of the range. "Better chance of me keeping the balls where they can be found."

He laughs. "Totally get it. Sure, go ahead. I'll let Mr. Murphy know."

"Thanks. I appreciate it."

He flashes a smile and moves back toward my basket to pick it up.

"That's okay. I got it."

As I grab the basket, he says, "I don't mind carrying it for you."

"Don't worry about it." I hoist the strap of the golf bag over my shoulder.

For a few seconds, he seems unsure about what to do. Finally he nods, says, "Thanks," and heads back to the hut.

I set my bag up at box five, pull out the 3 wood, and put a

ball on the rubber tee sticking up from the mat of artificial grass. I twist my torso a few times, stretching, and take several practice swings.

The only golf I've ever played was back in college with some buddies from the dorms. I was, to put it kindly, not good, but I did learn how to hit a ball. And in the years since, I have on rare occasions gone to places just like this to take some swings. It's not a bad way to blow off pent-up energy.

But the last time was probably over two years ago, so it's not a shock that my first ball travels farther vertically than it does horizontally.

I step back and take a few more practice swings. As I do, I glance at Cadillac Guy. He's about halfway through his basket. Given how long he's been here, it must be his fourth or fifth. He clearly knows what he's doing. His swing is smooth, and his balls are routinely flying well past the two-hundred-yard marker.

I move up to my ball again, and try to remember the lessons my friends taught me. This time I do better, and the ball almost reaches the marker at one hundred and sixty yards.

I watch Cadillac Guy take another swing. He must come out here several times a week.

He watches his ball sail down the range. After it lands, he glances over his shoulder and catches me looking at him.

"Sorry," I say. I'm not. This is exactly what I wanted to happen. "It's just...you really know what you're doing."

He smirks. "Years of practice." It's a humble brag. He's good and he knows it, and he wants everyone else to know it, too.

"That's what people tell me." I step up and prepare to take another shot.

Cadillac Guy grabs a ball from his basket and puts it on his tee, but I can sense him glancing in my direction.

I pull back my club and let it swing. This ball would have

bettered my last by at least ten yards if it didn't take a left hook halfway into its flight.

"You're taking your eye off the ball," Cadillac Guy says.

"Am I?"

"Among other things."

I laugh. "Maybe I should just give up."

"If it's that easy to do, then maybe you should."

"Nah. As bad as I am, I love it too much."

"Then don't take your eye off the ball."

For the next several minutes we take our swings in silence. He's right. I was taking my eye off the ball. My shots are flying much straighter now and I'm actually enjoying myself.

When Cadillac Guy reaches the last few balls in his basket, Paul runs over and says, "Another, Mr. Lyman?"

Without looking at him, Cadillac Guy—Lyman—pulls out a ball and says, "No more."

"Got it," Paul says and jogs away.

I get off five more shots before Lyman finishes his basket. With nothing left to hit, he shoves his club into his bag, wipes his hands on a towel hanging from the strap, and pulls out a bottle of water, which he drinks halfway down in a single swig.

As he starts to pull his bag over his shoulder, I say, "Thanks for the tip."

"Yeah. No problem."

"Hey, can I ask—where do you play around here?"

He looks at me, eyes narrowing, as if he's seeing me for the first time. "You not from around here?"

"Just moved. This is the first chance I've had to get out and swing a club. I'm Matthew, by the way."

He takes a beat before saying, "Robert."

"Nice to meet you, Robert."

He returns the sentiment with a nod, then says, "The county course is the closest. It's across the river, south of town.

But if you want to play something more challenging, Finch Lake is the place. It's about fifty miles west. You can google it."

"Thanks. I'll do that."

Another nod and he's off without a goodbye, as if I should feel lucky that he thought me worthy enough to speak to at all.

Chuckie's friend is another asshole? Shocking. *Shocking,* I say.

I pull out my phone to text Jar his name. Only there's a message from her waiting for me. She's already learned his name from his car's license plate.

To think I wasted all that charm on him when I could have just been concentrating on my form.

I hit my way through the two additional baskets I paid for, and then I head back.

It's Sunday evening, and the Prices' normally silent dinnertime is anything but.

The moment Kate sets the main course on the table, Chuckie snarls, his head twisting to the side as if he's smelled something bad.

"What the hell is *that*?" he asks.

"Butter chicken," Kate replies.

"Butter chicken?" He's apparently never heard the words used together before.

"Is-is there something wrong with it?" She looks at the serving dish, truly confused.

"It stinks."

"Those are just the spices. It's Indian. From India. I got the recipe from Angie. I thought we could try it out."

"What the hell, Kate? You seriously expect me to eat some messed up chicken from a Third World country?"

"I'm sorry. I-I can make something else."

She reaches for the dish but Chuckie waves her arms away. "And wait another hour? I'm hungry now." He pokes the casserole with his fork. "I'll force this crap down. But I don't want to see this again. Ever. Understand?"

"I'm sorry," she says again. "I was just trying something new."

Emphasizing each word, he says, "Do you understand?"

"Yes. We won't have it again."

"We'd better not." He serves a helping onto his plate, scoops some onto his fork, and lifts it toward his mouth.

"It smells good to me," Sawyer says, his voice just above a whisper. "Can I have some?"

Chuckie whips his head around, the bite still on his fork. "What did you say?"

"He didn't mean anything by it," Kate says quickly.

"The hell he didn't."

"He's only talking about himself, not you. It's all right." It's clear she's spent years trying to maintain the peace. You can both read it on her face and hear it in her voice.

"You think I don't know when something smells bad?" Chuckie asks Sawyer.

"I don't understand," Sawyer says.

"You implied I was wrong. Am I?"

Sawyer stares at his dad for a moment, then looks at his mom. "I don't know what that means."

"It's okay, honey," Kate says. "It's just a misunder—"

Chuckie's eyes shift to his wife. "Oh, so you're saying I don't understand my own son, is that it?"

Sawyer sniffles, water gathering in his eyes. "Please don't yell."

"This is *my* house," Chuckie says. "I'll yell if I want to."

The boy can no longer hold back the tears.

"Stop that," Chuckie said. "Stop that right now."

This only serves to make Sawyer cry harder. Kate gets out of her seat to comfort him.

Glaring at her, Chuckie says, "Don't you coddle—"

"Leave him alone!" Evan cuts him off.

Chuckie shoots his gaze to his oldest son. "What did you say?"

From the fear on Evan's face, I have a feeling standing up to his father is not something he does often, but he doesn't back down. "I said leave him alone."

Chuckie stares at him, anger intensifying, but he says nothing.

Evan endures this for about ten seconds before blurting out, "I think it smells good, too."

His father's eyes move to the side for a moment, then narrow back on Evan. "Did you finish the yardwork today?"

"What?"

"You heard me."

"Yeah. I finished."

"You mowed and swept?"

"Uh-huh."

"You emptied the bag?"

"I always empty the bag."

"You watered the plants?"

"Of course."

"Good, good," Chuckie says, nodding. "What about the gutters?"

"The gutters?"

"Did you clean them out?"

"You didn't say anything—"

"Cleaning the gutters is part of cleaning the yard."

"S-s-since when?"

"So, you're saying you *didn't* clean them."

"You never told—"

"Grounded. Two weeks."

"For what?"

"If I were you, I'd stop talking now."

"But—"

"Evan," Kate says, the look on her face pleading with him to be quiet.

"And since you like..." Chuckie looks at his wife. "What did you call this? Butternut chicken?"

A pause, before a hesitant whisper: "Butter chicken."

Chuckie turns back to Evan. "Since you like *butter* chicken so much, you can eat it all." He pushes the serving dish toward Evan and dumps his own helping back into it.

"Charles, no," Kate says. "That's too much. It'll make him—"

Her husband quiets her with a hard glance, then swivels his attention back to Evan. "Every last bit. And don't even try to get up before you finish." He looks back at Kate. "On second thought, I will have something else. I assume there's steak left from the other day. Make me a sandwich and bring me a beer." When she doesn't leave right away, he says. "Now."

Kate reluctantly leaves the room.

I wonder if there was a time when she would have stood up to her husband, or was her childhood also abusive and the ability to stand up for herself beaten out of her before she became an adult? Whatever the case, it's clear she's learned to operate from a position of accommodation rather than confrontation. It's probably a method that calms the beast more times than not.

Today is a *not* day. And I'm sure her only desire is to get her boys through the evening without things escalating.

When I was growing up, there were a few times when my parents didn't see eye to eye. I can even remember when a disagreement became a little heated once, but I have never witnessed one of them disrespecting the other. Kate faces this prospect day after day.

It's easy for an outsider like me to wonder why she hasn't taken her boys and left Chuckie long ago. One of the possibilities that comes to mind is that his reign of terror was not present at the start of their relationship, and that the abuse grew slowly over time. So now she's clinging to what little hope she still has that their life together will one day return to the way it used to be. It's a common theme, isn't it?

As for the boys, their pain and hurt and anger must be off the charts. I wouldn't doubt that Evan has more than once considered running away. Few would fault him for worrying only about himself in a situation like this. But I'm sure what's kept him from doing so is his desire to shield his brother from the worst of their father's ire.

We are going to end their misery. To this I swear.

Chuckie pushes his chair back but does not get up. Instead, he sets his dirty shoes on the table, laces his fingers together, and puts them behind his head. With a sickly smile, he says to Evan, "Go on. Eat."

The boy closes his eyes for a second or two, like he's praying, then takes a deep breath and shoves his fork into the food.

Jar and I have dug up several leads today. But that's all stuff I can tell you about tomorrow.

I'm sure there's only one matter on your mind.

Does Evan finish off the food?

He does. Every last bite.

Chuckie is there for it all. When his son swallows the last

bit, Chuckie simply removes his feet from the table and walks out of the room.

Kate makes Evan drink some Pepto-Bismol, no doubt hoping it will ease any stomach pains. It does not.

Less than an hour after Evan goes up to his room, he's sitting on the bathroom floor in front of the toilet, spilling his dinner and the Pepto into the bowl.

Honestly, that's probably the best thing that could have happened. At least this way he'll be able to sleep.

When I finally try to go to sleep myself, one thought keeps playing through my mind.

In how many other homes, where no one is spying on the people who live there, are situations like the Prices' playing out? In other words, how many others need help?

I don't know the answers.

I'm not sure I *want* to know the answers. The thought alone is nearly debilitating.

I really need to pay my parents a visit when I go back.

CHAPTER SIXTEEN

Our plan to this point, inasmuch as we've had anything specific in mind, has been to catch Chuckie in a moment of abuse and turn that footage over to the authorities. To be clear, we wouldn't just leave then. We'd make sure the information is followed up on first. If it's not, we would publicly release the footage and force the police's hand.

The incident with the butter chicken was definitely abusive, but I doubt it would be enough to get Chuckie even a slap on the wrist. We would need something worse.

The thing is, after witnessing it, I don't want something worse to happen. Allowing that in order to satisfy the need to report Chuckie would make us complicit. I cannot live with that.

So, we are shifting our focus.

We need to bring Chuckie down as soon as possible.

Thankfully, we already know he's up to something.

The note. The secret phone. The twice-locked door to his home office.

If what he's doing is illegal (and it sure seems to be), finding proof to back it up would give us a way to deal with him without even touching on the domestic abuse.

Here's what we learned yesterday.

Robert Lyman, the guy who gave me tips at the driving range, is a lawyer who handles everything from divorces to setting up trusts to criminal law. Being a generalist like this is probably the kind of thing you need to do in a smaller town. His practice has three other lawyers and he's the managing partner. He's also a Mercy native and was a year ahead of Chuckie at school, though he attended St. Catherine's High School while Chuckie went to MHS. Still, I'm sure they knew each other, or at least knew *of* each other growing up. We haven't found any business connections between them yet. Chuckie and Price Motors use the other "big" lawyer firm in town. Jar is still hunting around.

The golf ball guy's full name is Paul Bergen. He's another Mercy native, who, it turns out, *was* a classmate of Chuckie's. They were both on the football team, though Bergen—now and in his high school pictures—seems kind of scrawny to have received much playing time. So far, we've unearthed no other connections between them.

Travis Murphy is the guy who was working in the golf shop. He moved here for the job, from Pueblo, Colorado, three years ago. The driving range is owned by his uncle, who made his nephew the manager. Murphy is ten years younger than Chuckie, and we've found nothing that indicates they socialize outside of seeing each other at the range.

Jar has also identified the two men Chuckie met with inside his RV at the barbecue at Grayson Lake. Old Guy is Nicholas Huston, and In Shape is Kyle Decker. They both work for a company called RCHB Consulting. Huston is the managing partner. The kind of consulting they do and who they consult are things we're still working on. But it's not a stretch to think one of their clients is Gage-Trent Farming, since that's who sponsored the barbecue.

This thought led us back to the email exchange Chuckie had with Hayden Valley Agriculture. You remember—the one about him being turned down for...something?

Maybe his communications with them are unrelated to what's going on now. Or maybe that tickle at the back of my mind is correct and there *is* a connection.

There's only one way to find out, which is the reason that by eleven a.m. I'm on the road northwest to Denver.

Jar has remained in Mercy, where it'll be easier for her to work than from the passenger seat of the truck. We've agreed she won't try anything risky until I'm back, though I'm aware our definitions of what that might preclude are probably different. Hopefully, I won't find myself in the position of having to break her out of jail.

Most of my three-hour trip is made through endlessly repetitive farm country. It's still early in the growing season, so even the different types of crops look the same to my eye. I realize this is a flaw in my education. I've trained in so many different subjects, but the ins and outs of everyday farming is not one of them.

I see no signs of the Rocky Mountains until I'm almost to Denver. But even then the towering range is a mere hazy silhouette, low on the western horizon, its sight a welcome change to the flat world I've been surrounded by for the last week or so.

The regional office for Hayden Valley Agriculture is located in the Cherry Creek section of Denver, the area a mix of homes and businesses southeast of downtown. A quaint area of clothing stores and stationery shops and bookstores and bars and townhouses and apartments. The hotels seem to all be boutiques, like the Jacquard, where I have a room reserved. I'm not planning on staying the night, but it's always good to have a base.

I know that Vince Neuman, the VP Chuckie met with, is in town. I called before I left Mercy, pretending to be from a mortgage broker who had some documents Neuman personally needed to sign before the end of the day. The friendly receptionist told me he had meetings on and off throughout the afternoon and should be around.

Though I have not made an appointment, I have brought along something that makes me confident he'll see me.

I park at the Jacquard and check in, then head down Second Avenue to Men's Wearhouse, a place that specializes in men's suits. The one thing I didn't bring with me on vacation was any kind of business clothes. I know exactly what I'm looking for, but even then it takes me several minutes to find the style I want in my size.

Black, well fitting, nothing too fancy, but not cheap, either. And a white shirt with a dark blue tie.

A helpful clerk shows me to a fitting room, where I confirm I have indeed chosen well.

"I'll take it," I tell the man when I come back out.

"Excellent," he says. "I can take it to the counter for you if you'd like to continue looking around. Or will this be all?"

The weather outside is pleasant, but the forecast calls for a temperature drop of a good fifteen degrees over the next few hours. It's the harbinger of that storm Nicholas Huston mentioned to Chuckie at the barbecue. Tomorrow is supposed to be even cooler, with the rain hitting the plains sometime in the early hours of Wednesday and dropping a late May snow in the mountains.

"Do you have any overcoats?"

The clerk smiles. "Right this way."

Back at the Jacquard, I dress in my new clothes, and transfer my phone and false ID into the inside pocket of the suit jacket.

It's a nine-minute walk from my room to the offices of Hayden Valley Agriculture. The business is located on the top floor of a five-story building, across the street from a Wells Fargo Bank and a Whole Foods Market.

The elevator lets me off directly in Hayden Valley's lobby, which is decorated in soothing tones of off-white and brown. Eight leather chairs are scattered around in pairs, separated by white end tables. At the other end of the room is a circular desk, behind which sits a woman of perhaps twenty-five. Though she's wearing a mask, from the crinkles around her eyes I can tell she's smiling at me.

"Good afternoon, sir. How may I help you?" she says when I reach the desk.

"I'd like to speak with Vincent Neuman, please," I say.

Before she can ask me if I have an appointment, I pull out the leather case containing my faux FBI ID and show it to her.

"Oh, um," she says, "one moment."

"Thank you."

She calls someone and tells them in a low voice who I am and what I want. After listening for several seconds, she says, "Sure," hangs up, and looks back at me. "Someone will be here shortly. Would you like to have a seat?"

"No, I'm fine."

I seldom sit in situations like this. Remaining on my feet makes people nervous, and nervous people talk. Not that I'm expecting to learn anything from her, but she *will* be motivated to get me out of the lobby. If Neuman drags his feet about meeting with me, I can count on her not waiting too long to remind him I'm here.

This turns out not to be a problem. The door behind the desk opens a minute later, and a man in his mid-thirties steps out.

I've been looking at my phone like I'm checking email, when in reality I have an entirely different app open and have been waiting for this moment. I press the button that starts a voice recorder and slip the device into my suit pocket, microphone up.

The man exchanges a word with the receptionist, then walks over to me. "Good afternoon. I'm Isaac Davis. I understand you wish to speak with Mr. Neuman?"

"I do," I say, and show him my ID.

"Perhaps I can help you, Agent Springett."

"You can if you take me to Mr. Neuman."

"He's in a meeting at the moment."

"Then I'll wait."

"It may be a while."

"Like I said, I'll wait." I walk over to one of the chairs and, in a break from my previous policy, sit down.

This is not the response he was hoping for. He considers his options for a moment. "Perhaps you'd be more comfortable in our conference room?"

"I don't want to put you to any trouble."

"It's no trouble at all. Please, follow me."

Davis leads me into the main part of the office. On the walls are framed pictures of crops and farm equipment and smiling workers, creating an almost utopic image of the company. We pass several offices before we reach the conference room.

"May I get you something to drink?"

"Coffee would be nice." I sit in one of the chairs around the oval table.

Davis is not the one who brings me the coffee. The kid who does looks young enough to be in high school. An intern, maybe.

Whatever the case, he says nothing as he nervously places the cup and a small tray of sugar and creamers on the table in front of me before hastily making his exit.

I'm only halfway through my coffee when Davis returns, this time in the company of Vince Neuman. Even with the mask he's wearing, I recognize the man's eyes from his picture on the Hayden Valley website. He's older than in the picture, but not by much. I'd place his age around fifty-five.

He strides confidently over to the table and says, "Vince Neuman." To his credit, he does not extend a hand toward me.

"Special Agent John Springett," I say.

"I understand you have some questions for me?"

"If you have a moment."

"Is this about the company or something personal?"

"Company."

"Then do you mind if Isaac joins us? He's our VP of operations."

"Not at all."

Neuman sits in the chair across from me, and Davis takes the seat next to him.

"So how can we help you, Agent?" Neuman asks.

"It's our understanding that about a year and a half ago, you had contact with a man named Charles Price."

Neuman's brow furrows. "Who?"

Davis is also confused, though more, I think, because he recognizes the name but can't place it.

"Charles Price. You met with him on August eighteenth two summers ago."

"Two summers ago?" Neuman shakes his head. "I meet with dozens of people every week. I would have to consult my calendar."

"A larger man, right?" Davis says, the puzzled look on his face fading. "From...um..."

"Mercy," I say.

"Right," Davis says. "Mercy. I remember him." He looks at Neuman. "He interviewed for the southern rep job." When Neuman still seems confused, Davis adds, "He's the one we got the call about." As he says this, he raises an eyebrow, emphasizing the call's importance.

It takes only a second for Neuman to make the connection. "I remember now." He looks at me. "Sorry. I haven't thought much about him since then. Technically I never met him."

"But, Mr. Davis, didn't you just say he came for an interview?"

"I did," Davis answers. "For one of our area rep positions."

"What exactly is that?"

Davis glances at Neuman, who nods for him to go on. "Hayden Valley Agriculture is in over thirty states now. Our office's region covers Colorado, Wyoming, Kansas, New Mexico, and parts of Texas. It's one of the company's largest and busiest territories. It's further broken down into smaller areas, each covered by one of our reps, who travel between our farms, making sure everything is running smoothly. They're also often the first to check out potential land purchases."

"Sounds like an important job," I say.

"We like to think all our positions are important," Neuman says. "But, yes, some are more so than others. I think it's fair to say our reps fall into that category."

"So, Price showed up for this interview, and..."

"And I met with him," Davis said.

"We were under the impression the meeting was with you," I say to Neuman.

"Are we under investigation?" Davis asks.

I cock my head as if surprised, though I've been waiting for this question since the beginning. "Not that I know of. My interest is in Charles Price. We only became aware a few days ago of his meeting here. Before that, I'd never heard of Hayden Valley Agriculture."

"He's done something?" Neuman asks.

"I'm not at liberty to discuss that," I say, clearly conveying *yes, he has indeed done something.* "What I'm hoping for is your cooperation. What I'd like to avoid is having to return here with a subpoena and a squad of agents to go through your records, for what I'm sure will turn out to be only a small point of information in our case."

"Would you excuse us for a moment?" Neuman says.

"Of course."

The two men get up and exit the room.

Worst-case scenario, they're getting their lawyer to sit in on the rest of our meeting. Actually, worst would be them calling the local FBI office. I don't think I'd get into much trouble, thanks to several well-placed contacts I have in the government, but it could get a little messy. I'm confident Neuman and Davis won't do that, though. Almost no one ever does that.

When the men return, they're alone, the only thing different is the file in Davis's hand. They stop behind the chairs they were sitting in but remain on their feet.

"I'd like to apologize for my hesitation earlier," Neuman says. "We would be more than happy to tell you what we can." He glances at Davis. "Since Isaac was the one who met with him, as well as conducted the preliminary interview, I see no reason for me to be here. If you have anything you'd like to ask me after, I can always come back."

"That works for me," I say.

"Pleasure meeting you, Agent Springett."

"And you, sir. I appreciate your time."

Neuman leaves, and Davis settles back in his chair.

"The interview on the eighteenth was not the first you had with Price?"

"Candidates had to go through a series of steps. Application, background check, and initial interview conducted by our HR department. The people who didn't get filtered out then had a video interview with me, and whoever made the final cut received an invitation for a face-to-face interview with Mr. Neuman and me."

"Price made it to the final cut, then."

"He did," Davis says, regret in his voice. "He had a decent application, no blips on his records, and he interviewed very well."

"I would think someone up for that position would need a background in farming."

"According to his resume, he did." Davis opens the file he brought in and scans the top page. "It lists growing up on a farm in Mercy County, and a degree in agricultural business and management from Fort Hayes State in Kansas. He also provided recommendations from many in the Mercy area, including the mayor and his local member of congress."

"We may need to get a copy of what's in that folder," I say. "If that turns out to be the case, I'll get a warrant so that both you and the bureau are covered."

"If you do, contact me directly and I'll facilitate it for you."

I was hoping my assurance would get him to let me take a peek at it, but no luck. That's fine. I'm sure there are digital records of what's in that file. Jar and I can pull what we need from the company's server, if we have to.

"I get the impression that Mr. Neuman ducked out of Price's final interview at the last minute," I say. "Why was that?"

"Actually, there was no interview."

The perplexed look on my face is not an act. "You said you met with him on the eighteenth."

"I did, but only to tell him the interview had been cancelled."

"You'd given the job to someone else?"

"We did eventually, but that wasn't the reason the interview didn't happen. The night before, I received a message from someone claiming to have information I needed to know, concerning one of the candidates for the rep position. The message did not say which candidate, only that it was important for me to call back. It was the first time I'd ever received a message like that, and—I'm not going to lie—it worried me. These days, one wrong hire and a whole company can be stained by someone's bad behavior."

"You did background checks, though."

"Background checks are far from perfect."

He's not wrong about that. With the right skills or access to someone who has them, a person can hide a lot of things.

"I take it you returned the call," I say.

"First thing the following morning." He glances down at the file. "The caller identified herself as Cheryl. I have a feeling it wasn't her real name, though."

"Did she give you a last name?"

"No. And I did ask for it, but she declined to give it to me. Said it was safer for her that way."

"Safer?"

He nods. "She told me that Mr. Price's resume was full of misrepresentations and lies. And while he had attended Fort Hayes State, his major was general business, not agricultural business, and he had dropped out three semesters short of graduation. She also mentioned he'd been arrested several times for drunk driving but never charged, and had a mean streak—I believe that's what she called it—that had also gone unpunished. She said she could provide names and phone numbers of people who could confirm his behavior, if I wanted them."

Who had Chuckie pissed off enough to ruin his chances at the job? And why was he looking for a job in the first place?

"Did you take her up on the offer?" I ask.

He shook his head. "It wasn't necessary. Lying on his resume was enough to get him dropped from consideration. All I had to do was call the university. They verified that he had been a general business student, not focused on agricultural business, and had left before finishing his junior year."

While that was the right move from a corporate standpoint, it sucks for me.

"Why didn't you cancel the interview over the phone?"

"His interview was set for midmorning. By the time I finished checking with the school, he was already sitting in our lobby."

"How did he take it?"

A slight pause. "I would say his reaction convinced me we made the right decision."

"In what way?"

Davis looks uncomfortable. This is not a topic he wants to discuss, but it's hard to say no to the FBI.

"I thought it would be easier to tell him we'd filled the position, and apologized for him having had to make the trip. I even offered to reimburse him for his gas money. At first, it seemed as if everything was going to be fine. He asked a few questions, like why did we make the decision now? And who did we hire? I kept my answers vague and, of course, didn't give him a name.

"I remember him sitting there silently for several seconds, staring at the table, his face turning redder and redder. He finally stood up, looking angrier than anyone I've ever seen, and started yelling at me, telling me how unprofessional we were. How he wouldn't want to work for a company like us in the first place. How we owed him more than just gas money for wasting his time. There were other things, too. I can't remember what exactly, but it was crazy.

"Finally, two of the larger members of our staff rushed into the room with one of the building's security guards. I told Price that he needed to leave or we would call the police."

Davis falls silent, though I can see there's something else he wants to say. "Did he leave?"

A nod. "The guards escorted him out. As far as I know, that was the last time he's ever been in our building. I know I've never seen him again."

"And that was it? There was nothing else said?"

He winces. "I said something to him on his way out that I shouldn't have. But I couldn't help myself. His reaction had pissed me off."

"What did you say?"

"Something like, 'The next time you apply for a job, maybe try not lying on your resume.'"

"He didn't say anything to that?"

"No. But I could see he was surprised, then his face darkened again, and I thought maybe he was going to start another round of yelling. But he kept his mouth shut."

I give it a couple of seconds before saying, "I know you said you never saw him again, but did you hear from him?"

He looks back at the file and flips through a few pages before stopping. "Oh, right. I forgot about this." He looks up. "We received an email from him the next day. A quasi-apology for his behavior." He glances at the file again. "'I'm sorry for my strong reaction yesterday. I'm just a passionate person. I'm hoping we can put all this behind us and that, if a similar position comes up in the future, you will consider me again.'"

Chuckie, Chuckie, Chuckie. So willfully arrogant. So painfully clueless.

"He said nothing about the discrepancies in his resume?" I ask.

"Not a word."

I already know the answer to my next question, but Davis doesn't know that. "Did you respond?"

Another look at the file. "We had Mr. Neuman's executive assistant reply with a message telling him not to contact us again."

"And that was that?"

"As far as I know."

"Is there anything else you can think of that I should know?" I ask.

A shrug. "That's pretty much everything."

"If something does come to mind, I'd appreciate it if you would give me a call." I hand him a business card that matches my FBI ID, with another one of my numbers that routes to my phone.

"I will." He pockets the card.

"One last thing. It would be helpful to us if you and Mr. Neuman tell no one the reason for my visit today. This is an ongoing investigation, and you'd be surprised at how quickly information like that can spread."

"Of course. We won't say a word."

"I appreciate it."

As we both stand and walk toward the door, I decide to press my luck a little. "Would it be possible to get a copy of Price's resume?"

A pause. "I don't see why not. If you wait in the lobby, I'll run one off for you."

"Great. Thank you. Also, do you think you can give me Cheryl's phone number?"

Even though he's wearing a mask, I can see his smile slip. "I'm not sure I can do that."

"Don't worry about it, then. I understand."

Bummer. But again, Cheryl's number is probably on their server.

He leads me back to the lobby and tells me he'll be only a minute. It's more like two, but I'm not going to be upset about it. Because in addition to the resume, he has given me a present. On a Post-it note stuck to the copy of the resume is the letter C followed by a phone number.

CHAPTER SEVENTEEN

It's just after five p.m. when I exit the Hayden Valley offices, early enough for me to make one last stop before returning to Mercy.

The world my colleagues and I occupy is superimposed over yours. Like a ghost world, of which only those who need to know are aware. Our reality is a network of safe houses and secret hospitals and forgery specialists and transportation services and suppliers of all kinds of things.

And that network is everywhere.

Well, almost everywhere.

It most definitely is not in Mercy.

But it *is* well established in Denver.

Which is why, after I return to my room at the Jacquard, I put in a call to my friend Dave Cheeks.

Yes. It's his real name. Why would anyone ever choose that?

Dave is one of the good guys. He runs a nonprofit business that sends medical and other essential supplies to needy communities around the world. He does not make a lot of money for this, so it's a good thing that his husband, Mark, is a doctor.

That's not to say Dave couldn't make a lot on his own. He does have a side business, one that generates a high profit margin. But instead of keeping any of that money for himself, he funnels it all into the nonprofit. That's the kind of saint Dave is.

Puts the rest of us to shame. Well, me at least.

His side business is the reason for my call. He is one of the secret suppliers in my world, from whom I can get things that would be impossible to obtain elsewhere.

"You remember how to get here?" he asks.

"I think so."

"Then get your ass over here."

Before leaving, I call the phone number Davis gave me for Cheryl. I've been hoping the woman would pick up, but I'm not surprised to find the number has been disconnected. We can still try to find out who was using the number two years ago but that can wait.

I change out of my suit and take everything down to my truck, because I plan on leaving the city right after seeing Dave.

Rush-hour traffic on a Monday night usually means it would take me at least forty-five minutes to get from Cherry Creek to his warehouse, but with the majority of people working from home these days, I turn into his parking lot in just under thirty.

It's a big, rectangular building, three stories high with a sloped roof. Along the side I park on are several loading docks. Two of the slots have big rigs backed into them. The roll-up doors associated with these slots are open.

I see several people loading boxes and pallets into the nearest truck and I head that way.

The room beyond the door is huge, stretching a good two-thirds the length of the building and going all the way up to the rafters. Rows of shelves are filled with boxes of varying sizes and other items that are shrink-wrapped or bagged or otherwise contained.

While Dave does have a paid staff of about twenty, most of them work on the administrative side. The majority of the warehouse workers are volunteers. There's at least a dozen of them here tonight, all between sixteen and twenty-five years old.

The only old guy is Dave, who's in his late fifties but looks younger. He's right in the mix with the kids, moving boxes and singing along to the ever-present classic rock blaring through the warehouse (sixties and seventies stuff, nothing later). As I knew they would be, everyone is wearing masks and gloves.

When Dave sees me, he calls to one of the kids, hands him the box he's been carrying, and jogs over.

"Well, well, well," he says. "You're looking good, my friend." Dave, always with the compliments.

"Back atcha," I say.

"What's it been? Two? Three years now?"

"Something like that." It's been a while since a job last brought the team to this part of the country.

"You need to get out here more often. Next time, make a trip in the winter. We can go skiing."

"I'll put it on my to-do list."

"Come on. Let's get you taken care of."

I look at all the activity around me. "If you're busy, I can wait."

He laughs. "Are you kidding? They'll get things done at lot faster without me in the way."

"He's right," a girl who can't be more than twenty-one says as she walks by, carrying a box.

Dave shrugs. "What can I say? I'm an old man."

He leads me through the massive room into another one that takes up most of the rest of the building. It, too, is filled with shelves and boxes and other types of packages. We walk to a door on the right side of the room. Dave unlocks it and motions for me to enter.

From all appearances, it's an unoccupied office, with a desk and a chair and a phone. Dave has told me in the past it does get used when things get really busy, but most of the time it's empty like this.

He locks the door behind us, then pushes sideways on a section of the wall paneling, low behind the desk. After a click, a palm-sized panel swings outward.

Dave looks over to see where I am and nods his approval. As I learned to do on a previous visit, I'm standing as close to the exit as I can get. After he pushes a button inside the recess, the floor under the desk rises upward several centimeters before sliding forward. In the space where it was is a set of stairs leading down.

We descend to his secret basement, where the inventory for his side business is kept.

Dave stocks a lot of fun stuff. What he doesn't carry are guns, knives, and explosives. The only weapons he does sell are Tasers, expandable batons, cans of mace, and other less lethal devices.

That's fine. I'm not here for anything lethal.

The room is completely dark when we enter. A flip of a switch and overhead fluorescents flicker to life. The space is a miniature version of the warehouse rooms above—products stuffed onto metal shelves, which down here go from floor to ceiling.

"What can I get you?" Dave asks.

"Bugs, both tracking and listening, to start with," I say. "Cameras, too." Jar and I have all but depleted the meager supply we brought with us.

"Right this way."

Dave may have restrictions on the items he stocks, but those he does carry are all top of the line. I grab a box of thirty trackers, two boxes (forty each) of audio bugs, and two cartons of miniature cameras (one hundred total). The amount is way more than I think we'll need but I don't want to be caught short.

Next, Dave takes me to the directional microphones. They consist of a bowl that catches the sound, and a six-inch-long mic where the bowl sends the sound. Think of the bowl as a small satellite dish, made of clear plastic. They come in a variety of sizes. I choose two sets at the smaller end, as they'll be easier to carry in a backpack. I'm still annoyed about not having one at the picnic, and I will never leave home for a lengthy amount of time without one again.

As we peruse the shelves, I pick up a few other items. Will we need them? Hopefully not. But I guess we'll see.

"Anything else?" Dave asks as we near the exit.

"I think I'm good."

"Cool. Are you hungry?"

Dave talks me into joining him and Mark for dinner, and takes me to their favorite restaurant, Sam's No. 3. By the time I'm on the road back to Mercy, it's after nine p.m.

The majority of our missions occur in large cities, not so much in rural settings. When I'm home, I'm in Los Angeles, one of the top twenty metropolitan areas in the world. So being in the countryside is rare for me. And though this is the same drive I took this morning, at night with no moon it's completely different.

All I see around me are miles and miles and miles of darkness. It's as if the world has ceased to exist beyond the halo of my headlights. And yet, the sky is ablaze with stars.

It is both awe-inspiring and, I have to admit, slightly terrifying.

I'm not sure when it happens, but at some point, I realize

Liz has joined me in the cab. At first, I think she's come to tell me something, but she seems content to just ride.

I want to ask her where she goes when she's not here. I want to know if she's happy. But most of all, I want her to be honest with me about what she wants me to do.

Because for the first time, I realize I do want to move on.

It's when I have this last thought that she turns to me, a smile on her face, sweet and soft and filled with love and regret and understanding and fear.

I don't know what she's trying to tell me.

That it's okay for me to move on?

That it's not?

I take a deep breath and center myself. When I look over again, she's gone.

But of course, she was never there.

As much as I always look forward to seeing her, I know these illusions are holding me back. Wait, it's more than that. They're crippling me by preventing me from fully living.

I just don't know how to tell her goodbye.

A few minutes after midnight, I receive a message from Jar.

Where are you?

Using my phone's voice-to-text function, I respond:

Twenty minutes away. Maybe less. Everything okay?

Jar:

Something for you to see when you get here.

A few minutes later, the lights of Mercy begin to cut into the darkness ahead. It is a welcome sight. Soon enough, I'm driving through the quiet town and pulling into the driveway of our duplex.

With my new suit draped over an arm and the duffel bag with the items from Dave in my hand, I head to the house.

Jar opens the front door before I get there.

A sense of warmth fills me the moment I see her. I smile, but before I can say, "Hi," the oh-boy-have-I-got-a-story-to-tell-you expression on her face stops me. "What is it?" I ask.

She huffs a laugh, then motions for me to come inside.

The duplex has a small entranceway that opens into the living room. I step through this, intending to carry the bag over to the card table, but I get only a single step beyond the foyer before I stop and stare.

Sitting in one of our two folding chairs, wearing a mask, is Evan Price.

CHAPTER EIGHTEEN

I blink once. Twice. Then say, "Um, hi."

"Hi," Evan says.

We stare at each other, like two animals unexpectedly meeting each other at a watering hole, unsure of what the other might do.

I glance at Jar. She gives me a kind of I-warned-you shrug, but she most *definitely* did not. Not about this.

"Can you give us a moment?" I say to Evan. Without giving him a chance to respond, I lock eyes with Jar and jerk my head toward the back of the house, then walk into the hallway.

I'm tempted to go into the unused bedroom at the end of the hall, but if we do, we won't be able to know if Evan moves around. So I stop just outside its door.

As soon as Jar joins me, I whisper, "What's he doing here?"

"He says he wants to talk to you."

"I meant, how does he even know we're here?"

She shrugs again, this time it's of the more common I-have-no-idea variety.

"Did you ask?"

"I asked."

"And?"

"He only said that he would wait for you."

"How long has he been here?"

"Since about three minutes before I texted you."

"You could have let me know then that he was here."

"True. But it would have changed nothing. And it is more fun this way."

"Fun?"

A third shrug. It is what it is.

I take a deep breath and say in a calmer voice, "So he came to the door and asked for me?"

"Yes."

"And you let him in."

"It seemed like the right thing to do."

"And the only thing he's said since then is that he wants to talk to me?"

"He said, 'Thank you,' after I gave him a bottle of water."

"Now you're just trying to be cute."

"I was not aware that I needed to try."

It takes an act of God to prevent me from rolling my eyes. "Well, I guess we should go see what he wants, then, shouldn't we?"

I stash the duffel and my suit in the back bedroom and we return to the living room. We have only the one additional chair, which Jar claims, leaving nothing but the floor for me.

I think she's enjoying this.

Instead of sitting, I head into the kitchen to grab myself a bottle of water.

As I described before, the duplex isn't that large. The kitchen and living room are a single space, divided by a counter above which cabinets hang.

As I walk back into the living room, I say, "So, um, nice to see you again."

The words are barely out of my mouth when he asks, "What are you doing here?"

"We live here."

His mouth tightens in annoyance. "I don't mean this house. I mean Mercy."

"Same answer."

"That's not true. I would have seen you before."

"You haven't seen us because we're new here. We came for work."

"What kind of work?"

"We're web developers."

"You're doing that *here*?"

"The internet is everywhere," I say, sounding as disarming as I can.

He thinks on this for a second or two, and frowns. "Then it was complete chance you camped near us at the Grand Canyon?"

"Complete chance," I say, which might be the most honest answer I've given him.

He studies my face, eyes narrowing. "That's kind of hard to believe."

"I don't know what to tell you. Until we saw you that first time, we had no idea you and your family even existed."

"You didn't follow us here?"

"Did you see us following you?"

A downward glance and a shake of his head.

"Then how could we have done that?"

He looks at the floor. At first, he seems a bit lost, but when he returns his gaze to me, the intensity in his eyes has ratcheted up tenfold. "Okay, then. Why were you in our RV?"

This is the question I've been dreading, but there's no way he would leave it unasked. I have no good answers to give him, so I have little choice but to be at least semi-truthful.

"We were worried about you."

His eyebrows converge on each other. "What?"

"We saw what your father made you do at the Grand Canyon," I remind him. "That's not...normal. You seem like a good kid. When we realized you live here, we wanted to make sure the situation hadn't gotten any worse."

"He didn't do anything wrong," Evan says. It's a practiced line, a variation of something I'm sure he's learned to say a lot.

I can't come out this week. I have homework.

It's my fault I've been grounded.

I was clumsy and tripped. That's all.

He was even able to put some conviction behind it, though not enough to convince anyone who's met Chuckie.

Calling him on it isn't going to help our current situation, so I say, "I'm glad to hear that."

Seconds pass without any of us speaking, the tension growing. I don't want to be the one to break the silence. The less I say, the better.

To my surprise, it's Jar who speaks first. "It was a mistake."

Evan cocks his head. "What was a mistake?"

"Hiding under your camper. That was my idea. I wanted to make sure you and your brother were okay."

A defensive flare races through his eyes. "My brother? I can take care of my brother myself."

"He is on the spectrum, is he not?"

"Leave my brother out of this."

"I only say this because I am as well."

He looks at her as if she's spoken a foreign language. "What?"

"Your brother and me—we are the same."

"You mean you're..."

"Yes."

Evan doesn't seem to know what to make of this, which is a

feeling I share. Jar has never talked directly to anyone about the way her brain is wired. Not ever. Not even to me.

"You don't seem the same," Evan finally says.

"Every person is unique. Even those like your brother and me. He does have something that I do not, though."

"What's that?"

"A brother to watch over him."

Evan looks surprised by her response. "I'm-I'm sorry."

"Nothing for you to be sorry about. None of us can change the past. We can only affect the future. Which is why, after we realized you and your brother were here in Mercy, we checked on you. I'm sorry that my friend surprised you. But even if hiding in your camper was a mistake, I am not sorry that we did it."

Man, I could not have tied up that story better. And all of what she said is true.

Still, the explanation leaves plenty of questions unanswered. Like, how did we find out Evan and his family were in Mercy at all? How come we live so close to where they live? Why is there no real furniture in our house? Not to mention a dozen other loose threads that if tugged on would expose the fact there is more to why we're here than we're letting on.

Evan doesn't seem to be thinking of any of that, though. From the tears gathering in his eyes, I know Jar's words have resonated with him. I think he isn't used to people seeing his brother and their relationship as being something other than a nuisance or a burden. It's almost certainly the way his father sees things.

He wipes his eyes before the tears can fall. After a glance at Jar, he looks at me. "You shouldn't have done that." He means hide in the Winnebago. "He could have caught you. That would have been bad."

There's no question about who he's referring to. Part of me

wants to use his words as an opening to question him about his father. But to do so would draw him into our conspiracy, if even just a little bit. So instead I say, "I promise it won't happen again."

A bit of his defensive tone sneaks back into his voice when he says, "We're fine. Everything is fine. You...you don't need to worry about us."

"Good," Jar says. "That is a relief."

Whatever fight is left in Evan seeps away. He takes a deep breath and stands up. "I should get back home."

"Thank you for coming by," Jar says. "It is good to clear things up. If you ever need a place to get away to, you are always welcome here."

"Yes," I say. "Anytime. Day or night."

"Thanks." I can tell he's not really sure what to do with that information. But hopefully, if a time does come when he needs a hideaway, he'll take us up on our offer. We won't be here forever, but we do plan on staying until he and his brother are safe, after which a place to run away to should no longer be necessary.

"I wouldn't mention to anyone that you saw us," I say.

A quick, humorless laugh escapes his lips. "Are you kidding? Who would I tell?"

We walk him to the door. The whole time I sense he has something more he wants to say but is having an internal debate as to whether he should or not. Apparently, the *or not* camp wins out, because all he says as he steps outside is "good night" and then he's gone.

After I close the door, I say, "I don't understand how he knew we were here."

"I think I know," Jar says.

She returns to the card table, opens her computer, and starts typing without elaborating.

After a few minutes, she looks up from her screen. "It was my fault. I walked over to Central Avenue to pick up dinner, between five and five thirty. At the same time, Evan's mother sent him to the market. He must have seen me and followed me long enough to find this place."

She shows me the footage from the Prices' house of Evan's departure.

"You didn't notice him?" I ask. I'm not accusing her; I'm just surprised. Jar is normally very good at knowing when she's being watched.

"I did not."

Again, I get the feeling Evan's life under Chuckie has taught the boy skills most people never fully develop.

Jar plays another scene on her laptop for me, this one of Evan sneaking out of his house late at night, the only light on the one in the Prices' backyard. "He knocked on our door four minutes after this." She pauses. "Maybe it's better that he knows we are here."

"Maybe." Speculation from Jar is a rare thing, so I don't want to discourage her. But I'm not sure what to think about him knowing we're here. The one thing I am sure of, the sooner we can do something about Chuckie, the better.

Jar shares the progress she's made on the things she's been looking into, after which I brief her on my trip to Denver, then retrieve the bag of goodies I picked up from Dave.

Jar looks through it, nodding as if mentally checking items off a list.

When she finishes, she says, "Should we go now? Or do you want to wait until tomorrow night?"

It's been a long day and I could really use some sleep, but that's never stopped me from working before. Besides, now that we have the additional bugs, waiting twenty-four more hours to install them means we'd be needlessly throwing away an entire day of potentially useful information.

"Let me grab a quick shower first. Then we can go."

Price Motors stretches for an entire block. To be fair, it's not a long block, maybe sixty meters at most. The business consists of two basic areas—a car lot, which even at this hour is flooded with lights; and a rectangular building, with a big, glass-sided bulge in the center. The bump is the showroom, which is dark but for a few security lights inside. In the floor-to-ceiling windows at the front hangs a banner that reads: PRICE MOTORS—WHERE YOU'LL ALWAYS GET THE BEST PRICE. I wonder if Chuckie considered WHERE THE PRICE IS ALWAYS RIGHT. That seems snappier. But what do I know about marketing?

Jar and I are in the pickup, parked across the street about a half block away. Central Avenue is dead quiet, not a moving vehicle in sight in either direction.

Jar lowers the binoculars and hands them to me. "Looks clear to me."

I scan the lot, then focus on the windows of the showroom. The big question is whether or not the place has a night security guard. My money is on not. While I'd expect to see one at a car dealership in someplace like Los Angeles, in a small town like this it would be a waste of money. And if Chuckie is indeed having financial issues, he's not going to spend cash he doesn't have to.

"I don't see anyone, either."

Jar lowers her window, sends the drone into the sky, and gives the controls to me. I fly the device over the car lot, the camera pointed straight down. This allows me to see if anyone is hiding behind a vehicle. Once I determine the lot is deserted, I lower the drone so that it hovers four meters in front of the showroom windows, its camera pointed inside.

If there is a guard on the premises, he's in a back room, maybe even asleep.

I send the drone upward until it is twelve meters above the building and turn on sentry mode. Until this function is cancelled, the craft will hover where it is, its camera scanning the building and surrounding area for signs of movement.

As I'm doing this, Jar has been hacking into the dealership's security system.

"How's it going?" I ask.

"Almost there. He has several security cameras. Just creating loops."

Her keyboard clacks under her flying fingers as she creates video loops for each camera, ones that will show scenes with no one in them. She will feed these into the system so they will be recorded instead of the live shots while we are on the premises.

A minute later, she says, "We are good to go."

Leaving the truck's lights off, I put the vehicle in gear and drive us over to the side street just north of the dealership. There, I park and kill the engine.

The backside of Price Motors sits along a dark alley, the only light coming from a single flood positioned above the car entrance to the service department. The wide roll-up door is closed, as are the two pedestrian doors along the back. One of these doors is next to the roll-up, while the other is much closer to us. A sign above this last entrance reads: EMPLOYEES ONLY. I pick the door's lock and we step inside.

There's something invigorating about entering a place uninvited.

Hold on—now that I've shared that thought, I realize how that sounds. We're not criminals. Well, I mean, I guess we *are* trespassing. Breaking and entering, really. Which sounds worse. Plus, we'll illegally bug the place and likely look through a few drawers.

Um...

You know what? I'll just be keeping some thoughts to myself from now on.

The entrance has put us into a hallway about seven meters long. In addition to the door we've just come through, the corridor has four others—one at the far end, one on the right side, and two on the left. The last two are the men's and women's restrooms, both of which are empty. The door on the right opens into an employee break room, also unoccupied.

We walk to the end of the hall and carefully open the last door. To our right is the showroom, currently featuring a pair of SUVs, a pickup, and a sedan. Between us and the vehicles are several cubicles that I'm guessing are used by the salesmen. To our left are glass-walled offices for the higher-ups, like the sales manager and probably Chuckie if he doesn't hold that position himself.

We creep out of the hallway and make a quick sweep of the space to confirm we are alone.

In the far back corner near the service garage, we find Chuckie's office. Its walls are mostly windowed but covered by closed blinds. On the door is a plaque with the words CHARLES PRICE • PRESIDENT carved on it. Unlike with the other offices, this door has a dead bolt on top of the doorknob lock. Neither provides me with much of a challenge, and we are soon standing on the other side of the door.

I place four cameras in his office, aiming them to cover every inch of the space. While I am doing this, Jar hacks into his computer and inserts a program that will run in the background and allow us to see everything he does on the machine.

We spend a few additional minutes searching his desk and

filing cabinets. I'm hoping we'll find another secret phone, but if he has one here, he's hidden it well.

After we finish with his office, we scatter additional cameras and some audio-only bugs throughout the building, placing them in a way to prevent any dead zones in the coverage.

As you can imagine, that'll be a lot of data. And there's no way Jar and I will be able to go through it all on our own. Instead, a monitoring program developed by Jar and one of our colleagues will do the work for us. It will notify us of sections it thinks we should hear. It doesn't always get it right, but it should be sufficient for our needs.

I've just finished putting a camera in the service department waiting area when Jar appears at the other end, next to the cubicles, and signals for me to get down. I drop into a crouch and move over to her.

She has the drone feed up on her phone. In the corner, a red exclamation point blinks rapidly, indicating movement has been detected. A scan of the screen reveals a person standing on the sidewalk in front of the dealership, facing the building.

I'm pretty sure it's a man, though I could be wrong. The angle is nearly straight down, and the person is wearing a baseball cap.

"Where did the drone pick him up?" I ask. What I'm really wondering is if he's had the chance to spot us.

"When he was a block away," Jar says.

"How long has he been standing there?"

"Only a few seconds."

Which means it's unlikely our mystery guest has seen us moving around. Thanks to the cubicles between us and the glass walls, he definitely can't see us now. The problem is, we can't move anywhere else without risking exposure.

For another half minute, the person remains motionless, facing our direction. Then the bill of the baseball cap swivels left and right. When it returns to center, the person steps onto the car lot.

Crap.

I don't think he works here. If he did, why worry so much about being seen?

Any hope that he's just here to steal one of the cars disappears as he walks right by them, heading for the south side of the showroom, his gaze never leaving the building.

Staying low, I move along the cubicles to the corner nearest the showroom's south wall, then pull out my phone and attach the gooseneck camera. After pressing the video record button, I darken my screen so that it won't give away my position, and slide the gooseneck's lens around the corner, aiming it toward the door.

Jar has moved in next to me. Her screen is still on, though she's turned down the brightness. On it, we watch the visitor walk up to the entrance only five meters away from us and stop. I use this information to adjust the aim of the gooseneck camera, trying to get a look at the person's face.

On the drone's camera, the visitor unzips his jacket and puts a hand inside. Maybe I was wrong. Maybe he does work here, because I can't help feeling he's about to pull out a set of keys and unlock the door.

But it's not a set of keys. It's a piece of paper or perhaps an envelope. Hard to tell.

The bill of the cap moves back and forth again. Another check of the area. The person then moves close to the door.

We can't see what happens next because the visitor's body is blocking the drone's camera, but we can hear it.

The soft squeak of a hinge, a long scrape of paper, and then the sound of something light hitting the floor inside the showroom.

After a dull bang of metal, we see the visitor turn away from the door and hurry out of the lot. Thirty seconds later, he's moved beyond the drone's camera frame.

Jar and I remain where we are, in case he decides to make a return trip. The sidewalk in front of the dealership remains empty, but a minute after the visitor disappears, a car drives past, heading north.

It looks like an old Honda Accord but I can't be positive.

"Try to get the license plate," I say.

It's possible the car does not belong to our visitor, but I think chances are better that it does.

Jar sends the drone after it, but the car speeds out of the craft's range before she can get a good angle on the plate.

"Sorry," she says, annoyed with herself.

"It's okay. I couldn't have done any better."

She returns the drone to its previous position and sets it to sentry mode again. We check the feed and confirm the area is still deserted before we finally stand.

On the floor, just inside the showroom door, is the piece of paper that wasn't there before. We walk over and I pick it up. It's card stock. You know, like what's used for postcards, only it's cut larger than the ones you usually send to people from vacations. And it's bright yellow. On the side I'm looking at is a preprinted address for a place called Mercy Cares, and in the top right corner is prepaid postage.

I flip the card cover. On the other side is a form, with questions followed by boxes that can be checked. For example, under WHICH DAY WORKS BEST FOR YOU? are five boxes for the days of the week. (Weekends apparently not included.) There's another question asking for a preferred time, which also gives several choices. And a third asking WHAT WILL WE BE PICKING UP? Under this are checkboxes for ELEC-TRONICS, CLOTHING, APPLIANCES, TOYS, HOUSEWARES, and OTHER. The final question—ANY

SPECIAL INSTRUCTIONS?—is not followed by check-boxes but an empty area in which one's answer can be written.

These questions take up about two-thirds of the back. Below them is this:

Fill out the card and mail it back to us, or call the number below for faster service.

Mercy Cares sincerely appreciates your donation.

Your items will go to those in need or sold in our Mercy Cares Store. Any money earned will be used to fund various programs, such as job training, early start, and elder meals.

After this come the Mercy Cares phone number and nonprofit ID number for tax write-off purposes.

I've received plenty of postcards like this in my lifetime. It's the kind of thing that gets stuffed into mailboxes on what seems like a weekly basis. But it doesn't usually happen after midnight, nor are the cards dropped off by someone who clearly isn't leaving additional cards anywhere else in the neighborhood.

Jar, who's been reading along with me, asks, "What's that?" and points at a choice below the question about time. Specifically, at the box labelled 5-6 PM.

Beside the box are two small marks, each no longer than a quarter of a centimeter, one mark on top of the other like a tiny equal sign. They sit just outside the bottom right corner of the box, the bottom mark in line with the box's bottom line.

It could just be an artifact of the printing, but then Jar says, "And that?" She points at the checkbox for Tuesday on the days-of-the-week inquiry. It, too, has a mark but only one, lined up with the bottom of the box.

I scan the rest of the card, but none of the other boxes have marks. I do notice something interesting, though. The colors of the ink used for the message on the card and the marks are similar but not the same. The words are more a deep charcoal than true black and have a matte finish. The marks are definitely black, and when I tilt the card so that it catches direct light from the floods outside, the marks glisten. The marks and the message were not printed at the same time, so the former cannot be written off as a press error.

I would still be tempted to write off the marks if there was only one. Someone handling the card could have accidentally touched it with a pen at that spot. But three marks in corresponding spots next to two different boxes, especially given the way the card was delivered? The tiny lines are not so easy to dismiss.

"A message?" I say.

"It could be."

"Five to six p.m. Tuesday."

Jar frowns.

"What?"

She hesitates. "I was just thinking that since five to six p.m. is the latest time on the card, the two lines could mean even later than that."

It's not a bad thought, and would explain why the sender marked the box more than once. But does the extra line mean six to seven p.m.? Or does it mean double it to ten p.m. to twelve a.m.? Or does it have no meaning except later than six?

"Did you see this?" Jar touches the card again.

Make that four marks.

Not a line this time but a dot, which is why I missed it. It's between the words *various* and *programs*, and is made from the same darker ink. If it's a mistake, it's a perfect one, as it sits right in the center of the space between the *s* and the *p*, both horizontally and vertically.

Neither Jar nor I have any idea what it means.

I take a picture of both sides of the card, then place it back on the floor where we found it. After checking to make sure we've bugged everything we wanted to, we leave the building the way we came.

Once we're back in the truck, Jar resets the security system. There's going to be a blip in the security footage but it can't be helped. If anyone takes a close look, they'll see that at one second the floor beside the showroom door is empty, and in the next the card is sitting there. It's annoying, but at least *our* visit will go undetected.

It's not until we're back at the duplex that I look at the movie I shot of the visitor at the door. I've been hoping I caught his face, but the visitor's head is tilted downward the entire time, his features hidden by his cap. The only new piece of information the image provides is that the hat is black with a dark blue or purple bill, and displayed on the front is the logo for the Colorado Rockies baseball team.

CHAPTER NINETEEN

J ar lets me sleep in until eight a.m. That gives me about six
hours of rest, which is normally enough for me when I'm
working. I'm feeling a bit more sluggish than usual,
though, and it's another forty-five minutes before I'm showered
and dressed.

When I finally enter the living room, Jar says, "Coffee is in
the kitchen."

I go fetch myself a cup. After taking a couple of sips, I head
back out, feeling marginally more awake.

"Sit." She pats the empty chair, which she's pulled around
the card table so that it's beside hers.

As soon as I plop down, Jar plays a video on her computer
screen.

It's a shot from our camera in the kitchen of the Prices'
house. Right after it starts running, Chuckie enters and walks to
the outside door, carrying his briefcase. When he exits, the shot
switches to the camera in the garage. Apparently, Jar has had
time to make a movie for me. Chuckie walks into the garage, gets
into his twister orange Mustang, and leaves. The time stamp at
the top puts his departure at 6:03 a.m.

The shot switches again, to footage from one of the cameras at the dealership. This one is in the service garage. It picks up most of the service bays and the roll-up door, which is open. Two men in coveralls are doing something at a counter near the door. No one else is present.

Within seconds, both men look toward the big doorway, and a few beats after this, Chuckie rolls in behind the wheel of his Mustang. Time stamp is 6:09 a.m.

Both men give him a wave as he drives by. Chuckie pulls into one of the empty service bays, exits the vehicle, and walks over to the two men. They share a laugh, then Chuckie walks through one of the doorways leading into the rest of the building.

Camera switch. Chuckie walking through a hallway.

"Does popcorn come with this film?" I ask.

"No, it does not," Jar says. "Watch."

Another switch, this time to a camera inside Chuckie's office, a moment before he enters. We watch him set his brief-case on the desk and drop his keys beside it.

The next shot is from the showroom camera that covers the area between the glassed-in offices and the cubicles. Chuckie enters the frame, pauses for a moment and looks around, obviously checking for anyone else.

The shot changes again to the camera watching over the main part of the showroom. It's on the window near the banner (WHERE YOU'LL ALWAYS GET THE BEST *PRICE*), and is focused toward the cubicles and offices in the back. The shot also takes in the public entrance, where, as of the recording of this clip, the donation card is still sitting on the floor where we left it.

I know the moment Chuckie spots the card. It comes right after he circles the cubicles, when a smile springs onto his face. After he picks up the card, he can't help but look around again.

I think he's going to take a look at it right there, but he waits until he's behind the closed door of his office.

The moment Chuckie touches the card right below the two lines beside the 5-6 PM box, any question as to whether the marks are deliberate or not disappears. He isn't quite so obvious with the mark by the checkbox for Tuesday or the one between the *s* and the *p*, but I'm sure he's seen them.

Not only is he smiling now, he looks relieved, too. He folds the card and puts it into the inside pocket of his leisure jacket, then leaves his office and returns to the service department. The younger of the two men who were there at Chuckie's arrival has moved over to a bay and is working on a car. The other man is sitting on a stool behind the counter.

Chuckie walks up to the other side of the counter and starts talking to the man about the day's service appointment. Suddenly, the video speeds up.

"They say nothing important," Jar tells me.

The shot returns to normal speed a moment before Chuckie steps away from the counter and walks out the big doorway into the alley and vanishes from sight. Which is a problem. We didn't anticipate needing cameras out back so we didn't put any there.

The movie does not end, however. After a brief fade to black, a new shot cuts on. It's actually from the same camera as the last, but time has jumped forward twenty minutes to 6:37 a.m. The man behind the counter is now working at one of the bays.

Chuckie enters the garage from outside, carrying a large pink box, the kind that often contains pastries. He yells, "First come, first served!"

The two mechanics stop what they're doing and come over. Chuckie opens the box, revealing a variety of donuts. At least a couple dozen. Balancing the box on one arm, he pulls out a wad of napkins from his pocket and has each man take one before they choose their treat.

He then carries the box inside the main part of the building, and leaves it in the area where people wait for their cars to be repaired or their new cars to be ready for them to drive away. He chooses three donuts himself, makes a cup of coffee, and goes into his office.

This is where the video ends. Jar clicks a few keys and brings up a live feed from Chuckie's office. He's at his desk, working on his computer, the donuts no longer in sight.

"Unless he went somewhere while I was showing you this, he has not left," Jar says.

"Has he done anything with the card?"

"Only if it happened when we weren't watching him."

"Has he taken it out of his pocket at least?"

"No."

The leisure jacket is hanging on a hook on the back of the office door. If the card is important, and it sure seems so from his reaction to it earlier, it feels odd that he wouldn't keep it closer. Sure, he's the only one in the office, but the card is clear across the room, and if he gets up for some reason and leaves without putting his jacket back on, he'd be leaving the card behind. He probably has the habit of never going anywhere without his jacket. Otherwise, I can't see how the situation would feel comfortable.

Unless…

"How many donut shops are within a few minutes' walking distance of there?" I ask.

"Only one."

She brings up a browser window already showing a website for Sunshine Donuts. Jar and I once more in sync.

"It is two blocks away," she says. "Maybe a four- or five-minute walk."

I might be wrong, but it is possible he dumped the card when he went out.

"Feel like some breakfast?"

The card is not in the trash can outside Sunshine Donuts.

No, we don't pull off the top and rifle through it, but Chuckie wouldn't have removed it, either. So, the donation form should be near the top. But we see nothing there that's the same shade of bright yellow.

It's not going to be in the can inside the shop, either, because —like The Smiling Eyes coffee shop—Sunshine Donuts has turned its entrance into a service counter. Yes, he could have given it to the lady working the counter to throw away, but if it really is important, he wouldn't want anyone else to know he had it, right?

We purchase some donuts and put them in the truck, then walk the route Chuckie would have taken between Sunshine Donuts and the dealership.

We check the two city-owned trash cans we pass. Neither has much in it, and nothing bright yellow. When we turn down the side street that will take us to the alley behind Price Motors, I frown. There are no cans here at all.

Could I have been wrong? Is the card still sitting in his jacket?

We walk to the alley and look down toward the dealership's service entrance. A couple of dumpsters sit in a niche along the back of the building. They would be the ones used by the dealership. Putting the card into one of them means it would be surrounded by trash from Price Motors. Any half smart criminal would know that's not a good thing. And if Chuckie is anything, he's half smart.

Still, I can't let the dumpsters go unchecked.

A Ford Escape turns onto our street from Central. Jar and I pretend to be having a conversation as the vehicle slows and turns again, this time into the alley. When it reaches the open door of the service garage, it enters but stops before its back half is inside.

The pair of dumpsters is about three-quarters of the way down between us and the garage doorway. It's a little closer to the entrance than I'd like it to be, but hopefully the mechanics inside will be occupied by their newly arrived customer.

Jar and I stroll into the alley. The dumpster niche is just deep enough so that the receptacles aren't in the way of anyone driving past.

While Jar keeps an eye out, I lift the lid of the first dumpster and peek inside.

Ugh. The stench. It's like a science experiment gone bad.

I blink to keep my eye from watering too much, then scan the contents quickly. If the card is in there, it's out of sight.

I move to the other dumpster. A moment after I lift the lid, I hear a low whistle from Jar. I turn my head just enough to see someone has come out of the garage. I can't identify who it is at this angle, but the person is clad head to toe in the same shade of gray as the coveralls worn by the service department mechanics.

I already have the dumpster open so I give the interior a scan, pretending I just threw something in there. When I see no card, I set the lid back down and make a show of wiping my hands on the sides of my jacket. Through the corner of my eye, I can see the person glance in our direction.

"Let's go," I whisper.

We head back the way we came.

"Mechanic, right?" I say, my voice still low.

"Yes."

"Do we need to be worried?"

"I don't think so. When you started to walk away, he knelt down next to the car and looked at the rear tire."

Good. Likely he'll forget about us in a few minutes, if he hasn't already.

When we reach the side street, we turn the corner so that we can no longer be seen by anyone at the garage, and stop.

I felt positive Chuckie had dumped the card on his way to the donut store. I guess I was wrong. He must still have it on—

My gaze freezes on the entrance to the alley that runs behind the businesses on the other side of the street—including Sunshine Donuts. What if instead of approaching the shop via Central, Chuckie continued down the alley and reached the donut shop from the side street one block away?

We cross the street and approach the alley entrance. Before we enter, we glance back toward the service garage. The Escape is gone and the area is unoccupied.

We turn and start walking. Along the back of the shops are three more dumpster niches, these only wide enough for a single receptacle each.

The card is not in the first. But when I open the second, I see bright yellow paper sitting right on top. Chuckie has torn the card into quarters and tossed them in together, the pieces stacked in a single pile. I extract them and look at the questions on the back side, to confirm we have the right card.

Two lines by the box for 5-6 PM, one by the box for Tuesday, and a dot between the words *various* and *programs*.

Here's the assumption I'm operating under.

The note Nicholas Huston gave Chuckie at the picnic is a request for...something. Two somethings, actually.

Chuckie, acting as middleman, passed them on during his Sunday trip to the driving range. I'm thinking to Robert Lyman, the guy in the parking lot. Once Lyman arranged for the requests to be fulfilled, he informed Chuckie when this would occur by way of the donation card delivered to the dealership. One of the two requests, that is, not both. "Before and after?" Chuckie had asked Huston, to which the man had responded, "Right after." It had been clear they were referring to the storm. Which means the card must be about the event happening *before* the weather turns bad.

Though Lyman might have been our mystery man in the baseball cap, I doubt it. The man we saw early this morning didn't seem as broad or tall as Lyman. An assistant from his law firm, perhaps? Or some rando he threw a few bucks at to deliver the note?

The marks on the postcard indicate the initial event is going to happen on a Tuesday, probably sometime after six p.m.

Today is Tuesday, and tomorrow comes the rain. Unless we've completely misunderstood everything, the event will occur this evening, no earlier than six.

I would very much like to witness whatever they have planned. Which means we have about eight hours to find out where we need to be and get there.

Instead of returning to the duplex, we head out to our Travato at the farm. Chances are Evan isn't planning on paying us another visit today, but I don't want to be around if he shows up. The fewer distractions we have, the better. (And yeah, I haven't forgotten he's grounded, but Chuckie's at work, and I have a feeling Evan's mother might be willing to stretch the rules if he asks nicely enough.)

After a week of staying in town, it feels nice to be back in the RV again. I have the sudden desire to get on the road and just drive and drive and drive. What we do instead is sit down at the table, open our computers, and get to work.

Our first task is to determine if Robert Lyman is indeed the person to whom Chuckie passed the note. While the drone footage caught the handshake between the two men, it neither confirms nor rules out an exchange occurred. The driving range parking lot is not covered by any security cameras, so we don't have alternate footage to fall back on. The best we can do is try to find a strong link between the two men that would indicate they're doing business together.

After an hour and a half of diving through legal records, email correspondence, and the *Mercy Sentinel*'s database, we are no closer to that point. The two men have crossed paths plenty of times, but that's to be expected in a town the size of Mercy. We find nothing that even hints at them ever doing anything together beyond showing up at the same functions. Even if they're hiding a connection, I'm sure we would find something. There are few people in this world who can cover their tracks a hundred percent of the time.

I still consider Lyman to be our prime suspect, but without proof we are forced to spend some time investigating the two driving range employees—Travis Murphy, the manager; and Paul Bergen, the ball guy.

As we've already learned, Bergen has known Chuckie since at least high school, when they were on the same football team. Other than that, we find even less to connect the two men than we did for Chuckie and Lyman.

With Murphy, it's not just less, it's almost nothing. Chuckie is a member of Rotary Club, the Chamber of Commerce, and the Lion's Club. Murphy is not a member of anything, not even a church, as far as we can tell.

I'm starting to think that the idea Chuckie left the note for someone else to find later is what really happened. If that's the case, I have no idea how we're going to discover who that was.

Needing to clear my head, I grab my jacket and step outside into the cool afternoon. The sky is mostly filled with a layer of high clouds, the advance team for tomorrow's storm.

I walk around the barn, struck again by the emptiness of it all. So much land, and so few people. This is not an insult to those who live in places like this, but I think if I had to stay here permanently, I'd go crazy. We're all built differently, I guess. Me, I was put together to be surrounded by millions of others.

The quiet, I think, is what would be the worst. It's nice at first, but after a while it gets to you. Right now, other than the chirps of a few birds, I can hear nothing else. Not even the sound of a car driving by on the road.

I stop in my tracks.

A car on the road.

I stare across the nearby field, seeing nothing as I follow the thought. Could I be misremembering things? There's only one way to find out.

I hurry back to the Travato.

"Can you send me the drone footage from the dealership?" I ask as soon as I step inside. "I only need the part starting when the guy with the card showed up."

She shoots me a link containing an anchor that starts the video right as the visitor walks into the shot. I speed up the footage, rushing past his approach to the building, his delivery of the card, and his exit back to the street, then return to normal speed just before the car that drove by enters the frame.

It's on camera for a total of four seconds. One hundred and twenty frames.

I play the sequence at half speed, but this only serves to blur the video. I go back again, but instead of hitting PLAY this time,

I advance the clip frame by frame. Again, most of the frames are blurry. It isn't until I reach the fifty-seventh one that I find a clear shot.

It's a Honda Accord, the model at least a decade old. It's hard to tell the color since it's a nighttime shot, but it's definitely a light shade, maybe tan or gray or a pale blue.

When I played my memory of this shot through my mind outside, the car felt somehow familiar. Now that I'm looking at it on my laptop, the feeling is even stronger.

I screen-capture the frame and open it in my photo editing program. The first thing I do is brighten the shot as much as I can without losing too much detail. This helps eliminate blue as a potential color.

I enlarge the image until the car fills the window, and I slowly scan the vehicle.

My gaze stops on the driver's side rear fender. It's crunched in a bit, right at the very back, breaking up the otherwise normal outline of the car.

I know this damage. I've seen it before. Which means I've seen this *Accord* before.

But where? And when?

I stare into the distance, thinking. It was...recent. Like within-the-last-few-days recent. Somewhere here in Mercy.

Did I see it on the road when I was driving around town?

No, that doesn't feel right.

The Accord was...parked somewhere.

Try as I might to conjure up the location, it remains elusive. Thankfully, I haven't been to that many places in town.

I shut my computer. "I'm going to take a little drive. You want to come along?"

"Where are you going?"

I tell her about the car and how I think I've seen it before.

"Where?" she asks.

"That's the problem. I'm not sure. Thought I'd drive around to jog my memory."

She stares at me for a moment, then says, "That does not sound like fun. I will stay here." She looks back at her computer. "Pick us up something to eat while you're out. At least you will accomplish something."

"Thanks for the vote of confidence."

"Anytime."

The first two stops on my journey are the offices of our landlords, neither of which does anything to enhance my memory. Next, I head past The Smiling Eyes coffee shop, but I get no sense of *this-is-the-spot* there either. Walmart is next, followed by a drive through the neighborhoods around our duplex. Again, none of these places feels right.

I stop at a Subway sandwich shop in the same complex as the grocery store we've been using. This isn't where I spotted the Honda, but as Jar said, at least I can accomplish something. I grab a couple of sandwiches and head back on the road, with only a few places left to check.

One is the used car lot where I bought the truck. Maybe the Accord was also for sale there. But after I pass by, I know it's another write-off.

Next is Price Motors. Of course I have a memory of the car here, but that's from early this morning. Otherwise, it's a dead end.

I've saved the driving range for last, since I can hit it on the way back to the Travato. As soon as its parking area comes into view, a memory snaps into my head.

Me, pulling the truck into the driving range parking lot on Sunday. As I make my way to my parking spot, I pass several cars. The very first one, in the slot farthest from the pro shop, is a twelve-year-old, light gray Honda Accord, the paint splotchy and dulled by years under the sun. There's something else distinctive about the car. The rear driver's-side fender is dented.

That's it. That's the car.

The driving range is where I saw it.

A second memory floats to the surface.

The first time I laid eyes on this lot I scanned it from down the street, when Jar was with me. I play that memory through my mind.

I'm pretty sure the Accord was there then, too.

Things begin to link up. Huston's note in Chuckie's pocket. Chuckie at the driving range, where a Honda is parked. The same Honda that drove by the dealership last night right after the card was slipped through the mail slot in the door.

Is it all circumstantial?

Yes.

Does it make me think we're on the right track?

Also yes.

As I near the parking lot, I cock my head in surprise. Sitting in the very same spot it was in on Sunday is the light gray Accord.

A pleasant chill runs down my spine.

I pull into the lot. In addition to the Accord, five cars are present, all parked closer to the shop. I pause behind the Honda long enough to take a picture of its license plate, and then pull into the spot next to it.

Being at the far end of the lot, I can actually see the first two tee boxes of the driving range. Box one is empty, but an older man stands near the tee in box two, getting ready to take a swing. I'm a good thirty meters from the shop, and the only way someone inside could see me would be to press their face against the window.

I tap out a text to Jar.

Found it. Can you ID?

After sending it off with the license plate photo, I hop out of the truck and walk around to the other side, where I open the rear crew cab door like I'm going to pull out a golf bag.

I'm all but invisible now. The only people who could see me would be those pulling into the lot. But the road leading to the range is deserted.

I use the alarm detection app on my phone to see if the Honda has one. If it does, it's no longer working.

I've brought a few bugs with me, just in case I happen to find the vehicle. On occasion, I can be smart that way.

After attaching a tracker underneath the vehicle, I pick the driver's door lock. The first thing I notice is a baseball cap in the passenger footwell. It's sitting on its side, as if it was tossed there, so I can't see the front.

I slip an audio bug under the driver's seat, sticking it to the frame, and lean in far enough to flip the hat so that it's sitting upright. The brim is purple, the dome black. Embroidered on the front of the latter is the CR logo, denoting the Colorado Rockies. While I'm sure there are lots of people around here with Rockies hats, its presence in this car tells me I have found our mystery man.

I tip the hat back the way it was, then shut and lock the door.

―――――――

The car belongs to Frances Peterson, a seventy-eight-year-old woman residing in an assisted living facility seventy miles away, in Pueblo. She is the mother of Paul Bergen, the friendly golf ball guy at the range.

A deeper dive into Bergen reveals he has not had the easiest of lives. After high school, he enlisted in the army and lasted less than two years before receiving an OTH discharge—Other Than Honorable.

That's not good. We don't have enough time right now to find out the reason but it's easy enough to guess, given what happened to him next.

Nine months after leaving the army, Bergen was charged with possession of narcotics and sentenced to thirty-six months in prison, serving thirty before being released.

One of the conditions of his parole was participation in a drug rehab program. Though he completed it, it apparently didn't stick, because a year later he was back behind bars, serving a six-year sentence for the same crime as before. No early release that time.

He either righted himself after his second stint or learned how to hide his activities better, because he's managed to stay out of jail since.

Up until eighteen months ago, he'd lived with his mother and worked a series of odd jobs around town. Medical records show Frances was moved to the Pueblo facility due to a diagnosis of dementia, something that had been getting worse over the two years prior to her departure. Her doctors had been recommending for some time that she be put in a nursing home before Bergen finally heeded their advice.

Right after moving her out, he started the job at the driving range. It's both the longest he's lasted at a single job, and his longest stretch of full employment outside the army.

When I mention that I can't imagine the job pays him enough to afford his mother's nursing home, Jar looks up Frances's account. Her social security payments have been rerouted to go directly to the home. While this covers a majority of her monthly bill, it still leaves a shortfall of nearly a thousand dollars a month, which Bergen has been paying. That's more than half of what he brings home from the range.

"Does his mom have any money in the bank?" I ask.

"I found one account linked to her social security number. But it ran out of money last summer."

"Maybe Bergen has a savings account."

"He does. It has one hundred and fifty dollars in it."

"Okay, then. What about the house? Maybe they've taken a second mortgage out on it."

Jar checks the property records. "They do not own the house."

"Who does?"

"Ronald Mygatt."

"Mygatt?" It takes me a couple of seconds to place the name. "The newspaper guy's name is Mygatt. Maybe it's his brother or cousin."

Ronald turns out to be Curtis Mygatt's second cousin. He doesn't live in Mercy but in Dallas, Texas, and inherited the house from his parents. The rent on the place is a surprisingly low seven hundred dollars a month. But even then, there's no way Bergen can afford to pay that and the nursing home and still have money left to buy food and gas and whatever else he might need.

The picture this paints is pretty easy to see.

A former addict living at the breaking point and doing the best he can. His main job is not enough, which means he has to be bringing in cash from somewhere else. We've found no indication of a second job, however. Maybe he's slipped back into his previous life and is selling drugs. Or maybe someone is paying him to do something not quite as aboveboard as shagging golf balls. Someone who knows they can take advantage of his situation.

I stretch and check the time, and am surprised to see it's already after 4:30 p.m. We've been at this longer than I thought.

If something *is* happening tonight, it'll be soon.

I close my computer. "We need to go."

CHAPTER TWENTY

The sky has grown darker since lunchtime, thanks to a layer of low, gray clouds moving in from the west, like an automated roof closing over a stadium. I have a feeling the storm will arrive sooner than advertised.

Jar and I are in the cab of our truck, parked at Timothy Morgan Elementary School on Schoolhouse Drive. Since I'm not exactly sure who we'll need to follow tonight—it's probably Bergen, but it could be Chuckie—we've chosen the school as our standby location, because it puts us at the approximate midpoint between Price Motors and the driving range.

If the two of them end up leaving their respective work-places at the same time, we'll have to flip a coin on who to follow. The good thing is we have tracking bugs on both their vehicles, so if we end up choosing the wrong guy, we should be able to locate the other one without much trouble.

My initial plan was to use the motorcycle tonight, which would make it easier for us to get around in a hurry, but the probability of rain put the kibosh on that. The upside of taking the truck is that Jar can use her laptop instead of her phone to track the Mustang and the Accord.

I glance at my watch. "Okay, that's six p.m."

If our assumptions are correct, we've now entered the time range when whatever is supposed to happen will happen. But apparently the plan is not for it to occur right at six, because neither of the glowing dots on Jar's map has moved by the time the clock hits a quarter after.

In Chuckie's case, this isn't surprising. As we know, not once since we've been in Mercy has he headed home before seven. And lest you think we're putting too much faith on the idea he will drive only the Mustang, Jar is also spot-checking the video bugs at the dealership on the chance he decides to switch cars. But he is still in his office.

As for Bergen, we have no idea what his normal routine is. According to the driving range's website, the place stays open until nine p.m., so it's possible that's when his shift ends.

Six-twenty, nothing.

Six-twenty-five, nothing.

Six-thirty, nothing.

Six-forty-three. "Movement," Jar says,

I glance at her screen and see the dot representing the Accord exit the driving range parking lot and turn east onto Schoolhouse Drive, toward us. We duck below the dash until it passes by.

As I sit up, I say, "Chuckie?"

"Still at work."

Looks like Bergen is our target for now. I pull out of the parking lot.

The Accord heads south on Central Avenue through downtown, then turns west onto Lyons Lane. This puts him in the part of town where the house he rents is located, which, to the surprise of no one, is where he goes.

I've closed the gap between us enough that I'm pulling to

the curb just around the corner from his place at the same moment he's pulling his Accord into his garage.

"Drone?" Jar asks.

I scan the neighborhood. We seem to be unobserved, but I don't know this part of town at all and am not feeling confident. "Let's go for a walk. Bring it with us, though. Just in case."

The changing weather has lowered the temperature quite a bit, which works in our favor. In addition to our face masks, Jar is wearing a hoodie. She pulls the hood over her head, making it harder to see her face. As for me, I don my stocking cap, and pull it down until there's only a narrow band between the bottom of it and the top of my mask for my eyes to peek out of. Pandemic anonymity at its finest.

We turn onto Dewer Street, staying on the side opposite Bergen's house, and walk at a leisurely pace.

Though sunset is still over an hour and a half away, the menacing sky makes it feel like twilight. One benefit of the gloom: it allows us to see Bergen has turned on several lights inside his home. The windows along the front of his house aren't very large, though, and I have a hard time making out much of anything through them. I don't see any movement, so Bergen must be somewhere in the back.

When we reach the end of the block, we walk down the intersecting street toward the alley that runs behind Bergen's house. I'm hopeful we can get a look over his fence at his place.

Just before we reach the alley entrance, a motorcycle rushes out, the driver skidding to a halt when he sees us.

"Sorry," he says, his voice muffled by the face shield of his helmet.

He takes off again, but not before we see it's Bergen.

I curse under my breath. "Send up the drone and watch where he goes," I tell Jar. "I'll get the truck."

I run back to the pickup and then speed over to where I

left Jar.

As she jumps in, she says, "Head to Central."

I turn right and right again, all the while resisting the urge to shove the pedal to the floor.

"Do you still have him?" I ask.

"No. He moved out of range a few seconds before you got back. He was heading south."

Now that we're on the move, the drone's range can expand.

After I get us back on Central, Jar picks Bergen up again at the far reach of the drone's camera. He's still southbound.

As we're going through downtown, she says, "Lost him again."

"Did he turn?"

"No, still straight."

I say nothing more until we're nearing the southern edge of Mercy. "I'm running out of city. Do I go straight, or...?"

A beat, then, "I-I don't know." She looks over at me. "I am sorry. He's gone."

I've been involved in dozens of mission failures over the years. A few have been substantial, but mostly they've been small. No matter which, though, it's never a good feeling. And it's doubly annoying when the failure is caused by the overconfidence of thinking all one's bases have been covered. I was sure we'd be fine tonight. We have both Chuckie's and Bergen's cars bugged. What could go wrong?

What we should have done was taken an hour this afternoon and searched Bergen's place. If so, we would have found his motorcycle and put a tracker on it. *Then* we would have had our bases covered.

Bottom line, I screwed up.

We drive through the neighborhoods at the south end of town, on the off chance we see his motorcycle parked somewhere. Of course we don't.

To keep this evening from being a complete failure, we return to Bergen's place and sneak onto his property via the alley. We've sent the drone aloft again and put it in sentry mode.

Bergen's backyard is divided into two sections. The first is covered in concrete, and is meant to be a parking pad for a camper or a trailer, like the one over at the Prices'. It's not being used for that purpose here, though. Mostly, it's empty space. A smaller portion of the pad has been turned into a makeshift carport, consisting of an old portable cabana tent covering a section of oil-stained concrete where I'm guessing Bergen keeps his motorcycle. The other part of the backyard is covered by grass, with a few trees sprinkled around and some bushes growing next to the fence. It's well maintained, to the point where I wonder if gardening is a hobby of Bergen's.

Like the man's car, the house does not have a burglar alarm, and though the back door does have a dead bolt, the only lock in use is the one in the handle. A few seconds' work with my picks and we're inside.

Since we don't know how long Bergen will be away, we want to keep our visit short. We bug the place first and then do a quick search for anything that might be of interest.

The house is filled with cheap but functional furniture, and off-brand products that confirm his need to be frugal. Like the yard, it's all very neat.

The only reading materials we find are some golf magazines. Probably from the range. Neither Jar nor I discover any golf clubs, though, so I'm betting he reads the periodicals for work, to better understand the sport and talk to the clientele.

He has a TV and computer, both also of the cheaper variety. There aren't a lot of files on the latter, so he probably just uses it to get on the internet. Jar grabs a copy of his browser history and the few files that do exist to look through later.

We find no signs of drug use, no secret stash, not even a

single bottle of alcohol. This doesn't guarantee he hasn't fallen off the wagon, but he's not on parole now so why would he hide that kind of stuff in his private space?

Jar's phone vibrates rapidly, three times—an alarm from the drone telling us it's spotted movement nearby. After checking her screen, she says, "It's him."

We make sure everything is as we left it, then hurry out the back door and lock it behind us. We head over to the fence, but before we can go over, we hear voices nearby—a woman and a man talking. I chance a peek over the top of the gate. They're standing in the open doorway of a garage, two houses down. There's no way we can get out without them seeing us.

Go inside, I will them. But they don't move.

A few moments later, we hear the rumble of a motorcycle turning into the alley.

So much for being gone before Bergen gets home.

I look around and spot some bushes along the fence on the other side of the yard. Most are still growing new leaves, but a couple are ahead of the curve enough that I think they'll provide us with cover, especially with the darkening sky.

We hurry over and squeeze behind them as the motorcycle nears the RV-sized gate at the back of the property. Bergen kills the engine in the alley, then unlocks and opens the gate wide enough to roll his bike through.

After parking it under the covering, he closes the gate, stops, and looks around, his body suddenly tense, as if he senses he's being watched. Jar and I have not made a sound that would alert him to our presence, and I'm not sure what could have triggered him.

He pulls off his helmet and takes a step toward the fence, holding his ear out like he's listening for something in the alley. After a few seconds of this, his shoulders slump, and the unease in his expression turns into one I can only describe as regret, as if he's disappointed with himself for thinking someone might be following him.

If you're thinking that sounds odd, you're not the only one.

He locks the gate and goes inside his house. Curtains are drawn across all the windows along the back so we can't see what he's doing. But when a light comes on in what is obviously the bathroom, I take that as our cue to leave.

On our way out, I place a tracker on the motorcycle before we hop the fence into the alley.

We're driving north on Central, Bergen's place a few minutes behind us.

We're on our way to a revised midpoint between him and Chuckie, in hopes we haven't missed the event the postcard foretold. But I'll be honest. Given that Bergen was away from his house for nearly an hour, I have a feeling we missed our shot.

"Pull over," Jar says.

I glance at her. She's looking at a video on her laptop.

I ease to the side of the road and park in front of a darkened dental office.

She turns her computer toward me. "Look."

It's a shot from Bergen's house. He's sitting on his living room couch, his face in his hands. At first I think the picture is silent, but it's not.

He's crying.

I look at Jar. "This is live?"

"Yes."

As we watch, his body begins to tremble. He slouches forward even more, his head now hanging just above the space between his legs, and sobs rack his body in waves, like the swells of a tsunami hitting one after another after another.

It's an extremely personal moment, a letting loose that can only happen when one is alone. And I can't help feeling that by watching him this way, we are committing a violation. But I can't look away.

What could possibly be causing him so much grief?

At first, I barely register the sirens. They're coming from somewhere north of us. As they grow louder, I finally look up and see two fire engines and an ambulance racing toward us, southbound on Central.

Jar and I exchange a look, and I see the dread I'm feeling reflected in her eyes.

As soon as the fire trucks pass us, I pull a U-turn and follow.

The farm is four miles southeast of town.

We watch the flames from a road about a quarter mile away. Just a house this time. No barn. No outbuildings.

"According to county records, the property is owned by Hayden Valley," Jar says, glancing over at me from her computer.

If we have the tally right, this is only the second time Hayden Valley has been hit by the arsonist. But statistics aren't really what's on my mind right now.

The blaze couldn't have been going for more than an hour, probably more like half that, putting its ignition squarely in the middle of the time frame when Bergen was away from his house.

Have we just uncovered the identity of the Mercy Arsonist? *And* discovered there's not just one person involved, but at least three others?

Holy crap.

But why would they want to burn down farmhouses?

Is it some kind of protest against corporate farming?

If all the places hit had been owned by Hayden Valley Agri-culture, I could easily see it as a revenge plot by Chuckie for the denial of the job he believed should be his. But most were owned by Gage-Trent.

Did Gage-Trent also turn him down for a job?

Even if that was true, it still doesn't make sense. Chuckie appears to be the *middleman* here. It was the old guy at the barbecue, Huston, who gave him instructions.

Is this new fire starting at the same time Bergen was away from his house just a coincidence?

Eh, maybe. But experience has taught me to always err on the side of events being connected.

"Nate," Jar says. "The name of the family who sold the property to Hayden Valley is Penny."

I look at her, not getting the significance.

"As in P," she says, like that should clear everything up. It does not. She sighs. "The dot between *s* and *p* on the postcard? P as in Penny?"

Now I get it. If we understood the conversation at the barbecue correctly, the message Chuckie passed to Bergen listed *two* places. Maybe it was left up to Bergen to decide which one he does first.

"Okay," I say. "Let's assume that Bergen started the fire because Chuckie told him to, because Huston told *Chuckie* to. If so, then I'd say we've found the hammer to bring Chuckie down."

With typical Jar caution, she says, "We need to be sure first."

She's right, but we're a lot closer to doing that now. I put the truck in gear.

CHAPTER TWENTY-ONE

The rain starts right around two a.m. A smattering at first, but it isn't long before it becomes a steady downpour.

Jar and I use this as an excuse to finally stop working and go to sleep. Until this is over, we probably won't be getting much more rest, so even Jar is operating under the grab-it-while-you-can rule.

My problem is, I have so many thoughts running through my head that I'm not sure my time spent on the Travato's bed qualifies as rest, let alone sleep. My mind is looking for connections, trying to piece the puzzle together. This happens to me a lot, especially when I'm so close to figuring something out.

But answers elude me.

We did clear up a few items before heading to bed. From all appearances, Chuckie has never applied for a job at Gage-Trent Farming. He has had several contacts with them, both directly through Price Motors and indirectly via RCHB Consulting—the company Huston and Decker work for that counts Gage-Trent as a major client. His direct contacts center around selling Gage-Trent a dozen pickup trucks a year ago. It was the single largest vehicle sale at Price Motors in the last thirty months.

The communications we've found between him and Nicholas Huston are all very short and to the point. Messages like:

10 a.m. Monday.
Huston

Or:

Confirmed.
Price

Or:

Need meeting.
Huston

Regular novelists, these two.

The interesting thing is that their email exchanges had started up about three months prior to the first time the Mercy Arsonist struck. In fact, a survey of their communications—all as short and vague as those I just cited—shows that the number of messages increased in the days leading up to every fire and then dropped to zero afterward, anywhere from two weeks after the first couple of blazes to just a day after the fire I pulled Harlan Gale out of.

Again, all circumstantial, but the flashing neon arrow pointing at Chuckie Price and his friends is getting easier and easier to see.

I swing off my bed at 6:30 a.m. and shuffle into the bathroom. Outside, the rain continues to fall, thick and steady. I usually sleep great to the sound, and I can't help but feel betrayed by myself for not being able to do so this time.

After pulling on a clean shirt, I get the coffee going. When the aroma begins to fill the RV, Jar slowly sits up on the bed in the back, where she sleeps. After a stretch, she says, "I'll take a cup."

A few minutes later, we're at the table again, computers open, coffee mugs in our hands. Jar takes a sip, her eyes on her screen.

"We have a message from JP," she says. "He wants us to call him."

In case you forgot, JP is the forensic accountant I suggested Jar contact.

"Cool. Let's do it."

She calls him via video chat.

Two rings, then the screen goes blurry for a moment before resolving in a live shot of JP. He's sitting in front of a wall filled with paintings of various sizes, all of which feature preindustrial sailing ships. It's kind of a thing for him.

JP is a slight man with a short beard and a head of wavy hair, which has turned a lot grayer since I first met him several years ago. He's wearing square, wire-rimmed glasses and a dark blue V-neck sweater over an open-collar white shirt. He's English so he probably calls the sweater a jumper, and he lives in London, where he does most of his work from the basement office of his three-story Notting Hill townhouse.

"Greetings and salutations, my friends," he says with a beaming smile. I've never heard him start a conversation any other way.

"Hello, JP," Jar says.

"Hey," I add. "How are you doing?"

"Wonderful, as always. Beautiful day here. Just gorgeous." JP has a distinctive rhythm to his voice. Fast and clipped, and always filled with a bit of cheer.

"You have us beat, then."

"Have you finished?" Jar asks.

"Indeed I have," he says. "Where would you like to start?"

Jar looks confused. "We only asked about Charles Price."

"That is true. But every question leads to other questions. Branches, everywhere branches."

"Let's start with Price," I say, "and see where that goes."

"Right. Price it is. That makes the most sense." Though we can't see JP's hands, we can hear the clicking of a keyboard. At the same time, his eyes shift back and forth as he reads something. Then he says, "Your friend is not exactly the best businessman in the world."

"He is not our friend," Jar says.

"Ha. Of course, of course." Another pause. "Mr. Price took over Price Motors from his father fifteen years ago, who had owned it for twenty-five years prior to that point. The only year the senior Price had not been profitable was his very first. That's not to say the company was a...what do you all call it? A cash cow?"

"I don't think I've ever used that phrase in my life," I say.

"No matter. You understand what I mean."

"Price Motors was making money, but no one was getting super rich from it."

"Exactly. But it was more than enough for a decent life, especially in a lower-cost area such as eastern Colorado. Son Charles, on the other hand, has not been quite as lucky."

According to JP, the first few years of Chuckie's reign were much like his father's, then profits began to decline. Still, the company remained in the black until three years ago. To offset the early losses, Chuckie sold the farm that had passed from his grandparents to his father to him when his father passed away seven years ago of a heart attack. (For the record, Chuckie's mother died from breast cancer when he was a teen.)

"He's been using the money from the sale of the farm to

keep the business afloat since then, but that's almost all gone," JP says.

"Things have been that bad?"

"Actually, at the dealership's current revenue level, the money should have been able to last for another two years."

"Why hasn't it?"

"Because not all his money has gone to Price Motors."

I wait for him to go on, but JP can be a bit of a showman at times and he's clearly enjoying the reveal. Finally, I bite. "Okay, where's the rest gone?"

"That is the question, isn't it?"

"You don't know?"

"No, no. I do know."

I take a breath so that I won't lose my patience. "Then how about telling us?"

He smiles triumphantly, and does as I asked.

The missing pieces are starting to fill in.

Now we understand why Chuckie was looking for work. The company he'd been given by his father was crashing and burning. A well-paid job, like the Hayden Valley Agriculture rep position, would have gone a long way toward keeping that from happening.

It was soon after Davis told Chuckie he was no longer being considered for the job that the draining of Chuckie's accounts began in earnest.

The money he didn't put into Price Motors was routed to the account of a shell company in Dallas, Texas, called RS Shepherd, Inc. JP was able to peel back the layers, and found that RS Shepherd is really owned by Husnic Investments. If you pronounce the *Hus* like the word hews, maybe you'll see where this is going.

Hus as in Huston. *Nic* as in Nicholas. You know, like Nicholas Huston, Chuckie's barbecue buddy and managing partner at RCHB Consulting.

The total amount Chuckie has funneled to him is $465,000. Why he's been sending the money is not something JP was able to discover.

I can think of two possibilities right off the top of my head. One, Chuckie owes Huston the money for...well, something. Two, Huston could have something damaging on Chuckie and is extorting the cash from him.

I don't like the second theory as much, because when they met in Chuckie's Winnebago, there didn't seem to be the kind of tension and animosity you'd expect between an extortionist and his victim.

I also don't know why either of these possibilities would result in Chuckie and Huston having Bergen burn down farms.

There is the Gage-Trent Farming angle to think about, too. The company owns the vast majority of the farmhouses that have been hit. So why would the managing partner of RCHB order the destruction of his client's properties?

Dammit. You solve one piece of the mystery and you realize there's a whole other piece you didn't know about that needs solving.

The easiest way for us to figure it all out would be to corner Chuckie and make him spill it. Don't for a second think we couldn't make him do that. I've persuaded some pretty rough types to cooperate against their better interests, guys a lot scarier than Chuckie will ever be.

But I'd like to avoid damaging him too much, if we can, before turning him over to the cops. I would hate for anyone to feel sorry for him.

Besides, there's someone else we can talk to who might be able to shed a little light on things for us. And today is the perfect day to pay him a visit.

Which is why Jar and I drive back to Mercy.

In Southern California, our storms hit us in waves, and it's rare that a single downpour lasts more than an hour or two. Here in southeastern Colorado, it's been raining since we went to sleep seven hours ago, and according to the forecast, it won't let up until after midnight. If that happened back home, the governor would declare a state of emergency and people would be talking about it for years.

In Mercy, it's just Tuesday.

We head to the duplex first to pick up a few things. As I approach the door, I see the faint muddy outlines of two shoeprints on the mat that weren't there when we left yesterday. They're not dry, but they're also not as saturated as they would be if they were made in the last hour or two. I estimate they were created sometime between the wee hours of the morning and sunup. Our tell on the door has not been disturbed, so if our visitor entered our house, he or she did so somewhere else.

I pull out my collapsible baton, unlock the door, and push it open. I wait just outside, listening for movement. When I hear nothing unusual, I step inside, my eyes moving all around, searching the place. The living room is empty, as is the kitchen.

I head down the hall to the back of the house, checking windows and rooms. There is no sign anywhere of an intruder having tried to get inside.

"Looks like we're clear," I tell Jar when I return to the living room.

She fires up her computer. Though we haven't bugged our own house, we did place two cameras outside—one taking in most of the front, and the other the back. This was done more out of habit than for any other reason. I actually never thought we'd have to review their feeds.

Jar scrolls quickly backward through footage from the front camera until she spots our visitor. She plays the clip in real time.

Even without the time stamp, it's easy to tell the video is from early this morning. A steady rain is falling, like it was when the storm started and much lighter than it is now. A figure clad in a winter coat and hood steps onto the walkway to our door. Just shy of the small, sheltered area by the entrance, the person hesitates.

If I didn't already know the outcome, I would think there's a good chance of the visitor walking away. But of course the person steps forward, leaving the prints we found. After another pause, the visitor raises a hand and knocks, then fidgets while waiting for us to answer. When we don't, the visitor knocks again, this time longer. Another wait, and another knock, and when the door remains closed, a slumping of shoulders and a turn toward our camera.

Evan.

A hole in my stomach opens up as I wonder what caused him to reach out to us at that hour.

He steps away from the door, and moves over to the bushes in front of our living room window. He's trying to look inside but the curtains are closed.

Without warning, he jerks his head around, looking over his shoulder toward the street. It's as if he heard something and is worried about being seen. But all we can hear is the rain.

And then I see his mouth move.

Jar pauses the video, turns up the volume, and replays the last several seconds.

The sound of the downpour leaps from the speaker like the roar of a crowd in a stadium, drowning out all other noise. When Evan whips his head around, his voice cuts through the deluge but not enough for us to understand what's being said. Whatever caused him to look back, we haven't been able to hear —or see—it.

After he finishes speaking, he turns back to the window, unconcerned that someone has just seen him and even talked to him. He spends several more seconds trying to see inside before finally giving up and walking back to the street, out of frame.

Jar taps the fast-forward key, speeding things up slightly. She's trying to see if Evan shows up again. Much to our surprise, he does.

It's a brief appearance in the bottom right corner, near the location where he walked out of frame. We can see only a portion of him, shadowy and skewed because of the angle. And then he's gone again.

Four seconds later, he enters the frame for a third time, but now he's at the bottom left corner. He doesn't stay there. He walks all the way into the shot and up the left side, along the narrow strip of our driveway that's in the camera's view.

And he's not alone.

The framing of the shot is just wide enough to catch the arm of someone walking beside him. Someone *holding* Evan's hand.

When they reach the garage door, they walk along it to the left, out of frame. A beat later, the door shakes but does not otherwise move.

Did they just try to open it?

We watch for another full minute but nothing else happens. Jar increases the speed, and we rip through the next thirty minutes without seeing Evan or his friend again. Jar checks the backyard camera, but he and his friend never show up there.

"Let's see what time he left his house," I say.

It doesn't take long for Jar to find the shot of Evan leaving his backyard. It happened less than ten minutes before he knocked on our door, meaning he came straight to us. The surprising revelation is that his companion left the house with him. While the rain and the darkness make it impossible for us to see either of them clearly, the size of the other person gives me the sinking feeling it's Sawyer.

The skin on my arms and shoulders tightens, and the pit in my stomach is turning into a roiling black hole.

I'm positive Evan would not have taken his brother outside at that time of night—in the rain, no less—if he felt he had another choice. And it's the unknown reason for this that's scaring the hell out of me.

I almost ask Jar to search through video from the Prices' house for the triggering event, but first there's a more pressing matter.

"What time did they go back?" I ask.

Jar speeds up the footage, starting from the point the boys leave the house.

Three a.m. comes and goes. No Evan or Sawyer.

Three-thirty.

Four.

Five.

Six, and soon after, sunrise.

At 7:03, we see a flash of the orange Mustang go by on the small bit of the street that the camera picks up in front of the house. Chuckie off to work, right on time. I'm guessing no one had checked on the boys at that point.

Just before 7:30, Kate appears at the backdoor and looks around. She then disappears inside for a moment, leaving the door open. When she returns, she sticks an umbrella through the doorway, opens it, and dashes through the rain to the door of the RV. She tries to open it but it's locked. Apparently she hasn't brought the key, because she knocks. When no one answers, she hurries back into the house.

I expect to see Chuckie return in response to a call from his wife telling him the boys are missing, but the orange Mustang does not come back.

Jar starts to open the feeds from inside the house to see what Kate did next, but I say, "Hold on."

My gaze moves to the access door to our garage, along the living room wall, just this side of the kitchen cabinets. We've barely used it, but I move over to it now.

Very quietly, I undo the lock and push the door outward.

An exchange occurs between the rooms, light spilling from inside the house into the dark garage, and cold air rushing the other way.

My motorcycle is right where I left it. The last time I was here, it was the only thing in the garage. That is no longer true.

Evan sits on the floor in the back corner, opposite us, leaning against the wall. Stretched out on the ground beside him is his brother. Sawyer's head lies in Evan's lap. His eyes are closed, and his chest is moving up and down in a way that tells me he's asleep.

Not so his older brother. Evan's eyes are open and staring at me, as if half expecting me to start yelling.

I step into the garage, careful not to make too much noise, then walk over and crouch down beside the brothers. Evan's gaze stays on me the entire way.

In a quiet voice, I say, "Come inside. It's warmer there."

Evan's lip trembles as he says, "He-he hasn't slept much. I don't want to wake him."

"He can lie down on one of our beds. If he's tired, he'll go back to sleep." I glance at Sawyer and back at Evan. "That jacket may be insulating him from the cold concrete, but I doubt his pants are. Yours, neither, I'd bet. You'll be a lot more comfortable inside."

"O-o-okay."

When he doesn't move right away, I say, "Maybe it'll be better if I'm not here when you wake him up."

Evan nods, looking a bit relieved that he didn't need to suggest it. "Probably."

"We'll be inside. Join us when you're ready."

I give him a quick smile and go back into the house.

CHAPTER TWENTY-TWO

J ar and I are in the kitchen, looking for some food the boys might like. I'm sure they're hungry. I remove two bottles of water from the refrigerator and eye what food we have there. It's not much. Part of a Subway sandwich, a donut, and some tasteless-looking french fries.

From a nearby cupboard, Jar pulls out some granola bars.

They may not make for a gourmet breakfast but they're better than anything I've found, so I close the fridge.

From the garage. we hear hushed voices. I'm sure I could pick up a word or two if I tried, but I let them have their privacy. Soon footsteps approach the door.

By unspoken agreement, Jar and I stay in the kitchen, keeping the counter between us and the garage door, in hopes that will make us look less threatening. But even then, when the brothers enter the room and Sawyer sees us, he stops in his tracks and stares.

"It's okay," Evan says. "I told you. They're friends."

"I remember them," Sawyer says, his gaze not shifting. "They were at the Grand Canyon."

"That's right. They're the ones who helped me."

"When you saved Terry."

"Yeah."

Terry? Who's—

Then I notice the stuffed tiger squeezed tightly under one of Sawyer's arms. The same stuffed tiger Evan was clutching when we pulled him up the side of the canyon.

Terry.

Sawyer eyes us for another few seconds, then looks at his brother. "I'm tired."

"They have a bed you can use." Evan glances our way. "It's still okay, right?"

Before I can say anything, Jar steps toward the hallway and says, "I will show you the way."

She heads into the back of the house and Evan guides his brother after her. Sawyer's eyes return to me as they start walking and stay there until he and Evan move out of sight.

At one point, I hear Sawyer say, "That's not a bed."

Jar says something too low for me to hear. Whatever it is, it seems to do the trick, because when she and Evan return, Sawyer is not with them.

We have made zero improvements to the duplex's décor since Evan's last visit, and still have only the two chairs. Like before, I let Evan and Jar take them, then I bring out the water bottles and granola bars and set them on the table.

"I'm guessing you missed breakfast this morning," I say.

"Thank you," Evan says. He opens one of the bars and finishes it in two big bites.

When he looks at the others, I say, "Have as many as you want."

He takes a second one, polishes it off, and drinks half of one of the bottles. This seems to satisfy him for the moment.

"How about you tell us what you and your brother were doing in our garage?" I say.

He looks at the table, as if afraid to meet my eyes. "We...I mean, I..." He lets out a breath. "There was nowhere else close by for us to go. I'm sorry."

"Something wrong with your house?"

"No," he says tentatively. He's playing semantics.

"*In* your house, then?"

He glances up at me, then looks away again.

"Evan, did something happen that made you leave?" I ask.

His chest moves in and out faster and faster as his breathing accelerates. He swallows, trying to calm himself, and says, "I'm really sorry. I-I'll pay for the window."

"What did you do to the window?" I ask.

"It, um...it cracked in the corner when I pried it open. I'm sorry."

"Well, there goes our security deposit," I say.

I mean this as a joke, but Evan doesn't take it that way. "I'm so, so sorry. We didn't mean to cause you any problems. We can go now. That would probably be best. Thank you for letting us use your garage."

When he stands up, I say, "I'm the one who's sorry. I wasn't serious. And you haven't caused any problems. Really. Besides, wouldn't it be better to let Sawyer sleep for a while?"

He looks toward the hallway, seemingly lost in thought.

"You do not want to go back out in the rain, do you?" Jar says.

Evan sits back down.

"We *want* to help you," Jar says. "But we need to know why you and your brother left in the middle of the night."

Pain crosses his face as he tries to push past whatever is keeping him from saying what happened. It's heartbreaking and makes me want to wrap my arms around him and tell him everything is going to be all right. But that would be a lie. Nothing will ever be completely all right for him and his brother again. Or for their mother. I'm not saying we won't take care of the Chuckie problem. We will. Without question. What I mean is, the damage Evan's father has already inflicted will always be there in some way. The most I can promise is that things will get better. But I'm not sure he would actually hear that right now, so Jar and I wait out his silence, giving him the time he needs to work through the obstacles in his head.

After several seconds, he pulls down on the zipper of his jacket. It's warm enough in the house that he doesn't need it anymore. Underneath he's wearing a black cable sweater. When he pulls that off, too, I realize he hasn't removed the layers because he's hot.

Under the sweater he's wearing a gray T-shirt. Its short sleeves aren't long enough to cover the bruises on both of his biceps. Five on each. Each an oval, spaced apart in the distinct pattern of fingers wrapped around the muscles. They're dark. The person who caused them would've had to clamp down hard to leave marks like these.

Jar jumps up from the table and hurries into the back of the house, returning seconds later with two towels from the bathroom. In the kitchen, she pulls out the tray from the refrigerator's ice maker and pours some of the contents onto each towel. She wraps the towels around the ice and brings them over to the table.

"It's okay," Evan said. "I don't need anything. They're not that bad."

"It is *not* okay," Jar says.

She scans both arms, determines the left is worse, and wraps one of the towels around it.

"Hold this in place," she tells him. "I'll be right back."

After another visit to the rear of the house, she returns with two ACE bandages from our med kit. She wraps one around the towel and hooks the clasps into the bandage to hold it in place. She then applies the second towel of ice to his right arm and wraps it in the same way.

"How does that feel?" she asks.

"Fine. Cold, I mean, but fine."

She checks her work again, making sure it is neither too tight nor too loose.

When she finishes, Evan says, "Thank you."

"Are you hurt anywhere else?"

For a moment, he looks like a kid who's been caught with his hand in the cookie jar, and I know he's been hoping he wouldn't be asked this. He hesitates, and then tries to grab the bottom of his shirt, but the ice is making it difficult.

"May I?" Jar asks.

He grimaces and nods.

She lifts the shirt upward until we can see another bruise on his side, under his left arm. While it is larger than the ones on his biceps, it's not nearly as bad.

"I-I-I ran into a, um, bookcase," he says.

I raise an eyebrow. "Ran into? Or was pushed into?"

A downward glance is all the answer I need.

"That and the ones on your arms—from your father, right?"

A breath, then an ever-so-slight nod.

"What about Sawyer?" Jar asks. "Is he injured, too?"

"No. I, um...he.... It was my fault. That's all. I should have..."

I give it a beat before saying, "You should have what?"

Another breath. "It doesn't matter."

I know now is not the time to think about myself, but I can't keep from sending out a silent *thank you* to my parents for being decent people.

I lean forward, resting my elbows on the table. "Listen to me very carefully. Those bruises are not your fault. No one should ever do that to you. Especially one of your parents. You know that, right?"

Another nod, also slight.

"I mean it."

His head moves again, same as before.

I'm sure that intellectually he knows I'm right, but it's clear he's having a hard time applying my words to himself.

"What if it happened to one of your friends?" I ask. "Would you think it was their fault?"

He says nothing.

"What about the girl you were sitting with on the pier at the barbecue? What if her father was hurting her? Would she have deserved it?"

For a second, he looks surprised, but he can't be too shocked to find out I saw the two of them there. He already knows I was at the barbecue, after all.

"Of course she wouldn't deserve it," he says.

"Then neither do you."

"Maybe."

"Tell us what happened," Jar says.

"Why? There's nothing you can do about it."

"That is not true."

His eyes widen and he says in a rush, "You can't call the police!" More plea than demand.

"Why not?" I ask.

"They'll just let him go, and then he'll—" He stops himself and looks as if he wishes he could take back the last few words.

It's not hard to figure out what he was going to say.

"Why would they let him go?" I ask.

"Because Uncle Richard would tell them to."

"Who is Uncle Richard?" Jar asks.

"He-he's the chief of police."

"And he's your uncle?" I say.

"Not my real uncle. My dad's best friend from high school. They played football together."

No wonder Chuckie got out of his DUI. I doubt Uncle Richard would be able to cover up accusations of child abuse, though.

"We're not going to call the police," I tell him. "Not right now."

"Not ever," he says. "You can't."

"We'll see."

"Please. You can't do that. You have to promise me."

"Here's what I will promise you. We will only call the police if we know for certain that there is no way your father can ever hurt you again. Can you live with that?"

He grimaces but says, "I...I guess."

"There is one condition to this promise, though."

His eyes narrow. "What condition?"

"That you tell us exactly what happened and answer any questions we might have. Can you do that?"

A beat. "I can do that."

"Good. So?"

He gives himself a second to gather his thoughts, then begins. "It happened after dinner. I don't know the exact time, but before eight thirty. I was in my room, doing homework, when I heard yelling downstairs."

"Your father?"

"At first, but then Sawyer screamed. He, um, does that sometimes, when someone tries to make him do something he doesn't want to do." He flicks a glance at Jar, then as if realizing he shouldn't have, he quickly looks away again. "I didn't mean—"

"It's okay," Jar says. "I sometimes feel like screaming, too. Go on."

"I, um, I went downstairs to see if I could help. Sawyer listens to me. I'm not sure why but he always has."

"Because you're his big brother."

A shrug. "I guess." He pauses. "Dad had a few drinks before he came home last night, and more after."

"Does he drink often?" I ask. We haven't seen Chuckie take a drink since the family returned to Mercy, but I am again reminded about that unpunished DUI.

"Once every week or two, maybe. Not every night. And not always a lot...though the amount doesn't really matter."

"What do you mean?"

"He gets mean whether it's one beer or ten."

"Don't you mean mean*er*?"

He glances up. "Yeah, I guess."

"When he does not drink, does he get physical?" Jar asks.

"A little maybe, but not really. And not as rough, for sure."

"So, he had a few drinks last night, both before and after he came home," I say. Evan nods. "And then something happened that upset Sawyer, and that's what triggered your father?"

"He'd told Sawyer to go to bed, but Sawyer always goes to bed at eighty thirty and it wasn't eighty thirty yet. He likes things to..."

"Follow a routine?" Jar suggests.

"Yeah, exactly. If his schedule needs to change, we have to prepare him ahead of time so that he's expecting it."

"And your dad didn't do that?"

Evan shakes his head. "I don't know why he told him to go to bed early. He knows what happens when things are suddenly changed on Sawyer."

I bet I can guess why. A power play.

Chuckie was a little—or a lot—drunk so his inhibitors were off. (Celebration of another farmhouse burning, perhaps?) He probably saw Sawyer sitting in front of the TV and became annoyed that his son operates by his own set of rules instead of Chuckie's.

Or maybe the boy just looked at him wrong.

"When I got downstairs, it looked like he was going to grab Sawyer and carry him up to his bedroom," Evan says. "That would have been even worse than changing Sawyer's schedule. He'd be messed up for weeks. And...and I wasn't quite sure what my dad might do when he got to Sawyer's room."

An undercurrent of experience carries his last words. I don't sense he means sexual abuse but physical for sure.

"What did you do?" Jar asks.

"The only thing I could. I got in between them."

"What about your mother? Where was she?"

"She'd been upstairs, too. If she'd been with Sawyer, none of that would have happened."

"You know it's not her fault, either, right?" I say.

"I know," he says, but I can tell he does lay at least a small percent of blame at her feet. I have a feeling she's been doing the best she can, that probably without her interventions over the years, the situation would have gotten a lot worse a lot sooner.

I give him a nod to continue.

"Me getting in the way only made my dad more upset. He grabbed me and threw me out of the way. That's when I hit the bookcase. He turned back to Sawyer, but before he could grab him, too, Mom ran in and told him no. She said some other things—I can't remember what. It's all kind of...mixed up, you know? She did calm him down, though. She told me to take

Sawyer upstairs. I thought my father might try something, but all he did was glare at us as we walked out.

"I took Sawyer to my room and told him to lie on my bed. I do that sometimes when he has a bad day so he's used to it. I didn't want him to be in his room alone, in case our dad wasn't done with him."

"What happened next?" I ask.

"I listened to them yelling downstairs. Well, my dad yelling and my mom trying to smooth over everything."

"What was he yelling?"

"Things like how hard his life is. How none of us understand the pressure he's under. How we are all ungrateful, and we would all see real soon how stupid we've been to not give him the respect he deserves. He said some things about Sawyer and me, too, about how disappointed he is in us. How we're not turning out the way he wanted us to be."

"I'm sorry."

"Nothing I haven't heard before."

"I'm sorry for all those times, too."

He doesn't say anything to this, but for a moment he looks thankful.

"Did either of them come and check on you?"

"Mom did. Sawyer had already fallen asleep. He's good at that kind of thing. She said everything's going to be fine, but that we should stay out of our dad's way as much as we can for the next few days."

"Did you show her your bruises?" Jar asks.

"I didn't see the point. She was already trying to put it all behind us. It's the way she always does it."

"Because it's the only way she knows how to survive and how to help you two survive, too."

He grimaces at Jar. "It's not the only way."

"What I am saying is we all must find ways to keep going,

and this is hers. Remember she has been caught in this a lot longer than you."

Barely able to contain his anger, he says, "Then why didn't she leave a long time ago, when she realized he was an asshole?"

"From what I've learned about people, it is because it is not that easy." Jar sounds like an alien anthropologist, specializing in the humans of Earth. Which she kind of is. "I don't know what happened with your mother, but I do know people are often blind to certain traits in the ones they love, especially early in a relationship. By the time they truly see their partner for who they are, they've become trapped, or at least feel they are. At first by the inability to know what to do, or to even act at all. Later, by other aspects. Like children."

"Are you saying me and my brother trapped her here?"

"The choice to be born lies not with you or Sawyer. The two of you are not to blame for any of this. All I am saying is that she has been damaged and is trying to make it from day to day."

Evan thinks for a moment, his anger ebbing away, as he sees the truth in her words.

Wanting to get things back on track, I ask, "What happened after she visited you?"

"I couldn't sleep," Evan says. "I worried if I did, my father would come in. But even after I was sure he was asleep, I was too wound up. I began thinking about what might happen in the morning, and knew there was a good chance he would want to finish what he'd started. I wasn't going to let him hurt Sawyer. And the only way to be sure that wouldn't happen was to get my brother out of the house. I grabbed some of his warm clothes and a jacket, then we...um, snuck out." He's avoiding mentioning the actual method, but the only way they could have exited without having to turn off or trip the alarm was through his window, probably with Sawyer cradled between Evan's body and the wall.

"Did you leave a note?"

"In Mom's purse," he says, nodding. "I told her not to worry. That we were going somewhere safe and would be back later."

"Do you really think that stopped her from being worried?"

"Of course not. But at least she knows we were together and okay. I just didn't want her calling everyone, trying to find us."

"What if your father was the one who found out you were gone?"

"I...I don't know. I guess if that happened, I'll just have to deal with it."

"Are you really planning on going back?" Jar shoots me a sideways glance as she asks this.

"Where else would we go?" Evan says. "My plan was only to give Da...to give *him* a little more time to cool down."

None of us say anything for several seconds.

"Can I, uh, use your bathroom?" Evan asks.

"It's next to the room Sawyer's in," I say. "You can't miss it."

As soon as he enters the hallway, Jar and I go out onto the front porch, leaving the door open so we'll see Evan when he comes back. The rain is still hammering down and no one will be able to hear us.

"We cannot let them go back," Jar says, her voice low but full of urgency.

I look out at the street. I know she's right, but I need to get things straight in my head first. There are only two realistic directions we can move in now, and that's using *realistic* generously. Neither direction is guaranteed to remove Chuckie from his kids' lives forever, and both share a common problem—the lack of time.

The first option is taking immediate action by getting the authorities involved right now. A trip to the ER would be the most logical step. Doctors and nurses are required by law to report incidents of potential child abuse. At least they are in

California, so I assume the same is true here. But that would run into the whole Chuckie-is-a-friend-of-the-chief-of-police problem. We'd have to inform other agencies, both state and federal, to reduce the chance of the boys being reunited with Chuckie before a thorough investigation is conducted.

Once that is in progress, we would put together a package of everything we know or think we know about the fires, and send that to various law enforcement agencies, governmental departments, Gage-Trent Farming, Hayden Valley Agriculture, and dozens of press outlets nationwide. The package wouldn't be as complete as I'd like, but it would have to do.

I don't like relying on others to tie things up, though. Plus, I'd rather the immediate focus not be on Evan and Sawyer, which would be the case if we expose the abuse first. They've already gone through enough. Yes, it'll all eventually come out, but things would be a whole lot easier if Chuckie's outside criminal activities are the impetus for his arrest. Which explains choice number two.

For that plan to be successful, we need a little time. Actually, we could use more than a little, but I don't think we can push matters more than another twenty-four or, at the outside, thirty-six hours. Can we wrap up the Mercy Arsonist case and tie Chuckie to it so tightly that he can never get free? I think so. I...hope so.

Worst case, if we can't, we'll go back to choice number one.

Getting the extra time is the problem. Whether or not we rest on the shoulders of someone else, we have no control over.

I explain my plan to Jar and she agrees. We go back inside.

Evan is still not back. With the sudden dread that he and Sawyer have slipped out a window, I go check on him and breathe a sigh of relief. He's in the bedroom sitting next to Sawyer, who's fast asleep, an arm around Terry the Tiger.

I stick my head into the room and whisper, "Come on back when you're ready."

"Okay," Evan whispers back. "Give me a minute."

When I return to the living room, Jar plays me a series of quick clips from the Prices' house—Chuckie leaving the master bedroom, dressed for work; Chuckie heading downstairs without a glance at the boys' rooms; Chuckie pulling a raincoat out of a downstairs closet; Chuckie leaving by the side door; Chuckie entering the garage, where he gets into the Mustang and drives away.

In other words, he went to work without knowing his sons were gone.

Jar starts to play another clip, this one featuring Kate, but we hear Evan exiting the bedroom and closing the door.

I cut to the chase. "Has she called anyone?"

"No," Jar says.

"What's she doing now?"

Jar taps a few keys, and a live feed comes up from the Prices' living room. A cup of coffee and a piece of paper sit on the table in front of the couch. Instead of sitting, Kate is pacing.

"The boys' note?" I ask, pointing at the table.

Jar nods.

That's why she hasn't called everyone she knows, looking for her sons.

As soon as Evan enters the room, I say, "How's Sawyer?"

"He seems to be sleeping well. The mattress seems to be helping. Thank you."

I motion to the chair he used before. "Have a seat. We have something we need to discuss."

His eyes narrow warily.

"Don't worry," I say. "It's nothing bad. We want to talk about helping you."

"Helping? How?" He sounds as if he doesn't believe it's possible.

"By making your father never be a problem for you again."

He huffs a laugh. "Right. Like that's ever going to happen."

"This wouldn't be the first time we've done something like this."

His expression is still guarded, but also curious now.

"Have a seat," I say again.

CHAPTER TWENTY-THREE

M y phone sits on the table in front of Evan. I've changed
the settings so that our call will not be identified by a
number but only by his first name.

"Ready?" I ask.

He doesn't move.

"Evan?"

He blinks, looks at me, and nods.

"We can run through it again if you want," Jar says. We've
practiced the call several times, going over potential directions it
might take.

"No," he says. "Let's...let's just get it over with."

I've input the number already so I hit CALL and tap the
speakerphone function.

I look at Jar. She's sitting on the other side of the table,
looking at her open laptop. Neither Evan nor I can see her
screen, but I know she's watching the feed from Evan's house.

Before the call can ring a second time, Jar glances at me and
nods. Kate has picked up her phone.

A click, then, "Evan? Oh, my God. Evan, are you there?"

Evan wets his lips but doesn't say anything.

"Hello?" his mom says. "Can you hear me? Evan?"

The sound of his mother's voice has paralyzed him. I touch his arm. He blinks, takes a breath, and says, "I'm here."

"Thank God! Are you all right? Is Sawyer all right?"

"We're both fine."

"Where are you?"

He glances at me and I nod. We knew this would be one of the first questions.

"Somewhere safe."

"Tell me where and I'll come and get you."

"I...I can't."

"What do you mean, you can't? Is someone keeping you there?" With her last question comes a ratcheting up of her panic. "Are you in danger?"

"No, nothing like that. I just mean I don't think that's a good idea right now."

"What do you mean? I need to know where you are, right now."

I can see that defying his mother is taking every ounce of will Evan has, and he's on the verge of cracking. I crouch down to his level, silently convey to him that he's doing great, and encourage him to stick to the plan.

"Mom, I'm just letting you know that we are okay, and that you don't need to worry about us."

"You tell me where you are right now!" She, too, is on the verge of cracking.

"We're *okay*. I promise. Sawyer...Sawyer was scared last night. He-he kept thinking something was going to happen to us."

Kate says nothing. While I can't see the video feed, I imagine she looks shocked, maybe even horrified by what he revealed.

"I had to get him somewhere safe, that's all."

Everything Evan has said is true. The only thing he's left out is that he was also scared something would happen to them.

"No, no, no, no, no," Kate whispers. "My poor boy."

"He's okay, Mom. He feels better. He's actually sleeping now."

A breath from the other end of the line. Then another. "I-I... I'm glad to hear that." She is on the backside of her adrenaline rush, her voice calmer, tired. "As soon as he wakes up, I want you to come home."

Evan and I share another look.

He closes his eyes for a moment before saying, "I think it would be better if we wait until tomorrow."

"Tomorrow?"

"You don't understand. Sawyer was *really* scared last night. It would be better if we give him a little more time."

"Honey, I don't think that's—"

"Mom, please. It was bad last night." He pauses. "Sawyer and I *both* need a little more time."

"Oh." A beat of silence. "Evan, I'm sorry. You know he didn't mean anything by it. It's just the—"

"Stop. *Please*. Don't make excuses for him."

Her lips part, but she doesn't say anything.

"We'll come back tomorrow, probably in the evening," Evan says. "Just tell...Dad that Sawyer was invited to a sleepover, and that you sent me along to make sure he was okay."

Evan told me they had done that before.

"It's a weeknight," she said. "No one does sleepovers during the week."

"Say it was a group project, and the other kid's parents thought it would be easier if everyone stayed the night." Evan's doing a great job of sticking to our script.

"I...I guess. It could work. But he's going to want to know whose house you're at."

"Choose someone he doesn't know."

Silence again, Kate thinking things over.

"You'll be back by tomorrow evening?" she asks.

"Yeah."

"You need to tell me where you are, though. I won't do this unless—"

"No. You need to trust me, Mom. We're safe. I promise."

What he's leaving unsaid, though I'm sure they're both thinking it, is that it's better she doesn't know where her boys are. That way, she can't be forced to reveal their location to Chuckie.

The pause that follows is the longest yet. "I do trust you, honey. All right. You're responsible for Sawyer. You can't let anything happen to him."

"I won't."

"He...he's lucky to have you as his brother."

The words take Evan by surprise. Praise, I'm guessing, is not something he's used to receiving.

"We'll see you tomorrow, okay?" he says, a hint of tears in his voice.

"I love you. And tell Sawyer I love him, too."

"I will. I love you, too. Bye."

He disconnects the call before she says anything else. Then, without a word, he gets out of his chair and walks quickly toward the back of the house. A moment later, we hear the bathroom door close.

Jar turns her computer screen toward me.

Kate is standing in the dining room, crying. It's as if she knows the tidal forces that have been trying to rip her family apart for years are finally on the brink of success.

I wish we could tell her it'll all be okay. But she is a compromised vessel, a victim who has learned to survive by being accommodating. If we share our plan with her, she would be unable to avoid at least hinting to Chuckie that something is up. For her own good, and that of her boys, she needs to stay in the dark.

"You can turn it off," I say to Jar, then head into the kitchen where I can have a moment alone.

It's not even eleven a.m. yet and it's already been a hell of a day.

Things won't get much easier, though. Thanks to the excellent job Evan did when talking to his mom, we have gained the extra time we need to try to prove that Chuckie is one of the people pulling the Mercy Arsonist's strings.

Now we need to actually do that.

A plan for our endgame has been forming in my mind. I'm still foggy on some of the points but the structure is there, and if we can pull it off, Chuckie should be getting his first taste of prison food soon.

A lot of what we need to do cannot be accomplished from the folding chairs in our duplex, which means we'll have to leave Evan and Sawyer alone for a while. Since we have very little food in the house, I make a quick trip to the market and grab a bunch of things I think a couple of growing boys would like. (Don't worry—it's not all pizza and soda. I throw in a veggie tray, too.)

When Jar and I are ready to leave for our next task, I tell Evan, "Do not answer the door and don't go outside. Not even the backyard. And don't look out any of the windows. No one can know you're here."

It's a small town. Someone might recognize him or Sawyer and tell Kate where they are.

"We won't."

"And try not to break my laptop." I say this with a smile.

"No promises."

I like that he's joking with me. It's a good sign.

In case you're concerned he'll be able to access files he shouldn't, I've partitioned my computer drive so that several streaming services are available but not any of the sensitive stuff I have stored on the machine. Which actually isn't that much. Most of my important documents and media are in the cloud and there's no way he could ever get to it.

I've also told him to not contact any friends, which includes responding to any messages he might receive. He assures me he won't contact anyone or respond to anyone who tries to reach him.

I want to believe him, but he *is* a teenager. Changing his mind is part of his operating system. Which is why we've placed a few audio bugs throughout the house, and one video bug covering the living room. This way we can at least know if he does something stupid. Sure, it's an invasion of his privacy, but, um, that's kind of the nature of what we do. Besides, the goal is to keep him and Sawyer safe, not to overhear his deepest, darkest secrets.

What we've told Evan is that we have a few business-related errands to run and probably won't be back for several hours. No, we still haven't been completely honest about why we're in Mercy. Not yet anyway. We've only said there are some things we might be able to do to improve his and his brother's home situation, short of reporting the abuse to the police.

Honestly, I would like to never say anything about our reason for coming here, but I'm not sure how we'll avoid it. But that's for Later Me to worry about. Right Now Me has other things to focus on.

As I back the truck out of the driveway, Jar checks on Paul Bergen's location.

"He's in his Accord," she says. "About three miles east of town."

I tense, thinking about the fires. But there's no way he'd set one now, right? Not with the rain still falling and everything so wet.

"Tell me where to go," I say.

———

The Accord has been parked for twelve minutes by the time we near its location. We are now seven miles from Mercy, once more surrounded by farmland. Though the storm has dimmed the day, it's not too dark to see without our headlights, so I turn them off before we're in range of Bergen's vehicle. Another two minutes on, we find the Accord stopped at the side of a dirt road that's turned muddy in the rain. The car is far enough down that we wouldn't have noticed it from the main road if we hadn't put the tracker on it. A check through the binoculars reveals Bergen is not in his vehicle, nor do I see any signs of where he went.

"Give me a few moments," Jar says, typing on her keyboard.

I drive us another quarter mile down the main road before pulling onto the shoulder, next to a deep culvert filled high with rainwater. I glance through the back window. With the rain and the gloom, I can't make out much of anything beyond a hundred feet or so. Which means unless Bergen is hiding nearby, he can't see us, either.

A half minute later, Jar says, "Three farms are within easy walking distance of where he is parked. There. There. And there." She points back the way we came, her hand moving from location to location. One is on the other side of the road. The other two are on our side, one in the area between us and Bergen's Accord, and one beyond his vehicle. "The one closest to us"—she points at the second location—"is owned by a family named Lindon. The other one on this side of the road, beyond Bergen's car, is owned by Gage-Trent. And the one across the street from it by Hayden Valley."

"Any way to know if the last two have tenants?"

"There is nothing about that here. I could probably find that out from the companies' databases. It will take a little bit of time, though."

"Let's assume they're empty for now." I think for a moment. "If he's here to visit the Lindons, he would have driven up to their house. Which means he's probably at one of the other two. He's not going to be setting a fire in this weather, but he *could* be here to scope out the location of a future one."

Jar nods, agreeing.

"The question is, which place is he at?" I say. "What do you think?"

"That we can't know that yet."

"I'm just looking for your best guess."

She ponders this. "All but two of the prior fires have been at properties owned by Gage-Trent."

"So you're saying the Gage-Trent place."

"No. I am saying probability indicates that one." With a glance at her computer, she adds, "According to county records, the Hayden Valley farm has the larger house, and includes not only a barn but a separate workshop. The Gage-Trent property has only a house and a barn."

"The Hayden Valley one, then."

"I did not say that, either."

I snort a laugh.

"Why don't you tell me which one *you* think it is?" she says.

"No clue."

Even when we are at our busiest, it's fun to tease Jar. Not too much, mind you. She may be small but she can hurt me.

What I draw out of her this time is a gawk that quickly transitions into a steel-eyed glare. I sense no other imminent retaliation, however, so I'll take this one as a victory for me.

I make a U-turn and drive slowly down the edge of the road, stopping when we can see the end of the driveway that leads to the Hayden Valley property.

In truth, I would weigh the chances of which property Bergen is on at around sixty percent the Gage-Trent place and forty percent Hayden Valley. It would be more like eighty/twenty if Jar didn't add the info about the buildings at each location.

"Binoculars?" I ask.

She pulls them out of her backpack and hands them to me.

I scan the area, following the driveway through the fields and up to a house about a hundred meters from the road. As you can imagine, the rain isn't making it easy to see things, and while I can pick out the house and the two other buildings beyond it, all three look grey in the dreariness of the storm. As far as I can tell, none of them have any lights on inside. I also don't see any cars parked near the house.

The place looks unoccupied, which means it would fit the arsonist's pattern.

After giving the buildings one last look, I pull back onto the road and head toward the entrance to the Gage-Trent property.

As we pass the road where Bergen's car is still parked, Jar checks it through the binoculars. "No one. He's not back yet."

I go past the Gage-Trent driveway about one hundred meters and make another U-turn, then crawl back until we are about thirty meters from the entrance. Again, I scan the area through the binoculars, and again I see gray buildings with no lights on and a parking area with no cars.

As Jar indicated, the house here is smaller than the other one. Much smaller, in fact. It's only one story, and unless there's an entire wing extending from the opposite side that I can't see, it can't have more than two not very large bedrooms. In other words, it doesn't appear to be a very inviting target. The problem is, we don't know the deciding factor behind why certain properties have been chosen to burn. So it's possible this place *is* the Mercy Arsonist's next target.

I continue to watch for the next several minutes, hoping to catch Bergen exiting the house or barn.

"Nate," Jar says, her hand touching my arm.

I lower the binoculars

"Look." She points down the road.

In the distance, I see a small, bright red light—artificial, not a fire. It's off the side of the road, right where Bergen left his car.

Oh, crap.

I toss the binoculars to Jar, put the truck in gear, and tap on the gas. Since we are between Bergen and Mercy, I'm sure he'll be driving this way. And though he can't see us at the moment, because our lights are still off, he would eventually if we stay where we are. I don't want him to catch even a glimpse of us.

Keeping my foot off the brake pedal to prevent the brake lights from flashing, I turn down the entrance road to the Gage-Trent farm. From the cracks and divots, it's obvious it's been a while since the driveway last saw much use. My cautious side tells me to slow down with every bump, but I don't.

"Where is he?" I ask when we're halfway to the house.

Jar is looking through the binoculars, toward Bergen's car. "He's backing onto the road."

I floor it.

The truck bucks and skids through the water and mud but stays on the driveway. Less than twenty seconds later, we reach the house. I pull behind it and let us roll to a stop. Though the rain should be enough to keep him from seeing us, hiding behind the house will guarantee it.

Jar is twisted around now, the binoculars pointing out the back window. Several quiet seconds pass before she says, "There he is. No change in speed." Another few moments tick by before she lowers the glasses. "He's gone."

If Bergen was at the Gage-Trent property, I would have seen him walking back to his car. But I didn't.

Which leaves only one place he could have gone.

I swing the truck around and head back toward the main road.

———

Jar finds the unlatched window on the Hayden Valley Agriculture farmhouse. It's along the back at ground level. A basement window, narrow, but not too narrow for someone to squeeze through, especially someone wiry like Bergen.

He used a glass cutter to cut away a section just large enough for him to stick his hand through and undo the latch. We open the window and slip inside, Jar doing it with much more ease than me.

The basement is a dingy space, with a smattering of shelves that are mostly empty, though a few unused mason jars can be seen here and there. The floor is dusty, which allows us to see Bergen's footsteps. It also records our own, but I'm not worried about that. We'll do a little sweep on our way out.

We see no prints on the stairs leading to the first floor, so we know Bergen never ventured farther than this room. He did walk the entire perimeter, though. My guess is he was looking for the perfect spot to set the fire.

As I follow his route, I come across an old, rotting bench pushed against a cabinet built into one of the walls. The bench has not been there long. I can see the clean marks on the ground only a couple of meters away. Bergen must have moved it.

Jar and I carefully lift the bench out of the way and set it to the side. I open the cabinet.

"I don't think these came with the house," I say.

Inside are four bottles of lighter fluid, several rags, and a small wooden device that appears to be some kind of igniter that delays setting off the flames long enough for Bergen to get away.

We leave everything where it is, shut the cabinet, and put the bench back.

After obscuring our footprints, we climb back out and check the barn and the workshop. Both have entrances that Bergen has compromised so he'll be able to get in quickly when the time comes. Each structure also has its own fire-starting kit, waiting to be used.

Before we exit the workshop, I scroll through the pictures I've been taking since we arrived, and an idea begins forming in my mind.

"Why are you smiling?" Jar asks.

"Am I?"

"Yes. It's creepy."

"What would you say to a little tweak of our plan?"

"What tweak?"

I tell her.

Jar's eyebrow raises, then she smiles, too.

CHAPTER TWENTY-FOUR

L oud, dramatic music blares from the TV in Bergen's living room as I pick the lock to his back door.

When I'm done, I whisper to Jar, "Still on the couch?"

She shows me her phone, which currently displays the camera feed from Bergen's living room. He's still on the couch, all right, in the same position as the last time I looked—feet on the ground and arms on his knees. While his eyes are aimed at his television, he's not reacting to anything, and I wonder if he's even paying attention to what's on the screen.

I nod and Jar slides her phone into her pocket.

I silently count down from three on my fingers. When the last digit collapses into my palm, I turn the knob, push the door open, and we rush inside.

Either the TV is too loud or Bergen is so lost in his head that he isn't aware of the world around him, because he doesn't hear us enter the house. Even when we step into his living room, it takes a second before he jerks in surprise and falls back against the couch.

He raises his hands in front of him, palms out, and turns his head to the side as if trying to avoid a blow. "What the hell? Wh-wh-wh-what do you want?"

His response is in large part due to the dart gun I'm pointing at him. Also, it can't be doing his panic meter any good that Jar and I are both wearing ski masks. (Yes, mine is the same one I used when I caught Marco and Blaine at El Palacio Banquet Experience. And yes, I'm well aware I need to get rid of it and find something new to hide my face. But this and the spare I keep around are all we have on hand, and we certainly weren't going to pay Bergen a visit with only virus-reducing face masks. Those we're wearing, too, on top of the ski masks.)

I aim my gun at his thigh and pull the trigger. As he screams, the movie soundtrack on his TV swells, as if Bergen's real life is being scored. It's a nice touch I wish I could take credit for.

The dart is loaded with a very low dose of Beta-Somnol. A higher dose would knock someone out for anywhere from a few hours to almost a day. The amount we've given Bergen should only make him groggy. But apparently I've made a miscalculation, because his eyes close and his head lolls back after a few seconds.

No matter. He shouldn't be out for long.

We put one of his dining room chairs in the house's only bathroom. We've chosen this room because it's in the middle of the house and faces the backyard, and from there it will be a lot less likely for any of Bergen's neighbors to hear us. Still, for added insurance, we duct tape two pillows against the window.

Bergen we tie to the chair, securing his hands behind the chair's back.

While we wait for him to come to, we search the house again. On the dresser in Bergen's bedroom I find his wallet, and inside the wallet, the note Chuckie passed to him. I unfold it and look it over.

Huh.

I've been expecting to find two names on it. One being Penny, for the house that has already burned, and the other being the name of the original owners of the house Bergen prepped this afternoon. But there are four, separated into two columns. Column one has three names:

CREIGHTON

LUNDSTROM

PENNY

Column two has one: WHITTAKER.

I find Jar and show the note to her, pointing at the second column. "I'm guessing this is the person who used to own the house we were at today."

"I will check."

She gets to work on her laptop while I resume the house search.

The only other thing I find that wasn't here yesterday is a backpack, on the floor of the closet by the front door. I open it and find a few empty food containers, an uneaten Snickers bar, and a couple more of those golf magazines I've seen around Bergen's house. I also discover a stack of the large, bright yellow postcards used by the charity Mercy Cares. None have been filled out. I put the bag back in the closet but keep the cards.

"Look what I found," I say, waving the stack.

Jar glances at them for barely a second before looking back at her computer. "He had to have some somewhere."

I was hoping for a *good job* or even a simple *nice!* I guess I'll just have to pat myself on the back.

I return to the bathroom to check on Bergen.

He's starting to groan, low and weak. Without assistance, it would probably take him another ten minutes to become fully alert. But we don't need to wait that long.

I pop back down to the living room. "Anytime you're ready."

"One moment," Jar says. She clicks her cursor a few times, types something in, and clicks again. After she reads what appears on the screen, she says, "You are right. Whittaker is the former owner."

"Excellent." See, *I* can give praise.

Jar follows me to the bathroom, bringing her computer.

I grab a washcloth off the counter, soak it with cold water, and drape it over Bergen's nose and mouth. His head is tilted back, helping the rag stay in place. That is, until he tries to breathe in the rag. His chest heaves, and he lets out a combination snort-gulp that ends with his head whipping forward, his eyes popping open, and the cloth dropping into his lap. He sucks in as much air as he can, lets it out, and does it all again.

He then looks around to see where he is. I turn on the camera that I mounted to the medicine cabinet. It's framed to record a tight shot of him, mid-chest to just above his head.

Fear fills his eyes again, only now it's not asphyxiation he's worried about.

"What's going on? Why are you doing this?"

I pull out my phone and show him a picture of the lighter fluid in the Whittakers' basement, holding my hand just outside the video camera's view.

Bergen is still slow from the drug, so it takes him a moment to bring the picture into focus. When he does, he gasps and says, "Oh, shit. I-I-I—"

I hold up my other hand, stopping him, and nod at Jar.

As soon as she clicks her cursor, a clipped voice comes out of her laptop's speaker. It has a mid-tone range that could be either male or female and speaks without emotion. "Are you the Mercy Arsonist?"

Bergen's eyes dart around, an animal cornered, looking for a way out.

I show him the picture again, but he remains silent.

Jar's computer repeats the question.

Bergen hesitates, and then nods.

Jar types something and clicks. "Speak your answer," her computer says. "Are you the Mercy Arsonist?"

"Yes." He says the word as if it escaped his lips before he could stop it.

"You set off the fire at the home once owned by the Andrews family?" That was the very first house to burn.

Bergen wets his lips and starts to nod, but then remembers Jar's direction. "Yes."

One by one, she goes through each house, eliciting confirmations.

Finally she asks, "And your next fire is planned for the home formerly owned by the Whittaker family?"

His eyes are full of water now. "Please, don't."

"And your next fire is planned for the home formerly owned by the Whittaker family?"

He slumps forward, sobbing, his body held at an angle by his arms tied behind the chair.

"I'm sorry. I didn't want to. I never wanted to."

Jar plays the question a third time.

"Yes! All right? Yes. It's supposed to be the Whittakers'."

"When?"

He glances at Jar and me before his head droops down again. "Tomorrow night," he all but whispers. "If the rain stops."

The rain is due to end this evening.

Jar taps four keys and clicks again. "Why?"

"Because that's what—" He catches himself. "Because. That's all."

More typing, then, "You said you did not want to and that you never wanted to. What did you mean?"

Tears roll down Bergen's face. "Nothing, okay? I just...I just..."

From my pocket, I pull out the note I found in his wallet. He's looking at the ground again and doesn't see it. Once I have the paper unfolded, I rattle it in front of him.

He looks up, confused, then his eyes focus on the note and the color drains from his face.

"Who gave this to you?" the computer asks.

"How did you.... That's not...."

"Who?"

"N-n-n-no one. I...I...I..."

"You are lying."

He opens his mouth, but the words don't come.

I grab the Mercy Cares postcard that I put on the bathroom counter earlier and show it to him.

"This is how you let your contact know when you will set a fire," our voice says.

"That's...not...true," he whispers with absolutely no conviction.

Jar hands me her phone. I point the screen at Bergen and tap it once to play the video clip Jar has cued up.

He watches in disbelief. It's the shot from the other night at Price Motors, when he delivered the postcard. When it ends, I reach over to the counter and pick up another yellow postcard. It's the one Chuckie threw away, whole again thanks to a little tape.

I point at the marks he made.

"Tuesday's fire," our voice says. "After six p.m. P as in Penny."

Another whisper. "My God."

"Who gave you the note?"

"I...I can't. He'll kill me."

"Charles will never harm you."

His breathing picks up speed. "You don't know him. He *will* kill me. It doesn't matter where I—"

And this is the point when it dawns on him that we said *Charles*.

"You know," he says, surprised and scared. "Y-you know."

Jar taps her computer again. "Who gave you the note?"

He looks at us, panic hovering at the edge of his gaze. "Charles Price."

The rest of the story comes out in a rush. Jar needs to ask him a question here and there to keep him on track or clarify a point, but for the most part we just let him talk.

Chuckie has been manipulating Bergen for years. It started after Bergen's second stint in prison, when he came to Chuckie looking for a job. Instead of hiring his old football teammate to train as a mechanic or just to clean the offices, Chuckie used Bergen for odd jobs he needed done, promising to one day give him a full-time position.

It was a promise unfulfilled. What did happen was, the jobs Chuckie had Bergen do started drifting into the gray area between legal and not, and eventually crossed the line entirely. Sometimes it was a car from Chuckie's own dealership that he wanted Bergen to steal. Used ones, normally, that he'd make more on from the insurance and the sale of the car parts when the vehicle was scrapped than if he sold it outright. Sometimes it was tossing the office or the home of someone Chuckie was having a problem with.

Bergen hated doing these things, but he needed the money to help care for his increasingly ill mother. He tried getting regular jobs, but he was always let go after a few months or a year at most, usually for no reason he could understand.

He describes some of these instances to us and I have to agree—the grounds for his terminations sound dodgy at best. Of course, he could be painting a rosy picture that makes him out to be better than he is. But I wonder if there's an alternative explanation. Perhaps someone doesn't want Bergen to have the security of full-time work? Someone with influence in the community who needs Bergen to remain dependent on the odd jobs this same person hands out?

It's just a theory, but it's easy to imagine.

Once the jobs Chuckie had Bergen do veered into the illegal, Bergen was trapped. As a two-time felon, he would receive a harsh sentence and might never see the outside of a prison again if he was caught and convicted. To keep Bergen in line, Chuckie would dangle the possibility of tipping off the police. We didn't ask why Bergen didn't go to the police himself but I can guess the reasons. First, he would likely still end up in prison. And second, I don't think he has the fortitude to act against Chuckie.

At least he doesn't on his own.

He's not aware of it yet, but our presence changes things.

According to Bergen, he never wanted to be involved with the fires. But Chuckie exerted his pressure and Bergen gave in. Chuckie even showed him what to do, which makes me wonder if there are other fires in Chuckie's past. Together they burned down a few old buildings a couple of counties away. Once Chuckie was convinced Bergen had a handle on things, the Mercy Arsonist was born. Chuckie would give Bergen the names of the places he wanted hit and Bergen would scope them out, then inform Chuckie via one of the postcards when the fire would occur.

"Why does he want to burn these places down?"

"I'm not sure," Bergen says. "I do know they're all owned by big companies. I think that has something to do with it."

"Has he said anything about that to you?"

"Not really."

"Nothing at all?"

He thinks for a moment. "We don't really talk that much. Just when he comes to the range sometimes."

"What does he say when he's there?"

"I don't know. Little things, I guess. He'll usually say, 'I've got something for you.' Sometimes, 'Don't mess anything up.'" He pauses. "I remember one time, after he gave me the name for the next house, he said, 'Make it really good.' I thought that was kind of strange. Fires burn everything. There's not much else I could do."

"Which house was this?"

Another pause. "I'm pretty sure it was the Murphys' place."

I glance at the computer as Jar pulls up the list of the Mercy Arsonist's accomplishments. The Murphy farm was the third to be torched, but the first one owned by Hayden Valley.

I gesture at the keyboard, and Jar turns her laptop for me to tap in the next question. "Why are the fires happening faster now?"

"Huh?"

"Tomorrow's fire would be your fourth in less than two weeks. Before that, there was normally a month between them."

"Oh, um, because we're almost done."

I look at him for a moment, then type in, "Charles said this?"

"He said one or two more should be enough."

"Enough for what?"

"I don't know. He's never told me that. Honest."

He's a broken man, and I have no doubt he's told us everything he knows.

I don't want to feel sorry for him, but I do. He's been trying to get his life back on track for years, which made him vulnerable to a manipulator like Chuckie. But he's not completely blameless for what he has done. He could have made different choices, ones that would have kept him from making a third trip to prison. Sadly, that ship has sailed. But perhaps, if he cooperates with prosecutors, he'll receive some leniency. That's the best he can hope for now.

I type in another question. "When are you supposed to contact Charles again?"

"Tonight. He...he's expecting another card to confirm tomorrow night's, um, event."

"Fire."

"Yes. Fire."

"Another postcard?"

"Yes."

"That you leave at the dealership?"

"Yes."

Jar and I retreat to the living room for a quick chat. When we return to the bathroom, Jar is once again manning the laptop.

"Thank you for your cooperation," the computer voice says for us. "We will do what we can to make things easier for you, but do not expect much."

"Wait. You're leaving? Then let me go. I told you everything."

"You will remain here for the duration."

"What? The duration? I don't under—"

I shoot a dart into his thigh.

This one is loaded with a maximum dose and should knock him out until noon tomorrow, at least. As soon as he's unconscious, we untie him and I carry him into his bedroom, where we secure him to his bed, just in case he wakes before we return.

CHAPTER TWENTY-FIVE

T he question still nagging us is one of motive.

Yeah, there's the whole Chuckie getting spurned by Hayden Valley angle, but that doesn't explain why most of the burned-down buildings belonged to Gage-Trent. Nor does it account for the involvement of Nicholas Huston and Kyle Decker from RCHB Consulting.

Though we have enough evidence now to make life very difficult for all three men, I really want to know the reason they're burning everything down. Not just for curiosity's sake, but Jar and I like tying things up nice and neat.

Which is why we're back at the duplex, doing some deeper research into the two companies that have been the Mercy Arsonist's victims.

Evan and Sawyer are in the bedroom, watching another movie on my laptop while we're in the living room. We've moved the card table to a position from where we can see down the hallway, and will know if either boy exits the bedroom. Don't want to be discussing the wrong topic in front of them, after all.

It is nearly four p.m. when we uncover several emails and

memos that hint at the answer. But I want more than a hint, so I decide to make a phone call.

"Hayden Valley Agriculture," a woman says over the line. I have a feeling it's the same receptionist I saw when I visited the company's Denver office on Monday. "How may I direct your call?"

"Isaac Davis, please." I'm using the voice modulator again, the settings transforming my voice into that of a fiftysomething man.

"Who's calling, please?"

"Kenneth Gains, FSA." The FSA is the Farm Service Agency, part of the US Department of Agriculture.

"One moment, sir." I listen to hold music for about half a minute before the receptionist comes back on. "Mr. Gains? Mr. Davis will be right with you."

"Thank you."

It takes another two minutes before the line rings again.

"Mr. Gains? This is Isaac Davis. How may I help you?"

"I'm actually calling to see if there's anything we can do to help *you*, Mr. Davis." I'm not, but offering help is a great way to get someone to answer questions they might otherwise avoid.

In this case it works like a charm, and the final piece of the puzzle falls into place.

The boys request pizza for dinner, which I dutifully order but pick up myself, since we'd rather not have anyone coming to the door.

"Why do you have only two chairs?" Sawyer asks.

He and Evan are using them to eat at the table. Jar sits on the floor with a paper plate holding a slice, and I'm leaning against the kitchen counter, where my food is.

"Because there are only two of us," I say.

"There are four of us tonight."

"You got me there."

"You should get more chairs."

"We probably would if we were going to stay here for a while."

"You're leaving?" This is from Evan.

"Soon."

"How soon?" He actually seems disappointed, which is both touching and heartbreaking.

"As soon as we know you two are safe."

He scoffs. "Oh, so you mean you're never leaving."

I shrug, though I think there's a good chance we'll be gone by Sunday.

While the conversation veers off into other topics, every now and then I catch Evan giving me a curious look.

After we finish, the boys return to the bedroom to watch another movie, and Jar and I check the video feeds from the Prices' house, wanting to see how Chuckie is reacting to his sons being gone. Turns out he hasn't reacted at all because he hasn't come home, which is odd because it's well after eight p.m. and all the other nights he was there by now.

Jar pulls up a grid of the camera feeds from Price Motors.

"There he is." She points at the feed from Chuckie's office and brings it up full screen.

He's sitting at his desk, not doing much of anything other than looking pensive. We scroll back through the footage to see if something happened that may have caused his current mood.

Indeed something has.

At just after six p.m., he receives a visit from Nicholas Huston and Kyle Decker. They greet each other cordially, and Huston takes the guest seat across from Chuckie's desk. Decker closes the door and remains standing, a few feet behind the older man, like a bodyguard.

"I didn't expect you to come by this evening," Chuckie says. "Is everything okay?"

"I want to make sure we are still on track," Huston says.

"Of course," Chuckie says. "Right on track. No problems at all."

"It needs to happen tomorrow."

"As long as the weather cooperates."

"Let me rephrase," Huston says. "It *will* happen tomorrow."

"Okay."

"We are at a very critical juncture."

"I'll make sure it happens. Tomorrow. You can count on it."

"Good." Huston smiles, and then his expression turns somber. "There is the other matter. If you're still in, we need the remainder of your commitment within twenty-four hours."

"I'm still in. No question about that. I'm very excited. I'll, uh, I'll make the transfer in the morning."

Thanks to my phone call with Davis, we now know why the rush is on. And thanks to some quick research by our friend JP, we know what the transfer is about, too.

The smile is back on Huston's face, more businesslike but not unfriendly. He stands and extends a hand, which Chuckie immediately takes.

Jar shivers next to me. Probably because there's not a latex glove, bottle of hand sanitizer, or face mask in sight in Chuckie's office.

"I appreciate the way you always come through for us," Huston says.

"Happy to do my part," Chuckie tells him.

They let go of each other's hands. "As long as everything goes smoothly on your end, we should have a deal done by the end of the weekend."

"Everything will be smooth. I promise."

They say their goodbyes and Huston and Decker leave.

Chuckie waits a moment, then walks over to the door and peeks out at the showroom. I get the sense he's making sure his guests have left. When he leans back into his office, he closes the door and locks it. He picks up his briefcase from the floor and puts it on the desk. From inside the bag, he extracts a cell phone that looks very much like the one hidden in the file cabinet in his home office.

He types in a message and sits down, presumably to wait for a response.

Jar and I share a look, then I lift my bag onto the table. Bergen had two cellphones in his pants pockets, both of which we took with us, but not before we'd used his face to unlock them and reset the passwords.

I wake up both phones. The first is devoid of notifications. The home screen of the second one, however, shows seven text messages have arrived, all from the same number.

I return to the table and show it to Jar.

She fast-forwards the video from Chuckie's office until we reach the live shot again. He has been sending messages about every fifteen minutes. Seven in total.

I open the message thread. Starting from the earliest:

Need confirm re tonight

Followed by:

Important. Need answer.

And:

Now. Please!

And:

> Where are you?

And:

> Need confirmation!

And:

> Answer me!

Then finally:

> You had better have a damn good reason for not responding!

I could ease his tension by simply answering, *On for tomorrow*, but that does not fit into our plans. We want the confirmation to be a physical thing that can be found by investigators with little effort. Besides, it's kind of fun to let him stew for a while.

It is almost nine p.m. when he finally leaves the dealership. Instead of heading home, he continues south, past downtown. When he reaches Lyons Lane, he turns right.

Oh, crap.

That's Bergen's neighborhood.

Sure enough, the dot on our tracking app weaves its way onto Dewer St.

I rush across the room, grab my jacket and helmet, and head toward the garage door. If I ignore the traffic laws, I should be able to get there on my motorcycle in four minutes. Hopefully I can reach the house before Chuckie gets inside. If not, things could get messy. I don't want messy.

As I reach for the door handle, Jar says, "Wait."

I move over to the table to see what's up.

The dot is passing by Bergen's house at a crawl. I expect it to stop, but it keeps going at the same speed, as if Chuckie is looking for a place to park. Which wouldn't make sense. We've been at the house several times now, and each time there was plenty of street parking.

The dot picks up speed. At the next intersection, it makes a U-turn and heads back toward Bergen's house. Now I think he will stop.

But no, he just drives past Bergen's place again. When he reaches the end of the block, he turns toward Central Avenue and cruises off at normal speed.

When we left Bergen's place, we turned off all the lights, wanting it to look like Bergen wasn't home. Thankfully, it looks like it worked.

We watch Chuckie's dot head north on Central, and then turn toward his house.

Four minutes later, the Mustang is parked in his garage.

We switch to the camera feed in the kitchen. Kate stands in front of the running microwave, shooting glances at the side door. The timer dings a moment before Chuckie opens the door, and she pulls out a plate full of food.

"Hi, honey," she says as he steps inside. "Dinner's ready whenever you are."

If he's noticed the family is not waiting for him at the dining table, he makes no mention of it. The only thing he says is, "I'm not hungry." He walks past her and heads straight to his office. After closing the door, he locks it.

"Was that my parents?"

Jar and I look up.

Evan is standing just inside the hallway. I don't know how long he's been there because we never heard him leave his room.

He steps into the living room. "That sounded like them. It was, wasn't it?"

Jar touches a button that turns her screen black, and I smile. There are only three ways I can deal with this: lie, reply with a half truth, or be completely honest.

In most situations, either of the first two would be the way to go. Maybe one of them would work on Evan, but I'll never know because my gut tells me to go with option three.

"Yes," I say. "Your father just arrived home from work."

I can feel Jar look at me in surprise.

Evan's brow furrows. "How did you hear that?"

"I'll tell you, if you really want to know. But I'd like to ask you a question first."

"What question?"

"What do you know about your father's activities when he's not home?"

"I don't know. Work stuff. Meetings. That kind of thing."

That's not exactly what I was going for, so I decide to be a little more direct. "Why did you and your friends visit the scene of that fire last Friday night?"

He blinks, caught off guard. "How did you—"

"Why, Evan? Was it just to check it out because you thought it would be cool?"

He shrugs, like maybe that's the answer.

"Or was it something more?"

He glances at me, and then away. My question hitting closer to the truth than he wants.

"All right," I say. "How did you even know about it? It wasn't in the paper or on the internet yet."

Another shrug. "I don't know. Someone heard about it, I guess."

"Who heard about it? Was it you?"

"I didn't hear anything."

Looks like we're playing semantics again, because it's obvious to me he'd known something ahead of time.

"You want to know how we can hear what's going on in your house?" I say. "Because we've bugged it."

"What?" he says, eyes widening.

"Should we talk about this first?" Jar whispers.

I shake my head and say to Evan, "We're investigating the Mercy Arsonist, trying to find out who he is."

It's very telling that Evan does not respond with *why would you need to bug our house for that?* Or *my family has nothing to do with that.* Instead he asks, "You're with the police?"

"I can't tell you that. But I can tell you that we're not with the *Mercy* police."

I'm leaning heavily into the implication that we are law enforcement. And he's buying it. I don't think it has anything to do with how convincing I sound, but rather because it's what he wants to believe.

"That's why you were at the Grand Canyon, isn't it? You were following my dad."

The truth would only muddy things, which is the perfect opportunity to redirect the conversation. "Tell me again—who heard about the fire?"

"I wasn't lying. I didn't hear anything, but..."

I wait.

"I...I think my father has something to do with it."

"Why do you think that?"

"It's nothing he's said or anything. It's, um, it's the way he acts. He gets all tense about a day before a fire. Drinks more sometimes, too."

"How long does that last?"

"A day or two. I didn't put it together at first. It probably wasn't until after the fourth or fifth one that I began to realize there was a pattern."

"Like last night," I say.

"There was another fire, wasn't there?"

"Yes."

"I thought so." He grimaces. "Last night was worse than usual. I think it's because it's only been a few days since the last one."

"And you knew about that one because of the way he'd been acting?"

"Yeah."

"Still doesn't explain how you knew where it was."

"My friend Owen. He has a police scanner. I told him there might be one, so he was listening when the cops were dispatched."

"And you went out there...?"

"To see if there was anything we could tie to my dad."

"Did you find anything?"

He shakes his head.

"Who knows you think it's your dad?"

"Just Owen and Luis and, um, Gina."

"Those were the ones with you."

A nod.

"How many fires have you been to?" I ask.

"The last three. Well, the three before last night's, I mean."

"If you find proof your father was involved, what would you do with it?"

"Report it. Get him arrested. But not by our cops. By someone like you."

Looks like he's totally bought our cover. Not sure why, but I'm feeling a little guilty about that.

"Is he involved?" Evan asks. "Do you have evidence against him?"

I should probably tell him it's better if he doesn't know. But he's lived without hope for so long that I can't do that to him.

"Yes," I say. "He's involved. We're still collecting evidence, but we should have everything wrapped up by tomorrow night."

"Seriously?" he asks, a glimmer of hope in his eyes.

"*Should* have it wrapped up. Something could always happen that might draw the investigation out a little longer."

"But he's going to be arrested, right?"

I so want to say, *Absolutely*, but I can't. No outcome is ever guaranteed, no matter how much I believe that's what will happen. I settle for giving him a look that conveys my confidence without verbalizing it.

"I want to help," he blurts out. "What can I do?"

"You've already done more than enough by getting Sawyer out of the way." This is not the answer he wants to hear, so I add, "But there might be something we could use your assistance on later. No promises, but if we do, we'll let you know."

"Okay. Great. I'll do anything."

It's both heartening that he wants to help give his brother and mother a better life, and heart-wrenching that to do so means turning against his father. But those are the cards he's been dealt, and I'm just happy he's choosing to fight for what's right.

"The best thing you can do right now is to keep an eye on your brother," I say, "and make sure you both stay out of sight."

We get his assurances before he asks a few more questions, to which I give him only vague answers, making it clear there are a lot of things I'm not allowed to discuss. Of course, I don't mention that the person not allowing me to talk is myself.

As he heads back to the bedroom, I get the feeling this will be the best night of sleep he's had in a long time.

It's now up to us to make sure it's the first of many.

CHAPTER TWENTY-SIX

By 11:17 p.m., I'm back at the Hayden Valley farm formerly owned by the Whittaker family.

The rain has finally stopped, and the night sky has begun to emerge through the growing gaps between the clouds.

Everything is muddy, which is why I've brought along a second pair of shoes to put on before entering each of the buildings. Most of the work I do is in the basement of the house, but I also make stops in the workshop and the barn.

It takes me until just after midnight before everything is the way we want it. For the two outbuildings, this basically means locking the entrances Bergen left open.

For the basement of the house? Well, that's another matter entirely.

I hike across the field to where I left my motorcycle and ride back to Mercy.

My next stop is Price Motors.

I park a couple of blocks away and don the baseball cap from my backpack, making sure the brim is low. It's a Colorado Rockies hat, just like the one Bergen has. I could have used his, but that seemed unsanitary. Besides, the mini-mart I stopped at for drinks when I picked up the pizzas had plenty of them. I *am* wearing Bergen's jacket. I'm taller and broader than he is, but the jacket was big on him and fits me almost perfectly.

Mimicking his visit on Monday night, I make my way to the dealership. I even stop on the sidewalk in front of the lot and look at the building like he did, before stepping onto the property and approaching the showroom's side door.

From my pocket, I withdraw a Mercy Cares donation postcard. On the question side, there are two marks next to 5-6 PM, one beside the checkbox for Thursday, and a final dot between the words *earned* and *will—w* for Whittaker.

Keeping my head tilted down so the security camera won't see my face, I slip the postcard through the slot and leave the same way I came.

Though I know my disguise won't stand up to intense scrutiny—Bergen's and my size difference being the main problem—I don't think it'll be an issue. If Chuckie checks the security camera, he'll see exactly what he expects: Bergen delivering the postcard and leaving. It'll be the yellow piece of paper that is of interest to him, not the courier.

Jar's and my larger concern when we were planning was that Chuckie would be at the dealership waiting for Bergen, since he's been unable to contact him. But Evan's dad is in his office at home. My guess is that as much as he wants to be here, he knows he and Bergen should not be at the same place at the same time in the middle of the night.

Guess what? Chuckie *has* been checking his security footage. As soon as I'm on my motorcycle, heading to the duplex, Jar tells me he just accessed the camera system and is now heading to his car.

I don't want him to pass by me, so I take side streets all the way back.

When I walk into the duplex, Jar looks up from her computer and says, "He is almost there."

As interested as I am in watching what's about to happen, I'm a bit distracted by the fact Evan is sitting beside her, looking at her screen. And by *a bit*, I mean completely.

"Uhhhh," I say.

Jar looks at me, confused, then follows my gaze to Evan and scoffs. "You already told him everything. What is the big deal?"

I give her a look meant to convey it *is* a big deal, but she ignores it and says, "Hurry up. He's parking now."

I strip off my jacket and join her and Evan. I frown at him, which he returns with a sheepish grin before we both look at the screen.

Chuckie parks on the lot and enters the building through a side door. Jar switches between interior cameras, following him all the way to the showroom, where he stops and looks around.

"Anyone here?" he shouts.

He waits several seconds, and then slinks over to the yellow postcard and picks it up. Unlike last time, he doesn't take it to his office to read. When he's seen all he needs to, he takes a deep breath, relieved to know the Whittaker fire is set for Thursday night.

He heads back to his car and drives off. Jar switches to the tracking app to make sure he goes home.

"Shouldn't you be asleep?" I say to Evan.

"I wasn't tired."

I look from him to Jar and back. "You can never tell anyone you saw this. I mean anyone. Police, FBI, whoever. As far as you know, you weren't aware that anything was going on. And you absolutely can never mention us."

"Don't they know about you already?" he asks. "I mean, you're the ones doing the investigation."

"Do you know what a black ops mission is?"

"Um, it's a military thing, isn't it?"

"It can be, but not always. It's a secret mission. So secret that the agency who initiates it will deny its existence. Think of our investigation kind of like that. We're going to make it easy for the usual authorities, but they'll never know we had our hand in it."

"You mean you're not law enforcement?"

"We're on a whole other level than your normal law enforcement."

"I can keep my mouth shut, if that's what you mean."

He's responded to my nonanswer with a nonanswer of his own. Have I told you how much I like this kid?

"Yes," I tell him. "That's exactly what I mean. So, will you?"

"Yeah, of course. No one will ever know."

It's the best I can hope for.

"Now might be a good time for you to go to bed," I suggest.

"Oh, uh, sure."

It's good he's choosing to not press his luck by trying to stick around. Smart move.

"Good night," he says as he gets out of his chair. "And-and thank you again for helping me and my brother. I..." Whatever else he was going to say, he decides to keep it to himself and just gives us a nod and heads toward the back.

Once we hear the bedroom door close, I walk to the hallway to make sure he actually went inside the room. He did. But who knows? He might have his ear pressed against the door, hoping to overhear our conversation. I know I would in his position.

I return to Jar and say in a low voice, "Remind me about the part of the plan where we show Evan everything."

"I did not change the plan. You did."

Okay, technically she's right, but—

"I told him a few things to keep him satisfied," I say. "That's it. I didn't show him all that." I wave at her computer.

She grimaces. "I did not do it on purpose. I went into the kitchen to get some water. When I returned, he was at the table, looking at my screen. He is very quiet."

She's right about that. So right that I shoot a glance at the hallway, half expecting to see Evan lurking there.

"I thought it would be better to share with him some of what we're doing than to tell him to forget what he saw and return to his room," she adds.

Given the circumstances, it was the right call. Doesn't mean I'm any happier about it.

"We need to put a cowbell on that kid," I say.

"What is a cowbell?"

"It's a bell you put on a cow. You know, so you can hear where she is."

"Huh," she says. "Then we definitely need a cowbell."

"You mean we need *more* cow—you know what? Never mind."

She stares at me like I'm crazy, then looks at her computer. "Chuckie is home."

That's good news. The last thing we need is Chuckie wandering around Mercy. Especially since we have one more task to take care of tonight.

———

Jar and I put the still unconscious Bergen into the bed of our truck, which is backed into his open garage. I've moved his Accord a block away.

After we make sure his house looks like it normally would, we take him to the Travato, where we tie him to the bed in back.

Jar installs one of our remaining video bugs so we'll be able to remotely monitor him, and we head back to town.

The last item we need to deal with is Bergen's car. I want

things to look like he's not home in case Chuckie comes back, which means the Honda needs to be moved out of the immediate area. What I'd really like to do is move it out of town, but that's not an option.

"We really need to talk about getting you driving lessons," I say.

"I already know how to drive."

"A motor scooter, not a car."

"I have watched you. It does not look difficult."

I laugh. That's not a theory I'm willing to test tonight.

"I'll be right back," I say.

I've parked the truck several blocks away, on a street with a couple of auto repair shops and a construction supply outlet. It's the perfect place to hide Bergen's Accord. The walk back to his car takes me about six minutes, and the return drive less than one. I leave the vehicle in a spot in front of the supply company. By the time someone notices the car has been there for a while, it won't matter anymore.

I hop back into the truck and we head home to get some rest.

Tomorrow, after all, is going to be a big day.

CHAPTER TWENTY-SEVEN

The destruction of Charles Price begins on Friday at 9:04 a.m., with me on the phone.

My call is answered after the second ring. "Mercy Driving Range. This is Travis."

"Travis Murphy?" I say. Yes, I'm using the modulator. This time my tone is pitched a little higher and older, like someone in his sixties.

"That's me."

"Mr. Murphy, this is Anthony Ruiz. I'm a nurse at St. Mary-Corwin Medical Center in Pueblo."

"How can I help you, Mr. Ruiz?" The chipper tone in Travis's voice has slipped into something more subdued.

"I'm calling about Paul Bergen. I understand he's an employee of yours."

"He is. But he's not here right now. I'm expecting him at any—"

"Mr. Bergen won't be coming in today. He was involved in a car accident early this morning and was admitted here."

"My God. Is he all right?"

"Nothing life threatening, but he'll need to stay with us for another night or two. He was worried about work, so I told him I'd call you and explain the situation."

"I appreciate that. Let him know not to worry, and I'll get someone to cover his shifts. Tell him to concentrate on getting better."

"I'll do that. Thank you, Mr. Murphy."

I hang up.

At 9:17 a.m., Jar finishes reviewing footage taken that morning from our various bugs. Thanks to the postcard confirmation I left for Chuckie last night, he's much more relaxed this morning. Which is why it's the first time he realizes his sons aren't around.

"A school project," Kate says, playing it off as nothing important. "I sent Evan along to keep an eye on him, you know, just in case Sawyer...." She lets it hang.

"Whose house?" Chuckie asks.

"The Campbells'."

Frowning, Chuckie says, "I don't know any Campbells."

"They moved here last fall. Nice family. They go to the Methodist church over on Lincoln."

She's really good at this, which makes me think she's been weaving stories for years to keep the peace.

"What's the husband do?" Chuckie asks.

"Engineering, or something like that. Works for the county, I think."

I stare at the screen, looking for any signs Chuckie will explode about not having personally given the okay for his sons to be away. There's a moment or two when I think it could go in either direction, but he keeps his cool and only says, "Does he need a new car?"

"I don't know, but I can ask."

He grunts and returns his attention to his breakfast.

I'm pretty sure if there wasn't a fire scheduled for tonight, he'd be more interested in Evan and Sawyer's whereabouts, but he has a lot on his plate right now. In fact, I wouldn't be surprised if he's thinking it's a good thing they're not around to bother him.

Jar shows me two more sets of clips. The first is from 7:09 a.m., when Chuckie arrives at work. Like he did on the morning after he received the last postcard, he makes another trip to the donut shop. Though we don't have a shot of him getting rid of the card, I'm sure it's been ripped and dumped into a receptacle along the way, likely the same dumpster as before.

The second set of clips starts at 7:43 a.m., shortly after he returns with the donuts.

He's in his office, door locked. On the screen of his computer is the website for his bank. I watch as he initiates a transfer of thirty-five thousand dollars to an account at another institution.

"Let me guess," I say. "To RS Shepherd?" That's the shell company owned by Nicholas Huston.

"Correct," Jar says.

Thirty-five thousand dollars brings the total Chuckie has sent Huston to exactly five hundred grand. A nice round number.

When the clip ends, I tell Jar I'll be right back and head out to my motorcycle.

As I suspected, Chuckie has no imagination. The torn postcard is right where I predicted it would be. I put it in my pocket, pick up a dozen donuts at the shop around the corner, and head back.

It's 1:53 p.m., and we have a logistical problem we have not been able to solve.

That's not quite accurate.

Jar *did* suggest something that would work, but it's not a solution I want to use. Unfortunately, we're getting closer and closer to go time and I have yet to come up with anything better.

I swear under my breath.

"You are getting worked up over nothing," Jar says. "It will be fine."

I close my eyes, hoping another solution will suddenly pop into my head. When it doesn't, I say, "Fine. Let's talk to him."

Jar retrieves Evan from the back bedroom.

"What's up?" he asks.

I get out of my chair and motion for him to take a seat. "We may need your help."

His eyes light up. "Yes. Of course. Whatever you need."

"Do you drive?"

"No. Not yet."

"*Can* you drive?"

"I've tried. Once."

That's what I was afraid of.

He sees the disappointment on my face and says, "I have friends that do."

I already don't want to involve Evan. Bringing one of his friends in, too, seems more than a step too far.

I'm about to say as much when Jar jumps in and asks, "Do you have a friend who drives, whom you trust?"

He smiles. "I do. She's very trustworthy."

I look at Jar, as if she's crazy for asking him that question.

She looks at me and says, "There. Problem solved."

Twenty minutes later, Bergen shows signs of waking.

"We shouldn't be much more than an hour," I tell Evan. "Sit tight and don't talk to anyone."

He gives me a thumbs-up like we're members of a team.

Which in a way we are, I guess.

By the time Jar and I arrive at the Travato and climb in—ski masks *and* face masks firmly in place—Bergen's eyes are wide open, though he still looks loopy from the drugs.

As I approach the bed, he stares at me with the same fear as yesterday.

"Please," he croaks. "I need water."

I grab a bottle from the cabinet, drop it on the bed, and untie his hand.

He starts chugging the water bottle, a good portion of it missing his mouth and drenching his shirt.

While I was dealing with his water situation, Jar retrieved one of our camp stools from storage and brought it inside. She passes it to me now, and I place it by the end of the bed and sit.

I lock my gaze on Bergen's and hold my hand above my shoulder. Jar puts one of our dart guns in it, causing Bergen to suck in a breath.

"No, no, no, no. Please. Not again."

Jar pulls out her laptop and sets it on the counter. A few seconds later, our computerized voice says, "We trust you slept well."

"You guys can let me go now. I swear, I won't light any more fires."

We figured he might say something like this, so it takes Jar only a few seconds to adjust one of the responses we wrote and play it. "There will be no letting you go. You have committed crimes that you will need to answer for."

"No, please. They're never going to let me out."

This time, no extra typing is needed. "You should have thought about that before agreeing to help Charles Price."

"I didn't have a choice!"

A few keystrokes and our voice says, "You did, and you still do."

"What do you mean?"

"You can choose to do nothing and face the full consequences, or you can do something that may put you in a favorable light."

He blinks at this last part. "Like what?"

"This is from last night."

I hold up my phone and play a montage of our conversation with him at his house.

When it finishes, Jar plays another prewritten bit. "The authorities will likely be more lenient if your confession does not sound like it is being forced out of you. We can give them this, or you can rerecord, telling everything you know."

"That-that's it?"

Jar types again. "No. It is not."

"What else will I have to do?"

She plays him the other requirement, and the color drains from his face.

We may not be offering him the lifeline he wants, but it is one I'm positive he will accept.

We arrive back at the duplex at 3:38 p.m.

Bergen is still in the Travato, once more fully restrained. He is also unconscious again, though the amount of Beta-Somnol we gave him will keep him under for only a few hours. That's because he chose to do the right thing. If he didn't, he'd have received another full dose.

I pull the truck all the way into our garage this time. It doesn't quite fit, but it'll do.

"You got everything?" I ask Evan.

"We didn't bring much."

Sawyer is beside him, clutching Terry the Tiger to his chest. "Thank you very much for letting us stay here," he says. From the rhythm, I get the sense he practiced the words with his brother.

"You're very welcome," I say.

"And thank you for letting us use your computer to watch movies."

From the surprise on Evan's face, I'm guessing that part wasn't something they worked on.

"I'm glad you enjoyed them."

Sawyer turns to Jar. He's almost as tall as she is. "Thank you."

She nods. "The world might not always be easy, but you will figure it out. I believe in you."

He smiles at this. It's not much, but is more than we've seen.

"Let's get going," I say.

I enter the garage first and stand at the back end of the truck's cab, in the narrow walkway I've left between the vehicle and the wall. This prevents anyone outside from seeing Evan and Sawyer exit the house and climb into the backseat of the crew cab. Once their door is closed, I go around to the driver's door and get behind the wheel.

From the living room doorway, Jar watches us back out, and then activates the roll-down door once we're out of the way. There's no reason for both of us to go on this trip.

I drop off Evan and Sawyer three blocks from their house, in a parking area behind a closed florist shop, out of sight of the street.

"I'll let you know when I'm out," Evan says from the open doorway.

"If it becomes a problem, don't push it," I say. "We'll figure something else out."

"Don't worry. It won't be a problem."

He shuts the door, takes his brother's hand, and walks away.

I make it back to the duplex before the boys reach their house, so I'm able to watch with Jar in real time when they step inside.

Kate has been lying down in the master bedroom, but at the sound of the door, she hurries to the stairs. When she sees her boys standing in the foyer, she runs down to them.

There are hugs and tears from Mom, after which she looks them over, as if expecting them to be hurt more than they were by their father.

"We're fine," Evan says. "Don't worry."

"Where...where were you?" she asks.

"Mom, I told you. Someplace safe."

"We were with Evan's friends," Sawyer says. "They were very nice."

"I'm glad to hear that, honey."

"They let us watch movies on their computer."

"Oh?" Kate looks at Evan, concerned.

"Disney movies," Evan says.

"Okay," she says. "Good."

"I need to change clothes," Sawyer says. "I wore these clothes yesterday." I'm happy he's changed the subject. I was worried he'd give away more about us.

"Oh, honey, of course. Do you want to take a shower first?"

"It's not shower time."

"Right. It's not, is it? Go up and put something else on, then.

We'll do the shower later." She looks at Evan. "What about you?"

"I could use a change, too."

"And...are you okay?"

"I'm fine, Mom. Don't worry."

He follows his brother upstairs, but it's not long before he returns. He's dressed in dark clothes now like I suggested, a long-sleeve black T-shirt and indigo jeans. When he grabs his jacket off the hook by the door, Kate comes out from the kitchen.

"Where do you think you're going?"

"I need to take care of something."

"No. You need to stay here. You're grounded, remember?"

He sighs and shakes his head. "I've just spent two days taking care of Sawyer, making sure he's safe. I need a little time for myself, that's all."

We were sure she'd try to keep him home, so I helped Evan work out an excuse that would hopefully get her to relent. What he just said is not what we prepared. It's better. You can see its effect in how she looks ashamed. But instead of giving him the okay, she says, "Your father will expect you to be here. If he comes home and you're not—"

"I promise you—I'll be home before he is." Evan Price, king of semantics. He knows if all goes well, his father is never coming home.

His mother looks less than convinced by his words.

"I promise," he says. "If he gets here first, you can ground me for the entire summer."

She frowns. "Where are you going?"

"No place special."

She studies him and finally nods. "All right."

He smiles and starts pulling on his jacket.

"You'd better keep your word," she says.

"I will."

She hugs him and he heads out the door.

Ten minutes later, my phone rings.

"I'm out," Evan says.

"Good. And your friend?"

"She just picked me up."

"Last chance to back out."

"No way."

"Okay, then it's time to get into position."

"Roger. We're on our way."

"You don't have to do that. We're using a phone. And besides, we never say *roger*."

"Oh, then what do you say?"

"If we're on a radio, we say *copy*. But we're on a phone so we say *got it* or *okay*."

"Right. Sorry. I mean, got it."

"Evan, be careful."

He pauses before saying, "Okay."

CHAPTER TWENTY-EIGHT

I park the truck on the road that runs three hundred meters behind the Whittaker farm, and Jar and I walk in from there. The barn and the workshop have not been disturbed, the tells I put on their doors all still in place.

At the house, we bypass Bergen's jimmied window, pick the lock on the kitchen door, and enter.

I check my watch—4:57 p.m.

It's time.

I call Evan first, make sure he's where he needs to be, and tell him to be ready. Next, I place a call to Price Motors.

On Jar's computer is the video feed from one of our cameras in Chuckie's office. He's at his desk, going through a stack of papers.

"Price Motors, where you'll always get the best price. How may I direct your call?" The woman who answers is young and perky.

"Charles Price, please," I say. I'm using the same setting on my voice modulator as I did when I talked to Travis Murphy at the driving range.

"May I tell him who's calling?"

"Dr. Anthony Ruiz."

"One moment."

The phone rings in Chuckie's office. He reaches over, touches a button, and says, "Yes?"

From the speaker, the same voice that answered my call says, "I have an Anthony Ruiz on the line for you."

Chuckie pauses, trying to place the name. "What does he want?"

"He didn't say. Would you like me to ask him?"

"Yeah, that would be a good idea," he says, as if she should have already done so.

Chuckie's put on hold and I'm taken off.

"Mr. Ruiz, may I tell Mr. Price what this is regarding?" the receptionist asks.

"It's about a friend of his. Paul Bergen."

"Thank you. Please hold."

Chuckie and I flip phone statuses again.

"Mr. Price? He says it's about someone named Paul Bergen."

Chuckie snaps up his receiver to take the call off speaker. "Put him through."

Jar mutes her computer to prevent us from accidentally creating a feedback loop as the receptionist comes back on my line. "Putting you through now. Have a nice day."

A click, and then the line rings. On Jar's screen, Chuckie stabs at a button.

"This is Charles Price. How can I help you?" His calm voice does not match how tense he looks.

"Mr. Price, I'm calling on behalf of Paul Bergen. I understand he's a friend of yours."

Chuckie winces. "I would say more of an acquaintance. Why would he want you to call me?"

"I'm a nurse at St. Mary-Corwin Medical Center. Mr. Bergen was in an accident early this morning."

"Accident? Where?"

Interesting that this is what he asks first. I would have gone with *Is he okay?*

"Just east of Pueblo."

"What was he doing in Pueblo?"

"Um, well, it's my understanding that he had been planning on visiting his mother this morning."

"How is he?" Ah, finally. Some fake humanity.

"He was pretty banged up, but he should make a full recovery. Unfortunately, he'll be in the hospital for a few more days."

"What?" The full reality of what that means seems to have just hit him.

"He asked that I let you know that. He also wanted me to say he's sorry he can't be there but that everything you asked for is ready. I don't know what he meant by that but I assume you do."

Chuckie says nothing for a few seconds. On the camera feed, his free hand is now on his forehead, his eyes wide and staring at the phone. "I'd like to talk to him. Can you put me through?"

"I'm sorry but that won't be possible at the moment."

"It's important."

"That may be, but Mr. Bergen is resting and likely won't wake again until morning."

"I just need a couple minutes, that's all."

"I'm sorry, Mr. Price. The answer is still no."

"Shit."

The word was whispered, not meant for Dr. Ruiz to hear, so I pretend I didn't and say, "I'll let him know I contacted you, and if he's up to it, you can speak with him tomorrow. Have a good evening."

As soon as I hang up, Jar unmutes her computer.

Chuckie blindly sets the receiver down, his gaze fixed across the room. There is a chance he'll try calling the hospital back. If he uses the number programmed as my caller ID, the call would come back to us. But if he tries to do an end run around Dr. Ruiz and use the hospital's main number, we'll be forced to implement more advanced methods to get his call rerouted to my phone.

When he finally looks away from the wall, his first action is to look at his watch. It's eleven minutes after five. If the evening were to proceed as he expected, somewhere in the next hour and a half Bergen would be on his way to the old Whittaker farm, and before seven p.m. the buildings would be on fire.

Panic returns to his face. There's no way to know for sure, but I'm guessing he's thinking about Nicholas Huston's visit the previous evening, and the man telling him that the fire *will happen* tonight.

His eyes narrow. I'm guessing he just remembered something that I, as Ruiz, said. *Everything you asked for is ready*.

We are at the crossroads.

How Chuckie reacts now will determine the rest of the evening.

He sits there for nearly a minute, before huffing out a breath and picking up the phone again. But before the receiver is halfway to his ear, he pauses. I can all but see the gears in his head spin. No doubt he's playing out scenarios, in hopes of finding the one that will make everything right.

He blinks, then instead of raising the phone the rest of the way, he sets it back in its cradle. The panic and fear of moments ago have been replaced by a look of determination and, if I'm not mistaken, hope.

He stands, pulls on his suit jacket, and exits his office.

He's made his choice of which path to take. What that choice is, we will know soon enough.

While Jar follows him through the dealership via our cameras, I call Evan.

"I think it's time," I tell him. "Stay alert."

"Got it," he says.

Instead of hanging up, I put him on hold.

Chuckie has entered the service garage and is behind the counter, talking to one of the mechanics.

"Do you have the work order for the Garrisons' Explorer?" Chuckie asks. "It was in yesterday."

"It should be in the office. Is there a problem?"

"They just had a question so I wanted to see the details before I called them back."

"I'll go get it."

"Thanks."

As soon as the mechanic leaves, Chuckie looks under the counter and reaches into the space. When he pulls his hand back out, he's holding a wad of baby blue disposable rubber gloves, which he stuffs into his pocket.

"He's going for it," I say to Jar.

Her response is a noncommittal *mmmm*.

That's fine. I know I'm right.

When the mechanic returns, Chuckie takes the plastic folder the man has brought back and returns to the main part of the building. After dropping off the folder in his office, Chuckie goes into a room we don't have a camera in, and comes back out a minute later holding a key ring with a single key on it.

As he makes his way across the showroom to the exit, I take Evan off hold. "He's going outside now."

On our camera feed, Chuckie passes through the door. And on my phone, Evan says, "We see him. He's walking toward the used cars area."

That makes sense. Chuckie might not be the smartest person in the world, but he's far from being the stupidest. If he's doing what I think he's doing, he'll want to keep a low profile. Driving around in an orange Mustang is not the way to do that.

Several seconds pass before Evan says, "He's getting into a car."

"What kind?"

"The four-door kind."

"You mean a sedan."

"Yeah, I guess."

"I need you to give me a little more than that. Is it a Honda? A Chevy? A Ford?"

"I have no idea. I don't know cars."

"Your dad owns a *car dealership*."

"Yeah. Exactly."

I hear a muffled female voice.

"Gina says it's a Volkswagen Jetta," Evan relays.

"What color?" I ask.

"Dark blue...he's pulling onto Central now, turning left." Left would be north.

"Don't get too close, but don't lose him, either."

"We won't."

We can vicariously track Chuckie's progress via a bug I gave Evan that he put in his pocket. The dot progresses north one block, then two, then three.

Right after Evan and Gina pass the fourth intersection, Evan says, "He's turning right onto Sanford Drive."

And that would be east.

I allow myself a small smile. Mercy has only two bridges over the river. Sanford Drive leads to one. There's no question now. Chuckie has taken our bait.

"I'm going to mute our end," I tell Evan, "but stay on the line and give us updates."

"Okay."

"And don't get too close."

"You already said that."

I tap the MUTE button.

Jar hands me the drone, which I take out the kitchen door and set on the ground, on the side of the house opposite the main road. We don't need it yet but it's ready to go when we do.

Back inside, Jar and I pick up our things and head downstairs to the basement. While most of the cellar is a single open space, two rooms have been carved out at the far end, a bathroom in one corner and a separate storage area in the other. The latter is only about two meters square and lined with empty shelves. We've set up two camping stools inside. Jar and I each take a seat.

The two cars pass over the river and into the countryside. Evan gives us updates every half mile. Right before they reach the six-and-a-half-mile mark from Mercy, he says, "He's turning left."

That puts Chuckie only three-quarters of a mile away.

I unmute the phone. "Okay, Evan. We've got it from here. Head back to town. We'll let you know when it's over."

"That's it?" he asks, disappointed.

"You did exactly what we needed you to do. Now let us do our job."

"Are you sure you don't want us to hang around, just in case?"

"Not necessary. You've done great. Head on back."

A pause. "Okay. Um, well, then good luck."

"Thanks." I hang up.

While he and I were talking, Jar switched her screen from the tracking map to the feed from the one camera we could spare to put on the route to the Whittaker farm. About a hundred meters away, coming toward the lens, is Chuckie's blue VW.

"Be right back," I say.

I step through the doorway into the gloom of the main basement and shine a flashlight beam through the space.

The floor has been swept clean to eliminate any signs that we're here. If we were going up against a professional from our world, doing so would be a mistake, as the person would notice the absence of dust right away.

Even on a good day, I doubt Chuckie would make the connection, and today is not a good day for him. His plans have been upended, and he's undertaking a task he has no desire to be doing. If his blood pressure isn't skyrocketing, I'd be shocked. Better for him to see a clean floor than one with a shoe print we might have missed.

I walk through the space, making sure we haven't forgotten anything. As I near the other end, I feel Liz materialize beside me. She's tense. Jumpy, even. Liz does not—I mean, *did* not—hate many things. But right near the top of that short list were men like Chuckie—abusers who lay waste to those around them. She will not relax until she knows we are successful.

"He's almost here," Jar calls from the small storeroom.

"We've got this," I whisper to Liz, then retrace my steps through the cellar.

In my absence, Jar has launched the drone. Its camera is pointing west down the main road. The VW is about two hundred and fifty meters away, still heading toward us. The drone's camera tracks it as it draws nearer and nearer.

When the sedan is about thirty meters from the driveway, it slows.

I'll be shocked if Chuckie drives directly up to the house, but as we've come to learn, he doesn't always make the best choices. The VW continues rolling forward. When it reaches the driveway, it keeps going straight.

He must be checking to make sure there's no one here.

Another couple dozen meters down the road, the car picks up speed again. Chuckie drives about half a kilometer down the road and then makes a U-turn, where I'm sure he thinks he's out of sight. But our drone sees it all.

When he drives past the farm a second time, he slows again, though not as much as before. He goes down to the end of the large field west of our location and turns onto a service road, which he follows down to a spot where bushes grow about a meter and a half high on each shoulder. The foliage isn't enough to completely hide his vehicle, but it'll probably keep anyone at ground level from noticing it.

Several minutes pass without him getting out of the car. I'd think our screen has frozen if not for the fact a light breeze is gently blowing through the brush.

He's just sitting there, likely contemplating whether to get out or drive away. He's at his personal point of no return.

I feel Liz hovering behind us.

Another minute passes with nothing happening. Then another.

Then—

The driver's door cracks open.

CHAPTER TWENTY-NINE

Chuckie keeps to the back of the field, near a line of trees. Now that he's made the decision to actually get out, he walks quickly, likely hoping to get the task over with as soon as possible.

When he reaches the plot of land where the structures are located, he heads to the barn. The building has five entrances—big ones at the north and south ends, and smaller ones on the east and west sides, with the last having two.

Chuckie makes his way around the barn, checking each door, and is clearly surprised to find them all locked. He moves to the workshop and is stymied again.

When he looks to the house like he's wondering if Bergen lied about everything being ready, I fear I may have made a mistake by locking everything else on the property, and that after finding the other two buildings inaccessible, he'll leave.

He eyes the farmhouse for a good minute before he begins moving again.

Toward us.

I step over to the storage room door and put a two-by-four under the handle that will jam the door if he tries to open it.

When I return to Jar, Chuckie has just about reached the house.

In addition to the drone, we have two cameras set up outside the house. The sole purpose of these is to get shots of him casing the place. The remainder of our cameras are set up in the basement, to provide us—if all goes well—with footage that will be the proverbial nail in Chuckie's coffin.

Chuckie works his way around the house, trying doors and windows until he comes to the basement window we left unlocked.

When it slides up, some of the tension in his face fades.

As you might remember, Chuckie is a big man, and getting through the window is not exactly easy. The worst part is when his belly reaches the frame. He has to suck in a breath and tuck his gut over the sill to get it past.

Once he's in the cellar, he scans the room, using his phone's flashlight. From the irritation on his face, I'm wondering if he expected to see Bergen's arson materials sitting in the middle of the space, waiting for him. He hunts around and soon discovers the built-in cabinet.

When he opens it and sees Bergen's supplies, he lets out a triumphant *yes!*

He pulls out one of the bottles, opens it, and gives the contents a whiff. He jerks his head away, his face souring at the odor of the lighter fluid. As entertaining as his reaction is, we'll probably leave that bit of video out of our evidence package. It'll be better if he appears to already know what was here before he arrived.

He spends a little time examining the wooden ignition device, trying to figure out how it works. It's really not that complicated, but when he puts it down with a grimace, I have a feeling he still doesn't understand it.

What he does next is...nothing.

His gaze is on the items of the arson kit, but otherwise he doesn't move. Apparently, he's caught in another one of his mind loops.

There's one more thing we'd like him to do. It won't be the end of the world if he doesn't, but it would be a nice cherry on top of the other evidence we've collected. I pick up my dart gun, double-check that there's a dart in the chamber, and look back at Jar's laptop.

Chuckie continues to stare into the distance, his body rooted in place.

Come on, Chuckie. Snap out of it. It's what you've come here to do. Don't screw it up now.

Finally he moves, putting a hand on the cabinet door. He leans forward, pulls out everything, and sets it all on a nearby shelf. Once the cabinet is empty, he picks up one of the bottles and opens the top.

Looks like we'll get that bonus footage after all.

He begins squirting liquid on the shelves and walls.

Don't worry. I'm not letting him soak the place in lighter fluid. That would be stupid. Though there *is* lighter fluid in the bottles, most has been replaced by water. So it smells like lighter fluid but won't catch on fire. I also coated the bottom of the caps and the spouts of all the bottles with a healthy layer of undiluted fluid to boost the smell.

He finishes the first bottle and opens the next. We plan on letting him get through three of the five bottles before we put a stop to things. That should be more than enough to show intent.

He's only halfway through the second bottle when he suddenly stops and cocks his head to the side.

He's heard something, but I have no idea what because I haven't heard a thing. I look at Jar, but she shrugs and shakes her head.

Chuckie moves over to the base of the stairs and points an ear toward the door at the top. Is someone in the house?

I listen, too, but again I hear nothing.

Seconds later, Chuckie takes a step back from the stairs, no longer looking concerned, and resumes dousing the room.

Perhaps he just heard the wind or an animal. Whatever the case, I make an executive decision to revise our plan and pull down my ski mask. When he finishes the bottle he's holding, I'll step out and tag him with a dart.

The liquid is starting to sputter out the end of the bottle, which means it's almost empty. I quietly remove the two-by-four from the door, and glance back at the computer to see Chuckie walking toward the remaining supplies.

On the screen something dark rushes up to the window. Before I can adjust my gaze, a voice yells, "It's true!"

Chuckie's head jerks to his right as Evan drops through the open window.

Jar and I had stopped looking at the outside camera and were focused on Chuckie. Evan wasn't supposed to be anywhere near here.

"You're the one responsible for all the fires," Evan says, snarling.

Chuckie's anger flares. "What the hell are you doing here?"

I yank open the door and rush into the room just as Evan says, "I'm here to make sure you go to jail and never get out!"

Evan is between me and Chuckie, with Chuckie striding toward him.

I adjust my aim to avoid hitting Evan and pull the trigger. The dart would have hit Chuckie if the big man didn't swing a hand at his son. Instead, the dart skims across Chuckie's back, missing him by centimeters.

Evan has jerked backward, and it's enough for Chuckie's

hand to miss his face, but not enough to get out of the way of the elbow that follows.

Evan flies into the shelves where Chuckie set Bergen's supplies. The bottles and rags and igniter tumble onto the floor, while Evan falls in a heap near his father's feet.

From the window, where she's apparently been watching the whole thing, Gina yells, "Evan!"

Chuckie whirls around as she starts to climb in. Before he can take a step toward her, I break my no-talking-to-our-targets rule and yell, "Hey, Chuckie! Over here."

He twists toward me as I pull my trigger again. There's just enough time for his anger to turn into confusion before my dart hits him in the gut.

He looks down in surprise, grabs the dart, and pulls it out. Unfortunately for him, it's designed to inject its contents on impact so the damage has already been done.

He takes one staggering step toward me and falls to the ground.

Gina lets go of the window ledge, and when her feet hit the floor, she races past Chuckie to where Evan lies.

As I start to follow her, I hear a crackling sound, and smell an odor I definitely do *not* want to be smelling right now.

On the other side of the shelving unit Evan smashed into, flames are licking up the side. The igniter. It must have sparked when it hit the ground and set the rags on fire. The liquid Chuckie was spraying around isn't flammable, but the dry wood down here is very much so, and I can see flames rising from some of the shelves.

"Jar!" I yell as I rush over to Evan and Gina. "We've got to get out of here."

Gina looks at me in surprise, a man in a ski mask clearly not what she was expecting.

"I'm Evan's friend," I say as I crouch beside them. I look at

Evan. His eyes are open, but he's having a hard time breathing. "Hey. You're okay. You've just had the wind knocked out of you." He also has the beginnings of a nice bruise on his cheek, but that's not the info he needs right now. "Here, let me help you sit up." I put an arm around him and shift him to an upright position. "Deep breaths. Push your stomach out as you breathe in, and tug it in as you breathe out. That'll help."

He does as I suggested, not so successfully at first but that can take a little time.

I glance at the fire. It's only a few feet away and expanding.

"We need to get out of here. I'm going to stand you up, all right?"

Evan lets out a breath, nods, and sucks in air for a longer period than he did before.

I put an arm around his back and drape his arm over my shoulders. Gina does the same on the other side, and we lift him to his feet.

"I've got him," I say to Gina. "Climb out the window. We'll be right behind you."

She hesitates.

"Go," Evan ekes out. "I'll be okay."

She runs over to the window, where Jar—wearing her ski mask—is waiting with our backpacks.

"Can you walk?" I ask Evan.

"I-I think so."

I let him take most of his weight, but I hold on to him just in case.

By the time we get to the window, Gina is already outside.

"I'll lift you out," I tell Evan.

I grab him by the waist and hoist him up. I'm sure it hurts him but he makes no complaints. He grabs the frame and, with Gina's help, pulls himself outside.

"You're next," I say to Jar.

She glances over at Chuckie. "What about him?"

"I'll get him."

She narrows her eyes. "Maybe we should leave him."

I can't tell you how tempting that is. It would be so easy. But as poetic as it may be to rid the world of Chuckie this way, we both know we're not going to do that. Have we taken lives in our line of work? Sure. But only when there was no other choice.

I wonder if Chuckie will think our saving him is a mercy after the courts are finished with him.

I make a cradle with my hands and lift Jar to the window. After she's outside, I pass out our backpacks and turn back to Chuckie.

Most of the bookcase is on fire now, and the flames are flicking against the ceiling. Smoke is building up, too, and it won't be long before breathing down here will become impossible.

You need to get out of here, Liz says near my ear.

"You think?"

I roll Chuckie onto his back, and work his waist over my shoulder so that his legs will dangle down my chest. It takes an extra effort to get to my feet, but I manage it.

To get to the stairs, we have to go past the shelving unit that's on fire. As much as I would like to run to the steps, with Chuckie's bulk I'm limited to more of a plodding walk.

I don't know if it's the smoke or the heat or just plain stubbornness, but before I take more than three steps, Chuckie stirs. This would be more understandable if I hit him with the first dart, as that one contained only enough juice to knock him out for about thirty minutes. The one that did hit him contained a full dose, and was supposed to keep him under for half a day at least.

As he sways, I hear him mumbling. He's only half conscious, but he's moving enough to threaten my balance. I lean forward as much as I dare to lower my center of gravity, and continue toward the exit.

When we're about to pass the fire, Chuckie tries to slap me with his arms. He's an uncoordinated mess so he barely connects with me. He swings his right arm out again to gain some momentum—and rams it right into burning shelves.

Fire jumps from the wood to his jacket and he screams.

I want to stop to douse the flames, but the more pressing matter is to get us the hell out of here.

With a surge of adrenaline, I whack my elbow into the side of his head, cutting off his bellowing, and power the remaining distance to the stairs and the steps. Before I reach the top, Jar opens the door from above. Her eyes widen at the sight of Chuckie's burning sleeve as I cross the threshold.

She points to the right. "Side door is open!"

I lumber through the house and out into the yard, where I drop Chuckie on the grass and roll him back and forth until the flames go out. The sleeve of the jacket is ruined, and he has some fairly serious burns on his arm and hand. But he's alive.

I've been scorched a little, too, but not enough to leave a permanent mark.

We are still too close to the house, so Jar helps me carry Chuckie to the front of the workshop, where Evan and Gina wait.

"I thought the plan was to stop him before the fire started," Jar says after we set him down.

I give her the evil side-eye but say nothing.

So far, the fire is only visible through the basement windows. But it won't stay that way for long, and it's only a matter of time before someone calls it in. Which means we need to finish up here and leave.

I feel Liz nearby again. All her anger and urgency have left her. I sense concern and relief. Also...longing? I'm not sure—I think that's what it is. But for what, I don't know.

And then she's gone.

I turn my attention to our two interlopers. Evan seems to be breathing better, though both he and Gina look a little shell-shocked.

Keeping my voice calm, I say, "What were you thinking?"

"I'm sorry," Evan says. "I was...I was just so angry. I wanted to see for myself. I ran over to the window and saw him throwing all that gas around and I just...I'm sorry."

I can't blame him for what he did. After years of abuse, he just couldn't hold back any longer.

"It's all right," I say. "I'm just glad you're okay." I clap him on the shoulder. "Where's your car?"

"Next to your truck."

"Next to my truck? How did you—" I stop myself. "Never mind. We need to get out of here."

"What about Evan's dad?" Gina asks.

"We'll let the police give him a ride."

"Will they know that he..." Evan trails off, but I get what he's asking.

"They'll know. You won't have to worry about him anymore."

He nods, as if he still can't fully believe it yet.

Jar recalls our drone, which sparks another look of surprise from our honorary junior team members. We walk out the back of the farm to where our cars are parked.

"One last thing before you go," I say to Evan.

We go over what I want him to do, then I make him repeat it again before I put my phone on speaker and dial 911.

When the operator comes on, Evan says, "The Whittaker house is on fire." He gives the address and adds, "The man who set it is lying outside."

"Can you repeat that, sir? Did you say there's a man outside?"

"You should send the police, too. And probably an ambulance."

"What's your name?"

Evan looks at me, and I nod.

"Evan Price," he says. "The man who set the fire is my father."

You may be wondering why I had Evan make this call. The reason is simple. There's bound to be a lot of fallout after his father is publicly linked to the fires. The fact that Evan is the person who reported him could go a long way toward sheltering him and the rest of his family from being lumped in with Chuckie's deeds.

Is it a guarantee they won't have to leave Mercy to have a normal life? No. But it's a chance.

We say our goodbyes, and Evan and Gina head back to Mercy.

Jar and I have one more stop to make before we go back to town.

CHAPTER THIRTY

B ergen is awake when we arrive at the Travato.
"Are you ready?" our computerized voice asks him.

A hesitation, and then a nod.

He looks better than he did earlier today. Like he's accepted his fate and is okay with it.

He sits in the backseat of our crew cab on the drive back to town, his hands tied behind his back. Even if they weren't, I doubt he would make a break for it but we're not taking any chances. And yeah, we are still wearing our ski masks. The sun has set, so it's less likely anyone will notice.

As soon as we hit Mercy city limits, we quiz Bergen on the instructions we've given him. He's got it down, so everything should go smoothly.

I park on a side street a block from the police department and nod at Jar. When I look back at Bergen, she clicks her computer and our voice says, "Turn and we will untie you."

Bergen shifts around and I undo the restraints around his wrists.

Jar clicks again. "This is your confession."

I hold out a memory stick that holds a copy of the video we made of him this afternoon.

He takes it, stares at it for a moment, and nods.

Another tap on Jar's computer. "Do as we told you and it should go easier for you."

He nods again and reaches for the door, but stops before opening it. "Thank you," he says.

Sure, we're potentially saving him from a worse fate if we didn't convince him to cooperate, but I don't think that's why he thanked us. I think it's because we've stopped him from having to do anything else for Chuckie. It was a cycle he couldn't pull himself out of on his own.

He gets out and walks down the street to the corner. When he turns toward the police station and disappears, we pull off our masks. I drive us down to the corner, where we watch him enter the building.

"All right," I say. "Send it."

A moment later, I hear the swoosh of an email leaving Jar's computer, indicating the robust information packet we put together about the Mercy Arsonists has been sent to the Colorado attorney general, the FBI, the Mercy PD, the press, Gage-Trent Farming, Hayden Valley Agriculture, and the two companies' insurance agencies. The only thing not in the packet is Bergen's confession. If for some reason he decides not to give it to the police, we'll send it out, but hopefully he'll follow through with what we discussed, as it will be better for him if he's the only source of his confession.

I drive us to Central Avenue and head to our duplex.

I'm not going to lie. I'm a little annoyed.

Jar and I have developed a kind of trademark way of

handling situations like the taking down of Chuckie Price. We like our victims to know just how hopeless their situations are. Usually, this is accomplished by forcing a restrained perpetrator to watch a gorgeous multimedia extravaganza that we produce. For example, the one we played for Marco and Blaine at El Palacio Banquet Experience.

There are few things more satisfying than putting together a killer presentation, and I don't mean to brag but we've brought some of our intended audiences to tears.

Our need to unexpectedly flee the Whittaker farmhouse, however, meant Chuckie did not have the honor of viewing our work. At least not while we're there to appreciate his reaction. I'm sure someone will show it to him eventually. The presentation is, after all, included in the mass email we sent.

Still, I would have loved to see his face as the crimes he'd committed—and thought no one would ever know about— spilled across the screen.

For instance, we all know Chuckie was looking for work because the dealership was struggling. Instead of a job, though, what he found was an opportunity to invest in Nicholas Huston's side project. See, Huston knew his client Gage-Trent Farming was trying to acquire as many properties as possible in eastern Colorado. It's already the dominant farming corporation in Mercy County. Hayden Valley, on the other hand, has only fifteen properties in the area. Most of the new places they were buying weren't even in Colorado. Huston was sure they'd be interested in divesting from the area. He also knew they'd never sell to Gage-Trent. The companies had a bit of history between them that kept cooperation to a minimum. Huston's plan was simple: convince Hayden Valley to sell to one of his shell companies, then turn around and resell the properties to Gage-Trent at a nice markup. (We had some wonderful graphics that explained all of that. Such a waste.)

We're not sure exactly when the plan of burning down farmhouses was hatched, but that doesn't really matter. Probably it was sometime after Chuckie met Huston. Chuckie didn't have a ton of money but he did have five hundred grand, and Huston has been living by that old investor rule: whenever possible, use other people's money. Chuckie also came with two other assets: a built-in hatred of Hayden Valley Agriculture, and the willingness to do anything to screw them, no matter if it was legal or not.

What stumped us at first was why they burned homes belonging to both companies. Turns out Hayden Valley has its roots as a family business. In fact, a member of the Hayden family has held the position of CEO since the company's inception sixty-eight years ago. The company prides itself on respecting the histories of the farms it purchases, and in several states rents the farmhouses out to family members of the previous owners. Gage-Trent has no such allegiance to the past. In fact, in a majority of its holdings, it has torn down the structures to create additional farmland.

The arson plan worked off the premise that though Gage-Trent might be annoyed by the fires, the destruction of the buildings would ultimately serve the company's purpose, whereas Hayden Valley would be disturbed enough by the fires to pull out of the area.

The idea would have worked, if not for my phone call to Isaac Davis yesterday. What I learned from him was that Hayden was close to agreeing to sales terms with Huston's company. A few points still needed to be ironed out, but Davis had been confident a deal would be worked out. The reason Huston felt the need to accelerate things was that Hayden Valley had received inquiries about the properties from another company.

Davis told me the other company wasn't anywhere close to

making an offer, but it hadn't kept him from dangling in front of Huston's representatives the fact that someone else was showing interest. Since Huston didn't know how legitimate the other potential suitor was, he decided to ramp up the fires to put on the pressure, focusing the latest acts of arson on Hayden properties.

Until I talked to Davis, Hayden Valley had no idea Huston was behind the offer. The company was well aware of his ties to Gage-Trent, and would have never considered selling to him if it had been aware of his involvement.

Davis was *pissed*.

I performed some fancy footwork to get him to promise to not do anything for a few days. I went as far as telling him I would consult with Ag Department investigators and other appropriate federal agencies to see how they want to handle it.

One thing we were never able to pin down was the identity of the mysterious Cheryl, the woman who'd outed Chuckie as a fraud to Hayden Valley. We do know the disconnected number belonged to a pay-as-you-go phone, purchased at a mini-market in Mercy, but that was as far as we got. I have a feeling the caller was Kate. Either she didn't want him to get a job that would keep him away from home for long stretches, or—and I'd rather believe this—she just wanted to screw his opportunity for no other reason than spite.

Who knows? Maybe the police will figure that one out.

News of Chuckie's arrest leads the special edition of Friday's *Mercy Sentinel*. Our old friend Curtis Mygatt has written the story himself, which, in essence, is a rough outline of the information from Jar's and my email. There's even a picture of Chuckie in a hospital bed, his unburned hand cuffed to a rail.

It makes me smile. I think I might keep this copy. Perhaps I should even frame it.

The attention has done exactly what we wanted it to: keep Chuckie's friend—and Mercy chief of police—Richard Hughes from sweeping everything under the rug. Furthermore, I get the strong impression from statements made by the governor's office —also printed in the *Sentinel*—that the state will soon take over the investigation. The tidbit we included in our packet about Chuckie and Richard being buddies might've influenced this. But I'm not one to brag.

We stay until Monday to make sure nothing goes sideways. If anything, interest in the case has only increased over the weekend. A few news vans from TV stations in Denver and another from Prime Cable News are camped out downtown.

This story is not going away.

Before we leave town, I load my motorcycle into the back of the pickup and drive to Mercy Cares. When I tell the director I'm donating the truck to her organization, she's surprised but doesn't say no. It feels a bit like righting a karmic wrong done to the charity by Chuckie's and Bergen's use of its donation cards. Sure, the charity doesn't know anything about that, but I do.

When I return to the duplex to pick up Jar, I find Evan walking up to our front door.

He stops and watches me get off the bike and says, "Hey."

"Hey, yourself," I reply. "You know you probably shouldn't be here."

The front door opens and Jar comes out, carrying our backpacks and the duffel bag of the stuff we haven't already returned to the Travato. "Hello, Evan," she says.

"Hi. Are you guys leaving?"

"Yeah," I say. "Seems like a good day to hit the road again."

"I see." He looks down, trying to hide what appears to be disappointment.

"How's everything at home?" I ask.

"It's...weird, but I think we're all happy my dad's not around."

"Sawyer?"

"He's great. A lot less tense. He hasn't gotten upset about anything since we stayed with you. I can't remember the last time he's been calm that long."

"And your mother?"

He shrugs. "She's not saying too much, but I'm sure she's relieved, too. That video of me and my dad you sent out helped, I think. Though she did make me go to the doctor on Friday."

Jar had chosen to include the clip from when Evan called out to his dad through the window, up until just after the point Chuckie knocked him into the shelves. If she'd asked me first, I'm not sure I would have wanted it sent. But I'm glad to hear Evan's not mad about it.

"Someone put it on the internet and it's got like two hundred thousand views already," he says.

"You're a star."

He laughs. "I guess. Between that and the nine-one-one call, at least the police know I didn't have anything to do with it."

"You didn't tell them anything about us, right?"

"Not a word. I just said I got knocked out and when I woke up, I was outside."

"What about Gina?"

"She'll stay quiet. She's really good at that."

While we were talking, Jar pulled out a piece of paper and has been writing on it. She now hands it to Evan.

"That's your house," she says.

She holds it out so both he and I can see it. On the paper are rough outlines of each floor.

She points at one of the xs that are all over the place. "Wherever you see one of these, you will find a bug."

He blinks in surprise.

"I thought you might want to take them down," she says.

"Do they still work?"

"They do, but you would need the proper software and access code to use them."

"Oh, then what should I do with them?"

"Just throw them away." I say.

"Or I could send him the app and he could play with them," Jar suggests.

His eyes light up.

"Uh, no," I say. "That's *not* going to happen. And you know what? If you do somehow get them to work without the app, I'd better not find out you've been using them for anything illegal or just plain wrong. Understand?"

"I would never do anything like that. I promise."

"Yeah? Well, you promised me you wouldn't follow your father."

"I'll do better this time."

"I'm counting on it." When he doesn't say anything else, I say, "We really should get going."

"Right. Sure. I understand."

Jar and I pull on our backpacks and don our helmets. After I get on the motorcycle, she hops on behind me and puts the duffel bag between us. It's a little awkward, but we have only a few miles to go to reach the Travato.

"Hey," Evan says. "I just, um, wanted to thank you. I know this was just a job you were doing, but...thanks."

"I'm happy we were able to help you." I start the bike.

"Keep helping your brother," Jar says, "and he will do fine."

"I will."

"See you down the road," I tell him, and pull out of the driveway.

Neither Jar nor I say anything all the way back to the Travato.

After we load the Yamaha onto the trailer, I make calls to our landlords and tell them an unexpected opportunity has come up that requires us to leave town. When I also inform them we understand we'll be sacrificing our deposits, the financial fight they were probably preparing to have with me vanishes.

Jar and I stand outside, near the entrance of the RV.

"I think I've seen enough farms for a while," I say.

"They are not so bad. The rows of crops are very soothing."

"Fair enough. I could call Mrs. Turner back and see if we could stay out here a little longer."

Now I'm the one getting the evil side-eye. "That will not be necessary."

I chuckle. "How about we hit something else on your list? Where do you want to go next?"

She leans against me and puts her hand on the small of my back. This is not something she does often. "I don't care," she says. "Let's just go and see where we end up."

That's also not very Jar-esque, but it sounds perfect.

ABOUT THE AUTHOR

Brett Battles is a *USA Today* and Amazon bestselling and Barry Award-winning author of forty novels, including those in the Jonathan Quinn series, the Night Man Chronicles, the Excoms series, the Project Eden thrillers, and the time-hopping Rewinder series. He's also the coauthor, with Robert Gregory Browne, of the Alexandra Poe series.

Keep updated on new releases and other book news, and get exclusive content by subscribing to Brett's newsletter at his website brettbattles.com, (scroll to the bottom of the webpage). You can learn more about his books there, too.

And around the internet:

facebook.com/Author-Brett-Battles-152032908205471
twitter.com/BrettBattles
instagram.com/authorbrettbattles

Printed in Great Britain
by Amazon